Murder in the Melting Pot
Jane Isenberg

Oconee Spirit Press, Waverly, TN www.oconeespirit.com
All rights reserved. No part of this book may be reproduced or transmitted in any form
or by any means without written permission of the author.
Library of Congress Cataloging-in-Publication Data
Isenberg, Jane
Murder in the melting pot/ Jane Isenberg

1. Detective and mystery stories—Yakima River Valley (Wash.)
2.Antisemitism—Yakima River Valley (Wash.)

10 9 8 7 6 5 4 3 2 1
Printed and bound in the United States. The text paper is SFI certified. The Sustainable
Forestry Initiative® program promotes sustainable forest management.

Cover design by Dead Center Graphics

For Jordan, Lucas, Levi, Malcolm, Zev, and Joey

"The community wants to be protected by us. They don't want to be conquered by us." – Sue Rahr, Director Washington State Criminal Justice Training Commission, former Sheriff, King County, WA.

"Once you eliminate the impossible, whatever remains, no matter how improbable, must be the truth." – Arthur Conan Doyle

ACKNOWLEDGMENTS

The author wishes to thank the following people for their valuable contributions: Jane H. Bock, Forensic Botanist, LLC; John Boule, Director, Yakima Valley Museum; Beth Brooks, artist and former Yakima resident; Linda Brown, retired English teacher, A.C. Davis High School, Yakima; Apanakhi Buckley, retired Professor of Education, Heritage University; Rose Butterfly, former Yakama* Nation Advisor, Heritage University; Karye Cattrell, mystery author; Robert Christensen and Miriam Isenberg, Yakima Valley scenic tour guides; Steve Davis, retired Yakima Police Department officer; Pamela Fabela, former Yakama Nation Museum Program Director; Kate Flora, mystery author; Rabbi Yitzchak Gallor, Rabbinical Field Representative, Orthodox Union; Mary James, Associate Dean, College of Arts and Sciences, Heritage University; David O. Norris, Professor Emeritus, Dept. of Integrative Physiology, University of Colorado; Michael E. Schwab, retired Yakima County Superior Court Judge; Kathryn and Sol Sylvan, Belgian Malinois owners; Brian Stoner, car fan; John Vornbrock, Treasurer Temple Beth Shalom, Yakima; Daniel Zimmerman, Founder, Phoenix Art Restoration, Issaquah and Shoreline, WA.

Deborah Adams, Barbara Extract, Marge Graham, Daniel Isenberg, Jeanne Matthews, Michael Meltzer, Jeannie Moskowitz, Laura Peterson, Michael E. Schwab, Philip Tompkins, and Joyce Yarrow served as readers. Rachel Stoner and Shilyh Warren provided technical assistance.

Yakama Nation retains the original spelling of their name whereas *Yakima* refers to the city and surrounding valley.

CHAPTER 1

Johnson Farmhouse Restored
New Budget B & B Opens Soon
Visitors to Yakima Valley have a new overnight option tailored to the business traveler when Breitner's B & B opens in Sunnyvale this fall. Innkeeper Seattle-born Miranda Breitner is a big fan of our valley. "Here nature and business both thrive. I'm happy to be part of this magical place and to have brought this historic house back to life."
—YakimaHeraldRepublic.com

Carrying a plate of still-warm pumpkin scones, Miranda hurried out of her B & B to apologize to Oskar Hindgrout. That she'd managed to piss off a guy she'd never even met didn't surprise her. After two decades with only her grandmother, her mother, and a shrink to talk to, she was aware that at thirty-three, she sometimes behaved like the socially inept middle schooler she'd been when her life went to hell. That was why her mom had encouraged her to open a B & B. "You'll get to interact with lots of different people one-on-one. You won't get rich, but it'll be good for you. And you can do it. It's time."

Maybe her mom had been wrong. Even before Breitner's B & B opened Miranda had offended her nearest neighbor. Oskar Hindgrout owned the fruit processing plant right across the street, and in her rush to ready her place for guests she'd neglected to give him a heads up about the delivery of her appliances the day before. So when she checked her messages, she'd heard this guy barking into her answering machine about how the "damn" Home Depot truck delivering her "damn crap" was blocking access to the driveway that farm trucks use to deliver ripe fruit to his factory. Miranda hoped the scones would serve as a peace offering. Making a go of Breitner's was her hard-won second chance to live a productive and peaceful life and keep the promise she'd made to her dying mother.

At the edge of the road, she paused for a few seconds to contemplate her freshly painted mailbox. Slathering barn-red paint over the gang tags and then emblazoning her new name, Miranda Breitner, in white on the clean bright surface was the first thing Miranda did after taking ownership of the old farmhouse. Seeing that mailbox buoyed her confidence and she crossed the street. The gate to the plant's deserted parking lot was open, and beyond it was the oversized entrance for trucks. She figured the office was probably near the front door on the other side of the big building, so she followed the plant's chain link fence around the block. Miranda reached the heavy front door and managed to open it with one hand while balancing the all-important plate of scones in the other. Just inside, she nearly collided with a stocky gray-haired man charging at the door. "Oh! I'm sorry. I'm looking for Mr. Hindgrout. Can you direct me to his office?"

"Damn. I thought you were my temp. My girl's out again today." The drooping ends of the man's snow-white moustache formed parentheses around the thin lips through which he spit out his words.

"I'm Miranda Breitner. I own the new B & B across the street."

"Breitner? I'm Hindgrout, and I left you a message yesterday. You never got back to me."

To Miranda's dismay, he eyed not the plate of scones, but her paint-splattered blue tee shirt, khaki Capri pants, and lavender Crocs. She should have changed.

"I didn't check messages until late last night, but I'm getting back to you now. I should have called ahead to let you know I expected a delivery." She hesitated. "And here's my apology." She held out the plate of scones, more shield than offering.

He scowled at the pastry. "Sugarless?"

She shook her head and put the underappreciated scones on an empty desk just a step away in what appeared to be the reception area. "I'll leave these for your workers. I'm sorry I didn't let you know about that delivery yesterday." Defeated, she turned to go.

"Miss Breitner, wait. I'm even more disagreeable than usual this morning. Apology accepted."

She turned back to face him and saw the corners of Hindgrout's mouth twitching into just the hint of a smile. He was shaking his head. "But see, this is a big day here and I have no girl, no temp, and no patience." His starter smile faded when he looked at his phone. "And now I'm running late. The damn grapes are ripening even as we stand here yakking and tomorrow they'll start pouring in and they'll keep on pouring in." He scowled. "You're not having anything else delivered in the next two months, are you?"

Hindgrout's question was absurd, so Miranda ignored it. But she was relieved that he'd become relatively civil.

"See, Miss Breitner, for the next two months ripe grapes will be delivered here 24/7. You and I will have to work something out about keeping my driveway clear. Meanwhile, Rabbi Alinsky and his koshering crew are due any minute. I always greet them in the parking lot. So walk with me. We'll go around outside." He grabbed her elbow and she let him maneuver her out the door, locking it behind them. He released her arm and together they walked briskly back around the chain-link fence.

Miranda wanted to keep their dialogue going. "I heard about this grape-koshering crew from the clerk at the post office. It sounds like a pretty big deal."

"Yup. Big deal and big bucks. Rabbi Alinsky works for Rabbi Certified Kosher, Inc., and every fall he imports a dozen rabbinical students mostly from New York and flies them to Seattle. They drive here straight from the airport at the beginning of the juice grape harvest. And they stay in a motel until the end, could be as long as eight weeks. So koshering grapes costs. But you can't sell juice grapes without doing it." His sigh bordered on a groan. "These days, it's not only Jews who want kosher food and beverages. Christians, Muslims, foodies, health nuts, ecologists, and, would you believe, even prisoners, want food with a kosher seal on it like the RCK from Rabbi Certified Kosher, Inc. That's why five Yakima Valley fruit processing plants put out big bucks to have our Concords koshered by Rabbi Alinsky's crew."

"Who knew? I'm Jewish, but my family's never kept kosher."

"You're Jewish?" She nodded as he turned to look at her. "Not many Jews here, so what brings you to this side of the mountains? We got so much land and so few people out here that folks who show up usually want to lose themselves, find themselves, or start over."

Miranda felt his eyes linger on her face. Her stomach lurched at how close he'd come to her truth. "But now more and more people are coming here to open wineries and other small businesses. I'm opening a B & B. Besides, I'm sick of the rain in Seattle and here it's so bright…."

The opening bars of "Amazing Grace" sounded from Hindgrout's pocket, and he pulled out his phone.

While he talked, Miranda continued their conversation in her head, recalling her first sight of the verdant Yakima Valley, a unique combination of oasis and industrial park, reservation and barrio, Promised Land and Welfare State, hunting ground and wildlife sanctuary. The road she had taken spiraled down from the massive and ever-green Cascades through farmed plains and led finally to beige sagebrush-strewn hills. These gentle rises seemed to border a brown-bottomed bowl striped by rivers and canals irrigating fields laid out like cross-word squares. Once she'd made the descent into this sunlit basin, Miranda felt protected from her own difficult past by its womblike contours and encircling rim. It seemed a promising place to incubate and nurture her new beginning. The bright arid terrain reminded her of Israel, and she, who thought she'd lost all faith, could almost imagine God's presence in its familiar high desert beauty.

Hindgrout pocketed his phone and quickened his pace. "The rabbi and his crew just pulled in. They'll hit the restroom and meet us in the parking lot. But before they join us, Miss Breitner, I gotta ask, what made you decide to buy that decrepit eyesore of a house?"

Miranda laughed. "My realtor tried to discourage me. Said the place was a 'money pit'."

"That'd be Rosemarie Arnold. Rosemarie's one plainspoken woman."

Miranda marveled anew at how everybody in this small town knew every-body else. "Yes, and she was right. But the simple truth is I just fell in love with that old falling-down farmhouse. And it's not falling down any more. You should stop in after we open." Miranda was not about to explain that she'd made the old house over just as she'd made herself over or that she'd also been smitten by Sunnyvale, a tiny farming town where no one knew her and where her traitorous father would never think to look for her.

Once in the parking lot, Miranda watched as a bearded middle-aged man wearing black jeans, a black shirt, and a beige cowboy hat led his distinctively dressed and considerably younger crew out of the building. The sight of the formally attired men made her stiffen and rise to the tips of her toes. Since she was thirteen, the year everything changed, Miranda sometimes took to her toes as if she feared the ground beneath her was mined. It was her memory that was mined though, and the arrival of these other Jews threatened to detonate her explosive recollections.

But it took her only a few seconds to stave off the urge to revisit the past. She lowered her heels, and smiled as Oskar Hindgrout introduced her to Rabbi Alinsky. "Miss Breitner. She's opening a bed and breakfast place across the street, and she's curious about your operation."

Miranda knew enough about Orthodox protocols governing physical contact between men and women to nod, smile, and refrain from extending her hand. Returning her smile with one of his own, the rabbi was cordial. "Good to meet you. I noticed a change for the better over there." He tilted his head in the direction of the B & B. "Feel free to stick around and listen to my spiel."

Hindgrout lost no time before addressing the group himself. "Welcome! Welcome! For those of you who've never been here before, I'm Oskar Hindgrout, owner of Hindgrout's, Inc., and my workers and I welcome you. For those of you who are returning, we feel blessed to have you back. Not all of you will be working at my plant, but I speak on behalf of all the Lower Valley fruit processing plant owners when I thank you for coming such a long way to kosher our Concords. We all welcome you to our Valley. Rabbi Alinsky, my friend, hello again. It's always a privilege to work with you. Please contact me if there's anything my workers and I can do to help you and your assistants with your important task. God bless." The two men shook hands. His duty done, Hindgrout rushed off in a dither to find his temp.

Curious about how Rabbi Alinsky was going to transform bookish urban nerds who spent their days and nights studying the Talmud and the Torah into experts on turning grapes into kosher grape juice, Miranda stayed put. For sure these men knew what foods were kosher, but not how they got that way in the twenty-first century. And how would these city guys adjust to living in a remote rural valley where it would be far easier to get tortillas than challah? She figured Rabbi Alinsky had his work cut out for him. The black-suited rabbinical students gathered closer to the rabbi like crows roosting in a hospitable tree, leaving her just outside their circle. They didn't even glance at her black curls, green eyes, or ample chest.

Miranda was less circumspect. Once the presence of these guys no longer upset her, she looked them over. Some struck her as quite handsome, and their proximity reminded her of her own loneliness. She considered inviting them all over for a glass of cold fresh apple cider. Their dark suits must be magnets for the still-strong autumn sun. But this vision faded when she remembered that they would eat or drink nothing from her decidedly unkosher kitchen.

The rabbi began what she assumed was an orientation with a question. "Let's review. Ephraim, why do we kosher grapes but not apples or pears?"

A lanky fellow with a full dark beard cleared his throat. For just a moment, Miranda allowed herself to imagine that beard against her skin. "In the Torah grapes are special. Grapes make wine, so they're sacramental. Once they might have been used by idol worshippers in their ceremonies. That's why the grapes' journey from vine to juice must be carefully overseen by observant Jews for those grapes to be considered kosher."

This was another "Who knew?" moment for Miranda whose long ago aborted bat mitzvah studies had not included the Torah's take on grapes. She continued to listen attentively as Rabbi Alinsky spoke. "Thank you Ephraim. So, as you know, Rabbi Certified Kosher, Inc., sends out a *mashgiach*, a kosher supervisor. That's me. I'm the *Kashrut* Cowboy!" He poked his thumb into the graying red beard covering his chest and adjusted the brim of his Stetson. "And to help me obey the Almighty's commandment to process newly harvested Concord grapes according to his two thousand year-old dicta, Rabbi Certified Kosher, Inc., also sends a handpicked crew. That's you." This time it was a rabbinical index finger that he jabbed at the young men circling him.

"So we schlep all the way out here to central Washington right where the grapes grow, acres of them. You'll see. This valley is like an oasis, like Eden. Not for nothing they call it 'The Nation's Fruit Bowl.' But it's different from what you're used to, so I want to prepare you for your important and exacting work, for the factories, and for the Valley itself.

The rabbi didn't sugarcoat what lay ahead there for his crew. "As I told you during your interviews and in the e-mails I sent you, this valley is where you'll spend six to eight weeks, including our High Holidays. It's here in little farm towns thousands of miles from your families that you'll spend twelve-hour shifts in trailers and improvised factory offices. When you're not on duty, you'll sleep in a motel. On our holidays you'll fast in this valley, too, and pray here, and some of you will fast alone, pray alone, and blow your rams' horns alone in this processing plant or one like it." He waved an arm in the direction of the gray concrete building hulking behind them. "You'll warm make-do kosher meals on hot plates and trade your fedoras, suits, and wingtips for hard hats, jeans, and work boots. You'll wear hair and beard nets too. Safety first!" The rabbi glanced around the circle, locking eyes with each listener. "And as I've told you, you'll supervise folks who don't take Jesus jokes lightly." Miranda stifled her laugh.

She was unprepared for his next question. "Any of you ever meet an American Indian?" The men shook their heads. "Right in the same fertile valley and for miles all around is the second-largest Indian reservation in the U.S. It belongs to The Yakama Nation." This time the arm he swung to indicate the scope of the Nation's U.S. government-allotted territory nearly knocked the black fedora off the head of one of his listeners. "And this valley is also home to many, many evangelical Christians and many Mexicans too. There are even a few Filipinos and Japanese. And you know what?" He paused. "They've all been very helpful to us, especially on our holidays. They're friendly, kind, and curious. That's the good news.

"The bad news is…" his voice lowered just a little. "There are a few gangs here. They're mostly run by Mexican drug cartels and distribute for them. So don't make anybody mad, especially young guys you run into in stores."

Miranda had learned online that Yakima County had more gangs per capita than any other county in the entire country. Attracted by business opportunities in the vast under-policed rural areas, these gangs had expanded their operations east from Seattle and Tacoma. Their impact on the culture of the Valley was not to be underestimated. Every September, some middle school principals in the city of Yakima distributed lists of gang colors and other trappings that might warn parents of their child's growing interest in gang activities along with the usual lists of school supplies. Miranda had brushed off this news, figuring that if the gangs out there were like gangs in Seattle they mostly killed only each other or cops who interfered with their business. The "plainspoken" Rosemarie Arnold had also downplayed the impact of the gangs when she said, "Seriously, Miranda, my brother's a county sheriff's deputy, and he says if you don't mess with the gangs, they won't mess with you." So that morning listening to the rabbi, Miranda felt certain they'd never bother a few overdressed New York Jews koshering grapes.

Rabbi Alinsky's next words reinforced this assumption. "But, thanks to the Almighty, the gangs have never bothered us. Of course, it helps that we don't hang out in clubs and bars or eat in restaurants or use drugs. So on your days off, explore this Valley. It's full of Hashem's wonders. I have maps and guidebooks at the motel." He paused. "Okay, so I hope you all watched the video I sent you because now we're going inside where I'll demonstrate exactly what you'll do on each shift."

Miranda slipped away and crossed the street. Elated by the improvement in her relationship with Oskar Hindgrout, she strode purposefully through her tiny overgrown yard, the last vestige of the fields that once surrounded the farmer's home before giving way to Sunnyvale's slim strip of downtown. She wanted to take another look at the stuff inside her shed before speaking to her handyman about hauling it out. Maybe she could haul it out herself.

When she looked back across the two-lane road that had begun as a wagon trail she saw that Rabbi Alinsky had led the young men into the processing plant. They were out of earshot when she screamed.

CHAPTER 2

Breitner's in Sunnyvale is the B & B for visitors coming to the Yakima Valley on Business and a Budget! We're smack in the center of this sunlit farming valley, "The Nation's Fruit Bowl." Here in "The Palm Springs of Washington" we enjoy over 300 days of sunshine a year! At Breitner's you'll have Wi-Fi and private baths. We're also smoke-free and accessible, and our ample continental breakfast is locally sourced, homemade, and healthful." www.breitnersB&B.com

The low growl coming from the other side of the shed door stopped abruptly. Miranda swallowed her next scream and stood frozen with her hand on the rusty lockless latch. She turned and, leaning hard against the still-shut door, considered going back to the house for a flashlight and a broom so she could see and evict the critter inside. Then she figured she was probably overreacting to the sound of a stray dog scouting the shed for scraps. She told herself that even though there were wolves east of the Cascades, it was very unlikely that one of them was in her shed. Still, she stood there considering the possibility that the animal, whatever it was, was injured, maybe even rabid.

"Come in. He won't hurt you."

This accented invitation to enter her own shed, extended in a barely audible female voice, was more alarming to Miranda than the growl. Maybe it was the voice of a thief scrounging for scrap metal or something else she could sell. Or maybe it was the voice of a runaway. There could even be two people in there. They could be armed. They could be on drugs. And then there was the dog.

Emboldened by her recent success with Oskar Hindgrout whose bark had turned out to be much worse than his bite, Miranda pooh-pooed her fears. She turned, threw open the shed door, stuck her head inside, and ordered, "Come out where I can see you. And keep that dog under control."

From behind a tower of old wooden fruit crates, a thin, dark-haired girl emerged bug-eyed and pale. Dressed in a grass-stained white T-shirt and jeans, she couldn't have been more than twelve or thirteen. She appeared to be alone except for the large dog beside her whose collar she gripped in one fist. This dog, better groomed than the bed-headed waif, looked like a slightly skinnier replica of every quasi-descendant of a German shepherd Miranda had ever seen. The girl's blinking eyes focused on the sturdy woman in the doorway, partially blocking the sun and any hope of easy escape. Miranda stared back and noticed dark smudges beneath those eyes and wondered when the youngster had last slept. She recognized the all-too-familiar signs of a frightened girl in trouble.

"Please, don't call the police, Miss. I'll go. I was just trying to get my dog. He got off his leash, chased a rabbit in here. That's all. I'm sorry." She took a step toward the shed door.

Miranda often felt insecure in her new setting and her new guise, as if she were living a lie, had stolen someone's identity instead of reinventing her own.

And her own daily deceit sometimes gave her insight into others who were also lying. Like this girl. Miranda could tell by the way her trace of a Spanish accent became more pronounced and her grip on the dog's collar tightened when she said *police*, by how she hesitated and wiped her nose with her hand before she said *rabbit*, and by how her narrow shoulders shrugged when she offered to leave. That shrug told Miranda that this kid had no place to go, no well-heeled parents to bail her out, and that she was scared.

Even though Miranda suspected she was being lied to and even though she was hardly an observant Jew, she knew that feeding the hungry was a *mitzvah*, a commandment. Or maybe that was just an excuse, a rationale for befriending a total stranger and so, for a time, keeping her own loneliness at bay. She had let reason prevent her from reaching out to the young kosherers. But just a few minutes later it didn't occur to her that in these times and this place her response to this girl might be ill-considered, as in really dumb. "Come in the house. Tell me who you are and why you're hiding in my shed while I fix us something to eat."

The girl didn't move. Her whisper was more prayer than condition. "No police. I didn't take nothing."

"No police." For Miranda, no police was a no-brainer. When the girl still didn't budge, Miranda cocked her head in the direction of the dog. "Yeah. Him too."

Once inside, the visitor took the dog into the bathroom with her. When she emerged with clean hands and face, Miranda pulled a stool up to the counter, and her guest perched there like a sparrow prepared to take flight except that sparrows aren't often tethered to large dogs. Miranda had never been a big talker, but compared to this girl she was a chatterbox.

"My name is Miranda Breitner. You are?"

"Vanessa Vargas."

"And your friend?" Miranda pushed a bowl of water across the counter. "Put this down in the corner for him, okay, Vanessa? What's his name?"

"Rusty." Vanessa did as she was asked and returned to her perch. "Thanks."

"I hope Rusty likes scrambled eggs because I don't have any dog food, so he's going to eat what we eat." Miranda cracked eggs into a bowl and slid slices of bread into the toaster. She put a quart of skim milk, some cheddar cheese, butter, and blueberry jam on the counter. It struck her as odd but somehow okay that her first B & B guests were a skinny vagabond girl and a dog with neither reservations nor the wherewithal to pay. And they were having a late lunch, not breakfast. She served Rusty first, giving him a bowl of scrambled eggs, cheese, and crumbled toast.

Miranda plated eggs, put them on the counter, pulled over a short stepladder, and took a seat opposite her guest. "Vanessa, somebody must be worried about you. Do you want to use my phone to call anybody?" She held out her cell.

Tears welled in the teenager's brown eyes. She shook her head several times. "No, no."

"Okay then, who do you live with? Where do you go to school?"

Vanessa ignored the first question. "Green Hollow."

Miranda remembered only too well that Green Hollow was Washington's only state-run residential school for youthful offenders that included girls. It was in a suburb of Seattle. Twenty years ago she'd feared she might be sent there. She wanted to hear how Vanessa described it. "Is that a school?"

"It's a boarding school." Thus proving her gift for euphemism, Vanessa scraped the last bits of egg from her plate, spread her next slice of toast with butter and jam, tore it in half, and handed his share down to Rusty who'd finished his own meal and stretched out beneath his mistress's perch.

Miranda understood that she over-identified with Vanessa because the unlucky girl reminded her of herself at thirteen. She was scared too then and needed help. Vanessa must have been found guilty of a crime. While deciding how to frame the question about what crime it was, Miranda pointed to a bright yellow bowl of apples on the counter. "Have one. They're good for you." She hated interrogating this kid. While her sympathy battled with her suspicion, Miranda managed to keep her voice even. "Vanessa, Green Hollow is a school for juvenile offenders. Why were you convicted? What did you do?"

Vanessa shrugged and studied the apple in her hand while she spoke. "I brought two guns to school."

Miranda swallowed a gasp.

When Vanessa continued, her words suddenly flowed, and Miranda heard in her voice the familiar expressionless drone of a suspect who has repeated the same sad, unsatisfying story many times. "They wasn't mine though. One was my mom's and the other was my dad's. He don't live in the same house with us. My mom wasn't no *chola* when I was little and she didn't do drugs back then, but this Sureño started coming round, staying with us, and then selling to her and then she was using and she was like his girlfriend and the other Sureños started courting her, you know, to get her to join. For her initiation they wanted her to pop my dad. Basically, you know, blood in, blood out." Vanessa's barely perceptible shudder prompted Rusty to stand and nuzzle her leg. "My dad's always run with the Norteños. He was a block rep in jail, and when he got out he started dealing for them in South Seattle." Her voice lowered as if this were the end of her story.

Miranda was incredulous. "Are you telling me your mom shot your father?"

Vanessa inhaled and straightened her shoulders before going on. "Almost. Last year when my mom saw him driving around in a new Escalade she asked him for money for me to go to Catholic school." Vanessa's mouth twisted and she stopped talking.

"So did he pay your tuition?" As soon as the question left her lips, Miranda regretted it. "I mean…"

Vanessa soldiered on with lowered eyes, talking a little faster. "No. And right after that he got busted for carrying and while he was doing time the Sureños gave her a gun. When he got out, she was gonna meet him and blast him, but that day the girl who was gonna drive her had to go to court, and my mom, she couldn't get another ride. But I knew she'd keep trying, so that night I took that gun outta the bag of rice by the stove where she kept it." A tear slid down Vanessa's cheek. If this girl was lying, she was putting on quite a performance. Miranda handed her a napkin and kept quiet, willing Vanessa to continue.

"Right after that I went to see my dad, and I heard him bragging to his boys about how he was gonna give his latest bitch his gun and get her to blast my mom first. And, basically, that little *puta* is so young and so dumb, she'd do it too. She's gonna have another baby." Vanessa rolled her eyes either at the idiocy of her father's current lover or at the prospect of another half-sibling or both. For a nanosecond Miranda considered sharing the story of her own father's second family. But she wanted to hear Vanessa's tale, not reveal her own. To her relief, the girl kept talking, as if sharing her story with someone who wasn't judging her, was in and of itself rewarding. "So while they was partying, I took his piece right off his dresser. I went and stayed by Liliana, a girl from my school they don't know."

"Were you going to sell the guns?" Miranda regretted interrupting when Vanessa paused and shrugged. Again Miranda read defeat in the rise and fall of those narrow shoulders. When the girl spoke next, her voice was so low Miranda had to lean over to catch her words. "No. I wouldn't do that. I was gonna give both guns to the cops at one of those gun exchanges they have, you know? But until the exchange, I basically had to hide them." Vanessa took a deep breath as if inhaling strength to continue.

Miranda sat back and waited.

"I was gonna stash them in one of them broken-down trailers at my school. They don't use it now cause it leaks real bad. But this old custodian, he came in to sneak a smoke while I was trying to hide them and he saw them and ratted me out."

Miranda was quiet for a moment trying to absorb this twisted tale. She asked herself if it could possibly be true, any of it. Her new ability to recognize a lie when she heard one offered no help, but it would take her only a few minutes on the information highway to corroborate or disprove Vanessa's account. Miranda didn't want to reveal her distrust by working her smart phone in front of the kid though. And she did want to hear the rest of her story. "How did you like Green Hollow?"

"I'm good in school so I liked it there except for visiting days. Miranda saw tears well again and was surprised when Vanessa chose to go on. "I rather be at

Green Hollow than with them two. I don't use drugs. I don't deal. I don't gang bang. So, basically, we got, you know, nothing in common them and me. This is the only ink on me. See." She lifted her hair to reveal a small scroll, a diploma, tied with a ribbon and tattooed on the side of her neck. She dabbed at her eyes with the napkin Miranda had provided. "Green Hollow's cool."

Her tone lightened when she added, "I found Rusty there. They got this program training us to work with dogs, 'service dogs' they call 'em. We train 'em to go live with people in wheelchairs or old people who get around with walkers." Vanessa got down from the stool and sat on the floor beside Rusty and, as she continued, stroked his flank. "Him and me, we were tight from the beginning, weren't we?" She grabbed his snout and leaned over to brush it quickly with her own nose. Both she and Miranda smiled. "He didn't have a good childhood either, but he's good in school too, picked up everything real easy, and I learned how to take care of him and train him, right, Rusty?" She ran her hand down the dog's back and planted a kiss on his head. The picture of canine contentment, Rusty yawned and blinked.

"So why did you leave Green Hollow?"

"I had to. Rusty got adopted by this dude who told them at his interview he was gonna give him a good home with his dad who was in a wheelchair, but when I was telling Rusty goodbye, I overheard that same dude say on his phone that his dog would be staying alone in his country place with someone just coming by to feed him and let him out once or twice a day. That creep lied and faked his application. He really wanted a watchdog for this fancy vacation house he has out in the desert near here.

"But, basically, Rusty's a Belgian Malinois, a work dog." Vanessa's shoulders straightened with pride. "He's bred to have responsibilities, right, Rusty?" She spoke into one of Rusty's pointed ears. "Cops and soldiers use dogs like you to find bombs and drugs and stuff, don't they? I bet you once worked for a soldier." Miranda noted that Vanessa was no longer using gang slang and her accent was barely noticeable. She was glancing around the room, too, no doubt taking in the fresh paint on the bare walls, the unfinished floors, and the almost total lack of furniture. "And this type of dog's very social. Basically, he needs to always be with somebody, right Rusty?" Miranda waited to hear more. There had to be more.

"So I got a look at this guy's address and a few days after he picked up Rusty I snuck out of Green Hollow in a plumber's van. I got out when the driver stopped at a gas station and walked until I snagged a ride over the mountains with some old couple. The lady talked about Jesus the whole way." Another smile animated Vanessa's thin face. "She made me feel good because I know, basically, rescuing Rusty was exactly what Jesus would do if he was me. They let me out right by the library in Yakima. I told them my mom was meeting me there.

"I asked somebody going into the library where that address was and she looked it up on her phone. I got another ride out that way in the back of a pick-up truck. In front was two women going fishing. They let me off, and I hiked up to where Rusty was staying and waited out of sight all day for someone to come feed him and take him out. Finally a guy drove up with a girl and brought Rusty out and chained him up outside and left him like that while the two of them went back inside. Didn't even put his water dish out there." Vanessa frowned at the horny dog sitter's priorities. "But at least I didn't have to fight him. And I didn't see no rattlesnakes. I signaled Rusty not to bark when I came up, so he just licked my face off he was so glad to see me! I unchained him and we ran all the way back down to the road and hitched another ride with a couple of ladies who like dogs. They live in this town, and they let us out last night, and we found your shed."

Miranda noted that Vanessa had taken rides only from women and wondered if that was intentional. She also was very curious about what Vanessa's next move might be, if the kid had a plan, would ask her for a job. At the prospect of having the girl stay, Miranda felt her heartbeat accelerate. She could use a kid around to quiet the incessant ticking of her biological clock. She'd always loved kids. Now most likely she'd never have a child of her own and she'd never be allowed to adopt. And right here was a youngster in need of a family. Also once the B & B opened, if it stayed booked, Vanessa could help with laundry, shopping, baking, and cleaning. But this fugitive girl had serious baggage, and Miranda didn't want to literally invite trouble, couldn't afford to really. On the other hand, who'd know? She could alter Vanessa's appearance and give her a new name and backstory. Then she could home-school her and prepare her for college.

Before Miranda's lonely heart and raging hormones made an offer her brain might regret, her handyman Michael walked in. This godsend had been referred by Pauline Thurston, the friendly woman, who'd agreed to supply fresh eggs for the B & B's guests. "Michael Wright built my chicken coop, dry-walled our attic, and painted our kitchen. He's Indian, but I never let that bother me. He's a serious young fellow, a good worker, a great fisherman. He used to bring me a salmon once in a while, but now he's studying at Heritage U, so he doesn't fish as much. Here's his number."

The skinny, long-limbed nineteen-year-old's wire-rimmed old man's eyeglasses seemed out of sync with his black ponytail, jeans, and sneakers as he nodded at Vanessa and ruffled the fur on Rusty's neck. When he spoke, his voice was low and his words measured. He sounded like a much older person. "I have a class in an hour, so I'm quitting for today, but that last bedroom's done. I left the windows open, so don't forget to close 'em when you go to sleep." He was at the door before Miranda could introduce him to her visitor.

He issued another directive over his shoulder. "Check it out! The Jews are back!" She went to the window, tailed by Vanessa and Rusty. They watched the young men in black hats and suits and white shirts file out of the factory like a procession of penguins in a documentary she'd watched with her mother.

That night Vanessa slept on an air mattress in one of the B & B's unfurnished guestrooms with Rusty at her side. Miranda had carefully considered and worded her invitation to this odd sleepover. "Vanessa, you two can stay here tonight. I won't call the cops. Get a good night's rest." She resisted a powerful urge to lean down and kiss the girl's cheek as her mother had kissed hers each night of her childhood and as she had kissed sweet little Timmy's cheek whenever she babysat. So distracting were the conflicting feelings Vanessa inspired that until Miranda turned out the light and left the room it hadn't dawned on her that later on Vanessa just might sneak up the stairs, open the lockless door to the attic apartment, help herself to her sleeping hostess's laptop, smart phone, and wallet, and flee with them and her dog into the night. Or worse.

To ease her mind, once upstairs in the lonely privacy of her unpainted and barely furnished quarters, Miranda poured a glass of wine, went online, and did a search for *"guns Seattle school."* Vanessa had not fabricated a word of her improbable story. In late spring an unnamed female juvenile had been arrested for bringing two loaded handguns she took from her gang-affiliated parents to the magnet middle school for gifted tweens her guidance counselor had arranged for her to attend. This gun-toting juvenile claimed she planned to turn in her arsenal at the upcoming police-sponsored gun exchange. Nevertheless, bringing firearms to school is a felony in Washington State. She was sentenced to six months in Green Hollow. Her escape from the juvenile detention center was referenced in a small article in *The Seattle Times* and made headlines in a newspaper in the little town in the foothills of the Cascades where Green Hollow is located.

After much soul-searching and another glass of wine, Miranda repeated over and over to herself the speech she planned to deliver to Vanessa at breakfast the next morning: *Vanessa, I promised I wouldn't turn you in to the police, and I won't, but I can't harbor a fugitive either. You set out to rescue Rusty, which you did. Now you both should go back to Green Hollow. Turn yourself in and tell the people who run the rescue dog program how Rusty was being treated, and they'll find a better home for him. After you serve the rest of your sentence and any new time they give you, I promise I'll give you a job. Right now, I'll give you enough money for a ticket on the bus back across the mountains and a few meals. And I'll drive you to the depot.* This was the least she could do. It was all she should do. She wanted to offer to let Vanessa stay but she knew she couldn't. And she also knew that if she slept at all that night, she'd relive in a vivid nightmare the events that had changed her own young life.

It's an especially wet Saturday evening in February and she, then named Meryl Wein-traub, is babysitting for Timmy Schwartz. Things go badly from the start. A dimpled nineteen-month-old cherub with rolls of fat for thighs, Timmy usually grins at the sight of her. But tonight he's whimpering when she arrives and he doesn't stop when she kneels to play with him. His mom Kathy says, "No worries, Meryl. He's been that way all day. He's probably getting another tooth" and takes off with her boyfriend Charles. Says she'll call if she's going to be getting home after one. Meryl's relieved to have them gone because Charles, who has to be at least thirty, always ogles her as if she's the last M & M in the bag whenever Kathy turns her back.

She immediately changes Timmy's ripe Pamper and finds no trace of diaper rash. Next she examines his gums and sees and feels no emerging teeth. His forehead isn't warm to her touch. Maybe he's hungry. But Timmy ignores the fish sticks and mac 'n' cheese she arrays on his highchair tray. During his bath, he remains glum and whimpers, even when she gives him his precious rubber frog. Probably he's tired. She heaves Timmy out of the tub, swaddles him in a bath towel, and rocks him gently for a moment or two. Then she dries, powders, and diapers him and eases him into a blue onesie. She reads him <u>Brown Bear, Brown Bear</u>*, lowers him into his crib, kisses his forehead, and croons "Twinkle, Twinkle Little Star" five times. Timmy always falls asleep by the third time, but that night he doesn't fall asleep at all. Instead his whimpers become moans. Timmy isn't tired. He's sick, and she doesn't know what else to do for him. Her own parents are at a concert. She dials 911. When the EMTs come and take Timmy to the hospital, she leaves a note for Kathy and goes along.*

Much later Timmy's mom and Charles join her in the waiting room at Virginia Mason Medical Center's ER...

Miranda struggled free of this recurring nightmare only when she felt something rough scraping the sweat and tears off her face. At first she thought this sensation was a new and grim addendum to the nightmare, but when she opened her eyes she recognized Rusty, who was licking her cheek. With a start, she remembered her other unexpected guest. She figured Rusty probably wanted to go out, and Vanessa, poor kid, was still asleep. Miranda jumped up, peed, dressed quickly, and followed the big dog downstairs. Her eye fell on a still-life on the counter, a white paper napkin wedged between two of the red apples in the yellow bowl. She snatched the napkin and read the careful printing: "Take good care of Rusty. His leash is on a hook by the door. Thank you. Vanessa Vargas. He had his shots. He eats mostly Purina One."

CHAPTER 3

Toppenish Murals Tagged!
Gangs Deface Local Treasures!

When Pauline Thurston stormed into the B & B a few mornings after Rusty took up residence, Miranda was startled. It wasn't one of Pauline's regular egg delivery days, and a scowl distorted her usually serene features. By way of greeting, Miranda's first new friend in a long, long time shoved a copy of *Yakima Herald-Republic* across the counter. The outsize headline screamed news of the desecration of the famed murals in the neighboring valley town of Toppenish. "I can't believe it! Miranda, tell me you've already seen these incredible paintings because now they're ruined!" Pauline pointed at a photo of one of the old town's celebrated historical murals, the one depicting a pioneer woman hanging laundry. The housewife and her wash were partly obscured by a menacing black hieroglyphic scrawled over the once-white sheets ballooning on the clothesline.

Miranda poured Pauline a cup of coffee and gestured to a stool at the counter. "Yes. I saw them when I was house hunting in the Valley. My realtor insisted. They're amazing. Who would mess them up? Does it say who did this?"

Pauline's tone was derisive. "Who do you think? It says some wannabe gang member—a Sureño, probably—had to do it for his initiation." She patted Rusty while sipping her coffee. "I see you got a dog. Good idea." As if soothed by Rusty's presence, Pauline's scorn seemed tempered when she spoke next. "It's odd though. Those criminals are murderous, but they never touched the paintings before. Not in the twenty-something years those murals have been there. You know, Miranda, they were painted by real artists, western artists. They're works of art, and God always kept them safe. Why would He let this happen?" Pauline hesitated, perhaps searching for either a rationale or an excuse for the Divine's slip-up.

Miranda waited. She'd always been a good listener. It wasn't long before her patience was rewarded.

"Maybe it's a warning. Like the writing on the wall in the Bible."

"Could be. But the words on that wall were a warning to a tyrant. Is there a tyrant in this valley?"

"The gangs are the tyrants."

Miranda drew on her considerable familiarity with TV crime shows for another interpretation. "Or maybe this warning isn't from God. Maybe Gang A is warning Gang B about what'll happen if Gang B moves in on Gang A's turf."

Pauline didn't look really happy with this godless interpretation of the graffiti, but she calmed down enough to enjoy a cranberry scone with her coffee and to apologize for her intrusion. "I know you've got enough on your plate trying to get this place going. So thanks for letting me barge in and rant. Some mornings after Nelson leaves for work I need somebody besides my chickens to talk to." She looked at Miranda and then directed her eyes to the ceiling. "I feel blessed to have you nearby. See you tomorrow."

Having recently lost her mother, Miranda was moved by the older woman's affection and approval and intrigued by her faith. She just wished her new friend's spontaneous visit hadn't been prompted by the desecration of important public art.

Pauline wasn't the only one troubled by the mutilated murals. They were very much on Michael's mind when he came to work a few minutes later. Like many citizens of the Yakama Nation, Michael was born in Toppenish, and Miranda figured that was why he took this tagging personally. "Our murals are trashed! We finally got something besides the casino to bring in tourists, the type who walk around, have lunch, maybe even buy a few things. They go to our museums. They hike our hills. Hire our guides. They hunt and fish or go to our wildlife center and take photos. And now those sick Mexican assholes, they cover those paintings with their stupid tags. Those stinkin' foreigners don't even speak English. My ancestors were born here but they had to learn English, weren't allowed to speak our own language. Those lowlife gangbangers should go back where they came from and stay there." Before Miranda could respond to this usually soft-spoken young man's disturbing tirade, the floor sander arrived and his machine made further conversation impossible.

It wasn't until the next day that Miranda thought again about the vandalized paintings. The land-line phone reserved for bookings and power outages rang, and she took the call. "Breitner's B & B. Miranda Breitner, speaking. May I help you?"

"I'm Caroline Evans, President of the Toppenish Public Art Association's Board of Directors. I'd like to book a room. But first, welcome to the Valley, Miranda. And good luck with your new business."

"Thanks. Caroline. And I'm so sorry about what happened to Toppenish's murals."

"What 'happened' to our murals is that those ignorant goons desecrated them. They created another black cloud darkening a valley that prides itself on sunshine. There are over seventy fantastic paintings on buildings all over Toppenish illustrating our town's history! These art works promote civic pride, patriotism, tourism, and art itself. And they're so bright! They give new meaning to the term *local color*."

Miranda wasn't just being polite when she said she was sorry about the murals. They certainly did relieve the beigeness of the old desert settlement that is Toppenish. And with images of cowboys, hops farmers, Indians, and horses all over town, it was possible to credit Toppenish's claim to be a place "Where the West Still Lives." Even so, she was relieved when Caroline got down to business. "Actually, the murals are why I'm calling. I want to book a room for Stephen Galen, an art restorer." Caroline's voice brightened. "If you can accommodate him, he'll stay on at Breitner's at your weekly rate, to be billed to the Toppenish Public Art Association. I don't care if we have to fundraise until we drop. He'll stay until he gets the job done."

After e-mailing the reservation confirmation, Miranda had to acknowledge that, for her at least, the dark cloud Caroline conjured up had a silver lining. Breitner's was getting an extended booking out of it. For a moment she wondered why this guy wasn't staying at the motel near the Casino in Toppenish. It seemed odd that Toppenish's Public Art Association was putting him up in Sunnyvale. But she soon dismissed her curiosity to indulge her pleasure in being fully booked opening night. She looked down at her new companion stretched out at her feet, stroked his head, and told him, "This art restorer will repair the paintings. Like the lady said, 'That's his job.'" She caressed one of Rusty's silken ears and smiled at herself for talking to her dog.

Miranda had been dismayed both by Vanessa's abrupt parting and by her parting gift. At odd moments during the few days since the penniless girl had vanished into the dark—headed who knew where—Miranda had found herself looking up the road, hoping for a glimpse of her. She scanned news websites for any word about her. Vanessa was at risk from pimps, other traffickers, vengeful gang members, critters, hunger, and the cold autumn night air. And the poor kid had to face all these horrors without her precious dog.

As for Rusty, Miranda hadn't planned on having a dog at the B & B. In fact, she'd considered it and opted against the idea so as to avoid the additional responsibility and expense. She'd also worried that her guests might bring their own pets or have allergies. Or her dog might not take to meeting new people all the time. She'd figured that if she needed more security, she'd alarm the place. You don't have to walk, feed, or pick up after an alarm. Or take it to the vet. No, she hadn't wanted a dog. But Vanessa had entrusted Rusty to her, and Miranda vowed to deserve that trust.

She spent a couple of nights reading about dogs online. Vanessa had trained Rusty well. With the exception of mistaking toilet bowls for drinking vessels, he was really well behaved. In just a few days, Miranda and her new pet who had a survivor's honed ability to transfer allegiance from one benevolent owner to another, had become inseparable.

"Rusty, do we have time for a run?" At the word *run* Rusty bounded for the door where his leash hung. According to what she'd read about dogs of Rusty's exalted lineage, he required exercise. So, sloughing off the warnings of Pauline, Miranda ran with him through the supposedly gang-occupied streets of Sunnyvale whenever she could fit it into her frenetic countdown to opening. She slipped out of her Crocs and into her running shoes. "Let's do this, Rusty!"

Running just a couple of miles through the quiet tree-lined streets of small homes and the occasional field helped relieve her anxiety which was increasing as Breitner's opening approached. She imagined a series of scenarios that played out over and over in her head. In one, the B & B opens and nobody comes. All those with reservations have canceled at the last minute in spite of her carefully constructed cancellation policies. In another, a guest complains that her cranberry muffins are dry and her coffee weak. In other fantasies, a disgruntled guest criticizes his memory foam mattress and a woman insists she is kept awake by the efforts of a "rodent trapped in the wall behind the bed." In a particularly crushing vision, Miranda pictures columns of negative reviews posted online by these dissatisfied guests and scores of others.

But when opening day actually arrived and she looked around, Miranda was pleased with how the place had shaped up. She loved the refurbished oak counter and cabinet that doubled as reception desk and breakfast bar she'd found at an auction Rosemarie had steered her to. A new sink and range top were embedded in one end alongside a fridge and dishwasher. On the other side were barstools. A pair of cushy but faded red easy chairs flanked the defunct fireplace which Miranda had repurposed to frame a battered metal pitcher ablaze with orange dahlias, a gift from Pauline who'd stopped by to wish her luck. Beneath the front window, a few weathered wooden fruit crates stacked on the gleaming pine floor served as bookcases. Atop them her mother's plants, a flamboyant wandering Jew and a prolific spider plant, held court in the sunlight. Miranda was eager to show off her cozy lobby that also served as breakfast area and lounge.

She'd dressed for the big day, too, in good black jeans and a long-sleeved tee of green jersey that, her mom had said showed off her green eyes. She'd made sure to touch up her red roots and pencil over her red eyebrows to match her black curls. She took a selfie and then one of her and Rusty. Check-in time was at two, but it wasn't until a bit later that the first guest actually crossed the threshold. He was a tall lean man with a long sharp nose at home between his angular cheekbones. His face was weathered, his hair a pepper and salt stubble, and his drawl decidedly southern. "Steve Galen." A grin softened the sharp contours of his face.

"Welcome, Mr. Galen." She recognized the name as that of the art restorer.

"Steve. It's Steve. Thanks."

"And I'm Miranda. Mandy." She blinked when the unscripted nickname tripped off her tongue. She'd always wanted a zippy nickname. Now it was her turn to smile, because her mom had been right. She could do this. She could be an innkeeper. And she could have a cool-sounding nickname. She pushed the registration form across the counter as if she'd done it a thousand times.

"Nice to meet you, Mandy. And you too, big fella." Rusty had stationed himself beside Miranda. Done with the form, Steve's eyes swept the front room. Miranda stood behind the counter, hoping the décor would merit this artsy guy's approval. "I like what you've done here. You've taken shabby chic to a whole new level." The skin beside his eyes crinkled when he grinned.

Unaccustomed to banter, Miranda was uncertain how to respond, so she didn't.

"Seriously, Mandy, I like old things, things with a past. That's why I do what I do."

"Thanks." Miranda decided against telling Steve he was her first guest. Instead she followed his lead. "You're going to be working down the road in Toppenish? Removing gang graffiti from those historical murals?"

Steve nodded. "According to Mrs. Evans, some of those art works have been up for decades, and nobody's ever laid a finger on 'em till now. She thinks it happened during a gang initiation. It's a big job." He shook his head and frowned. "You won't be seeing the last of me for weeks."

"Well you're welcome here as long as it takes."

"Thanks. You don't have to do up my room but once a week. Don't want to spoil me, do you?" There was that grin again. "And is there a washer and dryer I can use?"

Miranda didn't want guests, even charming ones, in her apartment and that's where the washer and dryer were, so she made an offer she hoped she wouldn't regret. "Not to worry. When you need some laundry done, just leave it on your bed."

"Are you sure? The Toppenish Public Art Association isn't paying for my laundry."

"I'm sure. I do laundry most days. Do you need help getting your luggage?"

"Not yet. Ask me again in ten years. And thanks." With a wink he was out the door. When he returned he was wearing a large hiker's backpack. "My work stuff's okay in the truck. Nobody's going to break in to steal a couple of thousand Q-tips, right?"

"Q-tips?"

"Yep. Those little suckers are the tools of my trade."

Miranda nodded, pleased to think that if this charming man seriously intended to clean graffiti off those messed up murals with Q-tips, he'd be staying at Breitner's until she was eligible for Social Security. But all she said was, "Who knew? You're first to arrive today, so you can choose your own room."

She grabbed her keys and led Steve down the corridor. Her contractor had gutted the former farmhouse's kitchen and dining room and transformed those spaces into bedrooms, and then, per Miranda's instructions, he had given each bedroom, the two new ones and the two existing ones, a bathroom. "Wow! The farmer who used to live here wouldn't recognize the place." Miranda assumed Steve disapproved. After all, the man made a life's work out of preserving old things in their original state. But, on the other hand, this same man probably wanted to pee in a private bathroom whenever he felt like it, so maybe he appreciated her priorities.

After they walked through all the rooms, Steve chose one bright with sunshine. Miranda commented, "That afternoon sun is still hot this time of year, so turn on the AC if it gets too warm. The thermostat is to the left of the dresser. Here's your room key, a key to the front door, and there's a list of area restaurants in the lobby." She left him at the door, glad she'd advised him how to avoid roasting to death, glad he'd arrived, and hopeful that her other guests would also show.

They did. One was a fifty-something Canadian woman interviewing for an administrative position at Heritage University. As if rehearsing for that interview she told Miranda, "I know it sounds trite, but I'd really like a chance to make a difference."

Two guests were new grandparents from Issaquah staying for a week to help out on the farm while their son and daughter-in-law got used to their twin girls. "For nine months our son insisted they wouldn't need help, but the second he saw those two little cuties he changed his mind."

And the last guest to arrive was a client Rosemarie referred, Tom Buler, a middle-aged man from Seattle looking for property for a second home. "I'll tell you what I told Rosemarie. I hate having to go south for a little winter sunshine. I don't need a beach, just a ray or two of sunlight in February, that's all."

Before she climbed the stairs to her apartment that night, Miranda checked the home-made whole-wheat muffins, granola, and peach jam, the dairy-fresh butter, yogurt, and milk, the hardboiled eggs from Pauline's pampered chickens, the locally grown grapes and apples, and a few token imported bananas for the hopelessly banana-addicted. She checked her supply of Peete's coffee, assorted tea bags, and organic sugar. Her mother's mismatched but lovely old china and flatware ought to please Steve. She straightened the bar stools in front of the counter and, finally, locked the front and back doors.

Upstairs in her three attic rooms the walls were painted and the floors sanded and stained. Her little kitchen was operable as were the bathroom, the washer, and the dryer. She had her air mattress, her sleeping bag, a folding table and chair, her laptop, and her clothes, so she was okay. Rusty had his own new bed. She'd furnish the place when she had time and a steady income stream.

Things were going well. Her mother would be proud of her. They'd discussed this day often during Mona Weintraub's final months, months when Miranda was aware that Mona was focusing her remaining strength and considerable wisdom on enabling her troubled and reclusive daughter to live on without her. So that night a relieved Miranda opened her fridge and eyed the bottle of champagne Mona had given her. "Crack it with your first guests!" Her mom had issued this order with her warm smile followed by a phlegmy cough that left her spent and reaching for her oxygen. Fighting tears, the fledgling innkeeper decided it was too soon to celebrate.

CHAPTER 4

> *Guest book: "Breitner's is going to be this California girl's second home until I find the property I'm looking for. This B & B is clean and comfy and the breakfast is delicious, organic, and not guilt-inducing, a nice change." Gloria Derrinsman, Napa Valley, CA*

On a Sunday morning in late September, while the Valley's church bells tolled their last round and the final jubilant hallelujah of a nearby Baptist choir rang out in response, Miranda heard another sound so out of context she thought at first she'd imagined it. She dropped the sheets she was folding and hurried outside to her mailbox with Rusty, but the sound had stopped. Then there it was again, the piercing, staccato wail of the ram's horn. She pictured the ram Abraham had chanced upon, the unwitting creature ensnared in branches. Her lips whispered the familiar syllables the rabbi and congregation chanted in between blasts of the horn. *Tki'a. Shva'rim. Tru'ah* — The unmistakable ancient call to prayer and to the promise of forgiveness came from across the street, from inside the factory. It must be Rosh Hashanah. In her new self-imposed exile, without her mother or other Jews to celebrate with, and with a B & B to run, she'd forgotten. But by blowing his shofar in that cavernous factory, a pious koshering inspector, perhaps also feeling alone, reminded her.

Miranda was grateful to be recalled to prayer even though she wasn't quite sure why. As the prelude to Yom Kippur, Rosh Hashanah was a cue for her to repent and ask forgiveness from those people she may have wronged during the past year. Yom Kippur, or the Day of Atonement, itself is a day when Jews fast and repent for the sins they have committed against God. And people say Kaddish, the Mourners' Prayer, in memory of their dead loved ones. Some Jews only appear at synagogue once a year to say that prayer on that holy day, even though it is said at every Sabbath service. She would mark her calendar. She would fast and spend Yom Kippur at the Reform temple in Yakima she'd heard about from Rosemarie. Nobody knew her there. She could rise to her feet with that congregation and say Kaddish for her mother, her grandfather and grand-mother, and for Timmy. Meanwhile, even though she'd missed the Rosh Hashanah service, she stood at the mailbox and asked forgiveness for hating her father and for not taking in Vanessa Vargas.

Perhaps discomfited by the piercing shrillness of the ram's horn, Rusty seemed glad to return to the house, to lie at Miranda's feet while tears brought on by remembering her dad's treachery splotched the sheets she was folding. The sheets were from the room just vacated by Gloria Derrinsman, who'd stayed a couple of nights while looking for property suitable for a second spa she hoped to build similar to one she owned in the Napa Valley. Miranda'd been amused by how Gloria made her ambition sound like community service. "The folks who tour wineries appreciate life's special moments. They also appreciate spa treatments using only organic herbal emollients. Why not give visitors to Washington's wineries the same opportunity for special moments and emollients my clients in California enjoy?" Miranda put away the folded sheets and felt cheered as she recalled the accolade Gloria had written in the guest book and posted online. And she was further relieved when, tail wagging again, Rusty followed her into Steve's empty room to watch her make the bed and clean the bathroom. She was less pleased with her pet when she had to reprimand him for slurping toilet water and dripping it all over the floor.

Miranda wasn't the only person in the Valley working that Sunday. Michael was repairing her shed roof. And as Miranda was on her way out to run with Rusty, Steve came in and drawled, "Well, now that I've finished my business with the Lord, I just might change and put in a few hours on the murals this afternoon. I'm like a farmer. My job's a lot easier before it gets cold." As usual she smiled at his wit and wished she could think of something equally witty to reply. The smile would have to do. When Miranda and Rusty returned, the B & B was empty. That day's one new check-in had yet to arrive.

He arrived that evening and a police officer walked in with him. The sight of a uniformed law enforcement official, a holstered gun on his belt, in her B & B propelled the cop-phobic Miranda to the tips of her toes. He was a tall, broad-shouldered, unsmiling man of about forty whose buzz-cut seemed at odds with his chin, which was as long as John Kerry's. He approached her at the counter, blinked a couple of times, pointed to the badge on his belt, and proclaimed, "County Sheriff's Deputy Detective Alex Ladin. You the owner?"

"Yes. I'm Miranda Breitner." She couldn't imagine what he was doing there. Her architect had brought the old building up to code and she had the permits and bills to prove it. She also had her innkeeper's license and certificate of occupancy posted behind the counter. Fire extinguishers and smoke detectors graced every room. Her driving record was as spotless as her kitchen. Rusty had a license, wore a tag. She recalled reading online that the Sunnyvale PD had a history of corruption and personnel changes, but she didn't know much about the county cops except that there weren't enough of them. She hadn't worried about it. Smitten by the old farmhouse and the small-town charm of the busy but still-bucolic Valley, she'd put the local constabulary in the same category as she put the gangs, irrelevant to her and her B & B. She'd have little to do with cops or criminals unless they were featured in TV crime shows. Maybe one of her guests was in trouble.

The detective's voice was deliberately pitched to be audible to everyone in the room and, Miranda thought, to most people east of the Cascades. So she wasn't surprised when Steve and Angela Lacey, another guest, emerged from their respective quarters. The deputy nodded at the newcomers. "There's been a homicide across the street, in the processing plant."

Miranda flinched as fear dueled with denial in her head. Fear won. She feared her ram's horn blower had come to harm or maybe Oskar Hindgrout.

Then she feared her guests could be in danger. Their gasps and mutterings were audible and, in response, the deputy turned and pointed into the darkness. "The building's taped off. But don't worry. We'll be patrolling there from now on. We wanted to let you all know. Tell me, did any of you notice anything going on over there that seemed unusual?" He glanced around the room. When no one came forward, he added, "If you think of anything, call me." He tossed a few business cards on the counter. Miranda's hand trembled as she extended it to claim one.

"I can't tell you the identity of the victim because next of kin have not yet been notified." Detective Ladin turned again as if to leave. Then he pivoted and leaned over the counter, lowered his voice, and addressed his remarks only to Miranda. "I'll be talking to you again, Ms Breitner." His stare was intense and made her feel even more threatened than cops usually did. "Glad to see you have a dog." He reached over the counter to let Rusty who stood beside her sniff his hand. Rusty obliged and promptly ejected a stream of liquid feces at Miranda's feet. Withdrawing his arm, the detective said only, "Hmm, he might not be much help. Might want to think about keeping a firearm handy too."

Miranda paled. She didn't know what was scarier, the message that some-body was killed right across the street or the grim messenger who delivered it. And she didn't know what was wrong with Rusty, either. Even if he didn't poop like that again, she'd take him to the vet the next day. She didn't get to thank the detective before he made it to the door. Instead, she removed her shoes, took them outside, and reentered to clean up the dog shit, while speaking reassuringly to Rusty and her guests.

One of these guests, Angela Lacey, a very pregnant pharmaceutical rep who'd been at the B & B for a couple of days, approached the counter and, in a lowered voice, advised Miranda, "Don't worry. My girlfriends threw me a baby shower and gave me a nine mil and a whole lot of lessons on how to use it. Anybody tries anything here tonight, I've got your back." To her own amaze-ment, Miranda found herself nodding a thank you. But when she checked in her new guest Hank Ames, she felt sick. He was a reporter from a Boise paper there to review the B & B as part of a feature on the Valley as a "Winter Wonder-land." When he made a crack about the Bates Motel, Miranda had to force her lips into a smile.

The guests remained in the front room talking softly. Steve brought out a six-pack of Yakima Glory beer, Miranda heated and spiced cider for Angela, and they all sat around speculating about what might get a factory worker killed. Miranda blanched when Steve said, "Maybe it was a gang hit." He displayed iPad photos of the gang tags defacing the Toppenish murals he was working on. After a discussion about the prevalence of gangs in the area, they agreed the deceased had been the target of either a gang initiation or a gang avenger. The reporter typed steadily on his tablet. Steve more than redeemed himself in Miranda's eyes when he announced his intention to remain at Breitner's regardless of the "doings" across the road. And she wanted to cheer when he added, "I've been here for several weeks and I can assure you, this B & B is a gang-free environment. The only drug dealer at Breitner's is a pregnant lady pushing allergy meds."

At last Miranda tiptoed upstairs, shaken by the news of a murder right across the street from her start-up B & B, by the intimidating messenger who delivered that news, and by the coincidence that a reporter was there chronicling the killing. No doubt he'd discourage Idahoans from visiting the Valley at all, let alone from staying at Breitner's. For the first time since the B & B opened, she considered the soul-sapping possibility that Breitner's might fail. And, no fan of the police, she'd been further unnerved by the visit of a law enforcement officer to that same B & B and by the knowledge that he or one of his cronies would return to interrogate her. The only bright spot was that Rusty hadn't excreted any more liquid shit and seemed himself. He gulped the fresh water she provided and fell asleep.

But she knew that sleep would not come to her easily that night. She couldn't do anything about the homicide, but she could try to calm her fears about dealing with police. So she poured herself a glass of wine, groped in her still unpacked duffel for a moment, and withdrew a few pieces of yellowing paper preserved in a plastic envelope. It was an essay she wrote when she was sixteen at the suggestion of her therapist. "Writing it down in your own words may help you take control of this episode in your life, put it in perspective, and move on," she'd said.

My Interrogation

I'd been in the waiting room at Virginia Mason Medical Center's ER for hours before Timmy's mom and Charles finally showed up. Kathy was hysterical. They went into the room where I figured the doctor was still examining Timmy. Soon two big guys in suits showed up and went into that room and talked with the doctor, Timmy's mom, and Charles. When the two men came out, one of them told me they were both detectives and showed me a badge hanging on his belt. He said they had a few questions for me about Timmy's behavior during the evening, but he didn't tell me Timmy died or that they thought it was my fault. He just said they wanted to chat with me privately at police headquarters. In the car, he said I didn't have to chat with them if I didn't want to, but if I agreed to, anything I said could be used in court.

I wanted to help Timmy. I also didn't want to be rude. And I had no thoughts of court. I told him I'd be glad to talk to him, but I asked him to please call my parents and let them know where I was and ask them to come and get me. He said he'd call them a little later.

But he didn't call them until a lot later. They put me in a little room and for over twenty-four hours both detectives threw questions at me. They just kept asking the same ones, over and over.

"Did you force him to eat?"

"No. Timmy's usually a good eater. I just nuked his fish sticks and mac 'n' cheese and put them on his highchair tray."

"Was his food too hot?"

"No. I always let it cool before I put it on the tray."

"Did you get angry when he wouldn't eat?"

"No, but I was surprised because like I told you, Timmy's usually a big eater."

"Did you get angry when he wouldn't stop crying?"

"No. But I checked him at both ends, you know, like it said to in the training manual I got at the babysitting workshops I took. He didn't have a diaper rash and his gums weren't red either. He wasn't extra warm. There was no sign of a new tooth coming in as far as I could tell."

The first time they left me alone in the little room, I figured they had reached my mom and dad. But they came back without them. Instead they brought in a policewoman carrying a video camera and a baby doll in a dirty yellow onesie. They started in again.

"Show us how you lifted him out of the tub."

"How did you hold him when you picked him up this time?"

"Show us how you got him into his PJs."

"Show us how you put him into the crib."

"Did you drop him?"

Over and over I stood up and pretended the table was the bathtub or the crib and showed them how I had taken care of Timmy. The lady cop filmed this part. Finally they all left, except for the doll.

I hoped this time they really were calling my parents. I was so tired. The ham and cheese sandwich they brought from the vending machine was cold and gross, but I ate it. The same sour-faced woman who took the video came with me to the bathroom and stood right outside the stall while I peed. I could see under the door her foot tapping on the floor. When I washed my hands, I could see her sour face right over mine in the mirror. When we got back to the little room, she finally left. I hoped this ordeal was over, that my mom and dad were waiting in another room.

So I was confused when the bigger detective came back again without my parents. He sat down at the end of the table nearest me, leaned towards me, and started talking like he was my best friend. "Meryl, thirteen is a little young for babysitting. How does it feel to have so much responsibility so young?" Before I could tell him for the millionth time about the babysitting workshops I'd gone to and my certificate, he interrupted. "Have you had much actual experience taking care of babies?" I couldn't believe how rude he was, talking right over my attempts to answer him. His voice got louder. "Meryl, lots of people, adults even, have no patience with crying babies. No one can blame you for trying to make him stop bawling. Did you give that brat a little shake to make him shut up?" He sounded crazy. I was really scared. I shook my head and that's when I saw that my hands were shaking too and one leg.

That's also when he jumped up and started shouting down at me. Then he bent over me and yelled right into my ear. I can still feel his spit spraying all over my cheek and hear him yelling, "Show me, Meryl. Show me how you shook that kid. I can see why you'd do that. Anybody would. Show me!" For a minute I was confused again and I clapped my hands tight over the Timmy doll's ears so he couldn't hear, wouldn't be scared too. "Meryl, is that how you got Timothy to stop crying?"

I only learned Timmy was dead when I was charged with killing him and arrested. I learned later that this doctor thought perhaps little Timmy had died of a new condition called Shaken Baby Syndrome and so he called the police like he was supposed to. I was so sad to hear that sweet little Timmy was dead. And I just didn't get how anyone could imagine that I had shaken him to death. Shaking was one of the "Don'ts" listed in red in my babysitting workshop training manual.

When my parents were finally told where I was and what was going on, I'd already spent a night in jail. They hired a lawyer who argued successfully for me to await my hearing at home wearing an ankle monitor. This house arrest lasted six long months. But when my case finally went before a judge, he dismissed the charges because the evidence, including the video that lady cop made of parts of my interrogation, was inadmissible. Here's exactly what the judge said. "The detectives ignored well-established police procedure: A police officer cannot Mirandize or interrogate a child under fourteen without a parent or other adult representative present." So because the case against me did not go to court, I was not found guilty of killing Timmy Schwartz.

The shrink had been right. Writing about her interrogation and ultimate triumph had been helpful, and reading about it was still helpful. Meryl had been only thirteen, a kid. Two decades later she'd taken the new name *Miranda* because of the failure of those incompetent and bullying cops to Mirandize her properly, and this name had become a source of strength. So when morning finally came, she used that strength to get up and lay out an appealing breakfast for her guests. If necessary, of course she would talk with Detective Ladin. She told herself she could handle his questions. She hoped there was news about the identity of the homicide victim at the factory and that the police would find and arrest his killer soon.

CHAPTER 5

Yakima Valley a Winter Wonderland? Not so Much
*If your idea of a winter wonderland includes being greeted by a detective bringing news
of a gang-related killing directly across the street from the new inn where you've
reserved a cozy room, then Breitner's B & B is the place for you. Otherwise, keep
driving..... Boise Tribune*

Miranda slammed her laptop shut and produced a smile for Steve, who was
usually the first to hit her breakfast bar and the first to leave. But that morning
he had the pregnant and heat-packing Angela Lacey for company. In between
dollops of Greek yogurt, Angela glanced at her phone and declared, "They're
still not naming the guy who got killed across the street. Can't get in touch with
his family. They must be away or something." Miranda thought she knew
exactly what that "something" might be. She was startled to hear herself
speculating aloud. "There are quite a few Orthodox Jewish guys staying in the
Valley now to help in the fruit processing plants with the koshering of the juice-
grape harvest. And yesterday was the first day of Rosh Hashanah."

The rep's brow furrowed.

"It's the Jewish New Year and a very important two-day holiday." Miranda
was again startled, this time to hear herself explaining one of Judaism's High
Holidays. "It's kind of a Sabbath, too. Orthodox Jews don't answer the phone
on the eve of this holiday and for two days after that. It's a holy time."

"So these Orthodox guys wouldn't be working in the plants on this holiday,
right?"

Miranda had expected Angela's question. "Most likely the koshering inspectors are allowed to make their rounds, because the grapes have to be processed
as soon as they ripen. So the commandment to keep kosher trumps the
commandment to do no work on this day. But even though the inspector
himself could be working, his family wouldn't answer the phone." She fell
silent, recalling the lonely wail of the shofar that had spoken so eloquently to
her. Maybe the young man's ages-old solo had been more than a call to prayer,
had been a warning. Or a call for help. The fact that someone, maybe her shofar
blower, was murdered right across the street pushed her once again to her
tiptoes.

Before she could speculate further, Michael texted to say he wouldn't be in
to finish repairing the shed roof that day. He offered no explanation. This was
odd. But now that classes at Heritage had begun, perhaps he had a paper due or
a big exam to cram for. She was so preoccupied with staying calm and keeping
her guests calm that she didn't dwell on it.

Instead, she spent the next half-hour fielding questions about the significance of Rosh Hashanah and the basics of keeping kosher, and then, newly
enlightened, Angela went off to make her rounds of medical offices. So Miranda

was pleasantly surprised when Steve lingered over a bran muffin and a cup of coffee. She wanted to thank him for his beer and his endorsement in the wake of the detective's visit the previous evening. But before she found her tongue, he spoke. "Mandy, I'm tired of eating tacos or pizza by myself. Will you have dinner with me tonight? After your guests check in, of course."

Miranda was so astounded by Steve's invitation that she said yes. What she actually stammered was, "Okay. Okay. I only have one other party due tonight. If they get here before, say, seven, okay." Only later did she wonder how appropriate it was for an innkeeper to date guests or for her to end this already bizarre Rosh Hashanah by going out with a churchgoing Christian on the very first real date she'd had since her failed experiment with Jim in college. Jim was the obliging lab partner she'd contrived to lose her virginity to during her freshman year. After this sticky fiasco, also an experiment for Jim, Meryl had decided sex was overrated. But Miranda was beginning to rethink that.

As soon as Steve was out the door, she left the dishwasher unloaded, the goodies on the counter, and the guests' breakfast dishes piled in the sink. She was in a hurry to take her trusty companion to the local veterinary clinic. Rusty showed no signs of the malady that had caused him to squirt poop the evening before, but she knew she'd feel better if she had him checked out. And as soon as Dr. Cynthia examined him and announced, "He's fine this morning," Miranda felt better until the doctor asked, "Did he get into your household cleansers or rug shampoo or eat anything unusual outside yesterday?"

For an instant, Miranda was thirteen again and indignant at the suggestion that she'd been less than vigilant. Then she reminded herself that she was thirty-three and Dr. Cynthia was just doing her job. "No. On one of our outings yesterday he showed his usual interest in whatever crap littered our path, including the remains of a rodent." She winced recalling the little pile of bloody bones and fluff, perhaps dropped by a sated raptor to be picked clean by an earthbound critter. "I steered him away from it. And I keep my cleansers where he can't get at them even if he wanted to."

"Well, that makes sense." Dr. Cynthia fondled Rusty's ear as she spoke. "Next time bring me a stool sample if you can. If he's pooping liquid, try to catch it in a cup or bring me the rag or paper you use to wipe it up. You can put it in this." She handed Miranda a plastic bag with the clinic's name on it.

Miranda drove back to the B & B, relieved and eager to restore order to the kitchen which was also the lobby. She'd just opened the dishwasher when Detective Ladin returned. This time he didn't reach out to Rusty who stopped barking at a word from Miranda. The detective talked fast. "Like I said, Ms Breitner, I'm back. But while we talk, I need a favor. Can I charge my cell and use yours or your landline to make a quick call?" He held up his cell phone. "My damn phone's outta juice and I gotta report back to Sheriff Carson. Then I'll be free to question you." He made it sound as if being grilled by him was an opportunity she'd been waiting for all her life.

Miranda pointed to an outlet just below the countertop, moved the landline phone to where he stood, placed her cell next to it, pointed at a stool, and, as pleasantly as she could, said, "Coffee?" When he nodded and grabbed the landline's receiver, she poured him a cup of coffee, put out milk and sugar, and moved the plate of now-cold muffins to where he could reach it. When the detective nodded again, she took that as a thank you and, conscious of his narrowed eyes on her, resumed unloading the dishwasher while keeping her ears open.

"Sheriff, Ladin. I'm using the landline at the B & B across the street. Saving my cell. Rabbi Alinsky's not answering his phone, so I went over to the Finest Western where they stay to ask him to help me get in touch with the victim's next of kin, right? The receptionist told me Alinsky and his crew aren't around because today's some big Jewish holiday. Like their Sabbath only more extreme. That's why we couldn't get him on the phone." There was a pause. "Me either. But I'm tellin' you word for word what she said." He was silent again. "Yeah, I checked the rooms myself. According to this same receptionist, the rabbi drove all the koshering inspectors who aren't on shift over to Seattle right before this holiday started. So they're all in their church in Seattle praying."

Shelving dishes with her back to the detective, Miranda allowed herself an eye roll.

"I know, Sheriff, I know. We gotta get up front on this before the press... I get it that having a visitor, a Jew yet, iced most likely by a gang wannabe in the Fruit Basket of Washington just might turn off some tourists and business people." The detective nodded at Miranda who'd just refilled his coffee cup. She felt his eyes tracking her even as he responded to his boss. His scrutiny was more creepy than flattering. "No, Sheriff, I'm not being a smartass. But, Sheriff, we can't do anything without talking to next of kin." Miranda began counting the number of times he said "Sheriff."

"Yeah, Sheriff, she's sure they didn't go to the church they have in Yakima." Miranda tried not to smirk at the idea of a group of Orthodox Jews celebrating Rosh Hashanah in a Reformed Jewish temple where a female rabbi reads the Torah and men and women sit together. "I asked her twice. Yeah, Sheriff, but I got an idea. How about I talk to the kosherer on duty at the processing plant in Grandview? Then I'll meet you back at the crime scene. And here's a heads up. I just left there and the owner, Mr. Hindgrout, is totally steamed cause he had to stop production! But he can't stop the damn grapes from ripening. He wants to talk to you personally, Sheriff. He wants us cops and the victim off his factory floor." While apparently getting an earful, the detective took a bite of the blueberry muffin.

When he spoke again, his gruff voice was suddenly silken with reassurance. "No worries, Sheriff. I got this. I'll drive to the plant in Grandview and talk face to face to the koshering inspector at one of the two plants there. Maybe he can tell us how to reach the victim's family or the rabbi. Then I'll meet you at

Hindgrout's." With the blueberry muffin in one hand and grabbing his barely recharged phone with the other, he added, "I'm on my way, Sheriff. I'll be in touch." Pocketing his phone, he rushed out, saying only, "Thanks, Ms Breitner. I owe you one. I'll be back a little later."

This visit did little to reassure Miranda. How could a brown-nosing detective who couldn't even keep his cell phone charged possibly solve a murder? She knew it was unrealistic, but she wanted real detectives to be like the ones in *Blue Bloods, Rizzoli and Isles,* or *Law and Order* that she and her dying mom used to watch on TV. She still watched them. There the cops were smart and gutsy, hardworking and idealistic. But this real cop was so inept she was tempted to feel sorry for him until she remembered that inept policing was what got her arrested for a crime she didn't commit. She was surprised when Detective Ladin returned just before noon, looking pleased with himself. "Feel free to continue charging your cell," she offered, pointing at the outlet. "Need to use the landline? Coffee?"

"No thanks. And no on the coffee, thanks. Two a day's my limit, so I'm good. And I just briefed the sheriff in person across the street."

Miranda was disappointed that he wasn't going to give her another eavesdropping bonanza. She really wanted to know what was going on. "I couldn't help overhearing your conversation this morning. Were you able to connect with the victim's family?"

"Yeah, maybe. But it sure wasn't easy. Mind if I sit down?"

As he spoke, his eyes were on her. All of her. Again Miranda felt uncomfortable under such intense unacknowledged scrutiny by a cop until she reminded herself yet again that she wasn't thirteen anymore. She persisted. "With the crime scene being so close to my home and my business, I'd like to know what progress has been made."

"I can't talk about an ongoing investigation, Ms Breitner." He hesitated a moment before adding, "But since this one hasn't even started yet, I can tell you how I figure we just might connect with the victim's family."

"That's something. No one wants to stay in a B & B across the street from where somebody was murdered and with the killer still out there." Miranda sat in the other easy chair with Rusty at her feet.

"We're aware of that ma'am. We're working on it." The detective turned to face her before he continued. "When I got to the plant in Grandview, the place was humming. Trucks full of grapes kept coming and a machine was stemming them." He sighed. "Back in the day when I was growing up, me and my brothers and sisters, we picked grapes on the weekend right along with the Mexicans. Now it's all done by machine..."

Miranda settled back into her own chair. This was going to be a long story. "Anyway, I went in and tried to stay out of the way of all the boiling water splashing down. Inside there were mostly machines and big vats and lots of tubes, but I spotted this guy on a ladder, so I identified myself, flashed my badge, and yelled at him to come down. He was wearing all kinds of safety gear. Said his name was David Cohen, and he was the koshering inspector, but he looked young. I asked him to get the plant manager.

"Then I took them both into some kind of cubicle-type office the kid uses and made him sit down and told them both that the koshering inspector at the Sunnyvale plant was dead, murdered." The detective paused and lowered his eyes for a few seconds.

Miranda put her hands in her jacket pocket and jammed her nails into her palms. It wasn't the first time she'd used physical pain to relieve her emotional pain.

"Of course, at first the kid didn't believe me. So he says, 'That can't be. He just got married.'" Detective Ladin shook his head. "Like killers don't take out married people." His eyes rested on Miranda's face, perhaps to see her reaction.

Miranda understood how shock, sorrow, and denial could have crowded David Cohen's Talmud-Torah-honed reasoning skills out of his brain, but all she said was, "I guess he isn't going to be too helpful."

"That's what I thought, but here's the thing. He was a big help. All of a sudden this kid is out of the chair and telling the plant manager to ask the koshering inspector at the processing plant right across the street to oversee operations at both Grandview plants so he can go right away to Sunnyvale. He wants to sub for Isaac and stand by his corpse or something like that. He said that's Rabbi Certified Kosher, Inc., protocol." Before Miranda could reply, the detective continued. "Would you believe this koshering outfit actually has a protocol for dealing with the murder of an inspector far from home on a major Jewish holiday?"

Miranda grew up believing that Jewish brains and brawn could make the desert bloom and defeat enemies who vastly outnumbered them in only six days, so she nodded and added something she'd learned recently, "That's good, because to the plant owners the RCK seal means the difference between selling grape juice and not selling it."

"Yeah, but until a few weeks ago this kid probably hadn't set foot in a factory or a vineyard. And all of a sudden he's calling the shots. I'm telling you, Ms Breitner, that's when things got really hinky. I had my keys out and my car was right outside. So I told him I'd drive him." This kid looks me in the eye and tells me on this Jewish holiday he doesn't drive or ride!" The detective raked his head with his fingers, a reflexive gesture Miranda figured was left over from before he got the buzz cut. She was pretty sure she knew how that offer had gone over, but didn't interrupt. "He says it's only five miles from Grandview to Sunnyvale, so he'll walk! He'll be here in an hour. And he sheds his safety gear and sets off doggin' it. I run after him. I tell him we got a special situation here, we're in a bind. And the kid tells me that he can break the commandment not to ride only to save a life. But Isaac Markowitz, that's the victim's name, is already dead, so…" The detective threw up his hands. "I nearly lost it but that's when I came up with the solution."

"I figured you would," Miranda fibbed. "What did you do?"

"I asked David how about if Sheriff Carson called NYPD and got them to send an officer to Isaac's widow's house to tell her of her loss face to face and ask her to authorize an autopsy. He said she might be at her parents' house in New Jersey for the holiday. But he allowed as how that way at least no commandments would be broken, only the widow's heart. Can you beat that for a response?"

Miranda shook her head.

"It gets better. That's when David told me that even if Isaac's widow was at home, it's forbidden to mourn on this holiday, so she won't be free to mourn the death of her husband until the holiday's over."

She ignored his obvious contempt for a religious tenet he didn't understand. "But Sheriff Carson will make that phone call anyway, right?" She wanted a sign of progress.

The detective stood and checked the time before he answered. "Yeah. And then we'll begin investigating for real. So not to worry, Ms Breitner. Excuse my French, but we're gonna get the son-of-a-bitch who killed this Jew in spite of the fuckin' roadblocks those fanatics put up. But meanwhile, get yourself a handgun. Just to be on the safe side."

CHAPTER 6

Guest book: "Stopped On my way back to Sea-Tac after a two-week consulting gig at Manhattan Project National Historical Park on the Columbia. What a find this B & B is! A comfy bed, a fine breakfast, and no mention of radiation sickness!"
—*Dr. Joan Oneidas, National Park Service*

Once again, the detective's visit left Miranda worried that a provincial and short-handed county sheriff and his deputies were not equal to solving Isaac Markowitz's murder. Detective Ladin was so obsequious and inept as to be a caricature of a competent police officer. While he bumbled around like a bumpkiny version of a lobotomized Columbo, Isaac's family suffered and news of the homicide could seriously impact her business. Not to mention how sad and scary it was to know that a person, a Jew yet, was murdered right across the street. And on Rosh Hashanah.

Miranda regretted blanking on Rosh Hashanah, but there was one holiday tradition she could still observe even if she was a day late and a nervous wreck. After powering through her chores, she grabbed a couple of uneaten brioche buns and Rusty, fed her destination into her truck's GPS, and drove out of town to take Route 22 north towards Granger. Passing canal-watered fields of what Rosemarie had identified as alfalfa and baled hay, Miranda was reminded of how lovely the area was. Soothed, she turned into a side road and followed directions to turn once more. That second turn brought her to the closest somewhat-accessible body of running water, the Yakima River. She and a yelping Rusty scrambled down a break in the reeds and shrubs along the bank to where she could almost reach the stream below.

Her rush to running water was Miranda's attempt to perform *Tashlikh*. When the Rosh Hashanah service ends on the first day, worshippers meet at a nearby river, lake, creek, or beach and walk together with their rabbi to the edge of the water. There they follow the tradition that originated in a request the prophet Micah made of God to cast the Israelis' sins into the sea. Adults and kids alike toss small pieces of stale bread representing their own sins into the water to be washed away.

This was a ritual she and her mom had performed together every year until Mona Weintraub's lung cancer made her too ill to leave home. Even then Mona had torn apart a slice of challah and given Meryl the bread bits wrapped in a napkin to take to the lake and scatter on her behalf. A year later, standing on the bank of the swiftly-moving river with only Rusty yelping and straining at his leash, Miranda felt like a lone lemming. She crouched beside her restive companion. "No, you can't go for a swim, Rusty. Not today. But someday soon I'll bring you back here and throw sticks in the water for you to fetch." She found it odd that her closeness, soothing voice, and a wee chunk of brioche bun failed to settle him. Perhaps he sensed her disquiet.

Resolved to hurry, she held the leash tightly with one hand, stood, and silently asked God for forgiveness for any sins she might have knowingly or unknowingly committed. She asked forgiveness not only for sins she committed during the past twelve months, but for the ones that she committed long ago, like causing her parents' divorce, hating her father, going a little crazy with the cutting, and especially that suicide attempt. At the mention of each sin, she hurled a bit of brioche into the river and watched the current carry it downstream. She asked forgiveness for becoming a "pick-and-choose-Jew," one who kept only those commandments that suited her and ignored the less convenient ones like honoring the Sabbath and both of one's parents even if one's father happened to be an asshole. She updated her list by including a more current misdeed—not doing more for Vanessa Vargas.

Rusty's loud bark interrupted her. He wasn't usually this insistent. She assumed he wanted to swim or more brioche. Only as she turned from the water, did the faint sweet and sour scents of marijuana and vomit reach her. And only then did she become aware of the impossibly ancient little man standing beside her, so close that without fully extending her arm she could touch him if she wanted to. Rusty had been trying to tell her this aromatic phantom was approaching. How had this geezer managed to get next to her without her hearing him? Smelling him? He was too old and too emaciated to frighten her even when he began to sway and mutter. Miranda couldn't understand a word and wondered if maybe he was praying too.

Ears cocked, Rusty was doing his best imitation of a guard dog, but she could tell that her stalwart protector no longer considered this white-haired, wrinkled gnome a menace, in spite of the faded camouflage get-up he wore and his pungent yet putrid stench. In fact, he looked familiar. His sharp nose, straight lips, and even his hair—straggly white strands held together by a strip of what might be leather—all seemed familiar. "Hello."

She wasn't sure he heard her, so she repeated herself and added, "I'm Miranda Breitner. I live in Sunnyvale. I run a B & B there."

"Kamiakin." She had to lean in to hear.

"Kamiakin, like Chief Kamiakin? Are you a descendant of his?" While she and Michael painted the B & B's large front room, her handyman had filled her in on local history, on how "Kamiakin was the only tribal leader who refused to recognize the Treaty of 1855, the treaty that deprived the tribes who became the Yakama Nation of all but ten percent of their land, the treaty whose terms the American government violated over and over." Michael spoke of these events as if they had occurred only the day before.

The gnome nodded and repeated. "Chief Kamiakin."

Miranda thought she knew why this strange fellow looked so familiar. He could be Michael's grandfather, the tribal elder who told his grandson the stories he, in turn, passed on to her. But she couldn't fathom what this old guy was doing there alone or how he got there. She wondered if Michael knew where he was. She tried again to engage him. "My friend Michael Wright told me that your Chief Kamiakin dug a canal to irrigate his vegetable garden and the white settlers realized that they could irrigate the whole Valley the same way. Without Kamiakin this entire place might still be desert."

What might have been a grin or a grimace contorted her listener's lips, and he turned and walked slowly away. Miranda stared after him until he seemed to vanish behind or through, she wasn't sure, a screen of tall dried shrubs dotted with white thistle-like wisps into which his skimpy ponytail blended. She'd have to ask Michael about him. It wasn't a good idea for such an old man to roam around the countryside by himself. She wondered why he'd come to the river. Perhaps it reminded him of his days as a fisherman. Or, maybe like her, he had sins to cast away. For all she knew, he could be asking some ancient river spirit for forgiveness. She should've offered the old fellow a ride. She was starting the New Year off wrong. Damn.

It wasn't until she got back to the B & B that she read the local news on her phone. "Unidentified Student Rabbi Found Dead, Presumed Murdered." The reporter went on to note that detectives from Sunnyvale's Gang Unit and the Yakama Nation Tribal Police Department were joining the County Sheriff's detectives in the investigation. She'd have to ask Michael about the involvement of the tribal police when he came to work the next day. But when she checked her messages, she found one from him saying only that once again he wouldn't be in.

There were three other phone messages. Returning these calls assured Miranda three new bookings. Two were reporters from Jewish newspapers assigned to follow up on reports of a murdered Jew. The third was a food blogger eager to reveal the mysteries of koshering to her followers. Talking with them distracted Miranda from thinking too much about the dead man across the street or the strange old man at the river. But it didn't distract her from thinking about the charming guy she had a first date with that very evening.

This was not only her first date with Steve Galen, but her first real date period. As such, it was fraught with more than the usual amount of promise and peril. Miranda worried, because Steve was worldly, smart, and at least a decade older. Undoubtedly he'd had lots of experience with lots of women while she'd spent her youth as a screwed up recluse, sequestered with her grandmother and her mom. But a glance in the mirror reminded her that it was the red-haired Meryl Weintraub who'd lived that nun-like life, not Miranda Breitner. And Meryl was history. Miranda checked to make sure her roots weren't showing, washed her face, brushed her teeth, and then brushed her curls. She didn't want to change her clothes lest Steve think she was making a big deal out of a simple dinner date. But out of deference to the art restorer's reverence for old things, she removed her small, silver hoop earrings and put on Mona's antique gold ones embedded with tiny stones of black and red.

Downstairs again and awaiting her guest, Miranda was checking her breakfast supplies when Steve called. She feared he wanted to break their date, so she was relieved when he just changed their meeting place. "Hey, Mandy, let me know when your check-in gets there. If it's still light, you can meet me here in Toppenish and I can show you what I've been up to." Miranda often asked him how his work was going and was flattered that he wanted to give her a personal tour. "Then we can drive back to Sunnyvale and have dinner at that little Italian place near the highway. You like Italian, right?"

Waiting downstairs for her guests, Miranda visited Steve's website, hoping to find some useful conversation starters and determine if he was single or not. The list of his pleased clients who provided glowing reviews was extensive as was the photo gallery of art works he'd restored to their original splendor after they'd been damaged by time, weather, vandalism, fire and/or smoke. Steve's brief bio made no mention of family. Of course, remembering how easily she had fabricated her own totally fictitious Facebook profile, she realized he could still have a wife and kids or a girlfriend or both. But she hoped he didn't and noted that she didn't mind that he wasn't Jewish. She was certain that, although she longed for a child, with her problematic past, marriage wasn't an option for her. And a long-distance relationship wouldn't interfere with running her B & B.

Miranda's guests arrived well before the blazing sun began to sink. She checked them in, called Steve, and, leaving Rusty in charge, headed for downtown Toppenish. She was able to park her truck right behind Steve's on Elm Street where he had suggested they meet in front of a mural called *The Rhythms of Celilo*. While waiting, Miranda read the plaque next to the mural and learned that the once powerful Celilo Falls, formerly a site sacred to the tribes, cascaded in the background. In the foreground, native men stood on wooden platforms built out over the roiling waters net-fishing for salmon and clubbing their catch. Near the center of the mural, two men sharing a platform were partly obscured by swirls and zigzags of black spray paint.

Seeing this particular damaged piece up close, Miranda was upset and Steve showed up just in time for her to say so. "My God! This is an important painting, Steve. Michael told me that before the government dammed the Columbia, there were so many salmon here that people could walk across the river on the fishes' backs. Scribbling on this is like scribbling on history."

"And hello to you too, Mandy, why don't you tell me how you really feel?" He grinned. "Seriously, all the paintings are important. The ones that weren't damaged are important too. The taggers just didn't have time to spoil them all or they would have."

"So, how will you get that black paint off this mural without ruining the original? And don't tell me you're going to swab it off with Q-tips."

"But Mandy, I am. That's exactly what I'm going to do tomorrow." He was grinning again. As usual, Steve's grin made Miranda smile. "But first, I'm going to put on my powdered latex gloves and my apron. This is a messy business. Didn't you see that photo of me in the *Yakima Herald-Republic*? I look like The Cake Boss meets Jackson Pollack." He blew away the white powder escaping his gloves and sprinkling his windbreaker as he pulled them on and then donned his apron and bowed. "See?"

Miranda's smile widened to a grin.

"Next I climb up there on my rented ladder with my trusty Q-tips and a glass lab jar which sits on the ladder's shelf. In that jar is my magic potion. I dip a Q-tip in this brew, and start to scrub." He pulled off his gloves and untied his apron and shoved them into his backpack.

"What's in your potion? Seriously. I need to know in case they tag my freshly repainted B & B." She didn't mention that in her nightmares she pictured the one-time farmhouse emblazoned with gang graffiti and deserted by the roadside.

"I mix xylene and alcohol to make a solvent. It's a fancy paint remover."

Steve didn't seem to notice that Miranda suddenly frowned. Memories of helping her parents scrub nasty labels off the white fence around their yard flash-flooded her brain. The paint remover her parents bought took off the white paint as well as the blood-red letters spelling out "Baby Killer."

"Won't that solvent dissolve everything under the black paint too?"

"Not if I mix it right. And I do." Sotto voce Steve added, "That's why they pay me the big bucks." He cranked his volume up again when he spoke next. "My brew isolates, dilates, and strips away the freshest paint, the sprayed on enamel graffiti. It may take off a little of the protective varnish that the artist applied to the original too, but I varnish it when I'm done. And the solvent itself dissolves." He shrugged. Then he paused. "Now listen up, Mandy, because here's the part you're gonna really love." His next pause was mock-dramatic. "I work on only one half square inch at a time!"

"You're kidding!" Miranda admired patience, a virtue that sometimes eluded her.

They strolled from mural to mural along the nearly deserted streets of the dusty old town. A dress shop window ablaze with gleaming satiny *quinceañera* gowns of fuchsia and turquoise rivaled the murals for Miranda's attention. Diagonally across the intersection, the grim black-and-white sign "Center for Victims of Domestic Violence" offered a reality check. Steve was still focused on the murals as he pointed out those that had not been tagged as well as those he'd already restored.

His tone was reverent when he told her, "Commissioning these paintings back in the late Eighties was a brilliant idea. They tell the story of this town. Not everybody likes to get their history from a book or even a museum. But these works of public art bring the old American west to life." He stopped in front of a painting of a local doctor's early car next to a horse and buggy parked in front of the boxy building that had been Toppenish's first hospital. He pointed towards the lower part of the mural. "Look at how he's got the lighting just right! Everything has a shadow and those shadows show the strength of the sun. This artist, Jack Fordyce, is so good with lighting."

Miranda thought the shadows rather grim, but she was nonetheless impressed by Steve's obviously more informed view. It would be fun to go to an art museum with him. All she said was, "Yes. He is. And these paintings are a huge tourist attraction."

Steve didn't respond with more than a perfunctory nod, but Miranda interpreted his silence for agreement.

When he did speak it was to announce, "Okay. My stomach's telling me this tour's over. I'll meet you at the restaurant, okay?"

Back in her truck, driving past the strip malls, collapsing barns, flourishing vineyards, corralled cattle, gas stations, and churches that gave the Valley its unique mixture of blight and beauty, she missed Steve's company. It would have been fun to share her impressions with him, but she also felt relieved from the stress of attempting to be both flattering and flirtatious. On their walk around Toppenish, she had thought she was having fun. But alone again, she wondered. Running alongside Rusty was fun. Baking blueberry scones was fun. Getting a new booking was fun. Even answering guests' questions was fun. But overcoming shyness for hours at a time to make a longer conversation was work. Dating was work. Or maybe she just needed practice. She would get more of this at the restaurant where she'd also get a glass of wine. She was glad to see Steve waiting for her beside his truck.

A genial woman named Annette and the irresistible aroma of garlic welcomed them to Annette's Ristorante. She greeted Steve by name, gave Miranda the once-over, and seated them. They turned their attention to the specials she reeled off and then to the wine list and menu. Steve made Miranda's choice easy for her. "Have the lasagna, Mandy. Annie here makes it herself. It's great." He ordered a bottle of Bale Breaker Ale, and Miranda chose a glass of merlot from a new winery in Horse Heaven Hills.

"Thanks for the tour, Steve. You really know your stuff and you appreciate those paintings."

"These paintings are by real artists, not the kind who stuff a dead sheep with beer cans, spray paint it blue, and call it art. Real artists deserve to have their work respected, not defaced by a bunch of thugs, right?"

Miranda nodded. But she had just spent an hour confronting the destructive work of the gangs. Enough with the gangs already. On a night out, okay, a date, she didn't want to dwell further on the damn gangs. With an ease that pleased her, she changed the subject.

"So tell me, Steve, the murals are in Toppenish where there's a motel. How come you decided to bunk in Sunnyvale? At Breitner's?"

"I figured your B & B would probably be quieter. The one in Toppenish is near the casino. Besides, the Toppenish Public Art Association President, Caroline Evans, said you serve a really good breakfast, and she was right. I'll miss those breakfasts."

Miranda was not so naïve that she couldn't tell that this compliment fell way short of what she wanted to hear. She acknowledged it with a polite nod. "I saw that you've restored almost all the damaged murals. You'll be leaving soon."

"Yes'm, I will. That's why I wanted to have dinner with you tonight, to thank you. You've made me real comfortable for over a month. The grub's been great, and none of my socks has gone missing from my laundry either. I'll be sure to write something nice in your guest book."

Miranda managed to fake a smile. The prospect of Steve's leaving didn't sadden her as much as the realization that, for him, this evening wasn't a date. It was an appointment, an obligatory tax-deductible business appointment like when her realtor took her to lunch to celebrate the closing on the farmhouse or her attorney treated her to a drink when she won her lawsuit. What had she been thinking? Just so the evening wouldn't be a total loss, Miranda reverted to business herself. "Thanks, Steve. And please post that review on-line also, okay? Another good one on my website and on a couple of travel sites right now would really help what with all that's going on."

"Done. But update me, please. Exactly what is going on? What's the latest on the neighborhood dead guy?"

"Don't know. I just hope they at least took the poor young man's body away." Miranda sighed. "A Jewish burial usually occurs within twenty-four hours of the person's death. So the thought of this corpse decomposing on the floor right across the street from me for days without any respect for the human life it embodied is very sad." Miranda felt tears well.

Steve noticed them. "Did you know this guy? Is that why you're so upset?"

Miranda knew the corpse belonged to the solo ram's horn blower she'd heard the day before, a total stranger she'd felt a kinship with. But she wasn't about to try to explain that to Steve now, so she gave him another reason for her sadness. "No, I never met him, but his body's just lying there like trash. And his family...." She ferreted in her purse for a Kleenex. "Almost as an afterthought she added, "And having someone killed across the street isn't exactly good for business."

"Of course. Isn't that Jewish holiday over yet? If it is, the sheriff can make contact with the next of kin." Steve seemed eager to cheer her up.

Miranda looked out the window at the restaurant's red neon sign, a bright flare in the gathering darkness. She spoke with more authority than she felt. "Rosh Hashanah ends tonight at sundown, so the police here should have been able to reach someone from that young man's family already. In New York the sun set three hours ago."

When Miranda and Steve got back to the B & B, he said a cheerful goodnight and headed for his room, clearly satisfied that he'd fulfilled his obligation to his hostess/laundress. Miranda walked Rusty. Disappointed by the way the evening turned out, she blamed herself for Steve's lack of interest in her. *What's wrong with me? He doesn't think of me as a woman. At least not as an attractive woman.* Gradually she allowed as how her lack of experience with dating had left her inept at reading men's behavior. That realization led her to acknowledge that factors other than her lack of appeal might have prevented him from taking her in his arms and so becoming the missing actor in the drama that was her new life. *Like maybe he's married....*

Not until she and Rusty returned did she begin trolling news sites. She learned that poor Isaac Markowitz's young widow in New York had at last been notified of his death and an hour later authorized his autopsy, that Rabbi Alinsky was speeding back across the Cascades, and that Sheriff Carson expected the Yakima County Coroner to return to the crime scene any minute. Miranda stationed herself at the front window of her upstairs apartment with a glass of wine in her hand and Rusty beside her. The window framed the view just like a TV screen. It wasn't long before a van like the ones from the morgue on *Law and Order* pulled into a space between the many stacks of wooden fruit boxes standing sentinel around the flood-lit processing plant parking lot.

To the woman observing from her second floor window, everything going on in that parking lot looked eerily similar to scenes in the crime shows she and her mother had followed during Mona's long illness. But, as Miranda reminded herself, the two men getting that stretcher out of the van weren't actors. They were real. She shivered, pulled her dog closer, and raised her wine glass to her lips. She figured one of those guys for the county coroner and the other for his helper. Together they took the stretcher inside. She expected to wait, knowing the coroner would have to examine the body before they moved it.

After her Orthodox grandma died, there had to be an Orthodox rabbi present to be sure her wizened corpse was respected, as in covered with a sheet and minimally invaded before anybody examined or moved it. Later Grandma Minnie's friends from her shul washed her body and dressed it in the customary white shroud. Miranda shivered again and then sat quietly, sipping wine and reading online accounts of Isaac Markowitz's recent marriage to Eva and of the young widow's initial refusal to believe the NYPD officers who had staked out her apartment waiting for her to return so they could tell her that her beloved young husband was dead.

The coroner and his helper were still inside when the familiar white Subaru roared into the processing plant parking lot and stopped short. Rabbi Alinsky jumped out and ran into the factory itself. Miranda drank from her glass again and waited. She minded waiting less now that the rabbi was on the scene. It wasn't long before he walked out alongside the stretcher bearing Isaac's remains beneath a tent made out of what looked like a white sheet. The rabbi's presence didn't make the sight any less jarring. Miranda remembered how the pious ram's horn blower's sharp notes had reached into her gut and stirred the dregs of her girlhood piety. She put her empty glass on the windowsill and watched the rabbi climb into the back of the van with the corpse. Only then did she give up her vigil and refill her wine glass. She knew that with Rabbi Alinsky in attendance, the treatment of the body of the dead shofar blower would be, well, kosher.

Her sleep that night was fitful and her dream, as usual, formed of larger-than-life memories. Seeing the very real remains of Isaac Markowitz borne out of the factory on that tented stretcher triggered her recollection of her mother's body being borne from their home. In Miranda's Cinemax dream, Mona's skeletal sheet-swaddled corpse appeared as a ballooning cloud of white threatening to submerge the puny stretcher made for lesser mortals. This super-sized chimera continued to swell until it grew too huge to stuff into the waiting van. That's when Miranda awakened, teary and grieving anew. She didn't need a therapist to help her interpret that message from her subconscious. Mona had loomed large in her daughter's lonely life. She still did.

That's why disappointing her mother, even after Mona had been dead for over a year, upset Miranda. It upset her so much that she just wanted to pull her sleeping bag flap over her head and never emerge from that dark cocoon. Meryl Weintraub had been intimate with hopelessness and depression for years, and that morning, for the first time since she moved, their siren song sounded in Miranda Breitner's head. Lying in bed, she castigated herself as a total loser for trying to make a successful business out of a funky foreclosed farmhouse in the notoriously gang-infested and under-policed Yakima Valley. And then she lit into herself for being too unattractive and dull to interest the intriguing Steve Galen, and this failure left her feeling even more hollow and hopeless.

So when the first rays of sunlight slid between the slats in her blinds, Miranda closed her eyes and cursed these relentless heralds of yet another bright, bright day. She was sick of the sun's blaze, tired of slathering her redhead's fair skin with sunscreen in October, and tired of the seat of her truck searing the back of her thighs. Seattle's wet gray days made a more suitable backdrop to her tearful black mood. She would remain in bed with the blinds down and let her damn guests, including Steve Galen, post irate reviews online. Breitner's was doomed anyway.

But Rusty had other plans for his mistress. His nuzzles and nudges made it clear that he expected her to get up and dress and let him out to pee, so she did. And while she was up, she fed him and put out breakfast for her guests. By the time Steve appeared, she was able to greet him pleasantly. "Morning, Mural Man."

"Mornin,' Mandy."

She made small talk, just for practice. "The rhubarb bread is from a new recipe. Let me know what you think." Then she busied herself with one of the other guests, a blind wheelchair-bound veteran come to Central Washington for equine therapy from The Pegasus Project at a ranch in the Valley. This guy, Harlan Atkins, was accompanied by his brother Jerry, who wanted Miranda to suggest a lunch spot. Steve had eaten and gone to work before Miranda finished going over with them the menu of a good tamales place on the way back from the ranch. In such close proximity to the cheerful yet sightless Harlan, it was impossible for Miranda to continue to indulge her own self-pity.

That state of mind lasted until Detective Alex Ladin strode in, triggering painful, angry memories of the inept cops who derailed her life. He looked around, approached the counter, and spoke to whatever he could see of her as she bent over the dishwasher. "Morning. I'm back. Now I gotta finally ask you a few questions."

Miranda straightened up and met the man's intense dark-eyed stare. It made her wonder if she'd grown another head or literally had egg on her face, so she raked her curls with her fingers, passed the back of her hand over her mouth, and forced a polite smile.

"Sure. Have a seat. And here, try some rhubarb bread." She pushed the plate of bread towards him and he helped himself to a slice. "Coffee?" She pointed to the coffee pot and he filled his cup. Damned if she was going to wait on him. But she would be civil if it killed her. "I saw on the news that the victim's family has finally been notified. That's a relief. I really hope you get this guy, Detective Ladin. Nobody wants to stay at a B & B across the street from a crime scene."

"Yeah. I hear you. It would also be good to get a killer off the streets and bring some closure to the victim's family."

His sarcasm caught Miranda off guard. Or was he joking? Either way, this dumb all-eyes cop totally misunderstood her. He thought she didn't care about the dead guy, his family, justice, or the public good. Well, she did, but dammit, she also cared about her B & B. And, unlike his pea-sized brain, hers could hold more than one idea at a time. Besides, she had rights and she'd learned the hard way exactly what they were.

He met her glare, and when he spoke again his tone was conciliatory. "I understand, Ms Breitner. And, believe me, you're not alone. The victim's family, Sunnyvale's mayor, the sheriff, the Chamber of Commerce, the rabbi and the kosherers, and every parent, farmer and business-owner in the Valley all want us to get this killer." He paused to take a bite of rhubarb bread and wash it down with a gulp of coffee. "They want us to get him sooner rather than later and they don't want any more bloodshed or any more press. No pressure though." He shook his head. "You know we finished up at the crime scene and the sheriff finally got the okay from the family to let the coroner move the body. You had eyes on that last night."

Miranda paled. "You were watching me?"

"No. Like I told you, the sheriff sent me over here to make sure the coroner's people didn't run into any problems. So I was on patrol at the crime scene and in the neighborhood. From the squad car in the parking lot, I saw your upstairs light go on and a few minutes later there you were and the light disappeared. Kind of like that guy in *Rear Window*." His smile might have been friendly. Or creepy. "I'm glad you're keeping your eyes open. We need all the help we can get. That's why I have to ask, Ms Breitner, in the days and hours leading up to the murder, did you notice anything unusual going on in the neighborhood? See any strangers? Hear anything?"

Miranda hated to have to share her private experience of hearing the ram's horn with this hard-to-read cop. Nothing good had come of her frankness with the detectives investigating Timmy's death twenty years ago. But she knew better than to withhold information and in this situation, like that one, she really wanted to help. "I did hear something. It was late Sunday morning about the time church services were ending. I was inside finishing up some laundry when I heard a ram's horn."

Detective Ladin rolled his eyes and shook his head, not quite the reaction Miranda had expected. When he spoke, his voice was stern. "This is a serious matter, Ms Breitner."

Miranda resolved to hold her temper. "I'm not joking. I'm Jewish." She paused, waiting for a reaction. When there was none, she knew she'd have to walk him through Rosh Hashanah 101. "And the dead man was Jewish, right?"

The deputy nodded. "I told you, that's why we had such a hard time trying to get in touch with his family or the rabbi here. Because of a Jewish holiday."

"Yes. Of course I remember." She kept her voice even. "Let me explain. Sunday, the day of the murder, was the first day of our New Year and on that day part of the synagogue service involves someone playing a musical instrument from biblical times made from a ram's horn." She thought she saw the detective's lips twitch into a smile that he quickly suppressed. The ancient ritual she described must have sounded ridiculous to him, just like Jesus embodied in a cracker did to her. Miranda took a deep breath. "You can Google it. Anyway, the rabbi told the crew of kosherers that some of them would have to celebrate the holiday in the factories and that they could blow their rams' horns there."

Detective Ladin shook his head as if he found her explanation incredible. "How do you know what the rabbi told his crew? You got ears on him somehow, Mata Hari?" He smiled as if that and his little joke could smooth over the fact that he was questioning her honesty.

Miranda felt her face redden again. This guy played both bad cop and good cop all by himself. It was hard to keep up. "I was in the plant parking lot the day the kosherers arrived, and I heard him giving them an orientation speech."

"Thank you, Ms Breitner." The detective sighed as if he had been doing all the conversational heavy lifting. "I'm going to talk to Rabbi Alinsky and the other workers at the processing plant, and if they confirm what you've told me I'll report this info to the County Coroner. It may help the ME he hires to do the autopsy to determine time of death." He hesitated. "If you're the only one who heard it, that may make you a witness. Are you okay with that?"

Miranda felt her stomach lurch and reached over to rub her hand the length of Rusty's back. She wished she'd stayed in bed. "Doesn't that make me kind of vulnerable? On TV the killers are always trying to do in witnesses."

"Look, Ms Breitner, you said you wanted us to get this guy. To do that, we need your help." He paused. When he resumed speaking, his tone was softer but still stern, maybe even a little menacing. "Besides, like you said, you're Jewish, so if it's a hate crime you're already pretty vulnerable." His lowered voice did not soften the harsh truth of his words.

"Do you really think it's a hate crime? Here? In this Valley?" Miranda's stomach lurched again. She recalled Rabbi Alinsky assuring his new crew of how friendly and helpful Valley folks had always been to his kosherers.

"The investigation's just beginning, so I don't know, and we don't rule anything out." He paused. "Out here we got the occasional nutcase holed up in the desert waiting for the rapture, and once in a while they get bored just waiting. Like I told you the other night, it's a good thing you got this big guy looking after you." He nodded at Rusty and reached over to ruffle his fur. His hand brushed Miranda's, and she repressed her urge to flinch.

If the creep was trying to scare her again, he was doing a good job. She closed her eyes, took a deep breath, and spoke. "Okay, okay. I want to help. I'll do what I can. But I have a question."

He looked at his phone, probably checking the time. "I'll try to answer it if I can have a little more coffee." He refilled his cup.

"Why was the white sheet covering the body tented?"

"You don't miss much, do you? The kosherer who came to the plant to start the machinery again said that out of respect you Jews cover the bodies of your dead with a white sheet. He wanted us to do that as soon as he got there. But us detectives didn't want any trace evidence on the victim's clothes or skin moved or lost by putting a sheet in contact with the corpse, so, as a compromise, we tented it."

"That was nice of you."

"Thanks. We aim to please." He drained his coffee cup and placed it on the counter. "Now, tell me, did you see or hear anything else unusual?"

"Not that I remember, no."

"Were there any guests around that morning?"

"There were two for breakfast and one left early. The other one, Steve Galen, he stayed. He's the art restorer working on the Toppenish Murals. He ate, went to church, came home to change, and then he went to work. He's still staying here. You can talk to him."

"So there was no one else on the premises?" His eyes narrowed.

"No other guests, but a handyman was out back fixing the shed roof."

The detective's eyes flickered.

"He's a college kid who works for me sometimes. He's here a lot. He's real sharp. You should talk to him too. Maybe he noticed something."

"I'd love to talk to him, Ms Breitner, but I need a name." His tone was patient.

She felt her face flush yet again. "Oh, I'm sorry. Michael. Michael Wright."

"You're kidding?"

"No." The fool seemed to think everything she said was some kind of joke.

"Is he on the premises now? The tribal cops are looking for him." The officer stood, cast his eyes around the room, and nodded in the direction of the corridor leading to the back door and the yard.

"No. he hasn't been to work in a couple of days. Why do the tribal cops want to talk to Michael?"

"I can't discuss that with you. But call me right away if you hear from him, okay? Or if you think of anything else. Thanks for your help, not to mention the coffee and the rhubarb bread. That stuff really rocks, Meryl. Can you e-mail me the recipe? I want to give it to my wife."

"Sure. I have your card. I'll send you the link." Even though their parting was cordial enough, Miranda was relieved to hear his car start. And then her breath came short. Detective Ladin knew her real name and the sly son of a bitch had tricked her into answering to it.

CHAPTER 8

Guest book: "After a stay of over a month, I hate to leave this comfortable and centrally located B & B. The amiable owner serves up a locally sourced organic breakfast. My room was quiet, my shower had great water pressure, and I could control the thermostat. Luxury amenities at economy prices!" Steve Galen, Art Restorer, West Virginia

After Miranda realized that chameleon-like Detective Alex Ladin knew her secret and after her B & B's once merely dicey neighborhood became a recognized killing ground, she was more than ever convinced that Breitner's was doomed. If Ladin had seen through her carefully constructed new identity, others could. But they wouldn't have to, because it was just a matter of time before the detective would spread the word about her all over the Valley. And her newest guests, journalists drawn to the murder like addicts to their dealer, would broadcast it to the world. And then Breitner's would surely bomb.

Lynn Dinnerstein, a svelte reporter from Washington's *Jewish Transcript*, arrived hours before check-in, and Al Horowitz, a Woody Allen look-alike from *The Forward* in New York, wasn't far behind. Coincidentally, a petite Texan named Sally Slade who blogged about food and was eager to discover and share the secrets of koshering grapes, showed up way early too. Even before Sally deposited her bag in her room, she looked around and drawled a request. "Miranda, honey, my blog's called *Faith-based Food*, and I bet some of my fifty-five thousand followers would love this B & B. And, just so you know, Rabbi Alinsky's agreed to let me video my interview on koshering with him tomorrow. And then he promised me a tour of the fruit processing plant so I can see the grapes actually being koshered and film it for my followers. But he says the plant is often noisy. So may I invite him here to do the interview?" Sally pointed to the two red easy chairs flanking the fireplace. "This room is so cozy and peaceful. I love it here already. And the interview will only take about half an hour. Please..."

A day earlier Miranda would have welcomed the online exposure, but that day publicizing her moribund B & B seemed about as useful as making dinner for a corpse. Before she had a chance to politely refuse, she felt her phone vibrate. When she nodded in recognition of the caller's name and answered it, Sally mouthed a silent "thank you" and wheeled her suitcase to her room.

The caller was Pauline. Miranda figured she was probably canceling their date for coffee at her home later. Pauline, who often knew what went on in the Lower Valley almost before it happened, would have heard about Miranda. That bastard Detective Ladin had started defaming her already. Miranda assumed she'd just lost the first friend she'd made since she was thirteen. She felt her heart relocate from her knees to her feet.

She could hardly understand this new friend's seemingly hiccupped words. It took a moment to realize that Pauline was not hiccupping, but sobbing. "Oh, Miranda, the police have Nelson! They're holding him at headquarters for questioning. They suspect him of killing that poor young man."

Miranda silently chastised herself for being relieved at this news, so different from what she'd expected to hear. But when she spoke, her voice was warm with genuine shock and concern. She said what her mother would have said. "Oh my God, Pauline, I'll be right over. I'll bring coffee. Not to worry. Nelson's a saint." Miranda's sole contact with this man she was so quick to canonize had been when he came by once with eggs when Pauline was sick. "I bet Nelson will be home even before I get there."

On the way, Miranda reflected on the fact that she'd made two friends in her new community, Pauline, whose husband was being held by the cops for questioning about a murder, and Michael, who was a person of interest to the Yakama Nation Tribal Police. And they both worked for her. Would they be her friends even if they didn't? If they knew all about her? And what about Rosemarie? She was proving to be a good friend too. Would she continue to refer her clients to the B & B? Miranda saw her business going down the tubes for sure when Detective Ladin opened his big mouth and outed her to anyone who would listen.

Miranda shivered as she remembered her friends deserting her, because although she was not tried and found guilty of killing Timmy, she was not proved innocent either and no one else was charged. So her classmates and their parents continued to suspect and fear her and she spent much of her adolescence and young adulthood as a pariah. But as she pulled into Pauline's driveway, she realized that if somebody didn't figure out who killed the kosherer, Breitner's would fail and Detective Ladin's revelation wouldn't matter.

Pauline was hunched over the vintage Formica and chrome table in her sunny kitchen with only a box of Kleenex and a yard full of clucking chickens for company. Fearing that these fowl and Rusty might not take to each other, Miranda had left him home. She was sad to see her friend's eyelids red and puffy and her distinctive French braid only partly plaited, leaving half her gray mane straggling down her back. Miranda sat down and, with an apologetic nod to the chickens, handed Pauline a thermos of the chicken soup she'd made for herself in honor of Rosh Hashanah. "This is better than coffee. Now tell me what happened. What do the police want with Nelson? Is he a witness?"

"I wish." Pauline blew her nose. "I think he's a suspect." Before Miranda could ask why, Pauline continued, her voice low. "It's partly because he found the body and called the police."

"They probably want to ask him about what he saw and the time and things like that. They already talked to me." What she didn't add was that on TV crime shows, the unlucky person who finds the body and reports it is often a prime suspect.

Pauline sipped her broth. "Thanks for coming over. Your soup is good." Her shoulders stiffened with the effort of containing another sob. "But it's not just that he found the body. They're talking to him because he was friends with the Jew. They used to eat lunch together."

"Is that a crime? You're friends with me." Clearly Pauline had no Jewdar, wouldn't recognize a Jew if one walked into her kitchen and handed her a thermos of homemade chicken soup. Miranda figured she'd better make her religion clear in case her first new girlfriend in twenty years harbored anti-Semitic feelings.

It was as if she had not spoken. "Yes. But this murdered man, Isaac, was a kosherer, he was a Jew."

Miranda tried again. "I'm Jewish, not Orthodox like that fellow, but I'm definitely Jewish." She paused, scrutinizing Pauline's face. She was relieved when it registered nothing more than surprise.

"Oh. I didn't know…

"Well, I want you to know. But right now it's beside the point, isn't it?"

Pauline straightened in her chair and looked Miranda in the eye. "To Nelson and me, faith is never beside the point. It is the point. Nelson's a devout follower of Christ. He would never, ever kill someone." This protestation of her own and Nelson's belief seemed to strengthen Pauline.

Miranda was relieved to see her friend's despair evolving into indignation and decided this was not the time to begin a discussion of the Crusades or the Inquisition. Instead she said, "Pauline, the cops probably just want to see if Nelson learned anything about Isaac that would explain why somebody'd want to kill him." Miranda hesitated and drew on her own experience. "But you know what? Just in case, it wouldn't hurt to get him a lawyer. Do you have a lawyer?"

"My neighbor's son was in a car accident last year and he had a good lawyer, somebody from our church. I know his wife. I'll call him."

"Good." Miranda checked the news sites on her phone. "There's nothing on the paper's website about Nelson. Pauline, how did you find out about him being questioned? Did he call you himself?"

"Yes. Of course. He wanted to be sure I was sitting down, said he didn't want to upset me. Hah!"

"Finding that body must have been quite upsetting for him." Miranda waited, confident that Pauline wouldn't be able to resist repeating Nelson's account of his grisly discovery.

"He came home late that day all upset, and no wonder. He had to wait for the detective and talk to him. Tell him how he was going to meet with the kosherer, with Isaac."

Miranda nodded.

"It was Sunday, so Nelson had to miss church, which he hated doing, but during grape harvest…" Pauline shook her head at the tyranny of nature. "And it was some kind of Jewish holy day too, so Isaac also had to miss going to his church. But he could pray at work, had to, in fact. He even played this special instrument Jews always play on this holiday. He used to go into the storage room to pray in private and play it there. Nelson and the others heard it that morning during their break. Now don't take this wrong, but Nelson said it sounded like a ewe giving birth."

Miranda's smile faded when she remembered that Isaac's poignant solo that day turned out to be his last. But she was relieved to learn that she wasn't the only one who heard it.

"So at lunchtime Nelson went to meet Isaac in the storage room and see the instrument he'd heard. He really wanted to learn about it. That's where he found Isaac face-down on the storage room floor." Pauline's face seemed to fragment into pixels while she shuddered and swallowed a sob. She somehow pulled her features together before she spoke again. "Isaac wasn't wearing his hard hat and Nelson could see that his head was bleeding. "Nelson figured the young man had fallen and hit his head on that cement floor and would come to. My Nelson did what he's supposed to according to company protocol. He called 911 and then he called the plant manager, and then, when the kid still wasn't moving, he prayed to Our Lord to help his friend." Pauline lowered her head.

Nelson had not returned when Miranda left, but Pauline had made an appointment with a lawyer and called her daughter-in-law who was en route. Back at the B & B she pulled into her parking spot and saw Michael's truck, so she followed the sound of hammering to the yard. The young man knelt atop the shed, nailing new shingles to the old roof. "I'm almost done."

"Good. I'm glad to see you." Miranda paused. "Stop in, please, before you leave so I can pay you. And I want to ask you something."

She walked around to the mailbox and stood with her back to the factory looking at Breitner's B & B, its painted sign a faint beacon in the diminishing light. What would happen to the place when she left? She'd poured her heart and her mother's hopes, not to mention a big chunk of her hard-won reparation money, into this building. It was more than just her home. It gave her life purpose. She loved her round of housewifey chores, making breakfasts and beds, cleaning up, doing laundry, grocery shopping. She also loved keeping the books and breakfasting with guests. And she'd begun to put down new roots in this fertile Valley where farms and factories and different kinds of people were all neighbors. She didn't want to leave, had nowhere to go. She had a stake in solving this murder, damn it. She grabbed the mail and went in.

The B & B's guest book was on the counter where she couldn't miss it instead of on its shelf near the door. It was open to a nice review from Steve that doubled as a goodbye, because his keys were next to it. Miranda had not looked forward to a face-to-face goodbye from him and his bill was paid through the next morning, so his abrupt day-early departure was almost a relief. She got her cleaning equipment and, with Rusty at her heels, went to work to ready Steve's room for a new occupant. She threw open the windows to let in the fresh autumn air. With the brisk breeze gusting in while she changed the sheets and aired the quilt that served as a bedspread, Miranda felt a bit better. She had to shoo Rusty out of the bathroom where, in spite of her efforts to break him of his one bad habit, he greedily guzzled the toilet water.

Banishing him from the room by way of punishment, she cleaned the bathroom and then did her routine check of the drawers, certain that the meticulous Steve hadn't left anything behind, but checking anyway. She was wrong. In the night table drawer she found a small copy of the New Testament. Well, she'd just mail it to him. Then she opened it and read the words on the inside of the cover. Steve's scrawl seemed at odds with the formal somewhat archaic message it spelled out, *"For the next weary traveler to lay his head here... Rest At Home O Wanderer Alone!"* So he'd meant to leave it. Annoyed because the religious book violated Breitner's decidedly nonsectarian policies, she pocketed it to place in a drawer that already served as a lost-and-found for a few other items left behind by guests.

She was getting ready to take Rusty out when Michael came in. Miranda talked while she counted out the money she owed him. "A detective from the county was here this morning to question me, and he asked about you. He probably wants to know if you saw or heard anything unusual while you were working here the day of the murder. Also he said the tribal police are looking for you too. Said I should let him know when you show up."

"Thanks." He pocketed the cash. His next words came even more slowly than usual, as if he resisted having to say them, having to reveal his personal life to his boss. "The tribal police already talked to me. They're looking for my grandfather again." Michael's voice was low. "I'm sorry I've been kinda scarce around here lately. I've been trying to track him down too. He went missing a couple of days ago."

"That's worrisome. I'm sorry, Michael. Can you walk with us? Rusty's been waiting for this outing. And I want to ask you something about your grandfather." Michael nodded and they left the building, crunching brown leaves beneath their feet as they walked past the processing plant and the row of small houses, some nearly hidden behind weeping still-green willow trees. "You must be worried about him, Michael. Tell me, is he a very small old man who wears camouflage clothes and has a pony tail?"

"And smells like an alley where some pothead just puked? Yeah. That's him." Michael sighed and slowed his pace to match hers. "Where'd you see him?"

"I was by the river off Route 22 over near Granger with Rusty the other day. And this little old guy kind of snuck up on me. He looks a lot like you. We talked for a minute or two. He said his name was Kamiakin and that he lives on the reservation. He disappeared before I could offer him a ride... "

"That's him. His name is Joseph Wright, but they tell me he's been wrong ever since he got home from Vietnam." Michael shrugged off his bad pun. "He said he killed a lot of people over there and that made him way different than he was." The boy frowned and shook his head. When he spoke next his voice was weary as if the story he was about to repeat exhausted him. "He moved out of grandmother's house in town and ever since he's been squatting in an old cabin way out on the rez. Then after grandmother died, my mom died and my dad went to jail and died there." Michael rattled off this list of losses as if such losses were routine. "Then it was just me and my older sister at home. She took care of me for a while. When I got older, she moved away. So grandfather took me in. I had to walk pretty far every day to get to and from the school bus." Michael rolled his eyes at this memory. "Back in the day he still fished a little." Perhaps it was pride that made his voice rise when he added, "Taught me to fish before I went to kindergarten. So now I'm taking care of him. Or at least trying to." He kicked a stick out of their path.

Miranda was struck again by how old this boy sounded, old and tired. Keeping tabs on a geriatric alcoholic suffering from PTSD out in the middle of nowhere while going to college and working had to be at least as challenging as taking care of a dying mom in Seattle. Miranda pictured the smelly old man babbling to the river. "What was your grandfather like before he served?"

"They say he was a real warrior and our storyteller. Like Sherman Alexie, only he didn't write anything down." When Michael beamed at the thought of the celebrated Indian writer, Miranda realized she'd never seen him really smile before. "He knew the old ways and tried to teach young ones our religion, our Sahaptin language, our history, and, you know, the culture of our people. But when he came back from Vietnam, they say he'd turned into a ghost."

"Why didn't your sister take you with her when she moved?" Miranda didn't stop to consider that the answers to all her questions were none of her business.

Michael apparently felt he'd revealed more than enough about his personal life to explain his dereliction of duty, so his next answer was oblique. He bent down to pat Rusty who chafed at his leash. "I don't like the city. Out here I can fish."

Miranda was distracted by Rusty who'd stopped walking not to pee or poop, but to vomit. Miranda stood over the little puddle of glop and stroked his fur and in a moment the big animal resumed his search for a spot deserving of his perfectly normal-looking poop. Miranda was relieved that he felt better and that, because they were outside, there was no need to clean up his puke. She used her plastic bag for its intended purpose. Rusty was scheduled to have his teeth cleaned at the clinic the next day anyway, so to be sure he was okay, she'd take this stool sample and save herself the trouble of making a second trip.

She glanced at Michael who had seemed oblivious to Rusty's disgorgement. When the boy spoke, his expression had hardened. "The sheriff's deputy, he's trying to pin the Jew's murder on my grandfather."

"What? Why on earth would he think your grandfather would kill a Jewish rabbinical student from New York who's here for just a few weeks to kosher grapes?"

Michael sighed at her ignorance and naiveté. "They need to pin it on somebody fast and he's Indian. And it doesn't help that the only time he's in town, he's drunk or stoned and talking crazy." Michael hesitated before blurting, "Besides, the detective told the tribal police they found his fish club near the body at the factory. The thing is, Ms Breitner, my grandfather gave me that fish club years ago at my First Fish Ceremony. It's mine, but the cops, they don't know that yet. Somebody lifted it from my truck. It's worth something, you know? But I would never sell it. Whoever took it left my nets and rods." Michael's chin jutted forward and his shoulders straightened, so that his walk began to look like marching. "I gotta tell the detective it's mine. I can't let him take my grandfather in."

The thought of this bright and hardworking boy being falsely accused of murder and going to jail to protect his equally innocent grandfather evoked empathy in Miranda. She knew what it was to be falsely accused so a sensational murder case could be closed quickly. And she also knew that at this point she had little to lose, so she was in a good position to try to help Michael. If only the police would stop wasting time questioning convenient scapegoats, they could focus on finding the bastard really guilty of murdering that poor young man. Even on TV, it disturbed her when the police focused on the usual suspects and ignored other possibilities. And if the Seattle cops hadn't been so certain she'd hurt Timmy, they might have figured out who actually did. For a moment, her thoughts vied for expression with her bitter memories.

Her thoughts won, and she shared them in her own anger-fueled rush of pronouncements. "Well, Michael, you didn't do it and neither did your grandfather. You need a lawyer." Without waiting for him to reply, Miranda added a promise. "I'll lend you the money to hire one. You can work off the debt." In her eagerness to help, she forgot that soon she might have no work for herself, let alone for him.

Michael's shoulders went back even further, threatening his balance, and Miranda feared that she might have hurt his feelings by offering to fund his legal bills. After so many lonely years she had a lot to learn about how to talk to friends, how to be a friend. She knew she was right when he replied curtly, "Thanks, Ms Breitner. I got this."

Eager to change the subject, she queried, "So do you have any idea where your grandfather is?"

"I have some ideas, a few places I haven't tried. But now…"

"Aren't you worried about him? The nights are getting cold. And those gangs… " She remembered Vanessa Vargas and again hoped the girl was warm and safe.

Michael's answer relieved her. "My people have always known where and how to camp in winter. And the gangbangers are afraid of him. The way he, you know, appears and disappears they think he's a zombie and that bullets don't hurt him. Besides, they have their own problems now."

"And what might those problems be?" Miranda was delighted to learn that the gangs, had problems. She'd spent most of several nearly sleepless nights researching gangs online, and she was not above hoping these problems were serious enough to put an end to their murderous lifestyle. She shared her fantasy with this young man who had just shared some of his reality with her. "Did all the addicts in the Valley who buy drugs from them suddenly go into rehab? Did all the gang affiliates who smuggle drugs into Canada surrender to the Border Patrol? Is the legalization of pot in Washington going to destroy the market for the weed grown in the woods north of here that the cartels control and get the gangs to sell for them? So now the drug business in the Valley is so bad the gangs have no one to distribute to but each other?"

"Sorry, no." There was a grim twitch of one corner of Michael's mouth that might have been a smile. "But I heard they're questioning a Sureño in connection with tagging our murals."

CHAPTER 9

Guest book: "Because of the murder in the fruit processing plant across the street from this B&B, I couldn't do the interviewing and filming I came to do there, so I only stayed one night. But the innkeeper was very understanding, and I'll be back as soon as they lock up the killer." Faith-based Food blogger Sally Slade

Whenever she drove north out of the flat Lower Valley with its fields, farms, and factories, Miranda felt she was leaving semi-rural America and entering another universe, a city with a few high-rise buildings, a convention center, a museum, and a theater. Located in the hillier Upper Valley and with a population of over ninety thousand, Yakima is large enough to boast a synagogue. During her illness, Mona, with Meryl at her side, had found comfort in the rituals of her religious roots. Although Meryl had never regained her own faith, she attended synagogue willingly, grateful for the peace her mom experienced. In the months since Mona died, Miranda had not been to a single temple service.

But she interpreted the last blast of Isaac's shofar as a private and personal call back to prayer that she couldn't, didn't want to, ignore. She would pray and also fast as the holiday required. Most nights she nuked frozen pizza or a chicken pot pie and washed it down with a few glasses of wine in front of her laptop. But late that afternoon she poached a chicken breast and some mushrooms in white wine, roasted tiny new potatoes, and made a salad. It seemed odd to go to so much trouble for only herself, but she did. After enjoying her meal, she showered and put on her good pair of black pants, a black silk blouse, and the purple jacket Mona had always liked on her.

She'd made other preparations as well. The week before, Miranda had asked Pauline and Rosemarie to suggest a part-time worker to help out at the B & B when she had to be away for more than an hour or two. Rosemarie's referral, Darlene Baez, seemed perfect. "She's helped out in my office. She's a people person with office skills, experience, and a great work ethic." Rosemarie was right. A trim, graying Sunnyvale widow in her mid-sixties, Pauline had worked as a receptionist for a local dentist until he retired. According to the letter of reference he provided, as well as the one from her pastor, Darlene was reliable, bilingual in English and Spanish, personable, and at home with computers.

While interviewing her, Miranda learned that Darlene also loved dogs. She was working because she liked to give her grandkids a few dollars every now and then without dipping into her "old age fund" or her "church money." She even seemed unfazed by the murder just across the street. "I live alone now, so I know how to take care of myself," she said, patting her purse. Miranda envied her confidence and didn't mention that just the day before she'd had a locksmith put a deadbolt on the door to her own apartment. Leaving Darlene and Rusty in charge, Miranda had felt comfortable setting off for synagogue.

As she neared Yakima, she felt a little like a homing pigeon and a lot like a prodigal daughter. But Yakima's Temple Shalom was not her mother's imposing Seattle temple. Rather, it was a modest two-story house fronted in gray stone. It didn't stand out from the other dwellings on the quiet residential street except for a simple white wooden sign over the front steps on which *Temple Shalom* was printed in letters painted gold. The living room and dining room that served as the small sanctuary of the only synagogue within sixty miles was filling rapidly. Miranda assumed that, like her, on that night, the people sitting in the folding chairs sought forgiveness and redemption.

There was no cantor, so a mellow-voiced male congregant rose and opened the service singing the familiar mournful Kol Nidre prayer in which Jews request forgiveness for any promises they make to God but may not be able to keep in the year to come. Aware that Breitner's B & B could go under very soon, Miranda asked forgiveness for being unable to keep her promise to her dying mother to move, open a B & B, support herself, and finally be "at home in the world." To Mona Weintraub's still-grieving daughter, this promise had been a sacred vow. By the time the singer sat down, Miranda was teary-eyed and groping in her purse for a Kleenex. When the fellow sitting next to her pushed a whole packet of tissues into her hand, she took it and murmured her thanks.

She was relieved when Harriet Golden, a young visiting rabbi sent by the Union for Reform Judaism, began to lead the service. Rabbi Golden's flaming red Jewfro threatened to unseat her bobby-pinned skull cap, and her white robe stopped short of her white leather cowgirl boots. She introduced herself in a voice that spiced solemnity with confidence and excitement. Rabbi Golden made the Jews' annual fasting and anguished search for forgiveness and repentance sound doable, natural, and, even exhilarating. "After all," she explained, "during the days before Yom Kippur we have presumably sought and obtained forgiveness from the people we've wronged, so on Yom Kippur, we're free to seek forgiveness for our sins against God. What an opportunity!" Eyes agleam during her sermon, Rabbi Golden proclaimed that the holiday is not so much an orgy of breast-beating as a win-win occasion.

Listening to this exciting, young, red-haired woman, Miranda flashed back on the red-haired girl she had once been, a girl with her own share of chutzpah and spirit. Twenty years later in Temple Shalom, surrounded by total strangers who were also the closest relatives she had left in the world, this memory caused something heavy in her chest to shift. She actually felt this weight slide over a little, making room for a bit of the can-do spirit that had characterized her before her youth was stolen.

Even this fleeting channeling of her younger self inspired a surge of determination. This time around, Miranda wasn't going to sit by and let Detective Alex Ladin or anybody else define her. She wasn't going to let Breitner's B & B go down without a fight either. And if she fought hard and well, she might still keep her promise to God and to her mother. Driving home that evening, Miranda grinned at the realization that, after twenty years, she'd finally gotten some of her groove back. And it felt good.

On her return to the B & B, Miranda asked Darlene to stay a few minutes longer because she had an errand to run. While she changed her clothes upstairs, she rationalized what she was about to do. She needed to help get that murder solved or all her new resolutions would be meaningless. The county cops who were thinking at all seemed to be thinking inside their own familiar box where they kept the usual suspects. To help them find the killer, she needed to see the crime scene. TV's Laura Diamond always saw things the other detectives and crime scene investigators missed. She just might spot something. But Sally, the food blogger, had been denied access to the processing plant, even though they'd promised her she could tour it with the rabbi. Since the murder, they weren't accepting visitors, so Miranda would have to get in there on her own. She squatted beside Rusty, grabbed his ears, and spoke directly to his nose. "Sorry, Rusty. But I'm going solo. Tonight. Right now. Before I lose my nerve."

She hurried downstairs and waved goodbye to Darlene and the crestfallen Rusty. She trotted across the street and squeezed into a small recess formed by three tall stacks of wooden fruit cartons among the many stacks filling part of the parking lot. She knew this niche was there, because from her upstairs window she'd often spotted a female worker disappear into it and then noted puffs of smoke rising and dissolving into the clear sun-bright air. Miranda's dad had been a smoker too, and for a moment she shuddered at the memory of his dirty-ashtray aura and her mother's and her own useless attempts to persuade him to quit.

But that night the secret smoker's retreat was a perfect stake-out spot from which Miranda could see without being seen. She scanned the parking lot and as much of the interior of the plant as she could glimpse through the open entry. She hoped to avoid any factory employees or koshering inspectors who worked through the nights during the grape harvest. But if she did meet someone, she had a ready excuse for being on the premises. She rumpled her hair and pinched her cheeks to redden them.

Then, seeing no one about and undeterred by the NO TRESPASSING sign, she turned on her phone's flashlight and walked across the parking lot. She waved her flare to and fro and called Rusty's name every few steps. Ostensibly looking for her missing dog, she strode past a dumpster-like cart heaped with fragrant grapes and into the dimly-lit and seemingly empty processing plant. The noise of the machinery assaulted her ears and made her voice inaudible, but, sticking to her script, she kept hollering the two syllables of Rusty's name into the cavernous space while her eyes adjusted to the faint light and her ears to the racket.

The vats looming above her cast shadows on the walls and the concrete floor, making the sweet-smelling space really eerie. These same shadows made it hard to see the serpentine coils of tubes just overhead, so she kept her eyes low glancing up only occasionally to be sure the current kosherer or a plant worker was not about to accost her. She felt drawn to another smaller room, perhaps the storage room referred to in the newspaper as the place where Nelson had found Isaac's body. There was a doorway but no door, and once inside Miranda scoped out the large square room. Three walls were lined with round metal tanks that reached nearly to the ceiling. The wall broken by the doorway was lined with shoulder-high blue cylindrical jugs. She walked around the room, peering into the space in each corner.

She forced herself to look at the floor. If any of Isaac's blood still stained the cement, that stain was obscured by the shadows cast by the looming vats. Nonetheless, this cold, hard, concrete slab was where poor Isaac had prayed, played his final solo, and later died. Saddened by this image, she let her eyes flit from tank to tank and then to the blue jugs before leaving what was left of the crime scene.

Next she walked over to what she took for the kosherer's makeshift cubicle. Aware that the current kosherer might well be inside, she continued to holler Rusty's name into the well-lit din. Miranda peered through the glass window pane that was the top half of the cubicle door. The office appeared empty. She was about to try the door knob when abruptly the clanging ceased. The welcome silence was broken by the deep voice of God thundering from on high. "Stop where you are! Don't touch that dawr!" The startled Miranda reminded herself that God did not have a New Jersey accent. In fact, the voice belonged to Rabbi Alinsky, and she followed it to where the rabbi was scrambling down the ladder leading to the brim of one of the vats of boiling water. Without removing any of his protective gear, he sprinted over to her.

"Hello, Rabbi Alinsky. Sorry to alarm you. I'm Miranda Breitner, remember? I own the B & B just across the street. My dog's missing, and I think he might have wandered in here. He's done that before. I guess he can't read that *No Trespassing* sign." When the rabbi appeared oblivious to her joke, she called to Rusty again before saying, "Rabbi, I'm surprised to find you here at this hour on this night of all nights. Are you keeping an eye on your team after what happened?"

"I'm joining my team by substituting for Isaac Markowitz, may he rest in peace. I cannot ask my kosherers to work in this Valley if I don't set an example, show that Isaac's death was an aberration, that we're safe here."

"It doesn't look all that safe. What do you do up on that ladder? It's so high."

"I check the temperature of the water."

"I guess it's pretty hot. I've been trying to steer clear of it, but it overflows and splashes down."

"Koshering is all about purifying. So we have to purify even the exteriors of the vats. That's why we make them overflow."

"Wow! Even the outsides?" Miranda's awe was not feigned. "So that hot water pushes the grapes through the tubes and purifies them?"

"Yes. Hashem willing. And we keep checking. If even one grape goes through at the wrong temperature, we start that batch again. We have a sight glass that lets us see if the grapes are going through properly and a divert valve to stop the process if they aren't. And the koshering inspector, he has to check all these factors and then sign a seismograph printout that records the temperature fluctuations on each of his rounds."

"Not such an easy job."

"Oh, there's more." Rabbi Alinsky pointed to the office Miranda had been about to enter. "In there, he examines the RCK labels for the enzyme additives and counts the seals from RCK that he's going to affix to the newly-koshered grape juice and to the trucks that carry it away. It's a big job we do, but it is to fulfill a commandment." He paused as if he had just remembered something. "Wait right here, if you will, Ms Breitner, please. I have to restart the processing and then I want to ask something of you." Shaking his head, he entered the cubicle, closed the door behind him, and flicked on the light.

Even through the window, Miranda could see smudges of deep purple underlining the rabbi's eyes, his sunken cheeks, and the pallor of his skin. The man opening a laptop in that little room was a shadow of the zesty, self-assured fellow she'd seen from afar the day he arrived with his crew. Miranda's glance swept the cube, taking in the piles of paper, and the small flat boxes plainly labelled *RCK Seals*. She watched the rabbi as, without bothering to sit, he typed for a moment or two. The clanging resumed.

Just then a processing plant worker materialized out of the noise. He, too, looked tired and worn. If he was surprised to find Miranda in his workplace at that hour, he didn't give any indication, but merely nodded at her and stuck his head in the door of the little office. "Everything okay, Rabbi?"

"Yes. Not to worry, Peter. Ms Breitner lives across the street and she's looking for her lost dog. I just reactivated the heat exchanger." Peter nodded and left, and the rabbi returned to the office doorway, speaking quickly. "Ms Breitner, if I see your dog, I'll return him to you." He paused and then, with Peter out of earshot, he talked even faster. "My employers, the executives at Rabbi Certified Kosher, Incorporated, were not happy when they learned that one of our koshering inspectors was murdered on the job here or that the grapes in the processing plant were exposed to a dead body for several days or that goy detectives were in here alone with the fruit and the body. As I said, koshering is about purifying, and there is nothing pure about a murder and a corpse, even a Jewish corpse." He shook his still-helmeted head and went on. "And the press, even the Jewish press.... they're like vultures. The other day that miserable man staying at your place asked me if I had another job lined up after RCK fires me. *Oy vey!*

"I've been working Isaac's shifts even on this holy night. I've also been talking with his heartsick widow and his parents in New York and with his grief-stricken and frightened friends and colleagues here." It was Miranda's turn to nod. The rabbi lowered his head before going on. "And the police have kept me busy too. They're questioning all my kosherers, even those in temple in Seattle at the time of the murder, even those working in other plants." He paused and whispered, "Even me."

"They probably figure some of you might have been close enough to Isaac to shed light on who wanted him dead."

The rabbi nodded. "Perhaps they think we Jews know of a person who might do such a thing. But we don't. Isaac was a *mensch*, a good man, a brilliant scholar. He just got married. Who would want to kill such a person?" Miranda marveled that his beard did not come off in his hands, so hard did he yank at it. "This is a dark time." Then, as if obligated, he offered some assurance. "But like I told my wife, 'Yea though I walk through the valley of the shadow of death, I shall fear no evil. *Adonai* is with me.'" His deep sigh, a groan almost, belied his words.

And Miranda heard his next words as a plea for help from a man who wanted to cover all bases. "Ms Breitner, you have a front row seat at what goes on in this place." He gazed around at the tubes and dripping vats. "And I can see that you are bold and sharp-eyed. And surely, like me, you are worried about the effect of Isaac's murder on your safety and your business. Please, if you noticed anything odd or hear something, tell the police and help them find the killer who took Isaac's young life. This Valley must once again be a safe place for us all to live and work together. No more lives must be lost to this fiend."

At these words, Miranda found herself shivering. "From your mouth to God's ears." This expression, a standard of Mona's, flew from her lips like the prayer it is.

"I don't understand it. My team has never had a problem before in this Valley. People here are good. We must have faith. *Adonai* will come through for us."

Miranda replied tartly, "God may need a little help on this one, so I'll keep my eyes open and my ear to the ground, Rabbi. Let's keep in touch."

In her new guise as the Lord's helper and with her brain brimming with all that she had seen and heard, Miranda left the factory both exhilarated and scared. She wanted to help solve Isaac's murder if she could; in fact, had already decided to do so, but she didn't want to do anything that would raise her profile in the Valley. So for the benefit of whoever might notice, she continued to shout Rusty's name into the night when, for the second time that evening, a man's voice boomed out of nowhere. "Quit that yelling, Ms Breitner. You know damn well your dog's at home right where you left him. He hasn't stopped yapping since you walked out that door. You and I need to talk again, but I'm not being relieved for another hour. I'll stop by then. Don't just stand there. Get a move on before I arrest you for trespassing and disturbing the peace."

CHAPTER 10

Jewish Forward Blogger: "Checking in from Sunnyvale, Washington where most of the grapes in grape juice you and your kids blessed and drank tonight are koshered by twelve Yeshiva students imported for the occasion and their mentor, an Orthodox rebbe from RCK... But something's definitely not kosher here. I left my Upper West Side rent-controlled apt. and great neighborhood deli because one of those twelve kosherers has been murdered...."

Any satisfaction Miranda felt after her supposedly clandestine foray to the off-limits crime scene evaporated when she neared the door to her B & B and heard yet another male voice shouting inside. No wonder Rusty was barking. Breitner's was fully booked by the two reporters and four members of Spokane's Red Hat Society touring Valley wineries. Maybe Darlene let in some drunk without a reservation and he was badgering her for a vacancy she didn't have. Miranda unlocked the door, prepared to graciously refer the loudmouthed intruder to a motel, maybe even call ahead for him, and so peacefully eject him.

Instead, she froze on the threshold. A brawny young guy holding a gun stood over Darlene yelling at her in Spanish. His shaved head was partly obscured by a blue bandana spanning his forehead and leaving his thick tattooed neck exposed. The diminutive receptionist's right hand was out-stretched and her left hand gripped Rusty's collar. Her purse lay open on the floor, its contents strewn across the counter. Rusty, the first to notice Miranda, barked louder. She prayed all the noise would attract the attention of the detective just across the street.

At the sight of Miranda in the doorway, the gunman turned, pointed the revolver straight at her chest, and rushed towards her. Holding the gun with one hand, he shoved her hard to the floor with the other and then vaulted over her. Reanimated by her painful landing, Miranda reached up with both hands, grasped one of his feet and pulled, bringing her assailant to his knees just outside the door. Still clutching the gun, he kicked his foot free, jumped up, and raced cursing into the night. A car door slammed and an engine roared.

Relieved to be alive, Miranda hoisted herself up. Flexing her hands and rubbing her chin, she turned to Darlene. "Are you okay?"

Darlene nodded and let go of Rusty's collar. When she spoke her voice was doleful, defeated. "I'm okay. But are you alright, Ms Breitner? He knocked you down and kicked you."

"I'm okay." Shaken more than she cared to disclose, Miranda locked the front door. What had possessed her to tackle a gangbanger pointing a gun at her? She could still feel the heel of his high-top mashing her fingers, hitting her chin. Had she been grappling with the same brute who killed Isaac Markowitz?

Chilled at this possibility, she glanced at the tell-tale mezuzah she'd tacked on the door jamb and more possibilities filled her head. Perhaps that thug been

sent there to murder another Jew and had mistaken Darlene for the Jewish B &
B owner. Maybe Darlene had been begging him not to shoot her. Or maybe
he'd come simply to hold up a clerk and steal the B & B's meager stash of petty
cash and Darlene had been begging him to return her wallet.

"Did you let that criminal in at gunpoint? Did he get your wallet?"

Darlene shook her lowered head as she reunited her tote with its scattered
contents. She held up her wallet.

"Did he get the petty cash in the bottom drawer under the dish towels?"

"No. He didn't take any money from you. Just what I gave him." Darlene
looked up, enabling Miranda to see her grim tear-streaked face. "I'm so sorry.
Please forgive me." She inhaled. "It's because of me he was here."

"What do you mean?" While Miranda waited for Darlene to answer, a new
scenario formed in her head. The prim semi-retired receptionist Rosemarie
thought so highly of was a closet drug addict. She'd returned to the work force
to pay for her expensive habit and the gangbanger was her dealer who'd
followed her to the B & B to collect payment. Darlene's sweater prevented
Miranda from scanning the woman's forearms for needle marks, so she checked
her eyes for dilated pupils, and, when Darlene finally spoke, Miranda scoped out
her teeth for the discoloration that crime show coroners cite as a sign of meth
addiction.

"He's my grandson. Javier Baez." Darlene blew her nose and dabbed at her
eyes.

"Oh, my God!" Miranda was first astounded and then horrified. Which
was worse? Buying drugs from your grandson or selling them to your grandmother? But this time when she listened to her inner voice, she realized that it
was the voice of a crazy person jumping to crazy conclusions. She of all people
knew where that road led. Instead, she listened to Darlene.

"I have to call my son, Javi's father." Her voice weary, Darlene continued
to explain while digging in her purse for her cell phone. "I thought Javi came
looking for me to give him a little money like he sometimes does, so, of course,
I let him in. But when I opened my purse to get a few dollars, he grabbed it and
took my gun." Darlene's mouth quivered. "That damn gun is what he really
came for. I promised my husband I'd get a holster for it." She paused, nearly
choking on a sob. "I begged Javi to give it back. I'm afraid he'll hurt himself
with it."

"What?" Miranda was stunned anew by Darlene's latest revelation. Every
word she uttered confounded Miranda's earlier versions of what had happened.
"How would he 'hurt himself'? You mean shoot himself?"

Darlene reached for the silver cross suspended from a chain around her
neck. Her mouth trembled, and before she spoke again she bit her lower lip as if
to anchor it. "The police questioned Javi about tagging the Toppenish Murals."
Her voice quavered, making her sound like a very old woman. "He says he
didn't, but the cops say they got word on their tip line that he did. But they

don't have any proof, so they couldn't hold him. They're desperate to solve these crimes though, so they'll get proof. And they say they also heard Javi killed the Jew or knows who did. They're trying to get him to confess to that murder or give them a name as part of a deal." Miranda kept still, hoping Darlene would continue. "I swear Ms Breitner, Javi is a good kid. He has a good heart."

Having just been shoved to the floor at gunpoint and then kicked in the face by this cherub, Miranda bit her tongue.

"But he's being pulled by the cops and by the gang." Darlene shook her head and reached for another Kleenex. "You have to understand, Ms Breitner, the gangbangers are killers. They already killed his brother, Geraldo. And if the police find the banger who really killed the Jew, those thugs will think Javi gave him up. If Javi goes to jail for it, the Norteños'll get him there. If he's on the street…" She shrugged and pulled her sweater closer while her tears continued to fall. "The Norteños shot his brother Geraldo in the daylight on a street corner. I don't blame Javi for being scared." Darlene's exhalation was as full of hopelessness as a last breath. "Geraldo practically raised Javi while his mom and dad worked. Javi wants to join the Sureños only to get revenge."

Darlene squared her shoulders as if to face up to and assume the burden of all that she had said. "May I please use your phone? He must have taken my cell, and my car keys are gone too. I guess he took my car. I know he'll drop it off later. Meanwhile, my son will come for me." She shrugged and spoke again. "Are you going to call the police?"

Before Miranda could even begin to answer what, to her, would always be a loaded question, three mildly-inebriated red-hatted women and their designated driver streamed in chatting and laughing and oblivious to the two pale and shaken women who greeted them. Miranda was relieved to see that these guests had not interrupted the R-rated drama that had just occurred. She was even more relieved when Darlene told her that the two reporters had not yet returned. Reassured that word of an armed gangbanger's invasion of Breitner's B & B, assault on the innkeeper, and robbery of his own grandmother just might not go any further, Miranda considered Darlene's question and turned it back to her. "Are *you* going to report him to the police? He stole your gun."

Without hesitation, Darlene shook her head. "No. The boy is my grandson. *La familia.*"

Miranda flinched. Darlene's insistence on Javier's inherent innocence, her loyalty to him, to her family, even if, perhaps, misplaced, reminded Miranda of how her own father had believed the worst of her, believed she was a baby killer.

"So, Ms Breitner, are *you* going to call the cops? He assaulted you. You'll have bruises tomorrow."

"I honestly don't know, Darlene. I'll probably see a lawyer before I decide." She was silent for a moment. "I'd like to avoid any more negative publicity for the B & B and the neighborhood. If neither of us presses charges, maybe your grandson's visit here won't make the papers." She paused. "On the other hand, if he's a danger to others or, for that matter, to himself....." She sighed and, with hands trembling, handed Darlene the phone.

A few minutes later Darlene's son called back to say he was out front. As she stood to leave, Darlene patted Rusty and addressed Miranda. "Good night, Ms Breitner. I'm so sorry for everything that happened." She paused and lowered her head. "Of course, you don't want me to come back tomorrow."

Miranda had completely forgotten her intention to attend Yom Kippur services the next day. She looked at Darlene and said, "But I do, Darlene. What happened tonight wasn't your fault." Then, hoping she was right, she repeated one of Mona's maxims. "We don't get to choose our relatives."

Sorrowful and shaken, Miranda was loading the next day's breakfast offerings into the tiny fridge when the two reporters returned bickering. "You got this all wrong, Lynn. The Indian's got no motive."

"Who says? Isaac went to Toppenish the day before he died. Maybe he looked at this Indian kid the wrong way. Or maybe the Indian's *meshuganah* like his grandfather." Miranda nodded and smiled cordially at the two but did not encourage them to linger. She was relieved when they went to their rooms. Still reliving her own traumatic return and reviewing Darlene's sad story, she didn't want her trembling hands to evoke more negative publicity for the area.

When she left to take Rusty out for his late night pee, she nearly collided with Detective Ladin running up the few front steps. Standing on the same threshold where Javi had pushed her down and kicked her not an hour before, Miranda found herself face to face with another adversary, a detective who knew who she really was. And he'd seen her leaving the crime scene only an hour ago.

At that moment and in that spot it occurred to her for the first time that she was as viable a murder suspect as any of the rogues' gallery currently under consideration. She was a stranger with plenty of opportunity to enter the processing plant, with no alibi for the time of death, and with a previous arrest for infanticide on record. The probable murder weapon had been stored in a truck frequently parked on her property. But what possible motive could she have? She ran her finger along the thin scar under her chin. She was a long-term mental case, just like Joseph Wright. Such a person needed no plausible motive.

When her shiver became a shudder, she hugged herself and followed Rusty and the detective down the steps. "Better late than never," she remarked before realizing that she wasn't at all sure she wanted to share with this cop the scenario he'd missed.

"Sorry, but the guy who relieved me was running late."

Fortunately he had misunderstood her jibe, so her options were still open. She didn't have to tell him about Javier Baez's visit until she "lawyered up," as they said on TV. They began to walk. "I guess you're patrolling this particular processing plant because it's where the murder took place, right?"

"We're patrolling all of the plants koshering juice grapes for the duration of the grape harvest. Meanwhile, I can use the overtime, and I get to keep an eye on you, Miranda Breitner aka Meryl Weintraub."

There it was again. And this time he'd said it to her face, not as a threatening aside as he left. Miranda stood stone still in her tracks for the second time that evening. Only the reassuring presence of Rusty, who'd assumed his sentinel position at her side, kept her from running back into the B & B and slamming the door. But even Rusty's vigilance did not still her trembling.

"Here, take this." The detective removed his fleece and draped it clumsily over her shoulders. "You're shivering. It's not that cold. What are you afraid of? Has somebody threatened you? Why were you over at the plant tonight? I must've been on the other side of the building when you went in."

"I wanted to see the crime scene, that's all. Like I told you, I want this killer identified and caught sooner rather than later. I figured maybe if I saw the crime scene I'd notice something.."

"I appreciate your wanting to help, but I don't want you to put yourself at risk. If you just go about your business and keep your eyes open, that'll be very useful." The detective's response sounded formulaic and patronizing. Apparently her silence proved equally unsatisfying to him. "You're still shivering. What are you really afraid of?"

Standing there in the dark—tired and terrified—with a man she had every reason to mistrust, Miranda told him the truth. "I'm afraid of *you*. I don't want anyone to know my former identity. And somehow you found it out." She took a deep breath. "I want to know how."

"Back in the day I was on the other side of the glass when you were interrogated."

She felt her breath catch and forced herself to take in air.

"I was still in college and doing research for a paper. My uncle was a detective with Seattle PD, and he got me in to observe a few of their interrogations. Yours was one of them." He paused and stroked Rusty's head. "So that night when I saw you here, I thought you looked familiar. I mean underneath the dye job and the contacts. And of course, you, uh, filled out a little."

Even in the dark Miranda felt his eyes on her breasts, felt her face reddening.

"You really got to me. So I came back the next morning to make sure."

"You mean there was nothing wrong with your phone?" Miranda shuddered at how easily she'd been deceived.

"Like I said, I just wanted to scope you out, to make sure. Your voice is familiar too. But, I'm a good detective, so I checked the online videos they made of your interrogation and house arrest. You're that girl grown up." When she didn't speak, he continued. "And just last year I read that you sued SPD's asses and won some money."

Miranda cringed. The reporters who recounted her victorious lawsuit had detailed her cuttings and suicide attempt in the wake of her release from house arrest. And they had headlined the dollar amount she won. This cop knew about how much or how little she was worth. She whispered her next question. "Are you going to blackmail me?"

"Not exactly." He put a finger beneath her chin, tilting her head back, exposing her neck, and ran that same finger along the thin line there. Miranda jetted to her tiptoes which only made her mouth more accessible to the tall man who pulled her to him. Telling herself she had no choice, she made no protest, even considered responding to keep him quiet. But, there in the dark in his arms, she realized that she had no reason to trust this cop to keep her secret after he got what he wanted. His lips crushed hers and she felt his teeth behind them and then his tongue. She did not respond. Rusty's low growl only seemed to encourage him. His mouth pressed harder, but she didn't unclench her teeth. Nor did she raise her arms from her sides to push him away or cry out, even when his chin crushed her own bruised jaw. Only when Rusty actually snarled did the detective finally release her, step back, pick up his fleece, and walk away. Over his shoulder, his words were barely audible. "Good night, Meryl. I'll be in touch."

She stood shivering in the street wondering how long that one-sided kiss, any kiss, would be enough to insure the detective's silence. But she also knew that she now had a weapon to keep him at bay. She could charge him with sexual harassment, maybe even assault. It would be his word against hers. Damn. With her history, who would believe her?

CHAPTER 11

Guest book: "What a comfortable and quiet refuge! The proprietor runs a tight ship with the help of her sweet pooch and an obliging assistant. We especially enjoyed the breakfasts. And we felt perfectly safe in spite of all that hoo hah about gangs and a murder across the street. We all slept like babies and we'll be back when that new winery in Horse Heaven Hills opens." Joy, Diane, Greta, and Mimi, Red Hat Society of Spokane

"I saved you a seat. And I brought a couple of extra packages of Kleenex." A short, broad-shouldered thirty-something man with a dirty blond buzz cut, glasses, and wearing a prayer shawl over his gray suit, took possession of Miranda's elbow at the door of Temple Shalom. She figured him for the fellow she'd sat next to the night before and, flustered, allowed him to usher her into the part of the sanctuary that had once been a dining room. Only after they were both seated did he speak again. "I'm glad you came back. I'm Harry Ornstein." He turned to smile at her and held out his hand.

"Miranda Breitner." After a sleepless night reliving the events of the evening over too many glasses of merlot, she lacked the energy to make conversation. "I'm new to the Valley, so if you're on the membership committee, yes, I plan to join." Harry blinked and withdrew his hand abruptly, so she knew her message had registered as a rebuff. She hadn't meant to be rude, but she was there only to say Kaddish and hear Rabbi Golden's sermon. Then she'd rush home, eat, and go on-line to find a lawyer.

"I'm not on the membership committee, Miranda. I'm recently divorced, and I'm incredibly attracted to sobbing women..." He shook his head. "And you aren't wearing a wedding ring, so I was hoping to get to know you." He stared at her, taking in the bruise purpling her jawline and the matching circles beneath her eyes. When he spoke again, his smile was gone, but his voice was not unkind. "You may not want to get to know me right now, but here, take my card. You look like you could use a good lawyer."

That's when Miranda realized she'd forgotten to hide the bruise on her jaw. But she remembered that this was not a holiday for doing business. Glancing furtively around, she took the card he surreptitiously handed her. Then, from some long-suppressed reflex deep inside her, a girlish giggle bubbled up. Her lips stiffened in a futile effort to stifle her inappropriate merriment. This was not a holiday for giggling either. Besides, it hurt her sore ribs to laugh.

"What's so funny? Last night you were in tears and now you're all beat up and need a lawyer." He sounded angry. Did he think she was laughing at him? "I'm not only a lawyer, but a damn good one who's never lost a domestic violence case."

"You're right. I really do need a good lawyer." As soon as she began to speak, her giggle-fit subsided. "Now, drumroll, here's the funny part. I was

going to go home and go online to look for an attorney, but here you are, a real
live lawyer, sitting next to me. For a minute there I found that hilarious. I don't
know why. I guess I'm losing it."

"I don't know about that, but when this holiday is over, call my office and we'll set up an appointment. I represent Temple Shalom and…" He
scanned the faces crowding the sanctuary. "…at least four other people here.
You can find me online too." Holiday or no holiday, Harry was suddenly all
business.

Miranda knew she ought to check him out with a reference or at least vet
him on-line, but instead, she caved to convenience, telling herself she'd consider
this lawyer a gift from God, an answer to her prayers even. "Okay, but I need to
talk to you soon. Can we meet tomorrow?"

Harry nodded just as Rabbi Golden took her place on the *bima* and
the service began. When it was time to rise and memorialize one's dead loved
ones by chanting the *Mourners' Prayer*, Miranda stood with the other congregants
and let her own mourner's tears blot the pages of her prayer book. She could
tell by the rippling of the paper that her salty overflow wasn't the first to blur
the Hebrew and English letters. When Harry once again placed a pack of
Kleenex into her hand, she once again accepted it gratefully. She wept for her
beloved mother whose absence orphaned her anew every day. And she wept for
sweet little Timmy who, had he lived, would be twenty-something. Maybe he'd
be in grad school or teaching or, God forbid, in Iraq. Finally, she wept for poor
Isaac Markowitz, for his widowed bride, and for his anguished parents.

After another inspiring sermon from Rabbi Golden, she left Temple Shalom and headed back to Sunnyvale to break her wine-compromised fast with
lox and bagels, treats she and Mona had eaten together to mark the end of their
fast and of the holiday. As much out of curiosity as out of loneliness she invited
Darlene to share her lunch.

"Thanks, but my daughter-in-law is dropping my granddaughter Josefina
off here before she goes to work. I'll make us both something when we get
home."

The prospect of a visit from yet another one of Darlene's grandkids was not
appealing. "How old is your granddaughter?"

"Fourteen." Darlene had a question of her own. "But before she gets here,
tell me, please, have you decided whether or not you're going to report Javi?
Your face looks really bad today. I wouldn't blame you if you did." She lowered
her head.

"I have an attorney lined up. But the more I think about it, the less I feel
like doing it. I'll have to see what my lawyer advises."

"You must be mad at Javi. Like I told my son, he… he assaulted you." Darlene's lip trembled at the memory.

"I know. Believe me, I know." Miranda's curiosity overcame her discretion.
"Before you go, there's something I don't understand. "What made Javi's

brother, the one who got killed, join a gang? I can't imagine any relative of yours joining a gang."

Darlene sighed. "Luis, my son, had two years of college and he got a job in the office of the meat processing plant in Toppenish. His wife Mira works downstairs there on the plant floor. They had five kids, good kids. But Josefina, the one born before Javi..." Darlene took a call on her cell, and before she finished speaking, there was a loud banging at the door. "That's Josefina. I'll get it." Darlene rushed to the door and flung it open.

A teenaged girl with café-au-lait skin, long black hair, round cheeks, round brown eyes, and prominent breasts hurled herself into Darlene's outstretched arms. She embraced her grandmother with only one arm because the other clutched a large doll. "Kiss Josefina," Josefina demanded holding out the doll, a replica of her namesake and owner, except for the breasts. Darlene obliged, planting a resounding smack on the doll's forehead.

As Josefina approached Miranda with the doll, Miranda realized two things. First, this friendly effervescent girl in the body of a woman would remain forever four in her pretty head. Second, she expected Miranda to kiss the doll, so Miranda did. Only then did Josefina begin to give her doll a tour of the room, stopping to gape at the enormous spider plant.

"You can see she's... young for her age." Darlene's voice dropped to a whisper. Miranda nodded. "She's so pretty and friendly."

"Yes, but she cannot be left alone for a minute. My son and his wife, they found a boarding school for her in Spokane where the staff members are kind and watchful. She comes home sometimes to visit, but she's happier at school." Darlene blew her nose. "The Government pays a little, but Mira and my son, they work overtime to pay the rest. They sleep only a few hours each night. Geraldo raised Javier and Josefina. When they found the school, he wanted to help out more." Darlene rubbed her thumb and fingers together to indicate Geraldo's wish to earn more money. "He got a job downstairs in the meat plant, too, but he knew he could make more selling drugs." She shrugged at this sad fact of Valley life and then looked up. "Geraldo didn't use drugs himself or dress fancy or go to clubs or even drive a nice car. He was a good son, a good grandson, and a good brother. After he began dealing, he bought Josefina that pricey doll. She wanted it because on TV she saw it and it had her same name. Soon after, by mistake Geraldo went to meet a customer on the wrong street and..." Darlene snapped her fingers. "Next day he was shot dead."

Miranda surprised herself by enfolding the smaller woman in a hug. When she spoke she tried to return the conversation to the present. "I saw your car outside. Javier returned it?"

"Of course. It was already in front of my house last night when I got home. My cell and my keys were in my planter like always, but not my gun." She sighed. "He wrote "*gracias abuela te amo*" inside a candy wrapper and left it on the front seat like he always does. Here." She pulled out a colorful slip of crumbled paper from the pocket of her sweater and smoothed it out on the counter. Darlene's tears streaked her face and she excused herself to go to the bathroom.

While she was out of the room, Miranda photographed the note with her phone while Josefina sat cross-legged on the floor pulling out the guidebooks stored on the makeshift bookcases and showing them to her doll.

When Darlene returned, she finished her story. "Javi didn't go home last night. And his girl hasn't seen him." She looked over at her granddaughter. "Come on Josefina. It's time to go home and have lunch." Darlene began picking up the scattered books. "And then I'll wash and iron Josefina's dress, okay?"

The Red Hat ladies checked out, and Miranda readied their rooms for future guests while pondering Darlene's version of Javier's backstory. His family's predicament was wrenching, but the boy's disappearance made him a more likely suspect.

Later, while breaking her semi-fast alone, she allowed herself to recall her first kiss, technically a sexual assault by a cop. She wished it had been Steve Galen or maybe even Harry Ornstein, who had given her that first kiss. How would she handle the detective's next move? Soon he'd tire of her avoidance of his kisses and demand other favors. Even if she obliged, he'd eventually tire of her, discard her, and then blackmail her for money. And what about that wife he'd said he wanted to give the recipe for rhubarb pie to? Or had she been a convenient fabrication like his dead cellphone battery?

It was time to check out Detective Ladin online. What she found was not very revealing. He'd worked gang units in Tacoma and, more recently, Seattle. He'd left The Emerald City shortly after the arrival of the new police chief, a tough female cop, hired to bring the SPD into compliance with the Department of Justice's mandates for change. Miranda didn't have access to Ladin's personnel file where, she suspected, she'd find additional information.

Next she logged onto the B & B's website. There were two more cancellations and one new booking. She tried not to exaggerate the significance of either. Even though she had no love for journalists, she was glad the two reporters, whom she'd spotted in the back row when she left Temple Shalom, were still in residence.

The guest who'd booked a room that morning arrived. Rusty's ears stood up at the knocking and folded once Miranda unlocked the door. She could only gawk. This woman looked like a model in an Eileen Fisher ad. Tall and shapely with luminous honey-colored skin, she wore black leggings, a black turtleneck tunic, and sleek black boots. A barrette crafted of amber, gold, and onyx gleamed from atop her head where it kept her long black mane from obscuring her perfectly-proportioned facial features. Pulling a rolling duffel bag behind her, and with a black leather tote slung over one shoulder, she breezed in and addressed Miranda. "Hi. I'm C.S. Nikaimak. I've booked a room for the next few nights." Her voice was mellow, her diction precise. She was probably an actress. "And you must be Miranda Breitner."

"Yes." Inhaling the guest's spicy perfume, Miranda took the credit card as soon as this citrus-scented apparition handed it over. Her nails glistened with colorless polish and the diamond on her ring finger was impressive without being showy. The newcomer looked around. "Lovely what you've done with this old place. I hope business is good."

"Thanks. It's okay." Miranda tried not to sound grim. "Tell me, how did you learn about Breitner's?" She usually didn't ask this question until her guests had settled in, but this woman did not appear to be the budget-conscious business traveler she targeted in her promotional efforts, so Miranda was curious about what had brought her to Breitner's.

"My brother works here. He said it's a really nice place and that you're a kind person."

"You're Michael Wright's sister?" Miranda tried to keep her incredulity from somehow disparaging Michael. But how could this poised *fashionista* be related to the soft-spoken and scruffy handyman? And how could she be the granddaughter of that smelly old man Miranda and Rusty encountered at the river's edge?

"I am." The smile she flashed was, indeed, Michael's. In that smile's glow, Miranda could see Michael's chiseled features mirrored in his sister's face, his straight black ponytail in the glossy mane streaming from her barrette, and his scrawny physique echoing her lithe frame.

"Michael mentioned you. You helped raise him."

The stylish woman rolled her dark eyes. "I tried. That boy was wild, practically feral, and he acted like my condo in Seattle was a cage. Eventually I let him come back here and stay on the rez with our grandfather. They're two of a kind."

"Well, Michael's not wild any more. He works hard and his work is good and, as you know, he's enrolled in college. And now he looks after his grandfather too."

"Yes." C.S. Nikaimak twisted a tress of her hair. "And a great job he's doing of that. Now they're both missing."

"What? Michael was here just the other day."

"Well, he's not here now, is he?"

Miranda shook her head in case that had been a serious question.

"An old boyfriend of mine on the tribal police force called me. Jim usually plugs me into the loop when grandfather gets in trouble or either one of them gets sick. According to him, they've both disappeared and they're both murder suspects." She crossed her arms in front of her chest and widened her eyes.

If Miranda had better-honed social skills, she would have understood that the conversation was over and showed C.S. Nikaimak to her room. But she didn't. Instead she felt an urge to defend Michael from the harsh judgment of this beauty-queen big sister.

"I offered to help him pay for a lawyer for him and your grandfather, but Michael wouldn't let me... Said he had that covered."

"He does." C.S. Nikaimak sighed and held her hand out for the keys. "I'm their lawyer."

The big dog rested his head on Miranda's lap and kept it there so she could scratch between his ears as she sipped her second nightcap. Lawyers were emerging from the woodwork which she read as a bad sign. But she was glad Michael's sister was coming through for him. If she was as smart as she was pretty, he had nothing to worry about. And maybe she could help their grandfather too. His was a tough case. Miranda considered the strikes against Joseph Wright aka Kamiakin. He once owned the fish club the cops think is the murder weapon. He has no alibi. He drinks and smokes pot, and he probably has been arrested before. Miranda was all too familiar with the fact that recently everyone's history with the police had become a matter of public record available online. He also suffered from PTSD, so he was a little crazy. And if you're crazy, you don't need a motive. Chilled by the personal implications of this fact, Miranda stared at her companion for a minute as if expecting reassurance. She acknowledged to herself that Joseph Wright could have killed poor Isaac in a drunken fit, but what would he have been doing in the processing plant? Besides, according to Michael, Joseph was opposed to killing.

Rusty stood and stretched. He trotted to the door of her apartment where Miranda had hung a strip of leather fitted with bells and taught her pet to tug on it when he wanted to go outside. He tugged. "Good job, Rusty." He tugged again. "Okay, okay. I'm putting my shoes on." Once outside, Miranda continued to review the roster of suspects, but none, including Javier Baez, met the tri-partite crime show criteria by having motive, method, and opportunity.

As she and Rusty headed back to the B & B, the two reporters pulled up and parked. Instead of having supper alone upstairs, Miranda invited them to share her break-the-fast leftovers. Al, the older man, the one from the *Forward* leapt at her offer. "Lox from Barney Greenglass yet? Be still my New Yorker's heart."

Lynn was less enthusiastic. "Thanks, but I'm beat and we stayed for the break-the-fast potluck at that sweet little synagogue. I'm calling it a night. Go to it, Al."

Miranda knew that once Al got done slathering his bagel with cream cheese and piling lox, sliced onions, and tomatoes atop that, his mouth would be too full for him to speak, so she lost no time. "Any new leads? Clues? A new suspect maybe?"

"We both took the day off, but I did check in with the sheriff while Lynn drove us back here. And you know what he told me?" He paused and contemplated his creation, a bagel-based tower of old-school Jewish indulgence.

Miranda shook her head emphatically.

"Nada. They got nothin' new and nothin' old either." He had the bagel halfway to his mouth when, to Miranda's surprise, he spoke again. "And if you ask me, which you did, they just rounded up the area's usual suspects: a couple of Indians and a wannabe gangbanger who also happens to be Mexican-American. Meanwhile, the poor dead guy's family in New York wants answers. RCK too… Their competition is having a field day with this." A good sized chunk of the overburdened bagel disappeared into his mouth and he savored it in silence.

When the last bite was gone, Miranda brought him a cup of decaf and a couple of rugelach she'd defrosted in the microwave. "So what did you mean before when you said RCK's competition is having a field day with this?"

"Well, say the big fancy motel that is your only competition in Sunnyvale was suddenly infested with rats. Wouldn't you maybe find a way to spread the word and try to get their bookings?" When Miranda remained noncommittal, he explained. "There's a lot of internet chatter about RCK's sloppy oversight, violations of kosher protocols, that kind of thing. I mean, if you ask me, it's just sour grapes."

Miranda groaned.

"But competition is part of doing business in America, right?"

"So why aren't you competing with Lynn. You two act like you're best buddies."

The lines on the old newshound's face reorganized themselves into a grin. "We're closer than that. She's my wife's niece." He put his napkin on the table and stood. "One of these days, Ms Breitner, you'll have to tell me what a nice Jewish girl like you is doing in a relatively Jewless place like this valley. But not tonight. " He winked and stood. "I gotta get some shuteye. Thanks for the grub. Your rugelach has no competition this side of the Mississippi." And with that qualified compliment, Al went to his room.

Upstairs later, Miranda logged onto Checkmate.com and found what, undoubtedly, the county police already knew. Joseph Wright had been arrested many times for loitering and drunkenness and jailed twice for possession of small amounts of marijuana, but he'd never been brought in for anything more serious. Michael Wright, Nelson Thurston, and even the thuggish-looking Javier Baez had never been arrested at all.

Having done her due diligence, she was frustrated. It occurred to her that maybe she and the cops were all going at this the way detectives on shows like *Law and Order* or *CSI* would. Instead, maybe they ought to attack this case like profilers on *The Mentalist* and *Bones*. She poured the last of the merlot into her glass. Profilers are usually psychics or shrinks and they visit the crime scene, deduce from it the characteristics of the person who committed the crime, share their deductions with the detectives, and then those detectives go looking for someone with those characteristics. Mona had pooh-poohed profilers and Miranda didn't set much store by their extrapolations either, but she was tired of reviewing the same old suspects over and over in her head to no avail. She pulled up Word and began trying to create a profile of Isaac Markowitz's killer.

CHAPTER 12

Guest book: "No matter what anybody says, this place brought me good luck. I got my dream job while I stayed here before, so I'm back now to look for housing. Besides, the rooms are clean, quiet, and very affordable." Assistant Dean of Students, Heritage University

Before Miranda got beyond titling her profile, Rabbi Alinsky called. He was whispering so fast that Miranda asked him to slow down and pipe up. "Ms Breitner, I'm in the car across the street from you. My midnight shift begins in two minutes. But I know who killed Isaac, may his memory be for a blessing." For a split second Miranda dared to hope this whole mess might be about to go away. But the rabbi's next words dashed those hopes. "I don't know his name, but I know his motive. You know that Canadian koshering outfit?"

"No."

"Canadian-American Koshering Association. Their seal is CAKA. Well, CAKA's been trying to move in on RCK's processing plants here in the Valley for years, but, of course, my name was like a gold stamp and so was the RCK's until all this *mishegas*, so CAKA couldn't make any inroads. Now CAKA's sent a representative to talk to Oskar Hindgrout and the other plant owners RCK, Inc., works with in this Valley about taking over their juice-grape koshering."

"That's interesting."

"It makes sense. Koshering is big business with big money at stake. The method RCK uses to kosher these grapes is extremely effective and economical and unique to us. It was designed by my predecessor, may his life be for a blessing. CAKA must have sent an industrial spy to the plant disguised as a truck driver or a delivery boy or whatever. Maybe Isaac saw him taking pictures and asked a few questions, or tried to take his camera. They struggled and he hit Isaac over the head and left in a hurry."

Miranda tried to imagine an industrial spy using a Yakama fishing club as a murder weapon. Even with this caveat, the rabbi's theory was refreshing. If not exactly outside the box, it considered people and events in the wider world outside the Valley. A CAKA spy at least had a viable motive. Isaac wouldn't have been the first victim of capitalism. "Rabbi Alinsky, have you shared your suspicions with the police?"

"No. How does it look to the *goyim* to have a rabbi suspect a Jew of murdering another Jew? Besides if I'm involved, it looks like I'm just trying to save my job." He stopped talking for a moment. "Ms Breitner, I believe God sent you here to this valley to help us. You're our Queen Esther, someone the authorities here will listen to. Will you talk to the detective about this? And keep me out of it?"

Miranda had to smile at being compared to the beautiful legendary queen who persuaded her husband, the Persian King Ahasuerus, to spare the lives of the Jews and then fingered the villain who would have had them all slain. She knew she was being flattered, but she was intrigued by the rabbi's conjecture. "Okay, I'll talk to Detective Ladin and ask him to investigate your scenario but to keep his investigation quiet. And I won't mention your name."

"Do you trust the police?"

Miranda crossed her fingers and lied to the rabbi.

The next morning, with some trepidation, she considered leaving a carefully worded message for Detective Ladin asking him to stop by that evening. A small left-over-from-middle-school voice in her head kept telling her that now that the detective understood that she did not return his interest, he'd get over it and focus on his job. But there was a more contemporary practical voice that reminded her that she had an appointment with a lawyer that afternoon, so she could discuss what to do with this information with him.

Harry Ornstein proved to be an unorthodox lawyer. He'd agreed to see Miranda at what he labeled his "conference space," a scenic wonder called Cowiche Canyon in the hills just outside and above Yakima. "Meet me at the trailhead there at 3:30. Wear closed-toe shoes. It's still warm out, and the rattlers just love that mid-afternoon sun. We can walk and talk. Meanwhile, I'll e-mail you my rates and a form to fill out so I have your contact info."

When she arrived at the parking lot at the trailhead, Miranda was surprised to find Harry accompanied by Julia, his bright-eyed and pig-tailed little girl. He seemed so different from her previous lawyer who'd been her dad's peer, a suited and seasoned senior partner in a distinguished Seattle firm. Wearing jeans, hiking boots, and a Seahawks T-shirt, Harry was definitely buffer, younger, less conventional, and, alas, probably less experienced. Miranda hoped that his take on her questions would be useful.

"Today's one of my days with Julia," he said by way of explanation and introduction. "I just picked her up from school." He grabbed Julia's hand and pulled her back as she approached Rusty. "Wait, honey! Be careful. Let's see if he's friendly."

"Not to worry, Julia. He's very friendly. His name is Rusty and I'm Miranda." Rusty licked Julia's hand, sniffed her crotch and then sniffed Harry's, and, satisfied, positioned himself at the child's side, angling for a head scratch. At a word from Miranda, he stood as if to lead the way along the graveled trail between the steep sun-splashed canyon walls sprinkled with black lava, scruffy shrubs, and brush.

"I suggest you leash him. More dogs get bitten than humans."

"Thanks." As Miranda fastened the leash to Rusty's collar, she whispered. "Sorry, Rusty. It's for your own good."

Harry had restrictions for his daughter, too. "Julia, you know the drill. You have to stay with us, right?" The little girl nodded, her expression solemn. "No wandering off the trail, no running ahead. You can keep Rusty company, okay? Just watch where you walk." Wide-eyed, the child nodded again.

Once he'd scared the bejesus out of them, Harry turned out to be an enthusiastic and knowledgeable guide. "Cowiche Canyon is another gift from the glaciers when they gouged their way through here millions of years ago. Later on, this trail became a railroad track."

"It's amazing. I've recommended this spot to several of my B & B guests looking for something to do or see while they're in the Valley, so it's about time I'm seeing it for myself. Thanks for suggesting we meet here."

"I don't usually see clients when I have Julia, but…" He shrugged. "You did look a little the worse for wear yesterday. How're you feeling today?"

Before she could answer, two folks on horseback approached at a trot. Rusty herded his three charges off to the side of the trail as the riders slowed their mounts to a walk in passing.

"Much better. See?" She stopped and turned her face up so Harry could inspect the slightly diminished bruise. He took off his sunglasses to examine the yellowing blotch. He was exactly her height, so unless she closed her eyes, there was no way to avoid at least some eye contact. She closed them.

"Did he loosen any teeth?"

"No. I don't think so." She ran her tongue over her lower molars. Unaccustomed to being kicked in the face, Miranda hadn't even considered this obvious possibility.

Harry's phone apparently vibrated, because just then he pulled it out of his pocket and took a call. He shrugged his apology for the interruption. When he finished talking, he apologized. "Sorry. I had to take that call." He pocketed his cell. "So you're here to see if I think you should press charges against the animal that did this?" He pointed at her bruised jaw. She wondered if Harry knew he sounded a lot like *Blue Bloods'* Danny Reagan.

"Yes. But it's not what you think."

"Tell me what happened. Then I'll tell you what I think, and you won't have to speculate." They had arrived at a low wooden bridge over the meandering Cowiche Creek where, as if following some primordial rule compelling kids to throw rocks into water, Julia picked up a stone and did just that. She repeated this action many times while the adults, including Rusty, stood nearby waiting for her to tire of her game.

"When I got home on Yom Kippur Eve, I unlocked the door to my B & B and found a gangbanger waving a gun and yelling at the receptionist I'd just hired.…" By the time Miranda filled Harry in on Javier's appropriation of his grandmother's gun, his assault on her, and what she knew of his backstory, a few clouds had blown in on a breeze that chilled the air just a bit. Julia had tired of tossing stones and Harry provided her with a camera. She began photographing Rusty and then a tree-covered canyon wall ablaze with orange, red, and yellow foliage and the occasional wildflower blooming trailside.

"Hey, Julia, have a drink." She traded the camera for a pink water bottle and drank. Miranda poured some of her own water into the dish she carried for Rusty. When she raised the water bottle to drink herself, Harry reached over and tapped it with his, saying, "*L'chaim.*" He quickly raised his bottle to point at the sky where, as if on cue, two eagles soared in circles. Miranda smiled and repeated, "*L'chaim.*"

Then she continued talking until she had filled Harry in on how Darlene refused to press charges against her suicidal grandson.

"So if grandma is telling the truth, he did not break in and did not rob you or your business. At the time you didn't know that or know that he was a person of interest to cops investigating a homicide, so you tried to prevent him from escaping, and he assaulted you, right?"

"The first time he assaulted me I wasn't trying to do anything. I was just standing speechless and gaping in the doorway. He deliberately knocked me down on his way out. That's when I grabbed his foot to stop him and he assaulted me again."

"Jesus, Miranda! He was holding a gun! Do you realize you could have been killed?" Harry's voice was suddenly harsh. Rusty's ears went up and Julia stopped taking pictures to stare.

In the silence that followed his barked question, they all heard it. Clicking. Like ice cubes rattling in an empty glass. "Freeze." This time Harry's voice was low and urgent. He and Julia both halted midstride as if playing some weird game of Simon Says. Miranda pulled Rusty close to her and whispered to him to stay. His growl softened to a low rumble, but he didn't move. "On the left." Harry's whisper was barely audible. They stared transfixed as the snake, a mottled moving coil of beige on brown, unwound, slithered off a low-riding stone ledge about a foot from the trail, and disappeared among stalks of what Harry had told her earlier was white desert buckwheat.

Miranda had run but one step when Harry grabbed her hand, saying, "Slow down. Moving fast around snakes may scare them into striking." He turned toward Julia who was clinging to his other hand. "Good job, Julia. You were so brave and you remembered just what we practiced."

Miranda heard his words as if they were coming through the hand he continued to hold in his. She had just escaped a rattlesnake and was holding hands with a man who wasn't her dad. She'd never done either before. But she had once been part of a family, and for a split second that's what she felt they were as, hand in hand, the three of them slowly made their way to the trailhead with Rusty close beside them.

"Julia, tell Miranda how we practiced freezing."

"Daddy got a hiking video and we watched it and then we did what the hikers in the video did. Daddy said we could only come here if we knew how to act around snakes. But that wasn't a very big snake, Daddy."

"Even baby rattlers have poison in them that can make us pretty sick." Not for the first time that afternoon, Miranda realized what a patient and loving dad Harry was. Divorce hadn't soured him on fatherhood. For a moment she envied Julia. Only when they reached the trailhead did Harry release their hands, and when he let go of hers, she felt more alone than ever, even as all of them piled into Harry's car.

"Julia, see if Rusty likes being read to, okay? Then, we'll go for a frozen yogurt." Julia grabbed a book from a stash in a bag on the back of the driver's seat and began to read to Rusty, taking pains to explain each picture. Rusty yawned and then gave every appearance of listening attentively.

"So, you still want to know what I think?"

Miranda nodded. Seeing Harry elude the serpent in her post-Edenic valley had increased her respect for the lawyer.

"Okay. Here's how I see it. You operate a fledgling B & B in a neighborhood that's already compromised because of the killing across the street. If word of this intruder gets out, and if you press charges against your assailant, it will get out. That's bad for business. Nobody wants to stay in a B & B where a wannabe gangbanger assaults the owner and the receptionist is packing heat. The best thing for your business will be for the real murderer to be caught, tried, and locked up ASAP."

Miranda was grateful that, unlike Detective Ladin, Harry didn't seem to find her concern for her business a mortal sin.

But when he went on to say, "On the other hand…" she winced, expecting the worst sort of condemnation. "… let's look at this from the perspective of what's right. I mean you do have to live with yourself no matter what you decide to do. So if you press charges, this kid gets thrown in jail and disarmed. Maybe he kills himself some other way there or the gangbangers kill him. In either scenario, the murder gets pinned on him or he names the guy who maybe did kill his brother and gets his revenge that way and then is killed. The problem is that someone you're pretty sure didn't kill Isaac Markowitz goes down for it and, sooner or later, gets killed in prison."

"And the real killer walks," Miranda chimed in. "And maybe he comes back. Besides, Javier Baez is already a person of interest to the police. If they want to try to pin this on him just to get a conviction and put it behind them, why should I make it easy?" She stopped for breath "But, do you think if I don't press charges and Javier remains loose he'll come back? Do you think my guests and I are in any danger from him?"

"He could have shot you. He didn't. If you don't press charges and he kills himself with his granny's gun, you just have to remember it's not your fault. And if you do press charges he might still kill himself."

Miranda was relieved that Harry's assessment of her situation confirmed her own less nuanced one. She wouldn't press charges. At least not yet. "Thanks, Harry. I have one more thing to ask you."

"Okay, but before we move on, know this. If you press charges against Javier, your receptionist will get charged also for breaking the "conceal-carry" law that expressly states that one must not lose control of one's weapon. It must be carried out of sight in a holster or even in a waistband where one cannot lose control of it. Women lose control of their purses all the time. You don't sound like you want to bring any more grief to that woman."

"Who knew? Thanks, Harry. You're right. Darlene said something about how she should have had the gun in a holster."

"Okay. Next question. Fire away. Rusty and his tutor are happy."

"As you probably know, the cops investigating Isaac's murder are focused on only two suspects, a gang member and a Yakama. They just don't think outside the box. But both Rabbi Alinsky and a reporter from *The Forward* staying at my B & B think Isaac's murder may have been committed by an industrial spy."

Harry cocked his head and raised his eyebrows as he considered this possibility.

"They think a rival koshering company might be trying to discredit RCK and get the juice-grape koshering contract from all their Valley plants. And when I stop to think about this possibility, it doesn't seem all that implausible."

"No. it doesn't."

"So should I pass this lead on to the detective?"

Harry chuckled. "It doesn't sound like he's going to think of it himself. Why wouldn't you tell the investigator?" He took off his sunglasses and turned to look at her.

"I don't trust him." She hesitated. "I'm afraid of him."

"Why?" Harry's tone had a new edge.

Miranda chose her words carefully. "He's in a position to blackmail me and…"

"What? What does he have on you? A zoning violation or a DUI?"

Miranda felt her cheeks flame. "No. I've done nothing wrong. But he knows something about my past that I don't care for others to know. And if I don't…"

"How much did he ask for? You realize that if you pay him once, he'll keep coming back."

"Yes. I know. He says he doesn't want money." She studied the dashboard. "He wants to go to bed with me." She glanced at Harry and saw his pallor darken into a red flush. "But I figure if he keeps bothering me, I'll charge him with sexual harassment."

"If you do that, he'll try to defend himself by discrediting you and he might succeed. Either way, your secret will come out and you'll have legal fees." Harry paused. "As your attorney, I should know what he has on you."

Miranda kept quiet.

Harry picked up his glasses and studied them. He didn't look up when he spoke. "At least I should know this detective's name so I can check him out."

"Alex Ladin."

Miranda watched as Harry typed the name into his phone. "I looked him up and couldn't find anything except that he's worked on gang units in Tacoma and Seattle."

"I'll be able to get access to his personnel records. But Miranda, if you tell me what secret of yours he knows, perhaps I can give you better counsel."

Miranda suspected he was right. Acutely aware of the child reading aloud in the back seat, she leaned closer to Harry and whispered. "Twenty years ago in Seattle I was charged with shaking to death a toddler I was babysitting for. I was arrested." Harry's eyes, focused on her face, didn't blink. Having revealed her arrest and its cause, she resumed her normal position and made herself a bit more audible. "My case was dismissed for lack of evidence. But no one else was ever charged or investigated so whoever actually did harm Timmy was never caught. Everybody still believes I did it. But I didn't. I loved that little boy." Miranda's hands formed tight fists in her lap.

"So?" Harry's monosyllabic query was so understated that at first she wondered if he'd even heard her.

"So the next twenty years were very hard on me and my family. I'll spare you the details, but even with a college degree I still can't pass a background check and get work. Eventually I sued the SPD for mental anguish and won $215,000." Miranda paused, relieved to be nearing the end of what felt like a confession. Her words came faster. "Then I changed my appearance and my name from Meryl Weintraub to Miranda Breitner and moved out here." She watched Harry type her birth name into his phone. Soon he would see the video of her interrogation, read the press about her house arrest and the details outlined in her lawsuit. "I used the money from the lawsuit to buy and renovate an old farmhouse in Sunnyvale and open my B & B." She sighed. "But would you believe, Detective Alex Ladin just happened to have witnessed my interrogation all those years ago and he recognized me?"

"Bummer. And creepy. Okay, so here's my advice. "Don't go to the detective or Sheriff Carson with this lead.

Miranda bristled. "What? You said it was a viable lead. Their investigation's going nowhere. My B & B means everything to me...." Rusty repositioned himself so that his head loomed over the seat between hers and Harry's.

Ignoring the intruder, Harry reached over and put his finger to her lips. "Shhhh. Listen. It is a viable lead. But there's a safer way to bring it to the sheriff's attention. Crime Stoppers."

"The tip line?" She could feel Harry's finger on her mouth even after he'd removed it.

"Yes. Crime Stoppers enables people to report suspicious activity or actual crimes anonymously and without fear of retribution. It's very effective and safe. You should not be alone with Detective Ladin. Is that clear?"

Miranda nodded. She sat quietly for a moment, continuing to absorb Harry's proposal. Using an on-line payback-proof tip line was infinitely preferable to any more grappling with Alex Ladin, another bullying cop on the make, a voracious vacuum sucking her hard-won hope for a new beginning right out of her. Besides, the simplicity and efficiency of the tip line pleased her inner techie. "So after I fill out the Crime Stoppers forms, I just go about my business and pretend I don't know anything about anything?"

"Not exactly. The investigating officer may contact you online via a number they assign your tip. She or he may ask you questions which you answer online. This is all explained on the tip form. Just don't include anything in your tips that reveals your own identity, like references to your B & B. Also Miranda, don't talk about your new lead or anything else you send to the tip line with friends or family, okay?"

" Okay." She opened the car door. "And thanks for suggesting the tip line." Miranda was half way out the door and still talking. "Julia, I enjoyed meeting you. Seems as if Rusty did too. Thank you for entertaining him."

"Can you join us for some frozen yogurt? I mean I did save you from the fangs of a deadly viper." Stupefied by Harry's invitation, Miranda stood holding the back car door open for Rusty. This man knew the worst about her and was still willing to spend time with her, to expose his child to her. Maybe that was because he was a lawyer, her lawyer, and she'd won her suit against the SPD. Maybe he was giving her the benefit of the doubt. Or maybe, like Steve Galen, he was just being polite. Whatever his reasons for extending the invitation, she would have liked to accept it. "Sorry, I have guests checking in at six, so I have to get back. But I'll take a rain check." In a place where it rained only eight times a year, there weren't too many rain checks.

As soon as she welcomed her guests, Miranda went upstairs with her laptop to become an official Crime Stopper. She was pleased with her tip.

Commercially koshering foods is big business. RCK Koshering, Inc., which employed Isaac Markowitz is the biggest such company in the world. All the fruit processing plants that process juice grapes in the Yakima Valley have contracts with RCK. It is possible that another koshering company eager to take over these lucrative contracts sent an industrial spy to try to learn RCK's special process, developed by Rabbi Schnabel, predecessor of Rabbi Alinsky. Perhaps this spy was disguised as a truck driver or a delivery person and was taking photos and/ or trying to access enzyme samples when Isaac entered and caught him. The intruder hit Isaac over the head and fled. One company that may have sent a spy is the Canadian-American Koshering Association.

According to Crime Stoppers' protocol, as soon as she sent her message, she deleted it, making it untraceable. She wondered if her submission would elicit any questions or action. Supposedly if the police officer who read it had questions, he'd send them to her at her Crime Stoppers address and she'd reply and delete both messages. Meanwhile the experience of writing it, sending it, and deleting it was extremely satisfying.

C.S. Nikaimak showed up for breakfast in jeans and a gray sweater, her black mane constrained in a thick braid snaking down her back. Although she was still beautiful, she bore little resemblance to the *soignée* urban-Indian attorney who had checked in. Something of a chameleon herself, Miranda felt a kinship with this transformed woman whose dark eyes gleamed even before she helped herself to coffee. And if they were sisters under the skin, C.S was definitely the older sib because radiating from her glittering eyes were lines Miranda had been too dazzled to notice the day before. C.S. didn't speak until she refilled her coffee cup, and then her tone was urgent and unmistakably seductive. "Hey, Miranda, I'm going to look for my brother and our grandfather today. Those two goofs have literally gone off the rez. Care to come along for the ride?" She looked around. "It's pretty quiet here, and just plain pretty out there." She pointed at the sunshine streaming in the window. "Besides, I could really use the company."

Miranda figured that the quest C.S proposed might reveal something useful and relevant to her own search for Isaac Markowitz's real killer. She'd also see the area through C.S.'s Valley-bred eyes and the clincher was that she just might make another friend. For once her chores would keep. "Sure. Should I bring Rusty?"

"Probably not a good idea. We're going to be in the car most of the time."

"Okay, I'll arrange for someone to come and walk him."

In less than an hour the two women were cruising along Highway 97 in C.S.'s silver Audi S5. Miranda could have starred in an Audi commercial. "I love this car! The engine actually purrs. My poor truck's engine alternately sputters, coughs, and rattles."

"It's a good car." Having acknowledged the compliment, C.S. changed the subject. "Miranda, have you been to Horse Heaven Hills yet? It used to be a sparsely populated part of the rez. Now, trust me, these hills we're driving through are alive with wineries and ranches, even though most of them aren't visible from the road."

"It's really beautiful." The gentle hills were still golden with grasses. Herds of small horses flew down to race with the Audi along the roadside fence and then dash back up and out of sight. "Those must be the wild ponies I read about. They're beautiful too." She envied the wild horses their freedom and grace just as she envied the same qualities in C.S.

"Yep. They roam free out here, eating and reproducing like crazy. The ranchers go nuts because the ponies impinge on their grazing areas. But they are pretty. Pretty inbred, that is."

Miranda didn't know what to say to that sad factoid, so she asked, "Do you ride?"

"I used to. A lifetime ago I had a thing with a rodeo cowboy and he taught me." C.S was quiet for a while and then pointed at the scablands appearing in the distance. The gentle green and beige hills had given way to bare sunbaked ones, home to occasional sagebrush spheres and striped by dark rocky outcroppings. When she spoke next, her voice was reverent. "My grandfather told us that his elders said those scratches are the devil's handwriting."

Miranda shivered a little in spite of the sun. She was relieved when C.S. shifted the conversation. "So, tell me, Miranda, what made you leave Seattle, a haven now for start-ups, and come way the hell out here to open a business?"

Miranda had answered this question many times. Every word of her standard reply was true, but it left a lot unsaid. "I took care of my grandmother and then my mom for many years, and after they both died I really needed a change of scenery." Miranda paused. Back in middle school she had figured out that secrets were the currency of female closeness. So she inhaled and added to her spiel a few unscripted words. "You know, sometimes things happen and you just have to leave a place you're used to and start over somewhere new." Then she resumed her canned explanation. "I also needed a job, something where I could be my own boss. And I came into a little money. Running a B & B fit the bill. So I started exploring and fell in love with that old farmhouse. Even with renovation costs, it came a lot cheaper than anything in Seattle." She smiled as they whizzed past a herd of multi-colored ponies grazing just behind the fence. Then before C.S could ask her any more questions, Miranda turned the tables. "Enough about me. I'm sure everyone asks you this, but I want to know. What does "C.S." stand for?"

"My given name is Colestah. My mother and my grandfather named me after the fifth wife of Chief Kamiakin. She was a warrior, a healer, a bit of a shaman. The woman was legendary. In a major battle, a howitzer shell landed in a tree Kamiakin was riding under and a branch fell on him and unhorsed him. He was badly hurt. Colestah had been riding and fighting next to him, and she got him off the battlefield to a safe place where she nursed him back to health."

"Wow. That's a lot to live up to."

"Yes. And it's a pain professionally. Who wants to hire a female attorney named after an Indian woman/warrior/witch doctor? So I go by C.S."

"C.S. does sound very professional."

"I guess that means very male, right?" She didn't wait for a reply. "Friends call me Colestah."

"You're engaged and Michael's last name is Wright, so I take it *Nikaimak* is the name of a guy you were once married to?"

Colestah laughed. "I let a lot of people think that. But you're not 'a lot of people,' Miranda, so I'll clue you in."

Miranda was pleased to hear Colestah acknowledge their developing friendship. "*Nikaimak* is *Kamiakin* spelled backwards!"

"Who knew? But it makes sense for Colestah to have her namesake's last name too." Miranda considered telling this clever woman that she too had adapted a name with special significance to her, but Colestah redirected the conversation.

"You know, Miranda, if I'd been less ambitious I might have stayed out here and been a good caregiver for my brother and our grandfather the way you were for your family. Then maybe those two wouldn't be running from a murder charge today."

Colestah's guilt-ridden speculation assured Miranda that they were, indeed, getting to know one another, forging a friendship. She was glad she'd come. "You don't seriously think either one of them actually murdered that young man, do you?"

"No. But Indians get blamed for a lot of stuff we didn't do." Colestah hesitated. "And there's my brother's damn fish club...."

"How do you figure it got to the crime scene?" Miranda was hoping for some new insight into this conundrum.

When she replied, Colestah spoke slowly, seemingly reviewing aloud her defense of Michael. "My kid brother got that truck just a few months ago. Our grandfather gave him money from the VA that he saved just like he gave me money for board when I got a scholarship to law school. He wanted to be sure Michael could get to his classes at Heritage U. Until he got that truck, Michael hoofed it everywhere, even to high school. No wonder he dropped out." She shook her head at some memory she didn't share. "Anyway, the kid isn't used to having his own ride, so he probably forgot to lock the truck one day and someone took the fish club. But who's going to believe that?" She shook her head again.

"I do. And you're going to make the judge and jurors believe it too."

"Let's hope it doesn't come to trial. And remember, I don't want the cops to blame our grandfather, either." She paused. "Miranda, did your grandmother become demented before she died?"

"No, but she was a Holocaust survivor and that made her a little *meshuganah*. She hoarded food and hated doctors and medicines. After my grandfather died, she imagined that he was still alive and sleeping with other women and she'd berate him for it in public and in detail at the top of her lungs." Miranda glowered at the memory. "And when she got really old, she had to use a walker but she hated it, so she wouldn't, and then she'd fall and break an arm or a hip or a wrist. Someone had to be with her all the time." Miranda paused. "I understand now that she probably had PTSD most of her life." Her brow creased. "Michael told me your grandfather also suffers from PTSD. That's not exactly dementia, you know."

"A rose by any other name.... Look!"

Miranda turned and scanned the suddenly-flat expanse of fields on either side of the car. Looming in the distance was a huge white mountain. "I guess that's Mount Adams. Wow! I've got to tell my guests about this ride. Every view is a picture postcard." She hesitated. "Where are we going? Michael said Indians wintered in these parts for centuries and he had an idea about where your grandfather might be. Are we going to an Indian village?"

Colestah's response was arch, acidic. "You mean a rehab facility? Or a shelter? That's where half the Indians on the rez, including my grandfather, ought to be living."

Miranda didn't reply, didn't know how to.

"Sorry. No. We can't go to an Indian village because they've all been destroyed."

Bitterness infused Colestah's voice with an ominous undertone that gave Miranda the shivers again. "So where are we going?"

"We're headed for a kind of tribal ghost village. Back in the day the tribes gathered berries up in the Cascades in the fall and then wintered in the Ahtanum and Kittitas Creek areas where they hunted. But we're going to where they spent the summers, to the Columbia River."

"But it's not summer anymore. The salmon aren't there now." Miranda had studied the life cycle of the salmon in almost every grade until she left school.

"It's complicated, Miranda. The U.S. government finally allowed as how the treaties mandate that we be permitted to fish in our usual places. But then they built dams up and down the Columbia and those dams destroyed tribal fishing villages, fishing platforms, even our burial grounds and screwed up the salmon runs too."

Miranda flashed on the mural in Toppenish titled *Celilo Falls*.

"Now thanks to the efforts of the tribes as well as the government, some salmon are returning and there are thirty-one designated fishing sites along the river. But there's no affordable housing for us anywhere near these sites."

Miranda's stomach tightened as, for a second, Colestah took her hands off the wheel to throw them up in consternation.

"The government built new homes for the whites displaced by the dams, but not for us. What a surprise."

"I hear you," was all Miranda could think to say in response. When this assurance provoked no reply, she took her turn at rerouting the conversation. "So you think Michael and Joseph are camping at one of these fishing sites?"

Colestah made a sharp turn into a dirt road before she spoke. "Maybe."

They rode in silence until Colestah directed, "Look! Look at the river!" She stopped the car near a wide swath of white-capped dark water rushing furiously by a decrepit trailer planted in what looked like dried mud. A patchwork of faded blankets held down by a tire covered most of the trailer's roof. Miranda couldn't tell if the blankets were blocking leaks or drying in the sun. A torn tarp partially protected some equipment beside the trailer and a vintage wooden picnic table covered with dishes was positioned nearby. There were two rickety-looking canvas chairs between the trailer and the table. As Colestah and Miranda got out of the car, a woman seated in one of these chairs struggled to stand. Was she drunk or just old and arthritic? Or all three? Miranda couldn't tell.

Wearing a bright red-and-black plaid blanket as a cape covering her from head to midway down her gray ankle-length skirt, their hostess blinked at the silver car glittering in the sun. A scowl contorted her weathered face until she recognized Colestah. Then the scowl reversed itself to become a grin, and tears threatened to spill from her still-bright eyes. Colestah walked into an opening in the front of the blanket and the two women embraced.

When she emerged, Colestah made introductions. "MaryFrances, this is Miranda. She's Michael's and my friend." Miranda nodded and smiled. "Miranda, meet my friend MaryFrances. She was my mother's friend first. They went to boarding school together, right MaryFrances?" The old woman's nod was brief.

Having observed protocol, Colestah returned to the car and began unloading cartons from the back seat.

Miranda moved to help her and saw that these cartons, which she'd paid no attention to before, were packed with bags of pasta and rice as well as canned goods and coffee. One of them contained a first aid kit. Looking around, she noticed a few other dwellings as ramshackle as MaryFrances's trailer rising from the mud of the river bank.

As she worked, Colestah talked brusquely to MaryFrances. "We're looking for Michael and grandfather. The police are after them and we need to find them first. Michael's not taking my calls. Are they staying with you?"

"No." MaryFrances's voice was low and her eyes down.

"MaryFrances, this was Michael's blanket." Colestah pinched a corner of her old family friend's makeshift poncho. "I sent it to him for his birthday a few weeks ago. Looks like he gave it to you. Are you sure he and Joseph aren't here?" She glanced at the trailer as she spoke.

"Yes. They came but they left late last night." She shrugged. "Joseph is ready. He wants to die on Rattlesnake Mountain so his spirit can rise to the sky." The old woman looked up and smiled as if this grim message were good news. "Michael is driving him there. I didn't tell the police. They came here looking for them this morning."

"The tribal police?" Miranda heard herself ask before she realized that it was not her place to do so.

MaryFrances didn't reply until Colestah said, "It's okay. Miranda wants to help."

"Yes. Tall. Long hair. Long nose, too." She traced in the air a long nose extending from her own modest one. "The other one with him you know." She leered at Colestah. "They're driving a blue Toyota. Four doors."

"Right. Thanks, MaryFrances."

"Joseph says it's his time. He says Michael will come alone to fish with us next summer." She glanced at the cartons. "Thank you, Colestah. Take care of yourself." Just then a child, a little boy, emerged from the trailer rubbing his eyes and crying. MaryFrances faced him and held out her arms. As Colestah and Miranda turned to leave, the woman and the boy were bent over one of the cartons.

"That's the fishing site." Colestah pointed to some low wooden buildings a hundred yards away. "Let's pee there. I had a lot of your good coffee."

Appalled by the wretchedness of MaryFrances's encampment, Miranda had to ask, "If there are no salmon now and no villages, why is MaryFrances staying way out here with her grandchild?"

Colestah sighed and pointed at the other trailers and a shack. "She's not the only one. Some Indians came back to the river after the dams went up even though their homes were flooded. They and their descendants squat here all year round. They were born and raised near the Columbia and they see proximity to it as their birthright. It's their tribal home. They fish in the summer but in the winter they barely subsist, freezing in these beat-up trailers, shacks, and sometimes even tents. I suppose you could call it a village." Her snort was audible.

They walked along the river to three wooden buildings, the largest of which Colestah said was a drying shed. The next biggest may have been a smokehouse. The smallest housed toilets. "It ain't fancy, but it'll have to do. Here." Colestah produced a roll of toilet paper from her tote, ripped off some, and handed the roll to Miranda. "Leave it for MaryFrances and her grandson and the others. Don't sit and don't bother trying to flush."

Miranda followed orders. After each of them emerged from her stall Colestah turned on one of the taps in the sink, producing a trickle of undoubtedly frigid water. She turned it off again and handed Miranda a small bottle of hand sanitizer from her tote. When she spoke, her voice was sharp with outrage. "The State closes off the water here on October first, so the Indian "squatters" tap into the plumbing. This crummy sink is where MaryFrances and the others get their cooking and drinking water too. It's not exactly Board of Health certified." She paused. Then, right there in the bathroom, she placed a newly sanitized hand over her heart and in a low voice made what sounded to Miranda like a vow. "Come back in a few years, and we'll have decent housing here for Indians like MaryFrances and her family…"

Shivering in an off-season outhouse that made Honey Buckets look inviting, Miranda realized that Colestah probably represented the Yakama Nation in their ongoing negotiations with the U. S. Fish and Wildlife Service. No wonder she left the rez to become a lawyer. She hadn't been driven by personal ambition so much as by her determination to help her people. She must have felt she could do more for her family by leaving than by staying.

Colestah didn't speak again until they had almost reached the car. "Here's the thing, Miranda. I'd like to say goodbye to my grandfather." Her voice was at once low, urgent, and imploring, the way it had been that morning when she entreated Miranda to join her on her search. "But we might be a little late getting back. Can you handle that?"

Eager to be a supportive friend and to see this quest through, Miranda nodded. "I'll call and ask my dog sitter to turn receptionist and check in the guests due later today."

"Thanks. You better try to call now. There's probably not much cell access on Rattlesnake Mountain." Before they reached the car, Miranda had arranged for Darlene to spend the afternoon with Rusty at the B & B.

"Hey, would you like to drive?"

Colsestah's question took Miranda by surprise. "Would I?" Flattered by this seemingly impulsive offer and relieved by Darlene's willingness to remain at the B & B for a few more hours, Miranda slid into the already open door on the driver's side of the car. Her new friend's spontaneity was contagious. As she studied the dashboard and then pushed the start button, she felt free and excited. "Wow! This car takes driving to a whole new level!"

"I'm not sure about that, but it will take us to Rattlesnake Mountain. To go to a higher level there, we'll have to hike. There are no roads up that part of the mountain out of deference to its place in tribal history and culture, and we're always going to court to keep it that way. Yakama Nation boys have been doing their vision quests on that mountain forever. Michael did his there. Our grandfather too. That's why he wants to die there."

Behind the wheel of the powerful car, Miranda proposed a different agenda. "Don't give up, Colestah. If we get to your grandfather fast enough, we can take him to the nearest ER and get him medical attention. Then maybe you won't have to say goodbye. How far is it?" Miranda's efforts to keep her beloved mother's heart beating had tested the patience of even the kindest of the kind hospice nurses who came to the house to help Mona Weintraub die peacefully and painlessly.

"It's not the distance. We Indians believe it's natural for the old to die, and my grandfather is old now and not well. Michael and I understand that he's been getting ready to leave us since Michael started college. We don't see dying as a bad thing when one is old, sick, and ready. And it is good that his spirit begins its journey in a place he chooses. Michael was right to bring him to Rattlesnake Mountain."

Miranda was marveling at Colestah's ability to reconcile the values of her ancestors with those of modernity when a vehicle appearing and reappearing in the rearview mirror distracted her. "There's a blue sedan two cars behind us. It might be following us." For a second she wished she were back at her B & B doing laundry or making her one guest's bed.

Colestah turned to check out the cars behind them. "Damn. That's the tribal police. They were probably parked out of sight near MaryFrances's place waiting for Michael and Grandfather to surface. When we showed up and left so soon, they figured we'd lead them straight to their quarry. They'll bring them both in and grill them and then turn them over to the sheriff who'll grill them all over again and then lock one of them up for murder."

At the thought of an innocent and dying old man being subjected to police interrogation and possibly imprisonment, cop-phobic Miranda heard herself say, "I'm gonna speed up just a little. If they speed up, we'll know you're right. Then we can turn off this road and lose them." Miranda had braved a lot of tricky traffic while chauffeuring her grandmother and then her mother to and from various Seattle-area doctors and hospitals. Bolstered by that experience, her faith in the Audi S5, and a lot of adrenaline, she didn't wait for Colestah's permission. "Here we go! Hang on!" She gave the car a little gas and began weaving between the trucks and cars ahead of her until the Audi was in the right lane. Sure enough the blue Toyota followed their sinuous path the way the tail of a serpent follows its head. Miranda had seen enough car chases on NCIS to recognize such a tail. She was certain that in the Audi she could lose them. "Should I take a sharp right at the next road leading off this one?"

"No, let them get right behind us. Then signal that you're going to pull over, but don't actually stop. After that, when I say 'Go' pull out and really drive."

Miranda would always remember the next few seconds as if they happened to somebody else. Out of the corner of her eye she glimpsed Colestah deftly unbuckle her seat belt. "What the…" Miranda's voice was shrill and grew louder as her newly-unfettered passenger clambered nimbly into the back of the car. "Get back here! What the hell are you doing?" It was all Miranda could do to holler and keep the car on the road. Her shrieked protests provoked no response except for a rush of air as a back window opened and the sharp cracks of three gunshots in rapid succession. The tribal cops were shooting at them! Her heart clenched like a fist in her chest. Had Colestah been hit? Miranda only stopped praying when she heard her out-of-control passenger's imperative "Go." Colestah was alive—crazy, but alive.

Miranda glanced in the rearview mirror and saw the blue Toyota behind them spin and stop. No longer taking orders from Colestah, she stayed in the right lane. If her friend was wounded, Miranda would pull over and call 911.

With her heart still constricted, she heard Colestah close the rear window and scramble, apparently uninjured, back into the front seat. Miranda's peripheral vision afforded her a glimpse of her passenger sliding a black handgun into a holster strapped to her ankle. Only then did she grasp that the three gunshots she'd heard were fired by her new best friend who had been shooting at the Yakama Nation Tribal Police from a car she herself was driving! Had Colestah killed one of the cops? Praying once more, she pictured a man slumped in the driver's seat of the motionless blue car. Miranda felt her left foot begin to twitch and saw her knuckles whiten as she gripped the steering wheel hard enough to steady her hands.

Colestah buckled herself into the passenger seat and addressed Miranda calmly, as if nothing out of the ordinary had just transpired. "Nice driving. Thanks. I really didn't want those asshole cops to stop me from saying goodbye to my grandfather or make him spend his final hours in an interrogation room. You okay?"

"Colestah, did you kill the cop driving that car?" Miranda's voice was low, because she still wasn't breathing right.

"Of course not. I just shot up one of their front tires to slow them down a little."

Miranda made herself suck in air. At least she had not unwittingly aided and abetted this wild wack job in murdering a cop. But she had aided and abetted her in obstructing justice and shooting at a moving police vehicle occupied by not one but two officers. And, she, Miranda Breitner, was driving the getaway car. This time it was not the cops who were out to get her. Instead it was she herself who, albeit unwittingly, had taken part in an illegal and dangerous attack on them. This shift undermined Miranda's sense of moral superiority, but it also undermined her fear of cops. With these two facets of her worldview shaken, Miranda felt scared and off balance, the way she'd felt when, as a small child, by mistake she put her shoes on the wrong feet, took a step, teetered, and fell hard on her face.

Aware of her own mental state, as she drove she tried to get into her passenger's head or, in this case, heads. Miranda knew that changing one's name can be a catalyst for other changes. C. S. Nikaimak was as rational as she was beautiful. But Colestah Kamiakin Wright was nuts. Perhaps her loss-filled childhood and the impending death of her grandfather along with the arrest of her only other relative had turned C.S., law-abiding lawyer, into Colestah, sharp-shooting outlaw. C.S. could be disbarred and imprisoned for what Colestah had just done.

And Colestah's craziness could be Miranda's undoing too, could destroy her own carefully-constructed new persona. Hanging out with Colestah was not how one kept a low profile, kept people from looking into one's past. Under the spell of this witchy woman, the lonesome Miranda had completely forgotten the heavy burden that was her own history. She could pay a high price for a morning's illusion of freedom and friendship.

Apparently Colestah was a mind reader too. "Not to worry, Miranda. You have my word. This incident will not come back to bite either of us."

"I bet they've already put out a BOLO on this car."

"You lose. Those braves will never allow as how their vehicle got outraced by a lead-footed white woman and then disabled by a squaw sharpshooter who has championed their rights for years and who is on her way to her grandfather's death bed. Besides, I know a few things about the driver of that car that would cost him his badge if they got out. Chill."

Unconvinced, Miranda didn't reply but fumed and practiced breathing normally. When she could no longer hear her heart pounding, she gave voice to just one of Colestah's actions that infuriated her. "And you didn't tell me what you were going to do because you knew I'd never go along with it, right?"

"Wrong. If I told you, then you couldn't plead ignorance. In the unlikely event that they ever bring charges against me, it's in your best interest not to have known."

Miranda considered this lawyerly explanation, considered the possibility that having exorcised her demons by stopping those who would interfere with her plans, Colestah was giving way to C.S. Maybe the attorney was right. Ignorance was, if not exactly bliss, at least a possible defense. "Do you do this sort of thing often?"

"No, in Seattle I'm quite circumspect. But somehow when I come home what I face enrages me. Must be something in the water. Seriously, they say the manure from the dairies in the Lower Valley is polluting our groundwater. Then I look at MaryFrances and I remember my mom and how those years in boarding school messed her up. MaryFrances too. As girls they were uprooted from their families who were too poor to feed them and sent to a government boarding school at Fort Simcoe. They couldn't speak our language or practice our religion, and they were given meaningless new white names to boot. That's partly why my mother named me Colestah. There was never a white saint with my name." The bitterness in Colestah's voice further worried Miranda. "When they got out of those schools, they didn't know how to be family members or practice a religion. They had no tribal language to pass on to us. Hell, my mom drank herself to death and MaryFrances.... Never mind. The damn boarding schools are old news. Hey, want me to drive?"

"No. I'm good. How'd you learn to shoot like that?"

"An old boyfriend, the passenger in that car in fact, gave me this baby."

Miranda flinched as she glimpsed Colestah reach to pat her ankle.

"He gave it to me when I moved to Seattle and made me promise to take lessons. Turns out I've got a good eye, a steady hand, and quick reflexes, and that's what it takes."

"A little judgment wouldn't hurt either. Does your fiancé know you're armed and dangerous?"

"You don't give up, do you?"

Miranda heard annoyance in Colestah's tone.

"Yes, Roger knows I carry, but I probably won't mention this little episode to him. He's in politics and he wouldn't want it known that his fiancée shoots up the tires of cops when they get in her way. Lighten up, Miranda. Everyone has secrets. Even you."

Miranda didn't reply but drove on still trying to take in their recent crimes and the fact that her new friend was really two friends, and one of them was loony. But then, so was her Holocaust-survivor Grandma Fanny. Colestah's impoverished and virtually parentless childhood on the rez probably explained her impulsive, illegal, and destructive behavior.

Miranda took one hand off the wheel and ran it beneath her chin, tracing the line left by the razor. She pictured the keloids lining the inside of both her upper arms and inner thighs, recalled how the pain of each of those small slashes had brought her a few seconds of relief from her ongoing misery. But she also recalled the terror and pain her suicide attempt had caused her mom and how Mona had kept her alive and helped her get well. How would she have gotten through her own scarred adolescence alive without her fixer mom? Colestah had had no such mom.

Even so, Colestah wasn't Miranda's to fix, wasn't her child or even part of her family. She was a new friend. Real-world friends couldn't and shouldn't be "unfriended" like on Facebook or, for that matter, like her teenaged friends "unfriended" her years ago. And she couldn't "unfriend" Colestah and keep C.S. But she also knew she couldn't fix Colestah either.

By the time they got to Rattlesnake Mountain, a bald windswept hump overlooking a lake, the sky had darkened a little and the air had chilled. Miranda was glad she'd worn a jacket and that she and Colestah had scarfed down energy bars from the Audi's glove compartment. She parked at the trailhead next to Michael's truck and they began to climb.

The treeless, barren, uphill trail served as a memory lane for Colestah. "This is where Michael came to do his vision quest. That boy was gone nearly four days. I was worried sick, but our grandfather wasn't. He said Michael would be fine and would be a warrior when he came down and, damn it, he was right." Colestah paused and looked around. "My baby brother walked up this same grim path at thirteen. Back then he was a typical rez kid, an orphan from a screwed up family. He had bad grades, a drinking problem, and was being courted by a gang. But he really wasn't typical. He was luckier." Colestah's voice caught. "Joseph Wright, that, stinky, old pothead boozer dying up ahead, the Vietnam vet everybody thinks is crazy, had already saved my brother. He'd taught him to fish, to be at home in the wild, to know the ways of the salmon and the rivers.

"And he'd told him our stories." Colestah paused before continuing. "In fact, right before Michael went on his vision quest, grandfather told him the story about the warrior and the rattlesnake. He once told it to me too. So I figure Michael must've used the four days he spent alone up here to dry out and find his true path, because he didn't get bitten and he came down a warrior."

"That sounds like a bar mitzvah run by Outward Bound."

Colestah laughed. "Yes. It does."

"Tell me the story about the rattlesnake. I saw one last week."

"Kinda late in the season, but if there's sun…" Colestah sighed. "It's a story elders of several tribes tell kids to warn them off alcohol and drugs. As I said, back in the day grandfather told it to me too." She took a breath. "Okay. Here's the short version. A young warrior goes alone up a hill just like this one to make his vision quest. At the top it's cold like it is here."

Miranda shivered and zipped her jacket.

"At the end of his quest on his way down, the warrior finds a rattler immobilized and dying from the cold. The snake begs the warrior to carry him down the mountain to where it's warmer and so save his life. The warrior exacts a promise from the rattler that if he grants this request, once the snake regains mobility he won't bite his deliverer. So the warrior puts the snake on his shoulders and carries him down. When the snake warms up, he bites the warrior. As he dies, the warrior says, 'But you promised,' and the snake says, 'But that is my way and you knew what I was when you picked me up.'"

This story was different from the Jewish ones Miranda knew. God wasn't mentioned at all. Nor was sin. And there was no miracle. The warrior's mistake seemed to be ignoring what he himself knew out of either kindness or naiveté or both. "So the point is kids know what drugs and alcohol did to their friends and relatives and they shouldn't think it'll be different for them?"

"You got it. Thanks to my grandfather, Michael came down from this mountain with a plan. And it wasn't a pie-in-the-sky plan either. He said he'd try going to high school but if it was too far from that cabin he and grandfather were living in for him to go every day, he'd drop out and study for his GED. With that done, he'd apply to Heritage U and learn how to clean up the rivers and bring back the salmon."

"Sure sounds like a good plan to me. Dropping out of school could be a little risky, but…." Miranda reminded herself that she, too, had left high school and lived to tell about it.

"I think he knew that if he wasn't around town he'd be less pressured by the gangs too. At any rate, he left school in tenth grade. I bought him a laptop, and a rancher he still does odd jobs for let him charge it at his place and later on use the Wi-Fi there. I bought him books, too." Miranda realized that Michael's grandfather, his sister, and a kindly rancher had, in effect, home-schooled him. "But whenever Michael could get work as a handyman or a guide he'd take it, and summers when the fish were running… so getting that GED took him awhile, but he got it." She smiled, making no effort to hide her pride as she picked up her pace. "Miranda, let's walk faster. They can't have gone too much farther on foot. I don't want to be too late."

Miranda lengthened her stride. "This place is more moonscape than mountain."

"Yeah. It's early name was *Laliik* which means "land above the water." But let's walk, not talk, okay?"

It wasn't long before the wind in their faces smelled faintly of weed, and the two breathless women reached the ledge of rock where in the shadow of the mountaintop still ahead Michael sat next to Joseph Wright. Nodding at her brother, Colestah approached the wizened old man, sat down beside him, and took his hand in one of hers. With the other she accepted the lit joint Michael handed her and held it close to her grandfather's lips. Joseph stirred just enough to take a drag.

Miranda knew something about death watches, having sat quietly beside first her grandmother and then, years later, her mother as each, heavily sedated, took her last breath. She touched Colestah's shoulder and then, feeling very much the intruder, took a seat at the far end of the ledge, checking first to be sure no late-hibernating rattlesnake had a prior claim to the spot.

In a minute or two, Michael joined her, his face grave. "I said goodbye. It's Colestah's turn. Now that she's here, grandfather's spirit can leave him and rise to the sky, to the spirit world, as he wishes."

"It was good of you to bring him up here. Colestah says this place is of great significance to him."

"Yes. Here his spirit does not have far to go." Michael looked up. "He's ready to leave us. He'll go soon, before they can accuse him or me of murder, before he learns what I let happen to his fish club." He bent over, positioned his elbows on his knees, clasped his hands, and faced the earth. His voice was a whisper, so that to catch his words before the wind took them Miranda had to lean forward until her head was next to his. "He taught me to fish like his father taught him. That fish club once belonged to his father, my great grandfather. It has carvings on it. When I was a kid, I thought maybe they were a greeting from our ancestors to the fish or even to me. That club was dark with the blood of fish caught and killed by my ancestors. Once I started using it, man, my salmon died fast, without pain."

Michael flipped his hood over his head as the wind picked up. But he kept talking, so Miranda kept listening. "That club felt so true in my hands." He held out his right hand and closed it into a fist as if gripping the missing tool. Watching, Miranda felt in her own hands the carved handles of her great grandmother's wooden rolling pin, the handles that propelled the pin smoothly over even the shortest dough.

"Many people thought that club was really cool. Steve Galen said I could get a few hundred dollars for it. But I would never sell grandfather's gift. He presented it to me in front of the tribe at my First Catch celebration in the longhouse." Michael hesitated, perhaps summoning recollections of that occasion. "I was very young when I caught my first salmon, and Grandfather was very proud of me. I remember when he put that club in my hand, he asked me to promise to teach my own kids to fish and to pass it on to them." Michael's voice wavered for a moment before he continued. "The lady from our cultural heritage museum was there, and she asked me to let her display it in the museum every year when the fishing season ended. I shoulda let her. It woulda been safer there."

His next words jogged something in Miranda's head. "Now my grandfather's gift to my children is covered in human blood." Michael's voice broke and he stopped talking. Miranda resolved to think more about the fish club as murder weapon later.

When she heard Colestah's voice softly chanting what sounded like a prayer, she understood that Joseph Wright, aka Injun Joe, aka Kamiakin, had taken his last breath. His deathwatch had become a *shiva*, a time of mourning. She wanted to say something to console Michael for his loss and to appease his guilty conscience, but she could find no words. She knew how bad she felt at the prospect of being unable to keep the promise she'd made to her mom to start a new life and learn to feel at home in the world. So again she and Michael sat quietly for a few minutes until he stood, squared his shoulders, and joined his sister. The wind carried the murmur of their chanting to Miranda. When the murmur stopped, she went to where the dead veteran warrior still sat, his sightless eyes open to the sunless sky.

Colestah swiped at her tears with the back of her hand and took charge. "Michael, you'll have to stay here with Grandfather to keep the critters off him until the funeral home sends someone to retrieve him. That may take a while because he's over fifty and didn't die in a hospital, so I have to notify the cops first or maybe out here, the sheriff. But they all know how old and sick he is, so they probably won't bother to investigate his death. They'll tell me to call the funeral home to send someone to retrieve his body and we'll dress him and have a ceremony at the longhouse. Washington law forbids corpses in the longhouse, but the State won't mess with us. They never do. I'll make those calls as soon as I can get a signal on my cell."

All that said, she reached up and took hold of her brother's chin as if he were again a child and she held onto it while she continued. "I'm also going to call the tribal police to report that one of their fugitives is dead but that the other, Michael Wright, will be in with his attorney to talk with them tomorrow. They'll get in touch with Sheriff Carson who is also pretty interested in talking to you." She let go of his chin and he nodded.

"Get some sleep when you get home. You look terrible. I'll be out at the cabin first thing tomorrow morning to prep you for your meetings with those cops." Still giving orders, she shed her jacket and handed it to him. "Cover Grandfather with this."

"Here. Take mine for yourself, please. I don't need it." Miranda took off her own jacket and handed it to Michael.

Colestah looked around the desolate high-desert mountainside and asked, "Michael, do you have your rifle?" She scanned the ledge where the dead man's body had slumped.

"It's down in my truck." Colestah glared at him. "Yeah, I locked the truck. I didn't think I'd need the rifle. Besides, I had to carry him most of the way."

"Here. Take this." Miranda was hugely relieved to see Colestah bend to slip her handgun from her ankle holster and put it into Michael's hand. "In case there's a persistent critter. Take care of yourself. It's just us two now." She hugged her brother quickly, turned to Miranda, and jerked her head in the direction of the trail.

The two coatless women jogged down to the car without speaking. On the now familiar path, Miranda pondered the story of the warrior and the rattler as if it were a Torah portion. Now that she knew her complicated new friend better, understood that Colestah was capable of criminality as well as kindness, she would keep her guard up as she had with Vanessa Vargas and as she thought she had done with Detective Ladin. So the take-away for her from that grim cautionary tale designed to help teens stay away from drugs and alcohol was that if she learned to recognize danger, she could avoid it as Harry Ornstein had demonstrated so ably the day before. But Miranda knew that rattlers weren't always sunning themselves in the open. Rather, sometimes they waited coiled, camouflaged, and ready to strike an unwitting passerby.

CHAPTER 14

Guest book: *"Out here for some face-time with client and pleased with this new B&B. Good wi-fi and coffee. Nice room and client didn't balk at the tab." C.S. Nikaimak, Attorney at Law*

Joseph Wright was honored and buried so soon after he died that his funeral luncheon was over before Miranda saw the obit and realized that neither Colestah nor Michael had invited her. Colestah had been so busy in the days after Joseph's death that Miranda saw little of her. The day she finally checked out, she was early for breakfast, and Miranda greeted her with a question. "Colestah, I take it you persuaded the tribal and county cops that your brother and your grandfather had nothing to do with Isaac Markowitz's murder?

Colestah nodded.

"How did you manage that?"

Sipping coffee and helping herself to a slab of warm zucchini bread, Colestah gave a simple answer. "I told them they didn't do it."

"Come on, Colestah. Michael already told them that and they still kept after him."

"You're right. I phrased my message a little differently." She smirked. "I told them to stop their racial profiling and to stop harassing my brother if they wanted to avoid a lawsuit. And I reminded them that Michael has a solid alibi for Isaac's time of death, had no reason to kill him, was not in possession of the alleged murder weapon when it was allegedly used, and has no criminal record. I also reminded them that they had no evidence against him. Then I explained that our grandfather also had an alibi for that morning. He was out at Mary-Frances's place preparing for his journey. Easy peasy." She rubbed her palms together as if washing her hands of this matter once and for all. "Now can I eat?" She grinned, so pleased with herself that she hardly needed Miranda's approval. But Miranda, somewhat recovered from what she'd come to think of as their ride on the wild side, gave her a thumbs up anyway.

"And, so you know, Miranda, the luncheon went very well. State Law doesn't allow corpses in longhouses, but they never come down on us about that, so there he lay, wrapped in his father's Pendleton blanket. The whole longhouse smelled of grilled salmon." She shook her head. "Some of those folks hadn't sat down to a salmon meal ever. After that there was drumming, a lot of drumming… and we carried him out and laid him in Michael's truck. Then the vets came wearing their feathered headdresses and folded the flag and played taps and gave him a 21-gun salute. Finally Michael and I took him away and buried him." Clearly the details of Joseph Wright's private burial would remain private. Colestah drank her last few swallows of coffee and put her mug down. "Gotta pack. I'm due in court tomorrow in Seattle."

An hour later, Miranda was watering her spider plant when Colestah returned, dressed in her black pants and jersey, with her hair off her face and flowing down her back. Miranda put down her watering can and went to the fridge. "Here. I made you a doggie bag for your ride back over the mountains." She didn't usually do this for departing guests, but she was sure that Colestah would return to the Valley and wanted her to know she was still welcome at Breitner's. "Next time you come home, may it be for a much happier occasion. Have a safe trip." She refrained from adding, "And don't shoot anybody."

"Take care of yourself, Miranda. You've made a great little nest here. Thanks for sharing it with me." She took the bag Miranda handed her and turned to leave. After a few steps, she turned back. "As for that mess across the street…." She tilted her head in the direction of the processing plant and her lips curved in an enigmatic smile. "Don't let it get to you. Sooner or later you'll figure out who really did kill that koshering guy and you'll tell the cops, and they'll take the credit, and the whole thing will blow over." Miranda thought she heard wrong. How did Colestah know she was feeding the cops leads on Crime Stoppers? Maybe the woman really was a prophet who foretold events no one else even imagined. "And don't worry. I promise I won't shoot anybody on the way home." It was Miranda's turn to smile. She'd forgotten Colestah's mindreading expertise. "Seriously, Miranda, if you ever need my help… you have my contact info. I mean it." Colestah's hug was as unexpected as her offer, but surprisingly welcome. In a moment the Audi's tires squealed and she was gone.

When a week had passed after the trip to Rattlesnake Mountain, and no one had shown up to arrest her and there was no reference to the tire-shooting in the local news or blogs, Miranda acknowledged that Colestah was right. The two tribal police officers had decided not to publicize it.

By the end of that same week Detective Ladin hadn't shown up either. Maybe he regretted having forced his kiss on her. Or, as a newspaper reporter wrote, he was busy following "new leads." She suspected one was the one she'd sent via Crime Stoppers and that the other wasn't new at all but had to do with Javier Baez. Curious, she set out for a run with Rusty and headed straight for Darlene's house on the other side of downtown. Rusty trotted after her up the street just as Detective Ladin himself walked out the front gate. His eyes widened at the sight of Miranda. He nodded politely, but, to Miranda's relief, all he said was "Gotta run" and he kept going.

Darlene was surprised to see Miranda too, but not unhappy. Rusty enjoyed a reunion with her that included lots of head scratching and a bonus belly rub. She welcomed them both into what seemed more like a cottage than a full-sized house. Miranda reminded herself that, according to her realtor, many of the homes in Sunnyvale were built back when aspirations were modest and central heating and indoor plumbing were still luxuries.

The living room was neat and cozy, but Darlene was a mess. New lines transected her thin face, her complexion was sallow, and her eyes blinked in the sun-brightened doorway. The older woman's altered appearance brought out the fixer in Miranda. "You look like you haven't slept in weeks. I came over to see if you could work Friday night, but now I feel more like I should adopt you. Let's get you out of the house. Come for a walk with us. Tell me what's happened to Javier that's keeping you up nights and stealing your appetite."

Darlene obediently slipped a coat off a hook, grabbed her purse, and locked the door. "That man has been here every day this week, sometimes twice in one day."

"I'm so sorry. I read they were following new leads. Have they found Javier? Is he okay? I didn't see anything in the paper."

"No. They did not find him." Darlene's tone, suddenly resolute, was at odds with her worn face.

"Well that's a relief."

"No. They want to find him more than before because they think they have a new motive for Javier to kill that guy. It's more convincing even than the motives they made up." Darlene looked around her tiny yard, still blinking as if seeing the sun and the willow trees and the neighboring homes for the first time. "They think I know where he is."

Miranda thought so too. Darlene was smart and competent and probably quite capable of stowing that kid away somewhere secure if she had to. And she had to. Miranda didn't press her on it.

Darlene's voice was bitter. "I just wish they would concentrate on finding the real killer. Until they find who really did it, Javi is not safe in the Valley."

"You're right. Believe me, I know." Miranda swallowed her impulse to share her own experience with the police's affinity for premature incarceration. "What new motive have they dreamed up for Javier?"

"The dead guy and a friend, another kosherer, were walking around Toppenish looking at the murals on their day off. The dead guy , , ,"

"Isaac. His name was Isaac Markowitz," Miranda interjected.

"Now I remember. Yes. Isaac asked a girl walking by to take a photo of him and his friend in front of a mural, and he gave her his phone and she walked across the street and took the picture. Then she went back and returned his phone. But, Ms Breitner, one of Javi's amigos was driving by and saw this girl Alma talk to them and take the picture. As like a joke, he told Javi that Isaac hit on Alma." Darlene's voice had become low and desperate.

"Uh oh, that's not good."

"It gets worse. I'm telling you. It's like on TV."

"But Isaac was Orthodox. And he was married. Orthodox Jewish men barely talk to women they don't know. I'm surprised he even asked her to take the picture. I certainly don't believe he flirted with her."

"It doesn't matter, because Alma believed Javi got jealous. And right after that Javi went missing. And he didn't tell Alma he was leaving. He also didn't tell her where he was going. And he didn't take her calls. So Queen Alma was very angry." Miranda detected something almost like triumph in Darlene's voice. "That bitch always acts like she has him wrapped around her little finger. So she went to the police." Darlene stopped walking, looked at Miranda, and shook her head. "Can you believe that, Ms Breitner? That lying little slut told the police Javi killed Isaac for hitting on her. Can you believe that?"

Miranda nodded. All too easily she could imagine how Detective Ladin, eager to close this troublesome case, inflamed the hurt teenager's anger. "Yes, I can. Sometimes the cops can't tell the difference between closing a case and finding a killer."

"You're right. They keep questioning all Alma and Javi's friends and all us relatives over and over. They say he stole the fish club to use to throw them off his trail and they're talking to family and anyone else who ever so much as smiled at Javi or lent him money for a taco. My son and his wife are so afraid. They have already lost one son..."

When they passed a two-story house where some pumpkins and gourds were attractively arranged on one side of the front steps, Miranda broke their silence with what she intended as a distracting bit of small talk. "These stairs look good. I ought to get some pumpkins and gourds for the B & B's front steps and maybe for inside the fireplace."

Darlene didn't so much as glance at the house. "What looks good on the outside isn't always so good inside. On account of the people in that house who just moved here last spring, my granddaughter can't play in front of my house anymore and I've lived here for thirty-five years." She turned to look at Miranda and then back at the decorated stairs. "The kids who live in that house called my Josefina ugly names and took her doll and made her cry. Can you believe it?"

"What did they call her?"

"'Nigger.' 'Mud.' The child has dark skin like her father and grandfather. My husband's skin was dark." Darlene was shivering, so without interrupting her, Miranda turned and headed them back the way they came. "Those kids are old enough to know better, and when I phoned their mother and told her she apologized to me and made them give back the doll, but Josefina won't walk her doll's stroller out in front anymore even if I go with her. That mother's a nurse who works the night shift at the hospital she can home-school those two brats. The father, he's an engineer with the county. They're educated people. You'd think they'd teach their kids better than that." Darlene's sigh spoke of resignation and sorrow. "You can see why our Josefina's happier in her school. This world is not easy for someone like her."

Miranda, sobered by the realization that Darlene and her family routinely bore burdens that far outweighed her own baggage, put her arm around the grandmother's shoulders, and the two women walked the rest of the way back without talking, like mourners leaving a funeral.

Once inside, Darlene made tea while Miranda looked around admiring the many class, graduation, and wedding photos of young people and the portraits of unsmiling adults posing stiffly in their old-fashioned best clothes. Darlene seemed to find comfort in the ritual of feeding a guest, and she put out a plate of churros with the tea. "Help yourself." Her voice was deliberately cheerful. "Ms Breitner, I have another idea about who killed this Isaac. It's pretty simple. Want to hear it?"

"I'm all ears."

"Isaac's killer might have been a dismissed employee of Oskar Hindgrout's. He's the plant owner. You know, the killer could be like those psychos who get fired from the post office and go back and shoot everybody they used to work with."

"It works for me. I'm surprised the cops haven't pursued it. Or maybe they have."

"And maybe now this ex-employee's a junkie who stole the fish club from Michael Wright's truck to sell for drug money. Then, while in the neighborhood, he went into Hindgrout's plant to rip off some copper wiring or something else from a place where he had been so mistreated. He would think he knew how the plant operated too, that on a Sunday maybe there'd be fewer people around."

"Hindgrout does have a very short fuse." Miranda kept listening.

"Mr. Hindgrout could put together a list of fired employees, and the cops could find and question them instead of focusing only on my Javi. I know a lot of those ex-employees are back across the border, but still..."

"I agree. It's a new direction."

"Well those cops need a new direction. I keep telling that detective, if my grandson ever saw a fish club, he'd hit a baseball with it."

"Right. At least your scenario takes that damn fish club into account." She left Darlene's house only after the older woman agreed to send her suggestion to Crime Stoppers. She also promised to eat more and try to rest. "After all, you're going to be working all day Friday, and you'll need your strength to keep up with this guy." Miranda bent to scratch Rusty's head and run her hand over his back.

Later that day, she resolved to follow up on a new theory of her own. She called Nelson at home. Pauline took the call and insisted Miranda join them for supper. "We haven't seen you in too long."

After a delicious chicken dinner of which Miranda preferred not to know the provenance, she turned to Nelson and asked, "So did you ever get to actually see Isaac's ram's horn? Was it there in the room when you found the body? Was Isaac holding it?"

Nelson sipped his coffee before he spoke. "No. I don't remember seeing it. When I came in he was lying on the floor all bloody and not conscious and I went right to my phone to get help. I was pretty upset. I just don't remember seeing a musical instrument or any kind of animal horn near him. And that's funny, because he was really proud of that thing. It was his idea to show it to me. He told me it was a wedding gift from his father-in-law, some kind of family heirloom."

"Did you tell the detective who interviewed you after the murder that you were coming to meet Isaac just to see that ram's horn?"

"I'm pretty sure I did. But I'm not positive. I know I told him Isaac and I used to talk a lot when we were both on breaks. We talked about the Bible. He was my friend. And his poor young widow, Eva is her name, will always be in my prayers. He missed her so much."

"So you aren't absolutely sure you mentioned the ram's horn to the detective?"

"Right." Nelson's smile was wry, not mirthful. "I was scared the cops thought I'd killed my friend. And that new cop who interviewed me, he had a Spanish name. I understand Spanish accents, but he spoke with some weird accent that wasn't Spanish. So I just answered his questions as fast as I could to get out of that little room." Nelson's mouth began to twitch at the memory. "I prayed to Jesus to get me out of there before he got it into his head that I killed Isaac."

Miranda understood Nelson's desire to escape an interrogator. She hated interrogating him and they were both relieved when Pauline rejoined them at the table, even though she sounded annoyed. "I keep telling Nelson that cop was probably Filipino. They have Spanish names but they speak another language, right, Miranda?"

Uncertain herself, Miranda shrugged. "All I know is that the Philippines were once a colony of Spain, so it makes sense that lots of people from there have Spanish surnames."

"Yes. And now there's a Filipino family in our church and their last name is Gonzalez. The wife, she told me the health center keeps sending all their medical bills and test results in Spanish, and they can't read them. Our pastor got someone to translate for them."

At this, Nelson looked annoyed. "Well I don't know about that. All I know is I speak English and I couldn't understand that guy's English too good."

Miranda nodded, eager to avoid taking sides. She needn't have worried. When Nelson spoke next, he defused the domestic tiff by addressing Miranda. His voice was low and his tone apologetic. "Now, don't take this the wrong way, Miranda, but maybe one of the other Jews took the ram's horn to keep it from being, you know, desecrated by non-Jews like the cops. You people don't like non-Jews touching your grapes or your dead bodies, so maybe the rabbi or one of the other kosherers felt that way about the ram's horn, wanted to keep it, you know, kosher."

Miranda stiffened for a few seconds at Nelson's use of the phrase *you people* but she got over it. She assumed Nelson meant no harm. Even so, she didn't feel like explicating the complex commandments that governed the lives of Orthodox Jews just then. So all she said was, "The rabbi and most of the other kosherers weren't in the Valley when Isaac was killed, Nelson. And I don't think they would have removed anything from a crime scene even if they were here."

Nelson shrugged and nodded.

"Nelson, tell me, what's Oskar Hindgrout like to work for? I was talking to someone this morning who thinks the killer might be an employee fired by Hindgrout and holding a grudge."

"Hindgrout's a decent boss. He's got a temper, but he jokes about it. And from what I can see, he's real careful about who he hires, so he doesn't have to can too many people. I been with him over twenty years and he maybe let go four, five guys in all that time." Nelson sighed. "We got more machines than men now."

"Interesting. But I better get a move on. I'm going to Yakima tomorrow right after breakfast so I have to get my beauty sleep."

"Don't tell me there's another Jewish holiday."

Miranda grinned. "Yup. We have one every week. Friday night is the beginning of our Sabbath, so I'm planning to go to Temple in Yakima. They have a monthly service led by a visiting rabbi and a potluck dinner. But another reason for my heading up that way is the annual exposition and luncheon the Yakima Valley Chamber of Commerce gives to welcome new small business owners."

"Oh, yes. It's smart for you to go to that. You can spread the word about Breitner's and let them know you're prepared to ride out this mess, that you're not going anywhere. What are you wearing?"

"I'm going to go through my closet to see if I have anything a successful B & B owner would wear to such an event."

But at home, Miranda walked Rusty and then, ignoring her closet, spent an hour composing a tip to send to Crime Stoppers. She tried to make it simple and guileless.

I heard the kosherer was going to meet some co-worker in the storage room to show him his ram's horn. This is a musical instrument from the Holy Bible, played by Jews on their big holiday. But I also heard that the co-worker did not see a ram's horn with the body. So maybe the killer was a thief surprised by the kosherer, so the thief grabbed the ram's horn out of his hands and hit him in the head with it. Then probably the killer took it away.

CHAPTER 15

Guest book: "In the Valley for a family reunion on the res. Need a little me-time during these reunions. This B&B's rates are good. So is the breakfast. I'll be back next year." Colestah Wright

The exposition was in one of the older chain hotels near Yakima's Conference Center, and Miranda signed in, slapped her name tag on the lapel of the royal blue jacket she wore with her white sweater and trusty black pants, pinned a smile on her face, and went to set up her booth in the hall next to the dining room. She opened her laptop at the table fronting her booth and brought up the video she'd made for her website. She strewed the table with business cards and brochures, untied the box she'd lugged in, and assembled three platters piled with assorted bite-sized muffins she'd defrosted for the occasion. Then, taking a breath, she introduced herself to the burly young man arranging brochures, faucets, shower heads, and spigots at a neighboring booth. "Hi, I'm Miranda Breitner. I own Breitner's B & B in Sunnyvale. We opened in September."

"Oh my Lord! You poor woman! You're the one who bought the old homestead down in Sunnyvale across from where the Jew was murdered. They still haven't gotten that killer, have they?" He didn't wait for a reply. "How're things going now?"

"Isaac Markowitz's death was tragic. But it's business as usual at Breitner's. Reservations keep coming in. And satisfied guests send other guests. You know how that goes, I'm sure. Take a look at my video. Read the quotes from my on-line guest book. And may I have your card?" She handed him hers. "My B & B has five bathrooms and two kitchens, so I'll need replacements before long."

"I hope so." Laughing he added, "Seriously, I'll keep you in my prayers, Ms Breitner."

And so it went all morning. The business community in the Valley knew all about Isaac Markowitz's murder and the police's failure to identify his killer, let alone bring him or her to trial. Miranda dreaded more pitying looks and questions at lunch and was relieved when she read *Caroline Evans*, on the name tag on the cranberry-colored jacket of the graying woman seated on her left. She was really glad to find herself face to face with the President of the Toppenish Public Art Association's Board of Directors, whom she assumed was still an ally. "Hi, Caroline. I'm Miranda Breitner. Remember? Steve Galen stayed at my B & B."

"Of course I remember. Steve was very pleased with your place." She paused and picked at her salad. "He must have been. We offered to move him after that homicide across the street from you, but he wouldn't hear of it."

Miranda recalled how Steve had defended Breitner's to her other guests the night they learned about the murder. "He was an easy guest. And it was kind of you to recommend Breitner's to him."

"What do you mean?"

"He told me you suggested he stay at Breitner's because of my breakfasts."

"Good Lord! Don't let that rumor get around Toppenish. I tried to get him to stay at the place near the casino or even at the pricey ranch with the spa up in the hills, but he insisted on your place. Said he'd read about your breakfasts online."

Miranda's pleasure at learning that her website had been effective vied for her attention with her surprise that Caroline Evans hadn't referred Steve to Breitner's. "He did enjoy my breakfasts though. And if you didn't send him to me, I hope you'll send me other discriminating guests. I know you have the "Mural in a Day" event in the spring, and I bet there are artists who come to the Valley for that who'd enjoy Breitner's."

"I'll be honest with you, Miranda. As soon as the Sunnyvale police get their man, I'll feel better about making real referrals. But let's keep that under the radar. I don't want our Toppenish hotelier and our innkeepers to know I'm sending trade out of town. Between you and me, my artists are always looking for budget-friendly bunks and good cheap eats. Did I say cheap?" She winked. "And I have friends all over the Valley who often have family members and clients coming in. Your location and rates would work well for some of them too."

"Thanks, Caroline." Miranda made another go at her salad before asking, "So tell me, what brings you here today? Have you started a new business too?"

Caroline flicked her striking eyeglass chain. "Yes. I make these out of stones and seeds, buttons and whatever else I find. I sell them at fairs and flea markets as well as on-line. We boomers are mostly farsighted but it's really hard to find affordable eyeglass chains that are also attractive. Here's my card."

By late afternoon, Miranda's cheeks burned from smiling and her head throbbed from trying to absorb new names and faces while assuring vintners, grocers, organic farmers, restaurateurs, plumbing suppliers, woodworkers, gallery owners, antique dealers, accountants, periodontists, physical therapists, and a host of other entrepreneurs that Breitner's B & B was still open and going to stay that way. By the time she dismantled her booth and packed up her remaining materials, she'd posed for a photograph for the newspaper and another for the Chamber's website. Before she started her truck, she checked her B & B's website, something she was doing far too often of late. Many people had clicked on it that day and three of those had booked reservations. Her excitement died when she saw also that two long-standing bookings had been cancelled.

Miranda arrived at Temple Shalom just in time to join the other congregants clustered around Rabbi Golden, all singing a traditional melody, part of the pre-service blessing of wine. The familiar tune and the Hebrew words praising God for creating the Sabbath reminded her of how, as a girl, she'd stood close to her rabbi with the other kids and sung this same song. After the singing ended, two tweens, a pudgy boy whose yarmulke rested uneasily on his spiked hair and a tall, dark-skinned girl, recited the ancient blessing over wine. Two teenaged boys still awaiting their growth spurts carried trays bearing small glasses of wine to the adults and grape juice to the other kids. Just like their parents, some of the youngsters chugged their juice while others sipped. Swigging down her own wine, Miranda recalled a comment her grandmother had made in her Yiddish-accented English every single Friday evening. "Tonight Jews all over the Diaspora and all over Israel are raising glasses to celebrate the beginning of Shabbat."

Grandma Fannie's observation had often inspired the adolescent Meryl Weintraub to imagine celebrating the Sabbath in sunny Mexico or Hawaii or even Israel or on the French Riviera instead of in gray, wet Seattle. Sitting in a synagogue in the relentlessly sunlit Yakima Valley, the adult Miranda Breitner realized that she had gotten a version of what she had once wished for and that the other part of her girlhood fantasy was outdated. Contemporary Mexico spawned deadly drug cartels, modern France was full of anti-Semites, and Israel was both besieged and besieging. In spite of this disturbing realization, she tried to relax, to let the familiar songs and prayers welcoming the holiday distract her from both her global and personal concerns.

But when Rabbi Golden put down her guitar, adjusted her prayer shawl, and began her sermon, her words plugged into Miranda's own grim preoccupations. "Shabbat shalom. I won't begin with a joke tonight. We just blessed and drank the wine and grape juice the way we do every Shabbat. Both these beverages are kosher products. Perhaps they were even made from the fruit of vines grown right here in this Valley." She spread her arms as if to enfold the entire region. "As you know, since I was with you last, a young rabbinical student from New York here to help kosher juice grapes, was murdered just down the road in Sunnyvale. His name was Isaac Markowitz, may his life be for a blessing." Rabbi Golden lowered her head. Miranda was glad that the kids had disappeared, probably to a children's service upstairs.

"Why would anyone kill a law-abiding seasonal worker? An outstanding Talmud Torah student? A diligent employee? A newlywed? A visitor?" She looked around as if daring someone to respond. Miranda had been asking herself this question for weeks. Did this smart and with-it young rabbi know something she didn't? Or did the week's Torah reading, the prescribed topic of Sabbath sermons, hold a key to Isaac's killer? Miranda didn't even know what the week's Torah reading was. She leaned forward so as not to miss a word.

"Like Isaac Markowitz, I, too am a visiting worker here, an outsider. Perhaps that's why I'm astonished that no one, including the esteemed and grief-stricken rabbi who supervises the koshering of juice grapes for RCK, Inc., at several processing plants here, acknowledges publically the possible existence of anti-Semitism in your Valley." She leaned forward on the lectern as if to share a secret. "So tonight I'm going to talk turkey to you about anti-Semitism. Humor me, please."

Miranda was disappointed. What more was there to say about this tired topic? There just weren't any clues leading to overtly anti-Semitic suspects. She listened as the rabbi continued. "Some American Jews define themselves in response to the Holocaust and anti-Semitism. They see themselves as victims and often don't know much about pre-Holocaust Jewish history or anything at all about Jewish values." Miranda nodded. Her father was one of those people.

"Other American Jews deny the persistence of anti-Semitism in our country because here we Jews now enjoy more acceptance and success than ever before." Miranda nodded again. Her mother, may her life be for a blessing, had been one of these optimists. Rabbi Golden continued in a clear, strong voice. "And these glass-half-full folks are half right. We Jews should not allow the Holocaust and anti-Semitism to continue to define us."

The rabbi moved to the small space in front of the lectern and paced slowly back and forth as she spoke. "But neither should we deny the existence of anti-Semitism in this country, even in this Valley. Any American mother raising a black or brown son knows that racism in America did not end with the election of a black president." Miranda saw many in the seats in front of her nodding. "Sadly, like racism, anti-Semitism lives on, modified to suit the changing times."

Rabbi Golden stopped pacing, faced her congregants, and raised her voice just a little. As she spoke, Miranda felt the woman's eyes linger on her, heard her next words as a personal message, a mandate. "That's why you must stop denying the possibility that anti-Semitism exists here. Remember always those who refused to leave Europe because they couldn't believe that only death awaited them in their homelands. That's why you must ask law enforcement to consider anti-Semitism as a motive for killing Isaac Markowitz, to consider the possibility that his murder was a hate crime." While the Rabbi retraced her steps to the lectern, many heads stopped nodding. Miranda wasn't sure if it was the congregants' fear of taking a public stand or their unwillingness to confront even the thought of a murderous Jew-hater roaming their valley that stilled their nods.

"This week's Torah portion teaches us many things, among them that sometimes evildoers walk among us in surprising guises and disguises." Miranda felt the tension in the room dissipate, probably because finally Rabbi Golden had begun talking like a rabbi instead of a rabble-rousing prophet. "As many of you know, our Torah reading for this week tells the story of Isaac, old and blind, his twin sons Esau and Jacob, and his wife Rebecca. In biblical times it was customary for the father's blessing to go to his eldest son who then was named his heir. The slightly older and considerably hairier twin Esau was an outdoorsman, a hunter who often brought back tasty meat for their father to enjoy. Maybe this was why Isaac seemed to favor Esau. Jacob, their mother's favorite, was quiet and a homebody. Translators have described Jacob as homespun and/or simple and/or blameless, and so he seemed.

"The day Rebecca overheard Isaac promise to give Esau his blessing when he returned from hunting that afternoon, she told Jacob, and those two conspired to deceive Isaac. Rebecca killed and skinned a goat and cooked some of its meat. Then she covered Jacob's arm with the hairy goatskin. Thus disguised as Esau, Jacob entered Isaac's tent and gave their father the meat. Feeling the goatskin, the blind old man mistook Jacob for Esau and, so deceived, gave the wrong son his blessing." Rabbi Golden paused. "The consequences of Jacob's deceit were serious and often baffle scholars. But for tonight, it is only my purpose to remind you that Torah teaches us that wrongdoers are often those we least suspect.

"Aged patriarchs may be blind, but detectives should not be. The police here should be helped to see that it is possible that Isaac Markowitz's murder was a hate crime. And some among you should help them to open their eyes. Shabbat shalom." Rabbi Golden's green eyes met Miranda's for just a moment. Miranda broke into a sweat and was relieved when the clergywoman picked up her guitar and began strumming softly.

The kids, Julia Ornstein among them, reappeared and filed up front to watch the rabbi carefully wrap the Torah and return it to the simple Ark of burnished copper. At the sight of the children, some staring raptly at the scroll as Rabbi Golden brought its two parts together and slid them into the colorfully embroidered velvet tube while others twitched with impatience, Miranda felt queasy and disoriented. In that place at that moment the only voice in her ears was not Rabbi Golden's's but her grandmother's. Then Grandma Fannie's Yiddish-inflected words fused with the rabbi's and became the soundtrack for a nightmarish vision: Isaac Markowitz enters the processing plant's storage room carrying his ram's horn. He surprises a stranger tearing the seal off one of the jugs of enzyme additives. There's a vial on the floor beside the jug. In a flash forward, Jewish children in homes and synagogues from Yonkers to Yakima, swallow grape juice, throw up, moan and writhe, and die.

She'd been so absorbed in the service that she'd failed to notice Harry Ornstein when he took the seat next to her. So she was grateful when, seeing her teetering, he claimed her elbow. "Steady there. You look a little seasick. Maybe some dinner will help." When she winced at the thought of food, he added quickly, "Or not."

In her head she kept seeing these little ones, the pious and the bored alike, collapse to the floor in pain. Their moans sounded just like little Timmy's. To dispel this waking nightmare, she shook her head and looked away from the children. She focused on Harry's presence next to her and her head cleared although she remained shaken.

He waited until the blessing over the challah closed the service to actually greet her. "Shabat Shalom, Miranda. I was hoping to see you here tonight. We both were." Julia joined them and took her father's hand and began to pull. "Daddy, I'm hungry. Come on. Miranda too." She attempted to drag him towards the dining room where the potluck offerings were arrayed on a buffet table.

"You go ahead, hungry girl, and we'll be right behind you."

Miranda pulled herself together enough to return the greeting. "Shabbat Shalom, Harry. I'm glad to see you too." When Harry smiled, Miranda smiled back, stood on her shaky legs, and quipped, "Don't let it go to your head. You two are the only people I know here. Let's go eat with Julia."

"Are you okay? You look a little unsteady on your feet."

"Rabbi Golden's sermon really got to me." Miranda stopped walking and sat down in the nearest chair. Harry sat beside her. "When the kids were helping the rabbi wrap the Torah, I pictured them all having been poisoned by something in the grape juice. They were on the floor crying just like that little boy I babysat for. Then I pictured Isaac Markowitz's killer putting poison into the enzymes in the jugs in the storage room before Isaac came in…"

"Wow. No wonder you don't feel so hot. That's pretty scary stuff. I appreciate your telling me." He sounded grave, professional.

"I have no secrets from my lawyer. But I shouldn't make you work on Shabbat. Let's catch up with Julia. I'm sure I'll feel better after I have something to eat."

Together they walked a few steps to the onetime dining room where a table laden with casseroles and salads awaited. "Try Julia's and my whole-wheat challah. It's not bad." Harry pointed at a lumpy loaf of bread.

"Okay, but you should try my butternut squash lasagna. It's delicious in spite of spending the day in a cooler in my truck."

"It must be good. It's nearly gone. Are you trying to impress me with the fact that you can cook?"

His tone was joking, but Miranda wondered if perhaps she *was* trying to impress Harry Ornstein. It was a little late for that. He already knew she'd been arrested as a baby killer and now he knew that she fantasized about somebody poisoning kids.

After the depressing daylong Chamber of Commerce event, Rabbi Golden's compelling stares, Timmy's disturbing resurrection in her head, and her replay of this horror to Harry, Miranda felt unsettled and oddly reckless. Impulsive. She remembered feeling like this the day she opened the shed door to Vanessa Vargas and Rusty or agreed to accompany Colestah on her search for her family. She helped herself to salad, challah, a slab of salmon, and small portions of several casseroles while eyeing the bottles of wine on each table. No doubt a glass or two would restore her equilibrium. What the five glasses of wine she drank that evening restored was her long-latent libido.

She woke up the next morning naked, alone, and slightly hung over in Harry Ornstein's bed staring at a scrawled note he'd left on a pillow. *Shabbat shalom, Miranda, but there's no Shabbat for this poor Jew. I'm downstairs with a client. If all goes well, he'll be gone by nine. Then I'll make us breakfast and drive you to your truck. Meanwhile make yourself at home. The blue towels in the bathroom are clean. There's Tylenol in the medicine cabinet.*

It was 8:40 AM. Damn it. She found her phone in the pocket of her pants on the floor beside the bed and called Darlene. Miranda didn't feel especially guilty about having finally had sex. It was a pleasure she'd recently begun to look forward to, along with other personal indulgences like reading Yakima-raised Raymond Carver's stories, buying furniture for her apartment, and doing some volunteer work. But she did feel guilty for having abandoned her precious B & B to Darlene for the night. And her sense that she had gone AWOL didn't leave her, even after Darlene answered the phone and told her, "Don't worry. Everything's fine here. There's only one guest, and I made him a good breakfast. And just so you know, I had one too. I slept in one of the empty guestrooms. Rusty's fine. Everything's fine."

Alone and slightly hung over in her lawyer's bed, Miranda was not fine. She'd gotten drunk and seduced a guy she liked but hardly knew. But now he sure knew her. She remembered his hand caressing her breasts and then her belly, and then her thighs, and then moving slowly over her tell-all scars. She hadn't stopped him, but rather had guided that hand to her inner upper arm where she felt his fingers explore those welts too, deliberately, almost reverently. Exposing her long-concealed self-inflicted wounds, her secret self, to Harry, had excited Miranda so much that she had opened easily to him.

Under the shower with only Julia's plastic basket of tub toys for an audience, she rehearsed what she would tell him should he ask about her self-mutilation. He hadn't seemed disgusted or repulsed, but, though, he would be curious. As she ran her own soapy hands over those same capsule-sized lumps and the pill-sized bumps, she realized he might not care enough to ask. After all, she had taken advantage of his solicitousness and interest in her. First she got so sloshed at the Temple potluck in the company of his daughter that he'd refused to let her drive home. Instead he drove her to his house. He said he'd take her back to her truck after she sobered up. He dropped Julia off at her mom's. Before he even got back in the car, Miranda knew she wanted him. Remembering the intensity of her need, she winced.

The second they walked in the door of his townhouse, she had stood still with her back against that door and her phone in her hand. She caught his eye and put one finger to her lips. Looking straight at him standing within easy earshot, she phoned the B & B and asked Darlene to spend the night there. Harry met her gaze and, without changing the bemused expression on his face, took off his jacket and put it on the bannister. With her eyes still locked on his, she pocketed her phone and let her purse slide to the floor. She kicked off her heels, threw her jacket on top of his, walked over to her host, wound her arms around his neck, and kissed him. She remembered him tossing his glasses on top of their coats and pulling her to him.

She'd still been drunk. But not so drunk she didn't remember how, following her up the stairs to his room, he asked, "Are you sure you want to do this now? I'm not going anywhere. I'll be here when you, uh, sober up."

She'd actually retorted, "Good. We can do it again when I sober up." Where had that line come from? On the morning after, alone in the queen-sized bed, she had to smile at the realization that she had more wit drunk than sober.

Harry'd pulled a condom from a nightstand drawer and insisted on using it, even though she assured him she'd been wearing an IUD for years, another promise she'd made to Mona. Thinking of Mona made her decide to stop beating herself up. She'd wanted to have sex with Harry Ornstein and she did. They'd have breakfast, he'd drive her to her truck, and she'd go back to her B & B where she belonged.

There she'd figure out a way to word a tip that would convince Crime Stoppers to at least consider the possibility that Isaac's murder might have been a hate crime. The detective had mentioned that possibility to her early on, before the "evidence" seemed to implicate "viable" suspects who, surprise, surprise, just happened to be the usual ones. The county police were no more immune to hate-fueled bias than police in places like Seattle. She'd not wanted to think of her new home as a hotbed of barely-hidden hate and of herself as a paranoid Jew, so she'd ignored his warning, or had it been a threat? Whatever it was, she'd denied it. The good news in all this was that on TV if a murder is classified as a hate crime, the FBI often comes in and takes over the investigation.

Miranda dried off and dressed in the clothes she'd worn the day before. She glanced at herself in the bathroom mirror to see if she looked any different now that she had finally lost her virginity. No. Her eyes were not aglow, her cheeks not ablaze, and her smile not more knowing. The only difference was that she had no eyebrow pencil with her to color her copper-colored brows black. She was glad she'd told Harry that she'd altered her appearance when she left Seattle.

His bedroom was furnished simply with a few Ikea pieces. Only the sumptuous down quilt and memory foam mattress and pillows saved it from being spartan. She opened the bedroom door as soon as she heard the front door downstairs slam. She smelled coffee. Harry was halfway up the stairs. "Oh. There you are. I thought I heard the shower. I'm all yours now." She wondered if he stood still on the stairs because he expected a kiss, but then he said, "I'll make us omelets. Do you like omelets?"

Miranda nodded. How could he know so much about her and yet so little? "I love omelets, especially when someone else makes them."

While he cooked, she poured herself a mug of coffee and toured the townhouse's first floor, starting with the half-bath, a black-and-white tile cubicle with a decidedly earth-friendly soap in a spray bottle at the sink. There was what looked like a dining area reconfigured as a home office, complete with file cabinets, a double monitored PC, a printer, a copier, a shredder, and a recorder. Atop a bookcase Ruth Bader Ginsburg, Elena Kagen, Sonya Sotomayor, and Stephen Breyer looked on from a group photo between a couple of framed diplomas, one from Eastern Washington State and the other from the University of Washington School of Law. A portrait of Yakima-native Justice William C. Douglas hung on the wall. The living room was small and cozy with a sofa, a TV, and a couple of chairs. Ikea had probably been the chief beneficiary of Harry's divorce. Back in the compact kitchen, Miranda enjoyed Julia's bright drawings and photos covering the fridge door.

A perfect vegetable omelet oozing some good cheese, along with a warm chocolate croissant, a tall glass of water, and a bottle of Tylenol awaited her on the tiny kitchen table. "Eat. Mine's nearly ready." Harry looked rested and at ease in jeans and a long-sleeved green sweatshirt. Mona would say he looked "at home in the world." As he flipped his own omelet, he turned to face her and grinned. "I thought about kissing you good morning, but I didn't want to break the spell. You might decide I'm a toad or something." He chortled and shook his head as he spoke. "I sure as hell can't figure you out."

Miranda sat down and picked up her fork. "What's to figure? I'm sober now. Thanks for keeping me out of my truck last night and for putting me up."

His own omelet done and also perfect, Harry sat down across from her. "Any time, Miranda. But do you mind telling me what last night was all about? At our first meeting you were sobbing, at our next you were rude, and at our last you were in good client mode but not exactly personally accessible. Last night you were having visions but otherwise quite pleasant, and then you have a few glasses of wine and some noodle kugel and abracadabra! You're so warm and charming that everybody at our table is smitten. Julia loves the drawings you made on her napkin. She was so glad to see you again. You have a little more wine, and you're still charming, but I can't let you drive. So I drive you here to sober up, and you turn siren on me and make me an offer that I couldn't refuse even when I tried. And now I'm smitten, too. What was last night all about?" He caught her eye for just a moment before he stopped talking and attacked his omelet.

Harry's candid curiosity both pleased and alarmed Miranda. She appreciated his interest and wanted to give the right answer. It was her wish for his approval that, as soon as she recognized it, alarmed her.

When she didn't answer right away, he sipped his coffee, shrugged, and tried another tack. "It must be hard for the Markowitz family and for you to have Isaac's murder still unsolved. It's probably adversely affected your business already. I'm sorry."

This less personal comment she could handle. "Thanks. All day yesterday at the Valley's Chamber of Commerce's exposition for new businesses, people kept talking to me as if my B & B had already failed. It was pretty depressing. And then, as I mentioned, Rabbi Golden's sermon really got to me. I felt as if it was directed at me."

"Maybe that's why you drank so much. And why you wanted to get laid by a guy you hardly know. A little stress relief, right?"

"Yes and not exactly. Does it matter?"

"Yes. I've been trying to get to know you since I first met you on Yom Kippur. You have not been exactly encouraging, and then last night you...you were...very encouraging." He grinned again.

"Why on earth did you want to get to know me?"

"I'm single. I found you attractive. I still do."

"Why?" Miranda wasn't sure she was entitled to ask these questions, but her lack of dating experience made her really curious.

"On Yom Kippur you were crying over people in your life you've cared about and lost. At that service we remember our dead loved ones, but most of us do that in a very controlled and contained way. You struck me as very passionate. But you were also quite distant. You kept putting me off. So why were you all of a sudden so hot to get me into bed last night? Was it just the wine? I'd appreciate a straight answer."

Miranda put down her coffee cup, took a deep breath, and looked at him across their empty plates. "Okay. I like the little I know of you. I feel safe with you. I am a lot stressed and I was a little drunk." She hesitated and then blurted out her next words. "And I haven't had sex in a very, very long time."

"Okay. I'll take it. For now. But I want to get to know you better. And I want you to know me. Can we make that happen, Miranda?"

"Yes. I'd like that." She looked across the table at him when she spoke.

"Good." He refilled their coffee mugs. "But right now I want to tell you what I learned about why Yakima County Sheriff's Deputy Alex Ladin left SPD, okay?"

"Sure." Again she welcomed a topic of great interest to her but not so personal. And she was touched that he'd remembered to look into Detective Ladin's background.

"He left the SPD shortly after they hired their first female chief. A black burglar Ladin shot in the leg and arrested claimed Ladin shot him after he dropped his weapon and put his hands up. The burglar sued SPD. When questioned about it by the chief, Ladin claimed she "didn't understand how we do things here." Seattle paid up and she let Ladin go. She wrote a comment on his evaluation to the effect that he did use excessive force on unarmed blacks and that he didn't seem receptive to the government-mandated changes or "comfortable working for or with women."

"Wow. So why would Sheriff Carson hire him here?"

"Ladin's had all that gang experience. And he's from out here."

"Right. I get it. Thanks for checking him out."

"Well aren't you going to report him? Charge him with harassment?"

"No, Harry. I don't want people to know I was arrested and charged with killing a toddler. I came here to leave my past behind, to start over."

"I think you're making a mistake…"

"Harry, you don't understand what I went through. I don't want to lose my business."

"But…"

Miranda stood. "I have to get back, but that was a terrific breakfast." She didn't object though when Harry walked around the tiny table and kissed her. They didn't leave his house for well over an hour.

CHAPTER 16

Guest book: "Looking for business site in the area and Breitner's is a central base. Breakfasts healthy but still tasty, rooms comfortable, innkeeper pleasant but not intrusive. As for that murder across the street, I was two blocks from the Towers on 9/11. I don't scare easy anymore." Ex-New Yorker

Back in Sunnyvale, Miranda was too busy to moon over not hearing from Harry right away. Now not one, but two rabbis wanted her to help figure out who killed Isaac Markowitz. That was a mandate she couldn't ignore. She needed to talk to Rabbi Alinsky again, preferably face to face. So the next afternoon, she drove with Rusty to the Finest Western Motel and phoned him from the spacious lobby that served also as a breakfast area. She hoped he wasn't at the processing plant and so was relieved to hear his voice.

"Rabbi Alinsky here."

"Rabbi, this is Miranda Breitner. My dog and I are in the lobby of your motel. Could you join us down here for a few minutes? I have a new idea about how Isaac, may he rest in peace, was killed, and I'd like to run it by you."

"I'll be right down."

Now that their meeting was imminent, she fought off her anxiety about playing detective, and with an Orthodox rabbi yet. She hoped she could use their shared faith to their mutual advantage and that she could avoid offending his traditional sensibility with her decidedly more modern one. To him a good Jew was one who fulfilled the Torah's every commandment, even the most outdated, inconvenient, and seemingly irrelevant ones. To her, a good Jew was someone who adapted God's word to modernity and tried to repair our broken world. What would he think of her, a single woman, spending most of Shabbat in bed with a man she hardly knew? He'd think the same thing her grandmother would have thought. *Oy.*

To distract herself while she waited, Miranda strolled around the motel lobby. It was an outsized, newer, and less personal version of her B & B's front room. Rusty, ever alert to scents that promised scraps, sniffed the floor near the counter while she visualized the metal food warmers filled with dry scrambled eggs and greasy bacon. There were toasters and a microwave where guests could heat bagels and waffles next to urns for coffee, and the hot water they could mix with sugar-laced oatmeal from paper packets to concoct a version of the hot cereal. Her own simple fresh breakfast offerings were so much tastier. And Breitner's breakfast and check-in area was smaller, but way cozier. "Shabby chic," Steve Galen had called her lobby. Well this place was a plastic palace probably serving plastic food.

Miranda felt pretty smug until, seated at one of the tables near the floor-to-ceiling windows with Rusty at her feet, she looked out at the rows and rows of grapevines. Even bare they were an intriguing, more rustic sight than the fruit processing plant on view from Breitner's breakfast area. These vines must have looked and smelled lovely when they were still graced by clusters of ripe purple grapes suspended amid green leaves and oozing juice. And to her knowledge no one had been bludgeoned to death in this vineyard.

"Hope I didn't keep you waiting, Ms Breitner."

She started at the rabbi's voice.

"We're getting ready to check out early tomorrow. The grapes are all in and the last koshering shift finishes tonight at midnight. I'm glad you got ahold of me while I'm still in the Valley." Rabbi Alinsky, his skullcap slightly askew, seated himself. He seemed more *femisht* rabbi than Kashrut Cowboy.

"And hello to you too, Rabbi. Thanks for seeing me. I was out of town for a couple of days, so I didn't realize the grapes were all in and that you would be leaving so soon."

"Yes, and, sad to say, not soon enough for us. Usually we hate to say good-bye to this beautiful valley, but this year…" He pinched his lips together, shook his head, and rolled his eyes. This triple display of dismay mirrored Miranda's own misery over the terrible and as-yet-unsolved murder. "Tell me Ms Breitner, what's this "new idea" you have? I'm going to New York to bring the Marko-witzes Isaac's things myself. I'd like very much to bring them some encouraging news about the progress of the investigation."

Ignoring his query for the moment, Miranda posed a question of her own. "Rabbi, do you or any of your crew have Isaac's shofar?"

"No. Some of my inspectors bring their own shofars, but most of them use the ordinary ones I supply. I keep those in my suite in a drawer in the room upstairs that serves as our common area. It's where we cook and eat and study and pray together. But Isaac, may his life be for a blessing, brought his own special shofar. He kept it in his room. I was going to ask him to show it to me after the holidays, because it's supposed to be a beauty." He sighed. "Now the police have it along with his prayer shawl, his phone, his work clothes, shoes, and wallet. The rest of his things, his books and his other clothes, I'll pack and bring to New York with me. But I plan to ask the police to return those things of Isaac's that they still have to his family when the state crime lab finishes examining them. That includes his shofar. I hope they'll do that."

Miranda pictured the cardboard cartons full of stored physical evidence on *Cold Case* and suspected that until Isaac's killer was apprehended, Rabbi Alinsky's request would be denied. Because this prediction was only a suspicion, she didn't share it with him. Instead she gave him even worse news she believed to be true. "Rabbi, you know Nelson Thurston, the worker at the plant who found Isaac's body, right?"

"Yes. He's very nice, very diligent, a devout Christian, and always very help-ful to us. He and Isaac, may his life be for a blessing, used to discuss the Bible together." The rabbi lowered his head.

"Yes, and Isaac was meeting Nelson in the storage room on his break specifically to show him his shofar. But listen." Miranda paused to give her next words more weight. "Nelson says when he got there he didn't see the shofar with the body."

The rabbi raised his head and his eyebrows shot up. He sighed again, closed his eyes, and tugged at his beard.

"Rabbi, I need you to picture something, okay?"

She took his inhalation and the merest twitch of his head that accompanied it for a yes. "Okay. Here goes. Isaac comes into that room with his shofar to show Nelson."

Rabbi Alinsky mustered a recognizable nod.

"He surprises an intruder there, and this intruder grabs the shofar, and hits Isaac over the head with it. The shofar, not the fish club, is the murder weapon."

The rabbi blinked rapidly as he struggled to take in this ugly new scenario in which the horn that called Jews to worship for thousands of years is used to kill the pious Jew who played it. "But…but why…?"

Miranda held up her hand, imploring him to stop talking and keep listening. When he complied, she added a grisly finale to her already-disturbing word picture. "Then, because the shofar is bloody and has the killer's fingerprints on it, this intruder, now a killer, takes it away with him in his sack or backpack. But before he goes, he bloodies the fish club which he's recently stolen, and leaves it there to look like the murder weapon and throw off the police."

Rabbi Alinsky blanched and lowered his head to his hands. Miranda remained silent until he found a low voice and, finally, a few words. "Oy. Such madness! Who would do such a thing? And why? There's nothing to steal in that storage room. It's crazy." He looked up and shrugged.

Relieved that the rabbi was beginning to visualize her version of the crime, she let his speculation go without mentioning the copper wire so attractive to thieves. Instead she pursued her own line of inquiry. "Who among your crew has seen Isaac's shofar and could describe it to me? Would Isaac's family have a photo of it?"

"David Cohen was Isaac's roommate and he's seen it. He's upstairs doing laundry. I'll call him."

The phone call made, they waited for David to join them. "When do you return to the Valley, Rabbi?"

"I'm not sure. If I'm still employed, I supervise at different businesses out here throughout the year. But usually I don't spend the night, and I don't bring a crew. Why?"

"I want to share the rest of my thoughts with you before you leave."

He leaned forward. "I'm listening, Ms Breitner."

"Rabbi, what if the intruder was there not to steal something or to kill Isaac as part of a gang initiation or for revenge, but to commit a different kind of crime, one that would kill many Jews? And what if Isaac surprised him while he was doing it?"

Predictably, Rabbi Alinsky began shaking his head before she even finished stating her question. "Who else could he kill in there? Isaac, may his life be for a blessing, was the only Jew in the whole building."

Again his head sank below his shoulders and he supported it in his hands. Miranda leaned over to catch his next words, directed as they were, at the tabletop. "I've been fooling myself. Of course, killing Isaac was a hate crime. I'm not stupid, but I didn't want to believe that there could be racism and anti-Semitism here. Every year I bring young men here to do God's work, to fulfil his commandment... I'm like a shepherd leading his flock... And I never allowed myself to think we were in danger, Ms Breitner, even from the gangs." He raised his head to look at her through eyes filmy with unshed tears. "That's how much I wanted to do business here. And RCK, Inc., it does God's work, but still, it's a business." The mention of Rabbi Certified Koshering prompted the rabbi to yank really hard at his beard and, as if that vigorous tug let the air out of him, he slumped in his chair.

He managed to lift his head once more and continued to share with Miranda his anguished account of self-deception. "I kept telling myself and my crew that people in this valley like us, how we've never had anything but kindness here. So many Valley processing plants work with RCK, Inc. Year after year, we're always welcomed. This is true. And the manager of this nice hotel lets us kosher the oven in the room in my suite where we all prepare and eat our meals. And, Ms Breitner, the local police here have been providing us with security in case the killer returns. But let's face it. They're actually afraid the killer will come back to kill another Jew." He threw up his hands.

Miranda empathized. "Rabbi Alinsky, I understand, believe me, I get where you're coming from. I was in denial too. I wanted my own business here to succeed so badly that until Isaac was killed I felt immune to the gangs and the poverty and the drug trade and even the possibility of anti-Semitism. I told myself it was charming how these Valley towns seem lost in time, like Brigadoons of the Fifties." She paused for breath. "But then, after what happened to Isaac, I realized that there was more to the Fifties than saddle shoes and Sinatra. There was segregation. There was anti-Semitism. Women had few rights. You know, Rabbi, even when a county detective told me that Isaac's murder might have been a hate crime, I let him convince me that such criminals don't operate in the Valley itself, because that's what I wanted to believe. Talk about denial..."

Miranda was about to continue her rant when David Cohen arrived. Short, dark-haired, and heavyset, he looked to be about twenty-three or -four. He was sweating. For an instant, Miranda wondered if maybe he feared being accused of murdering his roommate after a squabble over an ambiguous Torah passage turned deadly. But she reminded herself that all of Isaac's carefully vetted colleagues not only had had clean records but also had very good alibis. They were either at a synagogue in Seattle or on duty in another processing plant when Isaac was murdered. At a nod from the rabbi, David joined them at the bare table.

"Ms Breitner, this is David Cohen. David, Ms Breitner. She wants to ask you a couple of questions about Isaac's shofar." David blinked, clearly surprised.

He and Miranda exchanged nods. "David, I'm sorry for the loss of your friend and I appreciate your joining us now. I know you have packing to do, so let me get to the point. I understand that you've seen Isaac's shofar?"

He nodded. Miranda began to wonder if he was speech-impaired.

"Would you describe it?"

When he spoke, his voice was low and he talked fast, as if he wanted to get his words out before his sorrow overcame him. "It's a real beauty, one of a kind..."

"Whoa! David, would you speak just a little louder and more slowly, please?"

On his next try he slowed down and spoke loudly enough for his tablemates to hear him but not so loudly as to attract attention from the one other occupied table in the dining area. "Isaac's shofar looked to be about two-and-a-half feet long if you straightened it out to measure it. He told me it was the horn of a Moroccan ram, not the horn of some other animal like a kudo or an elk. It has two twists." David drew a spiral shape in the air. "It also has lots of stripes and it isn't painted, but it's all different shades of brown from light like a latté to dark like, uh, like black coffee. Isaac said he liked to play it because it sounded like a tuba, kind of mellow."

"It must be very beautiful." Miranda had never before considered the aesthetic properties of rams' horns.

"Isaac said it was a family heirloom. Eva's dad gave it to him as a wedding present." David studied the tabletop. After a moment he looked up. "His father-in-law told him it's a very rare shofar, so Isaac insured it for over three thousand dollars. But what he really valued about it was that it was in Eva's family for several generations and he felt, you know, honored to have it. He said he'd leave it to their son when they had one."

Miranda flashed on Michael Wright's fish club, also an heirloom. "Thanks so much, David. You've been very helpful." The young man stood and, biting his lip, nodded his goodbyes before going back to his room.

"Rabbi, Eva or her dad may have a photograph of that shofar if they insured it. I'd really like to get my hands on a picture of it, the sooner the better. So I'd like Eva's phone number. I know she's still in mourning, so would you please phone her now and tell her or leave a message that I'll be calling her soon and encourage her to accept or return my call?" David's description, rough as it was, had given Miranda yet another new idea and with it came a new urgency.

"E-mail or text me and I'll send it to you immediately." Rabbi Alinsky jotted his e-mail address on a napkin he took from the counter behind him.

"How about giving it to me right now while you call her?" When he nodded, Miranda whipped out her phone, keyed in what he dictated from his, and read it back for him to check.

"That's it." He made the call and Miranda heard him leave a message alerting the widow to a call from a Ms Miranda Breitner and imploring her to take it. When he finished, he sighed and said, "I think she'll talk to you. She's eager for Isaac's killer to be brought to justice." Then he stood. "Thanks for your interest in this matter Ms Breitner. Don't hesitate to contact me if I can be of further help. And please, take care of yourself." But, his goodbyes said, he didn't walk away.

Instead, shaking his head, he sat down again and, looking around at the now empty lobby, spoke in an urgent whisper. "I mean it, Ms Breitner, be careful. I know from hate crimes. Here in Washington they range from painting swastikas on synagogues and schools and burning crosses on lawns to setting explosives at a Martin Luther King Day Parade and shooting unarmed women at the Jewish Federation." For the first time since they had begun to speak, his eyes bored into hers. "And it's not only us Jews these white supremacists hate. No. They're like the Nazis. Really. They admire and imitate the Nazis." This time the rabbi's whispered sigh was a breath of pure anguish. "So they also hate all people of color as well as immigrants, homosexuals, transvestites, bisexuals, the disabled, and even the mentally ill.

"White supremacists, they think we're all a threat to white America and pure white Americans. Obama, a dark-skinned mixed race President, is their worst nightmare come to life. Haters are afraid of whites becoming a minority, of America uniting with Mexico and Canada to form a new country different from the America they think they remember." Rabbi Alinsky attacked his beard again. "I'm telling you, now some of these Aryan supremacists may dress like gangbangers and have shaved heads and tattoos like them and drink and use drugs like them, but they don't have the cartels to answer to." On that somber note, he stood once more. Before he turned to head back upstairs, he looked down into her upturned face and spoke. "So Ms Breitner, you have my number. I have yours. Please take care and may Hashem be with you. I'll keep you in my prayers."

Miranda felt her eyes tear up. Her grandmother never let her leave the house without uttering those exact words. Sitting at the table alone, staring out at the rows of skeletal grapevines silhouetted in black against the blazing orange sunset, she briefly considered the rebbe's cautionary sermon. Then she nudged his words into a place in her head where she hoped they wouldn't paralyze her as she contemplated her next move.

Driving home, Miranda thought about the call she would make to the grieving young newlywed so suddenly and horribly widowed. She remembered how all those years ago her own Jewish community had turned their backs on her, and she suspected that Eva Markowitz would fare better. She recalled the rituals associated with traditional Jewish mourning. The week of sitting shiva was over, but maybe the widow had not yet left her home to reenter communal life, to visit her shul. Her fridge was probably still filled with casseroles and her mirrors still covered. She'd still be wearing black and playing hostess to relatives still staying with her. Even more important, Miranda was sure Isaac's widow still sobbed into her pillow every night. So it was with some trepidation that, once back at the B & B, she placed the call to New York. "Eva Moskowitz, please."

"Who is this?" The voice was soft, young, tentative.

"Rabbi Alinsky gave me your number. I'm Miranda Breitner from Sunny-vale, Washington."

"Yes. He left word I would hear from you."

"Eva, first, I'm so very sorry for your terrible loss." Miranda hated having to lay this formulaic bromide on the young widow, but she had tried and failed to think of better words.

"Thank you."

"Rabbi Alinsky probably mentioned that he and I are very eager to help the police find out who killed your husband. We need your help." How many times had she heard the cops on TV say this to the traumatized relative of a murder victim? Again, Miranda hated sounding so clichéd, like a rerun, like the cops who had questioned her about Timmy. For a moment she felt her focus slipping, but she resisted being sabotaged by her memories.

"How can I possibly help? I'm in New York." Eva sounded hopeless and angry.

"You can help a lot by answering two questions. First, do you know of an-yone anywhere who would want to hurt your husband?" Miranda threw that in just because she wasn't sure someone from the county police had actually asked it of the young widow, so determined were they to blame their usual local suspects.

"No. My husband was a good man. He helped everybody. He liked every-body. Everybody liked him." Eva sounded annoyed by this query as if Isaac's popularity were unquestionable or as if she'd answered it before.

"He certainly was very well-liked by his colleagues and others here." Miran-da paused and got to the point of her call. "Eva, I understand that the shofar your dad gave Isaac was very special and quite valuable. Is there a photo of it somewhere in your family's records? An insurance photo for example?"

"Maybe. Isaac insured the shofar before he left. He took it to an appraiser first. I can look for that report and see if there's a photo with it." She went on with a catch in her voice. "I know Isaac took pictures of our wedding gifts and I wrote the giver's name on each photo. That way I'd know who to thank for what." Miranda was pleased to hear this. "But I'm not sure if he took a photo of the shofar." Disappointed, she waited while Eva hesitated again. When she resumed talking, annoyance and impatience clipped her words. "But why do you need to see photos of the shofar? Rabbi Alinsky probably has it. Isaac had that shofar with him on Rosh Hashanah. He was going to play it in the factory."

"He did play it. I heard it from my house." Miranda remembered how profoundly the shofar had moved her. "I'm sorry to say, Eva, it wasn't with his body." Miranda would not burden the family with her theory that the shofar was the murder weapon until she could prove it. Besides, that bloody image seemed too ghoulish to inflict on the fragile young woman just then.

"Missing? How could that be?"

"The police aren't sure." That in all probability the police did not even know the shofar was either significant or missing Miranda kept to herself. "But Eva, please give me your e-mail address. I'm going to give you all my contact info too. Please, please look as soon as you can and e-mail or fax me copies of whatever photos you find. And a copy of the report from the appraiser would be very helpful too. I'll reimburse you for any expenses you incur making copies and scanning or faxing. And I'll return whatever you send me. Please don't discuss this with anyone. But you have my word, I'm going to find that shofar."

Eva's e-mail with a copy of the ram's horn's appraisal and photo attached arrived the next morning. The shofar appeared exactly as David had described it, large and twisted twice, with raised ridges in many shades of brown. It was appraised and insured for $3,500. Miranda was itching to begin her search, but had to finish her baking and other chores, check in guests, and walk Rusty, so it was evening before she was finally free to hunker down over her laptop.

Recalling Michael's half-joke about how, in order to get his fish club back, he'd have to buy it on eBay, she speculated that the person who took the bloodstained shofar learned it had value, cleaned it up, and sold it to a dealer. She further speculated that this dealer would then attempt to resell it online. So she would look for it and find it. Not a problem. With Rusty at her feet and a printout of the appraisal and photo in view, she sipped wine, and searched eBay, Amazon, and the websites of the many, many dealers who, to her amazement, traded in shofars. According to the appraiser, Isaac's ram's horn was exceptionally large and so, she figured, it should have been fairly easy to find. But when after several hours, she hadn't found it she feared the killer had already sold it.

That possibility was too defeatist to entertain for long, so she decided that Isaac's killer was waiting to sell the murder weapon until someone else was found guilty of Isaac's murder. But she also worried that if she weren't vigilant, the killer would decide to sell the ram's horn to a dealer who, in turn, would put it online for sale on the first night she didn't look for it, and someone else would buy it. Then the instrument and any evidence connecting it with Isaac's killer would vanish forever. So she asked Google Alert to notify her when the words and phrases that would be used to advertise the horn such as *one of a kind*, *Moroccan ram*, *double twist*, and *mellow like a tuba* appeared. Meanwhile she continued to scan the sites of the likeliest dealers each evening.

This scaled-down approach freed Miranda to pursue another line of research, one even more challenging and frightening. Rabbi Alinsky's impromptu sermonette about white supremacists and Rabbi Golden's reference to hate groups could take her only so far. She didn't doubt anything either rabbi said, but the thing was there didn't seem to be any news reports of un-gang-related skinheads in the gang-infested Valley. Detective Ladin had located the haters in the vast lonely regions surrounding the Valley, the isolated territory of survivalists, loners, fugitives, and land-rich ranchers. She went online and found nothing that spoke to her need to place hate groups in the Valley until she came across a book called *American Swastika: Inside the White Power Movement's Hidden Spaces of Hate* by Pete Simi. Where were these "hidden spaces of hate?" Were there any in Central Washington? In the Valley? In Sunnyvale? Miranda sent the book to her tablet.

That night it was snowing lightly, so she put on her Snow Traks when she took Rusty out to run. They were the only ones out enjoying the crisp cold air and the white world. They hadn't run far when a dark sedan pulled up alongside them. Miranda kept moving when she saw Detective Ladin jump out, leaving the car with the motor running in the empty street. He fell into step beside her. "Long time no see, Meryl. Care for a lift? It's cold out here. And with a killer still somewhere in the area… Tell me, did you get a firearm yet?"

"No, not yet." She kept moving.

"Good. Then you can't shoot me." He grabbed her arm and pulled her to him with one hand while his other hand groped at her jacketed chest. When that proved unrewarding, he crushed her clamped-shut lips with his toothy kiss. When Rusty growled, the detective released her quickly and loped back to his car, calling behind him, "You want it, too, Meryl. I can tell."

CHAPTER 17

> *"Exhibited at Farm Machinery Exposition and this B & B near Expo site. Breakfast choices good, room comfortable and clean, innkeeper helpful all at bargain rates, but neighborhood dicey. Seasonal worker killed across the street. Gang hit? Who knows?"*
> John Ingersall, Tractor Dude from WI

After being assaulted again by Detecive Ladin, Miranda's sleep had been uneasy. She wanted to talk to Harry and get advice on how to handle the Detective's continued attacks without having him blab about her past. But when Harry left her at her truck on Saturday, he'd promised to call soon and she'd not heard from him.

As if an assault, a bad night's sleep, and a broken promise weren't worrisome enough, that morning Meryl found not one but two of her worst fears confirmed. First, Breitner's finally got reviewed on Yakima County B & B's esteemed site only to be deemed unsafe. Second, no guests were scheduled to arrive that night. Not a single one. And the snowfall had let up, so there would be no walk-ins delayed in the Valley until the danger of avalanches was over and the mountain passes cleared.

A second look at her bookings validated her first. There really were no reservations for that night. There were three for the next night, and she'd had a full house the night before, so she tried telling herself this was a fluke, not a calamity. But it wasn't a good sign. That cold November night would be the first since Breitner's opened that all four guest rooms were guestless.

She resolved to visit every restaurant, vineyard, shop and museum in the Lower Valley and leave flyers. She'd advertise in…But what was the point? Until Isaac's killer was brought to justice, promoting her B & B seemed like an exercise in futility. According to Sunday's *Yakima Herald-Republic* the police had not turned up any new leads. That meant the missing Javier Baez remained their primary suspect and the investigation was stalled.

Frustrated and worried, she opened her tablet and clicked on *American Swastika,* hoping the slim creepily-titled book would shed some much-needed light on the disturbing possibility that Isaac Markowitz's murder was, in fact, a hate crime. In between her daily round of chores and errands, she read, spurred on by amazement and curiosity. At lunch, over her egg salad sandwich, what she read rendered her stereotype of hate group members outdated. According to the authors' research, the burly, tattooed, undereducated and underemployed, drunk and/or drugged skinhead haters Miranda and Rabbi Alinsky thought of as Aryan supremacists were still around, but they were decidedly old school. Twenty-first-century white supremacists encourage other white power enthusiasts to hide their Aryan affiliations so as to insinuate themselves into the social and work lives of their communities.

Miranda read that, like her, they give themselves makeovers. They let their hair grow and conceal their tattoos. Instead of going to jail, they go to college, get good jobs, and raise their kids in solid, structured traditional families and homes. She cringed when the authors explained that in these homes the newly-respectable haters feed their kids a steady diet of racist ideology embedded in their home-school curriculums, reading material, the conversations of their white-only friends, kids' birthday cakes in the shape of swastikas, and the lyrics of white power music. Miranda checked these lyrics out online and found, in addition to a melodic anthem in praise of Nazi hero Rudolph Hess, many songs such as *Jigrun* by a band named Bully Boys. It's first two verses are:

> Whiskey Bottles
> Baseball Bats
> Pickup Trucks
> And Rebel Flags
>
> We're going on the town tonight
> Hit and run
> Let's have some fun
> We've got jigaboos on the run
> And they fear the setting sun

To white power folks non-whites are *niggers* or *muds*. Miranda remembered Darlene telling her how her neighbors' children had tormented Josefina, calling her *nigger* and *mud* and taking her precious doll. She also recalled Darlene's shock at how educated people, a nurse and an engineer, could have such rude and mean kids. *Nigger* was a common enough epithet, but *mud?* Miranda'd never heard that slur before, even on TV. Like their idol Hitler, white supremacists believe that mixing with people of other races, creatures whom they believe to have been created out of mud, defiles the racial purity of whites. Darleen's neighbors could very well be closeted white supremacists. Remembering Colestah's chilling story about the rattlesnake, Miranda shivered. Like that inherently deceitful and venom-spewing reptile, hidden white supremacists did not change their essential identities. Even verses of their lullabies, their children's games, and their holiday songs malign dark-skinned people.

Even though *American Swastika* was a depressing and frightening read, Miranda kept returning to her tablet while she was on hold waiting to talk with the scheduler who made appointments for Rusty's vet or for her mechanic at the car repair shop to answer his phone, or even for the dryer to finish. And that evening, upstairs in her apartment, she read while picking at a frozen lasagna she'd nuked. She'd nearly finished the book and finally understood that the "hidden spaces of hate" in *American Swastika*'s subtitle are the homes of under-the-radar post-skinhead haters. To Miranda, the really scary thing was that clandestine Aryan supremacists aren't just wackos holed up in the desert or the mountains as Detective Ladin had led her to believe. One could be your doctor or your kid's teacher or your neighbor. Or Darleen's neighbors. A nurse or an engineer could very well be a hidden Aryan supremacist.

This suspicion didn't allay her growing anxiety as she contemplated taking Rusty out for his run. Even though she trusted her dog to deter another assault by Detective Ladin, if Isaac's killer really was one of these closeted anti-Semites she'd been reading about and was still in the area, she was now the only Jew around. Miranda knew she couldn't live cocooned with her dog in her B & B, so instead of spooking herself silly, she would protect herself. She took Rusty with her to the shed where Michael had stored painting and spackling tools. Using her phone for light, she selected a hammer and a couple of easily portable pocket-sized razor blades to have handy just in case. She made sure to lock the shed behind her. Ever since she'd found Vanessa Vargas and Rusty in there, Miranda'd kept the little building padlocked.

Once back inside the B & B, she put the hammer on one of the easy chairs, threw a patchwork quilt over it, pocketed one razor blade, and put the others in a drawer with the flatware. Next she checked to be sure that all the windows in those eerily empty guest rooms were locked. She considered calling Pauline and Nelson and asking them if she could spend the night at their house, but decided not to. She couldn't do that every time she had no guests. She reminded herself that she'd spent the whole summer alone in the B & B without coming to harm. Then she reminded herself that that was before Isaac Markowitz was murdered across the street.

She pulled her Snow Trax over what she called her geezer sneaks because they closed with Velcro, put on her parka, leashed her excited dog, locked the door behind them, and pocketed her keys. Finally she took the impatient Rusty out for what she hoped would be a restorative run in the cold night air. Once on the steps, she eyed her mezuzah. Even though the little scroll identified her as a Jew, she would not take it down. Instead, she did something she'd never done before. She kissed her gloved finger and tapped the mezuzah with it, transferring the kiss. But it was not the stern donor of the Ten Commandments she was hoping to channel. No, it was the vigilant shepherd of the Twenty-third Psalm whose protection she sought as she and Rusty ran through the streets of what she had come to think of as the "valley of the shadow of death." She was struck by the silence of the processing plant now that the 24/7 work of koshering was done. No lights shone within, but the big building's exterior was lit so that the stacks of fruit crates cast eerie shadows in the parking lot.

As they descended the front steps, Rusty's ears went up, his tail went down, and he growled what Miranda thought of as his "pay attention" growl. She looked around. Outside the newly locked gate to the newly lit plant parking lot she made out the silhouette of a man. One of those stacks of crates was so high its shadow transcended the chain-link fence, offering the outsider a hiding place. Who was he? Should she call 911? But what if the big man lurking there was Detective Ladin stalking her to claim another kiss or more for his silence? She didn't dial 911, because if the man wasn't the detective, a call might give that creep Ladin an excuse to reappear. It occurred to her that she was more afraid of the police than of the murderer at large. Miranda stroked Rusty's head to calm herself.

More likely this guy was a homeless prowler looking for shelter and unable to access the secured plant. That must be why he faced the B & B. Would he see her leave and try to break in there? Or, worst case scenario, could the man lurking in the shadow really be poor Isaac's killer looking for another Jewish victim? She fumbled in her jeans pocket and fondled the razor in its cardboard sheath. Then she transferred the blade to her jacket pocket where it was more easily accessible. When she looked up, the man was getting into a car that soon sped down the road towards Toppenish.

Relieved, Miranda and Rusty took off too. The cold dark streets seemed more deserted than usual. Even the inked young men who hung out at the convenience store weren't around. And across the highway Darlene's house was unlit because she was in Spokane visiting her granddaughter. Most of her neighbors were home though, their presence illuminated only by glows visible through the curtains on their front windows. Miranda pictured moms and dads who'd put their kids to bed and then collapsed on the sofa to snuggle and watch TV. As usual, she envied the imaginary contentment of these imaginary couples.

The house with the pumpkins stood out not only because it was bigger than the others and its stairs were seasonally decorated, but because it was all lit up. Rusty loped past it a little faster. Miranda figured his sharp canine ears were offended by the muted blare of rock music barely audible to his owner. A few more cars and trucks were parked in front of that house and across the street than elsewhere on the block. It was definitely party time in there. But who parties on a Sunday night? Miranda answered her own question. A nurse who works the night shift most other nights and home schools her kids. That's who.

The authors of *American Swastika* explain that home-based gatherings offer these hidden haters a rare chance to express their real feelings in a safe environment where they can get support and affirmation among like-minded friends. Sweatshirts emblazoned with *Heil Hitler!* and swastikas don't cut it at the office Christmas party, the church picnic, or the PTA meeting. As she ran, Miranda began to take her suspicion that the people in the pumpkin house were hate group members even more seriously. It wasn't all that far-fetched. And if those people partying in there were hate groupies, it was just possible that one of them might have killed Isaac Markowitz.

She ran on, her second wind putting wings on her feet and her eagerness to find Isaac's killer lighting a fire in her belly. She wanted to see for herself if the inhabitants of the pumpkin house really were Sunnyvale's hidden haters. Adrenalin, endorphins, and not a little chutzpah kept her running until she'd formulated a plan. Then she turned around and they headed back the way they came.

As they ran, Miranda reconsidered what she was about to do. In a way it was nothing she hadn't done before. No one but her would be hurt, and she'd recover. But it was crazy, a little kinky even. It was every bit as crazy as Colestah's shoot-'em-up car chase, and that had worked out just fine. Besides, unlike Colestah's caper, what she was going to do probably wasn't really illegal, although maybe her lawyer Harry Ornstein would disagree. So what? He obviously didn't care for her, thought she was some kind of self-slashing nut job anyway. She had nothing to lose. The worst thing that could happen was that her planned foray would prove useless like the cops' bogus leads. She took it as a good omen that most of Darlene's neighbors had turned off their TVs and gone to bed. She was too preoccupied to imagine, let alone envy, what they might be doing there.

She and Rusty ran right past the pumpkin house, turning into Darlene's gate to her tiny front yard and front steps. There they stopped abruptly beneath the willow where that tree's web of low-lying leafless branches partially screened them from the street. Miranda extricated the razor blade from its cardboard sheath. Next she took off her gloves and stashed them at the base of the tree. She spat several times in both palms and bent to rub the salt-strewn path to the front door until her moistened hands picked up some grit and grime. Then with a practiced twist of her wrist she deliberately slashed the skin of the palm of her non-dominant hand just opposite her thumb. Aware that she was charting new territory on her scarred body, she noted that for the first time, the burning sensation brought no relief. It only increased her sense of urgency. Working fast, she intentionally brushed her cheek with her wounded hand, leaving a streak of grime and blood. That done, she and Rusty resumed running under the streetlights. A glance behind her showed that, like bread crumbs in a fairy tale, a trail of crimson dots on the snowy sidewalk marked their route back to the pumpkin house.

Miranda bounded up the stairs to the front door and rang the bell. The doorbell was no match for the loud music, so when no one answered, she tried turning the door knob, but it didn't yield. She banged on the door and rang the bell over and over until finally a big white man with a semi-circle of ear-length brown hair surrounding a gleaming bald spot and whirling an old-fashioned glass empty of all but ice cubes opened the door and greeted them with a step back and a scowl. He recoiled at the sight of her dirty bloodstained face and the bloody hand she waved like a banner. Or it could have been the large dog alert at her side that spooked him. Miranda also thought that maybe her host simply registered the fact that she was a stranger crashing an invitation-only party.

To be heard, she shrieked over the blare of sound blasting through the open door. "Oh! Thank the lord! I just fell, and since you all're still up, I wonder could I wash this off and get a Band-Aid real quick?" She figured it was only his fear of Rusty's barking waking his sleeping neighbors that made him usher them in and slam the door shut. She kept shouting. "I left my gloves and my cell at my boyfriend's house, and I don't want to go all the way back now...."

"Tammy, come here!" The man bellowed this order over his shoulder, but even his bellow didn't make it through the earsplitting amplified rock music, because Tammy didn't appear. To Miranda, still standing at the door, he hollered. "Follow me. My wife's a nurse. She'll fix you up. Is he, uh, you know...." The man jerked his head in Rusty's direction and then glanced down at the shoes and boots piled on a towel near the door and at the immaculate pale blue carpet. He looked at the blood dripping from her hand.

Miranda pulled off her knit hat and covered her wound with it. She slipped out of her running shoes and Snow Trax and added them to the heap while yelling, "He's friendly and he just peed. He'll bark if I leave him outside."

The man gestured to her to follow as he hustled through a disappointingly ordinary living-dining room where a few men, fewer women, and at least four kids of assorted ages stood around watching a video of a really loud rock band. Her host moved too fast for Miranda to make out the logos on any of the guests' sweatshirts, but a few of the lyrics with their references to "muds" and "niggers" would stay in her head forever. These slurs set to music reassured her that in spite of the neat but bland décor, she'd come to the right place. She noted the mostly empty platters and casserole dishes on the table. Between the living room and the kitchen was a short hall, its walls lined with photos, and a door to what she assumed was a bathroom. Before she could get a look at the photos, the door opened and a curvaceous forty-something blonde emerged. She flinched at the sight of the two party crashers. Her husband reassured her. "Relax, Babe. The dog already peed outside. This lady needs a Band-Aid. Fix her up and send her on her way."

Tammy nodded and gestured for Miranda to follow her back into the bathroom. "Your dog can come too. There's no carpet in here." She closed the door behind them, effectively lowering the decibel level a little and imprisoning them in a cell of sea-blue tile. Even the soap bottle was blue. Rusty headed straight for the toilet where he guzzled water until Miranda reprimanded him. Tammy ignored him as she retrieved a first-aid kit from the cabinet beneath the sink. Setting it on the counter, she took Miranda's hand in hers and studied it. "That salt and sand mix on the sidewalks is nasty stuff. I'll just clean this out."

Tammy turned on the water in the sink and began to push up her sleeves and then, apparently thinking better of it, tugged them down again. Miranda, who hadn't worn a sleeveless T-shirt in decades, recognized the behavior of someone else eager to censor a body part that told too much. For a second she felt Harry Ornstein's hands reading her own body's braille, decoding its most secret messages. The rush of cold water on her wound returned her to her current sea-blue reality. Tammy, who'd pulled on latex gloves, was flushing Miranda's cut under the tap and then took her other hand and rinsed that too and swabbed the blood off her face with a gauze pad. Satisfied, she soaped each of Miranda's hands, and Miranda rinsed them under the cool water. Tammy dried her patient's uninjured hand with a blue towel and the other with a gauze pad. With the deft nonchalance of a nursing professional, she wrapped gauze around the bleeding hand while Miranda babbled about leaving behind her gloves and her cell. She tried not to stare at the writing on Tammy's faded blue sweatshirt, "Martyrs Day 1984." She remembered seeing something about Martyrs Day in *American Swastika*, but she'd been reading so fast she couldn't remember what it was.

"Here, take this. I've got plenty." When Tammy stuck the remaining roll of gauze in one of Miranda's jacket pockets, Miranda stopped breathing, fearing the nurse's adroit latex-covered fingers would find the razor. But hiding the tool she'd used to cut herself was an old habit, the kind that dies hard, and in a second or two Miranda recalled stashing the bloody blade with her gloves under the tree at Darlene's. Only then did she resume breathing.

"There, you're good to go. Keep that cut clean with soap and water and keep it covered. You don't want a scab."

"Thanks. Just let me pee and we'll be on our way. Not to worry. We'll let ourselves out. And I really mean it, Tammy. Thanks so much. It's some kind of miracle that I fell in front of a nurse's house, right?"

Tammy smiled graciously. "Glad to help. You take care now. If it gets red, see your doctor. And hold that flusher down for at least ten seconds, okay?"

Alone in the locked bathroom with Rusty, Miranda liberated her phone from the inside breast pocket of her parka with her good hand and pointed it at the rows of vials and tubes in her hostess's medicine cabinet just as any TV detective worth watching would have done. With the thumb of her injured hand, she clicked a couple of times and shoved the phone back in her hidden pocket. Then, even though no one else could possibly hear, she dutifully held the flusher down for ten seconds, waited a few more seconds, and left the bathroom just in time to let in a waiting guest with the initials AH beneath the swastika on his sweatshirt. Chilled to the bone, Miranda was glad this Hitler fan would see water eddying in the toilet.

The hall was empty and mercifully quiet until she heard chanting and stamping from the living room. She couldn't make out the words, but it sounded like some kind of rah-rah football cheer. She looked at the photos set out on old-fashioned molding that once probably displayed a former owner's "good" plates. The photos appeared to have been taken at rock concerts, Christian rock concerts according to the signage that figured prominently in several of them. The rock concert in the living room began again and that's when she saw it. The snapshot of Tammy, her husband, and another couple set Miranda's heart beating so hard and so loud, she could actually hear it over the percussive pounding of the music in the next room. She wanted to take a picture of this photo, but didn't dare. What if someone else with a bursting bladder came along? She'd said she had no cell phone. But what if she didn't take the photo? Could she steal the actual picture, frame and all? Too bulky. Besides, then it might be inadmissible as evidence. She wasn't sure. But without that picture, who would believe her? It was the missing dot that just might enable her to connect all the others. She had to photograph it.

So with her pits dripping sweat and her heart throbbing in her throat where it threatened to choke her, she took out her cell and pointed and clicked a couple of times. Just as she saw the knob on the bathroom door turn, she jammed the phone back in her pocket. Only a step ahead of the unsuspecting guy leaving the bathroom, she led Rusty quickly back through the living-dining room to the front door, trying to look at the guests without any of them seeing her and, perhaps, recognizing her. Could that smiling woman swaying to the beat in a white sweatshirt with a coiled snake on it be the genial farmer's wife who sold homemade jam from a roadside stand near the Thurstons' house?

Miranda squatted with her back to the group as she pressed down the Velcro on her sneakers with her good hand. These sneakers were geeky but convenient, especially that night. It would've been hard to tie the laces on her other running shoes with one hand bandaged. Before leaving, she slid what looked like a flyer from atop a stack of paper to the right of the pile of shoes and shoved it into her pocket.

She gave Rusty a quick head scratch as soon as they pulled the door shut behind them. The smiling man posing with Tammy and her husband and an unknown woman in the photo that had set her heart to hammering was Steve Galen.

CHAPTER 18

Guest book: "We just closed on a house in the Valley so we can be near our twin grandbabies. We're gonna miss staying at this B&B. After a day with those two, we love to come back here where it's peaceful and cozy and we don't have to do a thing! Thanks, Miranda!" Gram and Papa Harrison

Back at the B & B Miranda pulled the crumpled flyer she'd filched from the pumpkin house out of her parka pocket and studied it.

Martyrs Day Commemoration!
December 8th
Rock and Remember those who came before us!
5 bands!
Tyler's Ranch
Between the Okanagans and the Cascades
RaHoWa!

A quick flip through a chapter in *American Swastika* reminded her that *Martyrs Day*, the two words in navy blue on Tammy's sweatshirt and touted on the flyer, was a haters' holiday commemorating the shooting of Aryan terrorist Robert Matthews. He was gunned down in a battle with federal authorities on Whidbey Island, Washington, in 1984. Who knew? This information convinced Miranda that the inhabitants of that house and their guests were, in fact, Aryan supremacists. No wonder their kids had bad-mouthed dark-skinned and developmentally-challenged Josefina. Kids notoriously forget that when their parents tell them "What you hear at home stays at home," they mean it. She recognized *RaHoWa* as what she had heard the pumpkin-house partiers chanting and there it was on page one of *American Swastika*! It was coded shorthand for *Racial Holy War*, and chanting it promotes solidarity among white supremacists.

Running back to the B & B with Rusty after reclaiming her gloves and razor from Darlene's front yard, she'd been as elated by her own chutzpah as she was by the discovery of Steve Galen grinning at her from a photo on the wall of a "respectable" local family. That family had undoubtedly told Galen about the kosherers' annual visits to Sunnyvale. The photo and the flyer validated Miranda's own impulsive reconnaissance mission. No wonder the art restorer wanted to stay at her B & B even though his work was in Toppenish. It wasn't her great website or delicious breakfasts or comfortable, quiet rooms or low prices. It was the B & B's proximity to the processing plant and its koshering operation. He wanted to be able to observe the comings and goings there without being observed himself before striking. No wonder he'd selected the room facing the street. How many times had he donned a skullcap, climbed out of his first-floor window, and entered the plant before he found the storage room and figured out when it was empty? Her own foray into the pumpkin house had led her to a breakthrough in her entirely unauthorized investigation of the murder of Isaac

Markowitz. The familiar voice in her head telling her she must be crazy was muted by a louder one congratulating her on her cleverness and daring. She couldn't recall when she had felt so pleased with herself.

But later, upstairs in her apartment while giving Rusty a belly rub, this flood of self-satisfaction ebbed along with her endorphins, and her exhilaration gave way to skepticism. Steve Galen was an esteemed art restorer, an accomplished and personable man with a website full of references from satisfied clients. Maybe he was just a friend of Tammy and her husband, unaware of their beliefs and with no reason to kill Isaac Markowitz. But if he, too, was a white supremacist that would be reason enough. Nurse Tammy, aka Babe, was so kind and competent. She would never teach her kids to torment children like Josefina. But they had. And Tammy did work at the local hospital and have access to poisons. By the time Miranda covered her bandaged hand in a plastic bag, showered, and crawled into her sleeping bag, she had calmed down enough to realize that getting the cops to take Steve Galen seriously as a suspect in a carefully-orchestrated hate crime would not be a slam-dunk.

To Miranda, the art restorer's affiliation with Tammy and her husband was grounds for further investigation into Steve's past activities, but that affiliation alone might not prompt Sheriff Carson to authorize his finest to investigate him. One of her TV detectives would show them that Steve Galen had the opportunity to commit this murder by placing him at the crime scene. That would be a problem because she herself had given him a partial alibi by mentioning to Detective Ladin that the pious art restorer had chatted with her on his return from church. Damn.

And then Miranda remembered something. She thought on it for a few minutes. It was a long shot, but so was her visit to the pumpkin house. Reassured, she burrowed into her cocoon. There, in spite of the racial slurs set to music that she still heard, her fear of being exposed, the throbbing of her self-inflicted wound, the four empty guest rooms below, and the guy she'd spotted lurking in the shadows across the street, she slept dreamlessly until she felt Rusty's wet nose nuzzling her neck.

That morning was the first since Breitner's opened that she had no guests waiting for breakfast. This might have inspired yet another bout of self-pity. But instead, Miranda was up early enjoying a mug of hot chocolate and a couple of eggs-over-easy mopped up with a buttered cinnamon bun. This orgy of sugar, fat, and white flour energized her as she crossed the street and walked around the block to enter the fruit processing plant's front door. She presented her card to Oskar Hindgrout's receptionist, who looked a lot younger than Miranda expected.

"Do you have an appointment?" The woman consulted her laptop." I don't see any appointments for this morning. Mr. Hindgrout's at a meeting."

"I'm not here to see Mr. Hindgrout. I'm here to see you." Miranda smiled and pushed her card across the desk. "I'd like to talk to you outside for just a few minutes. Can you take a break?"

The young woman shook her head firmly. "No. I'm a temp." She barely glanced at Miranda's card. "This is only my second week here. I'm hoping to get hired permanently. What did you want to see me about?"

Miranda was disappointed to learn that this pert and ambitious gal was not the woman she wished to see. "Never mind. Thanks anyway." She snatched her card back and left. Before she'd made her way across the road, she'd figured out an alternate source of the information she wanted. Nelson would know the former receptionist. Miranda preferred to ask him rather than Hindgrout, who might not feel free to divulge personal information about a former employee. Also she was sure Nelson wouldn't tell the police about her inquiry, whereas Oskar Hindgrout just might.

She had Nelson's cell number and left word for him to call her during his morning break. While she waited, she e-mailed the photo she'd taken the night before to herself to get it on her laptop, enlarged it, and printed out several copies. She also made copies of the flyer. That done, she attacked her inn-keeper's chores with one and a half hands. She was watering plants when she heard her phone's distinctive bleat. "Nelson, thanks for getting back to me. I need some information but I don't want anyone to know, even Pauline. So this call is between you and me, okay? We can tell Pauline later."

He hesitated. He didn't keep many secrets from Pauline. She was pleased when he said, "Okay. What do you want to know?"

"The name of the receptionist who used to work for Hindgrout. I need her address too."

"Carmen. Carmen Esposito. Catholic. She's strict, like a school teacher. But she's a nice lady. Been at the plant almost as long as me. Now her mother has cancer and has moved in with Carmen. That's why she left work."

"Thanks." Miranda appreciated this unsolicited thumbnail description, but pushed for just a little more. "Do you have an address for Carmen?"

"Don't know her exact address, but I always drove her home when her car was in the shop. I could find the house again." Pauline often said her husband didn't know how to say no, and she was right. Nelson sounded resigned to his own acquiescent nature when, even before Miranda made a request, he complied. "I'll call you when I get off work. Follow me in your truck. I'll show you where her house is."

"I owe you one, Nelson." She figured her injured hand would complicate driving a little, but as long as she stayed on local roads, she'd be fine.

That evening with three precious guests royally welcomed, Miranda drove across the little town to the beige house Nelson had pointed out to her earlier. There were lights in the back, probably in a bedroom or the kitchen, and a light on the porch too. Before ringing the doorbell, she braced herself to meet a cancer patient, sure that the sight of the sick and suffering woman would evoke painful memories of her own mother's last sad months.

The brown-haired fifty-something woman who opened the door did a double take at the sight of Miranda. Clearly she was expecting a different visitor. Her cryptic dismissal was barely civil. "Please go away. You're wasting your time. I have all the make-up I need. I'm Catholic, and I'm not converting. And the election's over." She held the side of the door in one hand, ready to slam it.

Miranda stuck her foot over the threshold. "Carmen, I'm not an Avon lady, or a Mormon missionary, or a campaign worker. I'm Miranda Breit…"

"How do you know my name? Are you from the government? I was born here. I'm a citizen. What do you want?"

"No, no, I'm not from the government. I own the B & B across the street from Oskar Hindgrout's plant. My name is Miranda Breitner. And what I want right now is to come in and talk to you for just a few minutes. You're letting all the heat out of your house, and I'm freezing out here."

Carmen grudgingly opened the door and moved aside as Miranda stepped in and found herself in the line of fire of a rifle held by an emaciated gray-haired woman in a lime-green nightgown not two feet away from her. For the second time in a month Miranda froze speechless in a doorway fearing for her life. The gun rested on the would-be shooter's shoulder, and she gripped it in two hands, one tethered by tubes to an IV pole teetering behind her. Even the unlikely shooter's thick Spanish accent, raspy whisper, and the tubes pushing oxygen into her nostrils didn't keep Miranda from understanding her every syllable. "I not letting you bastards deport me. I gonna die right here in this house. I not going back."

"*Mamacita!* Put that gun down. What're you doing out of bed and sneaking up behind my back? You're not going anywhere. How many times do I have to tell you?" Gently, so as not to detach any of the tubes festooning her mother's blue-veined hand, Carmen wrested the rifle out of her grasp and tossed it onto the sofa where it lay among the cabbage roses decorating the fabric covering all the living room furniture. Miranda ventured a breath and closed the door behind her. Carmen's resigned tone indicated that this was not the first time she'd had to disarm her mother and talk her back to bed.

"Let me help." Shaken, Miranda approached the gasping patient and, with a practiced hand, untangled the tubes and checked their connections to the bags and bottles while Carmen dragged over a walker. Unbidden, Miranda walked ahead of mother and daughter to the ammonia-scented back bedroom where she expected to find a rumpled hospital bed. She was right. She lowered the mattress and, with her good hand, straightened and tightened the flowered sheets, plumped the pillows, and cranked the bed back up, so that by the time the groaning old lady and her sorrowful and embarrassed daughter appeared, it looked almost inviting.

Miranda left the two women alone and retreated to the cozy living room. She made sure to seat herself on the plush easy chair across from the sofa rather than on that sofa next to the rifle. On the mantel, children and elders smiled at Miranda from a line-up of family photos, while in a large portrait hanging above the rose-strewn sofa and the gun the Madonna kept an eye on her. A slightly smaller painting of the Stars and Stripes hung next to the one of Mary.

Just as Miranda heard the emphatic musical prelude to *Law and Order*, Carmen returned. "I'm sorry my mother scared you. She's pretty scared herself now and the meds are making her act crazy. When death comes for her, she'll probably try to shoot him too." Smiling bitterly, she picked up the rifle and manipulated its mechanism, making it click and open. She extracted and pocketed several bullets. "I don't know which of her friends is bringing her ammo," Carmen complained. "I try to keep this hidden, but she always finds it. I keep it around because of, you know, the gangs. I'll be right back." She left the room with the rifle and a pocketful of bullets.

When she returned, she sat down on the sofa. Up close and in the light, Miranda noted that Carmen's thin nose protruded beneath a forehead pleated with lines and that one of her hands, empty on her lap, trembled. When she spoke she sounded put upon. "Please, tell me your name again."

"I'm Miranda Breitner. I own the B & B across the road from where you used to work."

"Did Mr. Hindgrout send you? That man is stubborn." Carmen shook her head. "I keep telling him I can't come back until..." Her voice broke. She pulled herself together and added. "Tell him I'm really sorry. He should get somebody else."

"Mr. Hindgrout didn't send me, Carmen. In fact, I don't want him to know I was here. I don't want anyone to know."

Perplexity added even more lines to Carmen's crowded brow. "So what do you want?"

"Carmen, when you worked, you used to go out to the plant parking lot every day during your break to that little space between the stacked fruit crates to smoke."

Carmen's jaw dropped and she hugged herself with both arms. "You were spying on me?"

"No. I was just looking out a window in my apartment on the second floor of the B & B. I used to see you race in there, and then I'd see smoke from your cigarette rise in puffs."

"So? I was on my break." Carmen's tone was the defiant yawp of a teenager caught smoking behind the barn. "On my breaks I went out there and had a smoke. So what?"

"And during the grape harvest, you worked seven days a week, right?"

"Yes. I was Mr. Hindgrout's administrative assistant and receptionist. Since 2009 I had to do both jobs for one paycheck." She snorted. "But my mother kept getting worse so I took a leave and moved her in here. I quit smoking." In an instant, her defiant voice thinned to a wary, anxious whisper. "Are you from my health insurance company? Are you going to raise my rates?"

"No. I'm not here from the insurance company." Having learned to interrogate from pros, Miranda stayed on track. "You left your job soon after Isaac Markowitz was killed, right?"

"Yes. That's when my leave started, but I was glad to go after that happened. I was scared. Not too much difference between killing a Jew and killing a Mexican or an Indian, whatever." She shrugged. "That boy's death was a terrible thing. Nothing like that ever happened at the plant. We never even had an injury worth dialing 911 for. All the workers were scared after that. They wonder if they'll be next. Mr. Hindgrout worries too. He put up lights and an alarm. The cops still didn't get the guy who did it."

Without explanation or ceremony, Miranda took the enlarged black-and-white photo from her purse and placed it in her hostess's lap. "Carmen, when you were in the parking lot on your break, did you ever notice any one of the folks in this photo go into the plant?"

Carmen stared at the picture and then, intrigued by something she saw, picked it up and held it close to her face for just a few seconds before lowering it to her lap again. "That one." The tip of her index finger, a sorry digit, its nail bitten to the quick, obliterated Steve Galen's grinning puss. "I saw him go in a couple of times. He's one of the Jews, so he went in through the parking lot entrance. Not the front way where my desk is. I remember him because he even looks like a Jew." She pointed to her own longish nose. "And he always wore one of those little round hats they sometimes wear, so I figured he was meeting with the rabbi or one of the other Jews."

"Did he show up on the Sunday Isaac was killed?" Miranda struggled to keep her voice even and her words measured.

"Yes. Yes. He did. I saw him leave, and that day he was in a big hurry. It was like somebody was chasing him but nobody came out after him. I didn't even know that boy was dead, so I didn't think anything about it and nobody asked me. The cops only talked to the men on the plant floor. They're not thorough like the cops on TV."

Miranda silently cursed the cops for their lack of imagination. She saw no point in explaining that Steve Galen wasn't Jewish. She had a different goal. "Carmen, would you be willing to share with the police the fact that you saw this man at the plant a few times and that just after Isaac Markowitz was killed you saw him rushing from the building?"

Carmen gaped as if Miranda had just asked her if she'd like to dance naked on the moon. Then she picked up the photo and, holding it gingerly between her thumb and forefinger the way she might hold a live toad, she released it into Miranda's lap and abruptly changed the subject. "Like I told you, I'm expecting my cousin and I thought you were her. She's late and she hasn't called." The distraught woman stood and began pacing between the sofa and the front door.

Miranda put the photo back in her purse and kept quiet. When Carmen's cousin did show up, the jittery Carmen, a reluctant witness and a secret smoker, would be free to leave the house and light up. She tried again. "Would you tell the police what you saw? It would help them put Isaac Markowitz's killer behind bars."

Carmen sat down and, looking straight at Miranda, shook her head. "No. I don't want cops coming to the house. My mother came to this valley to pick apples over a half century ago without papers. She never left." She shrugged. "Who knows what else police might want to know? I promised her she would die right here in this house."

"I got that." Miranda knew a lot about promises made to dying moms. "But the officer who came to talk to you would be a detective in street clothes. And your mother wouldn't even have to meet him. Or you could go to the police station and your cousin could stay here with your mother."

"No. I don't want more trouble. What if this guy I saw finds out I gave him away? Maybe he's in with the gangs…"

The doorbell rang and Carmen catapulted off the sofa to welcome her apologetic cousin. Miranda stood and buttoned her parka. "I'll go now, but please think about what I asked you." She looked around the comfortable living room, a veritable rose garden. "It looks like this country has been good to you." Miranda paused and then, thrusting her card into Carmen's hand and, glancing at the watchful Madonna, added a zinger. "Maybe Jesus is sending you an opportunity to give something back by helping the cops bring a killer to justice, Carmen."

In her truck, she brushed away her own guilt over preying on another woman's guilt by recalling how Mona had always insisted that guilt is a building block of conscience. And then Miranda returned to the moment, and what a Laura Diamond moment it was! She had strung together two dots, neither one of which had been visible to anyone but her, and so found someone who saw Steve Galen rushing out of the plant at approximately the time Isaac Markowitz had been killed! Now the cops would have to refine and widen their investigation. She figured that Detective Ladin would be able to persuade Carmen Esposito that it was in her and her mother's own best interests to testify to what she'd witnessed.

Miranda herself was glad she wouldn't have to endure another tête-à-tête with Detective Ladin. She hated the fact that he knew her secret. Even his desire for her seemed more insult than compliment. But she didn't dwell on her aversion, because now she could use Crime Stoppers. Home again, she ran with Rusty and then poured herself a glass of wine, popped a frozen mac 'n' cheese into the microwave, and checked her bookings. There were three new ones!

And on her cell there was a call from Pauline inviting her to share their family's Thanksgiving dinner.

To her astonishment, there was also an e-mail message from Harry Ornstein. "Miranda, I've got some explaining to do, and I want to do it over dinner. Tomorrow night? Wednesday night? Thursday night? I'll drive down to your place, and we can go somewhere in the Lower Valley. Please." Hearing from Harry, like the new bookings and the dinner invitation, was a decidedly pleasant surprise. But of all the mail in her in-box, it was the Google Alert notice that excited her most. Her fingers flew as she clicked her way to the website of a ram's horn dealer known only as TheShofarDude.com.

CHAPTER 19

Guest book: "This place has the best rates in the Valley and the best location. I'm in sales, so location matters. After the murder across the street, I stayed someplace else, but my boss went ballistic over the hike in room rate and mileage, so I'm back. When I told Miranda her blueberry scones are to die for, I meant it!" Road Warrior

ShofarDude.com
Moroccan ram's horn measures just over 30 inches around the double twists! Biggest ram's horn that the SD has ever seen! Many shades of lush brown. Natural rugged finish. Has a big mouthpiece so it's easy to play and big mellow sound to match like a tuba! To hear this one-of-a-kind, collector's shofar call (718) 783-4464 Only $3,7000!

The ram's horn in the photos on the shofar dude's website looked identical to the one in the appraisal photo that Eva Markowitz sent. Miranda crossed her fingers. Aware that it was nearly midnight in Brooklyn, where the shofar dude's area code indicated that he lived, she didn't call him right away. If he kept his stock in trade in his home and worked from there, she didn't want to risk waking him or his family. She was tempted to buy the ram's horn without hearing it so no one else would get to it first, but she hoped that by talking to the vendor about the horn's previous owner she could learn something of the seller or at least get a physical description of him. So she e-mailed the shofar dude, saying that she wanted to hear the horn, and that, if she liked its sound and what she could learn of its provenance, she would buy it at once at the listed price and have it overnighted to her. She left her number and asked him to call her the next morning on PST.

Because she'd learned early on not to expect much from the world, Miranda could keep her hopes in check overnight. It was harder to justify spending thousands of her dwindling dollars on a shofar. With that money she could easily have the B & B's chimney made operable and maybe even buy herself a real bed. But why do either if Breitner's was soon to close? Finally she told herself that what she was doing was investing in the future of her own business, in her own future. If she didn't, who would?

Miranda's three guests were finishing breakfast early the next morning when Pauline materialized for coffee. She arrived eggless because her chickens were "on strike,' which was how she referred to their seasonal "off-time." Miranda sat down with her friend, hoping their chat would distract her from the fact that she hadn't heard from the shofar dude yet, even though in Brooklyn it was already almost noon. She placed her cell phone on the counter next to her coffee cup. "I'm expecting a call. But I have to tell you, I'm really looking forward to Thanksgiving with you and Nelson and your kids and the grandkids too." She hesitated before adding, "This is my first Thanksgiving without my mom, and your invitation means a lot. What can I bring?"

Pauline, who had helped herself to a gingerbread scone, looked around at the used cups and plates piled on the counter and sipped her coffee. "You have to feed guests every day, so why not take a day off? Bring a couple of bottles of local wine, or a six-pack of beer even. The young people always want to try the latest vino, and Nelson and I enjoy a little local brew now and then, too."

"Are you sure? I can make something besides breakfast, you know."

"I'm sure. My daughter-in-law likes to bring the sides and my son in Spokane likes to make the pies. I do the turkey, gravy, and stuffing. The guys do the dishes, would you believe? So we're good."

"I really appreciate your including me." Miranda paused again. "You know, Pauline, I almost called to ask if I could sleep on your sofa the other night. I had no guests and, for the first time, I got spooked here all by myself."

"I don't blame you, given what happened across the street. Why didn't you call? Or just come over? You now have a standing invitation. Our spare room is your spare room. I'm sorry you had no guests, though. That's probably not what spooked you, but it's a worry, isn't it?"

"Yes…" Just as Miranda was considering sharing with Pauline her discovery about the pumpkin house people and Carmen Esposito's revelation, her cell phone sounded. She glanced at the name of the caller, put the phone to her ear and shrugged. "Sorry. I have to take this."

Pauline chugged down her coffee, wrapped her cape around her, and waved goodbye, still munching the scone in her one ungloved hand.

"Hello."

"Hello. This is The Shofar Dude otherwise known as Louie Blitzer. Are you MBreitner@ gmail.com?"

"Yes. Thanks for getting back to me. Is it still for sale? I'm buying it for my father's fiftieth birthday. He always blows the shofar at our temple. May I hear it?"

"Yes. Yes. Of course. Listen, I'll play it now on speakerphone. "

Miranda listened recalling how powerful the familiar bleats had been when she heard them coming from the processing plant and how, even on speakerphone from Brooklyn, they resonated with her. "It sounds very good. Can you tell me anything about who owned it last?"

"*Goyim.*"

"Really? What would a non-Jew want with a shofar?"

"Not to worry. She only had it a few weeks. Before that it belonged to a *rebbe*. A woman called me and said she just bought a house that had once been owned by a rabbi and this ram's horn turned up in a box in the attic. The box was labelled *shofar*. So the new owner, she Googled *shofar* and, of course, she found me." Miranda recognized Louie Blitzer's pride in his website's reach.

"Right away she e-mailed me pictures, and I was glad to take it off her hands. It's a beauty, isn't it? And it's in perfect condition, too."

Miranda pictured Steve Galen researching shofars, fabricating this story to explain how he came into possession of the distinctive horn, and then getting some perhaps-unwitting accomplice to agree to e-mail the pictures and then arrange the transaction. "It looks great in the photos. Did she ship it or bring it in herself?"

"She mailed it. From California yet. But not to worry. Remember, it came all the way to this country from Morocco undamaged. Then it went to California without so much as a scratch. And I told her how to wrap it, and it still doesn't have a mark on it. I'll get it to you in mint condition. You have my word."

"I believe you. But I have one more question, Mr. Blitzer. What does <i>natural finish</i> mean?"

"It wasn't polished. Lots of shofars are polished by machine. This horn is just like it was when it was on the ram, a little rough and ridged. The ridges add interest and texture to the surface."

Ridges, especially thin, narrow ridges, might be hard to wipe completely clean, even for an art restorer with a toothpick fetish. Miranda grinned into the phone as she pictured TV's Temperance Brennan shining her luminal light on the shofar and turning a miniscule crevice in the curve of the instrument the telltale blue indicative of blood. "It sounds perfect. I'd like you to overnight it to me. But before I give you my credit card information and address, promise me something. I don't want anyone to know you sold it, let alone sold it to me."

When he responded, he sounded a little miffed. "Of course. I bought this beauty from the woman and paid her via PayPal. We have no further business together."

"Okay. But also, can you keep it on your website for a few more days, a week maybe?"

"Sure. Why not? Like I said, it's a beauty. It makes people want to buy something nice, something classy."

Miranda gave him her credit card information and address. When she finished the call, she allowed herself a few moments of pure satisfaction. She was certain that by the next day she'd have the real murder weapon in her possession. Surely that and her photos would convince the cops to expand their unsuccessful investigation into Isaac's murder, to treat it as a hate crime, to look into Steve Galen's past. This purchase was a good investment.

But before she presented the fruits of her own research personally to Sheriff Carson himself, she decided to talk to her lawyer. In spite of the immediate wave of pleasure and relief she'd felt when she read Harry Ornstein's e-mail the night before, Miranda reminded herself that he'd disappointed her in the boyfriend department. She'd not asked him or even expected him to call, but then he'd said he would and he didn't. Clearly he didn't care for her. She got that. But, she told herself, he was still her lawyer and she needed one. Colestah was too volatile for her and not as close by. So she e-mailed Harry that she'd have dinner with him that evening but only to discuss "an urgent legal matter of great concern to me." She told him she couldn't leave the B & B until the night's guests showed up.

She made a dinner reservation for two at Annette's. It was close by and quiet and the food was good. It was also not too expensive and, since she planned to pay for her own meal out of her very much depleted funds, cost mattered to her.

Miranda rushed through her chores and errands. She wanted to get to her laptop and buttress her case against Steve Galen by digging beneath the first layer of his website. She knew that an in-depth examination of her own online persona would eventually lead an insightful and persistent researcher to either a dead end or, worse yet, to Meryl Weintraub. Steve Galen's on-line presence was probably equally permeable. She began by calling a few of the people who'd authored the glowing references that lent the art restorer's site its considerable credibility. She claimed to be considering hiring him to restore some sand-and sun-scarred murals on the barn of her ranch in Arizona.

The mayor of Robertsville, a small town in rural Ohio, took her call and said, "Oh, yeah. Galen did a good job. That statue of our founder Jed Roberts was weather-beaten and had some graffiti on it, and he prettied it up in time for our centennial Fourth of July festivities. We were real pleased." The city official who praised Steve's work on a mural on the wall of a police station in a farming town in Iowa was at a meeting, but his administrative assistant, said, "I'll have him call you if you want. But we all thought Steve did a fine job. I saw the paperwork. He came in under budget and finished early too. You can't go wrong with him." Miranda made a few more calls with similar results from the references she was able to reach. She was disappointed to find that everyone she contacted appreciated the art restorer and his work. She was certain that getting information from the man's alleged alma mater, the University of Delaware, would be impossible without police or alumna credentials.

Miranda was cheered by the fact that Tom Buler, the last of her guests to arrive that evening, was returning for his third stay at Breitner's. Apparently the killing across the street hadn't soured him on the place. "Good to see you're hangin' in, Miranda. I'm not giving up either." Tom was determined to continue his search for the ideal spot to build his dream vacation home. "Our realtor has three promising sites to show me this time. Maybe I'll get lucky."

When she next opened the door with Rusty at her side, Harry Ornstein was standing there, his face mostly hidden behind a clay pot of yellow chrysanthemums. "Hi, Miranda. These are a peace offering. They'll do well outside during the day and indoors at night. Where should I put them?" His eyes glommed onto her bandaged hand. "Sorry you're hurt. How'd that happen?"

She ignored his reference to a peace offering and to her hand. After all, she was more client than friend. She didn't inquire after Julia either. "The fireplace doesn't work, so I usually put flowers in there. I'll move these outside in the morning. Thank you." She heard the primness in her voice.

"You're welcome. Do you want me to take off my shoes?" He hesitated just inside the door.

Miranda saw Harry's barrage of logistical questions as his attempt to dispel the awkwardness between them. "No. We're leaving right away. My guests all arrived, and I made us a reservation at a place nearby for 7:30."

Once he'd deposited the mums in the fireplace she could see Harry's face. A grayish pallor replaced his tan, and blue-black semi-circles beneath his eyes were visible behind his glasses. He needed a haircut and a good night's sleep. The man must've been working extra hard. He'd always looked and acted totally at home in the world, as Mona would have put it. But that night his misery was palpable. Was he sick? She couldn't control the pangs of concern she felt.

"I was hoping for a tour. Maybe after dinner?" His words were casual, but his tone was tense.

She made herself stick to business. "I want to show you that building across the street, especially the parking lot, and the side of the B & B facing it. Let's walk over to the gate there and then head for the restaurant. That way I can take Rusty out before we leave. It won't take long." She noted that Rusty had no misgivings about Harry, and lobbied him for a head scratch.

She threw on her parka, leashed her dog, and the three of them crossed the road and stood at the gate, staring through the chain links of the fencing. "See the big square in the side of the plant? That's the door where the fruit containers, the kosherers, and most of the other workers go in and out. The front entrance is just a normal-sized door on the other side. Now look at those fruit crates stacked all over. See the three over there?" Miranda pointed. "There's a little space between those three stacks where one former employee used to go on her break to smoke. Just file that picture in your head."

Rusty had peed, so they crossed the street again and Miranda pointed at the old farmhouse. "Check out the windows in the B & B that face the processing plant." She brought the dog inside and left the disconsolate pooch lying at the front door gnawing a fake bone and already waiting for her return.

"Follow me. Then you'll have your car." For reasons she didn't care to explore, it was important to Miranda for Harry to see that she could limit her drinking so as to be able to drive herself home and for her to remember that they were going their separate ways right after dinner.

Was it disappointment or surprise that widened Harry's eyes for a second? "Whatever you say."

They entered the restaurant together. "Hi, Annette. Good to see you again. We have a reservation for two under my name."

"Sure. Nice to see you too, Miranda." The glance she gave Harry was inquisitive. "Right this way please."

When a young man came by to take their drink order, Miranda requested a glass of Roussanne from Coyote Canyon, a winery in Horse Heaven Hills. She also asked for separate checks.

Harry flinched and ordered a cup of black coffee. "I don't drink when I'm working."

Miranda thought he sounded self-righteous. Anyway she was used to drinking alone. Her own wine couldn't come soon enough.

"What's good here?"

"The lasagna. It's homemade." She hesitated for barely a second before she heard herself saying, "But Harry, are you ill? You look terrible. What's wrong?"

"This is how I look every time my life turns to shit. Just listen." She had no choice. His words rushed out too fast to interrupt. "About an hour after I kissed you goodbye and you took off in your truck that Saturday, I got a call from my dad, who was traveling in Amsterdam with my mom." His voice turned husky. "She'd thought returning to a place he'd once enjoyed would jog his memory, rejuvenate him. Ha. She died over there in her sleep. He was in his PJs, lying on the bed next to her corpse when he called me. Phoning me was the last rational thing he did."

"Oh my God, Harry." Miranda was helpless to prevent her eyes from tearing up. She pulled a Kleenex out of her pocket and dabbed at them.

"It's weird. She died in his sleep, too. Poor guy. I mean, he woke up and there she was, still lying right next to him, but dead." Harry's voice softened. "He's been losing it for about a year and she'd never been really sick, so he wasn't expecting this. Neither was I. He's the one with the heart condition. Go figure."

"Were you and your mom close?"

Harry held up two fingers and crossed them. "But my mother not only died, she died six thousand miles away. It was totally surreal. If my dad hadn't been demented already, this shock would have unhinged him." He clenched his fists as if to defend himself from this memory. "I called Julia's mom and my sister Holly in Seattle and booked a flight to London. Then I drove to the airport. From there I called my part-time secretary to ask her to postpone everything. I flew to London, and then to Amsterdam. I got there very, very late the next night." Harry's voice lowered. "When I walked into my parents' hotel room, my poor dad was still in his PJs on the bed talking to my mom's corpse! Jesus!"

Miranda reached across the table and took his hand.

"I tried to make him understand that she wasn't going to answer him. Ever. But I didn't want him to have a damn heart attack. Then I had to get a doctor to declare her dead, make the Dutch cops understand that my dad hadn't killed her, change their flight arrangements, and get all of us back to Seattle. I should have called you then." He frowned at this missed opportunity.

"Harry..." Miranda squeezed his hand. When their server returned, she ordered lasagna for them both.

"Let me finish. I stayed with my dad in their condo arranging my mom's funeral while Holly worked the phone. My aunt and uncle came from Toronto with their kids and grandkids. Julia and her mom drove over, too, with a couple of my dad's brothers and my mom's cousin, who was her best friend. We had a private graveside service and sat *shiva* for two days in my parents' condo. I should have tried to reach you and at least left a message, but I was in this bubble of family and funeral and..." Harry grimaced.

"Harry..."

"The night of the funeral my dad left the condo in his PJs to look for my mother. My uncles and I had to go out and search for him. I found him outside a Starbucks she liked, waiting for it to open." Miranda kept squeezing his hand. "Holly moved into his condo for a while and we hired an agency to send caregivers there while she's at work. Then we started trying to figure out how and where dad should live so he could be safe and not too miserable and not make Holly crazy either. We don't think he's going to get better." Again Harry's face contorted. "Holly's fabulous and super-close to my dad, but she's got a demanding job that keeps her sane. Besides, my sister will tell you herself, she's not exactly caregiver material. She doesn't want kids. She doesn't even have a pet."

Miranda was tempted to tell Harry how her dad took off and her mom needed her to look after nutsy Grandma Fanny, but she wanted to hear more of Harry's story and he clearly needed to tell it.

"When I got back to Yakima, I really should have called you and explained everything. But I had to catch up with a few clients I'd bugged out on and at the same time deal with Julia's total despair." Harry took off his glasses and rubbed his eyes. "Julia and my mom were very close too." He inhaled as if hoping to gather strength from the air. "Would you believe my poor five-year-old kid is wetting her bed again and seeing a goddamn grief counselor?"

"With so many people to worry about, no wonder you look so terrible. I just wish I'd known. Maybe I could have helped somehow."

Harry's reply was barely audible, so Miranda leaned closer to listen. "I sure could have used at least a text from you wondering what happened, why I didn't call. Once I got back here, I felt like I'd waited so long that I'd broken that spell we had, our spell." He actually hung his head. "I figured either you weren't really interested in a serious relationship with me or you were hurt and pissed at me. I imagined all that passion that attracted me to you in the first place turned against me. And I was right. It was." He ran his hand through his hair and looked up. "But Julia kept asking about you, and then last weekend she wanted to know if you'd died like her nana." He lowered his eyes. "That really got to me, so I manned up enough to e-mail you."

Julia's obvious affection for Miranda was as precious to her as Harry's attraction. "I'm very glad you did."

Harry actually smiled. "You could've fooled me." But his smile faded, and when he spoke next his voice was still low but surprisingly stern. "Listen, if a girlfriend of yours said she'd be in touch and didn't follow through, you'd have worried about her, tried to reach her, right?"

"I guess so, but I'm not exactly up to date on how to communicate with friends or dates. Since I was thirteen, I lived a kind of monastic life with my mom and my grandma."

"You did mention that you were shunned by your peer group for a while."

"For years. I was a pariah. Even my dad actually thought I'd shaken little Timmy Schwartz to death. My parents divorced and I felt that was my fault. My dad married a much younger woman and they had a baby, a little girl. When his trophy wife wouldn't let me pick that infant up or be alone with her, my dad didn't contradict her. That's when I began cutting myself, but you know that."

"I wondered about why. Did it help?"

"It helped for a few seconds. But then that little relief wasn't enough and I wanted to die. I slit my throat."

"Yeah. I saw that too. At the Canyon. Right under your jaw. The line. Was that a cry for help?"

"It must have been, because it worked. My mom was a fixer, a PT. She fixed people for a living. She got me to a therapist who specialized in adolescent depression and also home-schooled me so I didn't have to go to high school. She encouraged me to apply to college and graduate. I did, but I was so worried about being Googled that I kept a very low profile. After that, when I couldn't get work, my mom made me a caregiver for my grandma and kept me on at home. She encouraged me to sue the SPD, to move and open a B & B. Last year she died of lung cancer." Miranda paused. "I'm telling you this not to get your sympathy but so you'll understand why I don't always do or say the right thing."

"Sometimes the truth is the right thing." Now it was his turn to squeeze her hand.

Miranda nodded and was relieved when Harry changed the subject. "So what's this urgent legal matter you want my opinion about?"

"I've been looking into the murder of Isaac Markowitz, and what I learned points to a different suspect than the only one the county sheriff and his detective are still considering. I want to take Rabbi Golden's advice and inform Sheriff Carson of my findings and make him understand that Isaac was a victim of a hate crime. Then he'll have to expand their investigation. But before I submit this tip to Crime Stoppers, I want to run my findings by you."

She didn't stop except to shovel food into her mouth until they had each polished off lasagna and salad. She was ordering espresso when Harry spoke. "Okay. So I'm going to recap what I heard to be sure I understand. First. The sheriff's currently considering only one suspect, a wannabe gangbanger with no priors who's disappeared. So Carson's investigation seems to have stalled.

"Second. You listened to two different rabbis talk about anti-Semitism, read one book on hate groups, and heard about a single local incident involving racial slurs. Your business is hurting. So on a hunch you maneuvered your way into the home of a respectable local family with possible ties to Aryan supremacists, one of whom you think is an art restorer. This individual was here to remove tags from the Toppenish murals and was in residence at your B & B on the day of the murder. Without your hosts' knowledge or consent, you took photos in their home and then stole a flyer advertising an Aryan supremacist event."

Miranda registered his sarcasm but didn't take offense. It was a lawyer's job to be skeptical.

"Third. You don't believe that the murder weapon is a bloody fish club found at the crime scene. Instead you think the real murder weapon is a shofar that was not found at the scene. You shared this suspicion with the sheriff via Crime Stoppers. Now you've paid some east coast online shofar-selling stranger almost four thousand dollars to send you what you suspect is this "real" murder weapon which you hope arrives tomorrow.

"Fourth. You know a woman who saw the art restorer flee the crime scene around the time of the murder but she's unwilling to even talk to the police let alone testify, because she's harboring an undocumented Mexican relative. She also fears reprisal if the man she saw in a yarmulke is somehow gang-connected."

Miranda admitted to herself that Harry's accurate recitation of her findings did make them seem preposterous. And he wasn't done.

"Finally you want to go to Sheriff Carson with the photo, the flyer, the shofar, and the names of your suspect and his accomplices and the name of the reluctant witness and say what?"

"That he should use these findings as a basis for widening his stalled homicide investigation, that Isaac Markowitz interrupted a hate crime and was collateral damage. Sheriff Carson should be looking into a hate crime, maybe even a series of hate crimes. Look, Harry, I know the city and county cops depend on the Washington State Crime Lab for practically everything, but it's notoriously overbooked. So, if this crime is treated as a hate crime and the man who committed it operates in many states, which I believe he does, Carson might get the FBI to lend their people and their fancy lab equipment to dig deeper into Steve Galen.

"All his references seem okay, but most of them are from officials in little rural towns where he's worked. These towns are like Sunnyvale in that they have small undertrained and overextended local and county police patrolling huge areas. She hesitated, suddenly aware that her voice had become insistent, strident. "And maybe they're also a little biased against people who seem different. We're surely aware that some cops aren't immune to bias." Warming to her topic, she couldn't resist adding, "Seattle cops are finally being monitored by the feds for, among other things, excessive use of force against minorities." She was gratified to see Harry nod.

Encouraged by that small gesture of agreement and energized by her espresso, Miranda kept talking. "So I bet if the FBI looked, they might discover that while Steve Galen was in those little burgs, bad things happened to some of the area's minorities. Maybe he worked in cahoots with their local hidden haters to orchestrate crimes that would never be associated with someone as 'respectable' as he is. I poked around online this afternoon and in just a few hours I found a burning cross on the lawn of a lesbian couple, a bomb in a knapsack on the parade route for Martin Luther King Day, and swastikas on the windows of a shoe store owned by a Jewish family. These events all happened in places Steve Galen worked at the time he worked there. But to do that research in depth would take me ages. A good forensics lab has the software and the people to do it quickly and, probably, more accurately. Also they could use facial recognition software on Mr. Galen. He's probably using an alias."

Miranda considered it a victory of sorts that when he spoke, Harry's tone was slightly less sarcastic than it had been. "Somewhere between the lasagna and the salad, you said something about how you thought this Steve Galen didn't go to the plant that morning to kill a Jew but only did so when Isaac surprised him. What do you think he was 'really' up to when Isaac walked in on him?"

"The nurse who bandaged my hand works nights at the local hospital. She probably has access to poisons…."

"So you think he went there to poison the grape juice? Like in that vision you had? That makes you a prophetess!" Harry's tone was incredulous again, but his eyes narrowed.

His conflicting reactions mirrored what Miranda knew. The scenario she described, like that vision she'd had, was both preposterous and possible, like flying jet passenger planes into the Twin Towers or incinerating millions of men, women, and kids. "I think he was experimenting to see how much of what poison would work. If he got away with it, a different person could return every autumn, stay at my B & B, sneak into that plant, and poison more grape juice, more Jewish kids." She shuddered. "And no one would ever suspect him. Of course now that Hindgrout's ramped up security I doubt that can happen. But if Isaac hadn't walked in on him…."

"How would your hypothetical poisoner know if he succeeded? That grape juice is shipped all over the country, all over the world in fact. And, if I understood you, the enzymes get diluted when they're poured into those vats."

"He'd do a search of Jewish newspapers and blogs to see if there's a reference to children getting sick after the Shabbat kiddish. Think about it, Harry. Every Friday evening, Jewish kids like your Julia drink grape juice at synagogue or at home. If he got the right amount of the right stuff into the enzymes, eventually some of those kids are going to get sick, maybe even die. There might not be enough of the poison to do in an adult, but even a little bit might make a kid sick. Until then, what has he to lose? He'd never be suspected. Here everybody blames the gangs for everything."

"That's because the gangs do a lot of bad things, kill a lot of people. They're a big problem here and everywhere else they go. Think about it, Miranda, if it weren't for some gangbanger tagging those murals, the art restorer wouldn't have had a reason to come to our valley."

"Oh my God, Harry!"

"What?"

"The local cops are trying to blame the same gang wannabe for tagging the murals. But suppose he didn't. Suppose no gangbanger did. They never touched those murals before this. Instead, suppose this art restorer came to town and stayed with his friends in the pumpkin house and went out one night and tagged those murals himself? Late at night I bet there's hardly anybody there. Hell, there's hardly anybody in downtown Toppenish in the daytime." She felt her face flush with excitement as her words rushed to keep up with her thoughts. "An agile artist dressed in black with a can of spray paint could tag those murals real fast with nobody the wiser. Gangbangers tag stuff all the time without anybody catching them at it. Steve Galen knew everybody would blame the gangs and he'd have a legitimate reason to come here." She finished her espresso, dazzled anew by her latest realization.

Harry sat opposite her, shaking his head. But she couldn't stop. If she couldn't convince him, how would she convince the cops? "Listen, Harry, I have a couple of samples of this guy's handwriting. One is in a New Testament he left in the drawer of his night table and the other is his review in my guest book. I'll Xerox them too. Maybe a handwriting expert could compare them to the photos of the tags on the murals or other handwriting of his."

"That would be a twofer." When she looked puzzled, Harry explained. "If he tagged the murals, he'd inflict pain on two targets on his most-hated list, Mexican immigrants and Jews." He paused. "Okay, just suppose you're right.

How did this art restorer get the Toppenish gig? I'm sure the Toppenish Public Art Association had a search committee and that they put this job out to bid."

"Maybe somebody on the search committee, another hidden hater, recommended him. So the committee interviews him and checks the impeccable references on his website. Then, cued in by the hidden hater on the search committee, he slightly underbids everybody else, which seals the deal."

Harry had removed his glasses and was rubbing his bloodshot eyes. Then he stared at her as if she had just alighted from a UFO. "I honestly don't know whether you're a lunatic or a genius or maybe both, Miranda. We've been so out of touch that I had no idea that you were still involved in this mess." He ran his hand through his every-which-way hair.

"But maybe I can help. Friday night, come to Shabbat services and bring the shofar… if it actually arrives." Harry rolled his eyes. "Don't even unwrap it. I'll have it checked out ASAP at a private lab, and if their techs find enough blood on it to get uncontaminated DNA, I'll have them contact the sheriff who can see if it's Isaac's. And maybe the sheriff can make a deal with the witness that'll get her to testify. But with or without DNA, I'll have the lab send the shofar to the sheriff." He stopped for breath. "This way, Miranda, if and when the cops finally do charge the art restorer with homicide and defacing public property and maybe even with the intention to commit a hate crime, you won't be forced to extinguish flames on a cross his buddies plant in front of your B & B. "

Miranda hugged herself to control the shaking this nightmarish scenario evoked. It was not one she'd ever envisioned. And there would be another consequence of convicting Steve Galen of Isaac's murder that she'd not thought about either, her own collateral damage. "It'll become known that this ghoul stayed at Breitner's. For weeks." Miranda was surprised that she hadn't thought of this before. "I guess I'll have to live with that."

"You can capitalize on it by hosting mystery weekends."

Ignoring his attempt at levity, she sat quietly for a moment absorbing Harry's proposal. Maybe she'd get the investigation expanded without exposing herself. Isaac's murder had become a voracious vacuum sucking her hard-won hope right out of her and she'd be glad to be out of its path, to have it solved. "So once again, after I fill out the Crime Stoppers forms, I just go about my business and pretend I don't know anything about anything?"

"Right. But instead of filling out one Crime Stoppers form, do three. In the first, accuse the art restorer of tagging the murals himself. In the next, accuse him of hitting Isaac with the shofar and killing him when Isaac interrupted him trying to poison the juice. And in the third, accuse him of attempting a hate crime. Three crimes attributed to one person will get Sheriff Carson's attention. Also e-mail me copies of the photos of Galen and the shofar, a copy of the flyer, and a copy of the inscription in the Bible. I'll snail-mail them to Carson anonymously from Seattle where I'll be tomorrow." He paused. "Have you already talked about your suspicions to friends or family?"

"No. One friend got me the name and address of the witness, but he doesn't know why I wanted to know. "

"Good. Once the sheriff's people get your tips, things may happen fast. There may be press. You'll have to be vigilant and discreet so no one knows you've had anything to do with exposing any of the people you suspect of being involved in any aspect of these matters." He paused and fiddled with his empty coffee cup. "You do realize, Miranda, that nobody wants Isaac's murder to be called a hate crime except you and Rabbi Golden, and she doesn't even live in the Valley. So many small businesses are incubating here now, the orchards are thriving, and the new vineyards have brought a flood of new tourists. Hate crimes are bad for business."

"Unsolved murders are worse," she retorted. "Denial is worse. Rabbi Alinsky has always feared Isaac's murder was a hate crime, but he tried to deny it even to himself. It's like when some European Jews didn't leave even after they saw what the Nazis were up to." She got off her soapbox long enough to look across the table where Harry was paying the check.

"You know, Harry, I can't let you drive back up to Yakima tonight. You're too exhausted." She was rewarded when he looked up with a twinkle in his bloodshot eye.

"Miranda, if you'd gotten out more, you'd know about make-up sex."

"Huh?"

"But don't worry. I'm going to follow you back to your place and bring you up to speed."

She didn't protest.

The shofar arrived as promised. Per Harry's instructions, Miranda didn't unwrap it, and late Friday afternoon she schlepped the large package to Temple Shalom. She felt protective of the instrument, the last object poor Isaac had touched. Rather than bring the bulky bundle into the service with her and answer a lot of questions about it, she locked it in the cab of her truck under an old blanket. She entered the little house-turned-synagogue and glanced around in search of Harry. The sooner she transferred the shofar to the trunk of his car, the better.

Julia found her before Miranda spotted the child and her dad heading for the kitchen. She knelt to hug the little girl. "Hi, Julia. I'm so glad to see you." Julia wrapped her scrawny arms around Miranda's neck and hung on. Miranda held her and bit her own lip so as to stem the tears the child's wordless greeting, a claim really, evoked. Hunkered down with her chin on Julias' small bony shoulder, Miranda just kept on hugging until Harry said, "Julia, please take our challah to the kitchen and give it to Emily. She'll put it on the table when they bring out the food."

"Wanna come, Miranda?" The child's voice was soft and tentative, her red-rimmed eyes imploring.

"I'll be right here when you get back. I promise. It's your dad's turn to get a hug." She stood and Harry opened his arms. She walked into them and, again, held on for a few seconds. Miranda and Harry waited hand in hand until Julia returned from the kitchen when the three trooped outside to transfer the shofar to the trunk of Harry's car. Julia eyed the large package which acted on her as a kind of Rosetta Stone. "Is that a present for Daddy? Or for me? Is it a Hanukah present? Are you a Christmas person or a Hanukah person, Miranda?"

"No, Julia it's not a present for anybody. It's something related to a legal matter your dad is advising me on. He's my lawyer. And I'm a Hanukah person, but we haven't even had Thanksgiving yet. Do you like turkey?"

"Nana's turkey. I like Nana's turkey." Her soft voice got even softer.

"I bet your nana was a good cook. My grandma was too. She made the best chicken soup in the world. And when she died she left me the recipe so I can make it."

"Your grandma died too?" Julia's eyes widened.

"Uh-huh. A long time ago. And I still miss her."

The child nodded and hugged herself against the cold air and the coldness of death. Having stashed the shofar, Harry joined them as they reentered the synagogue where the wine had already been blessed and the service was about to begin. Julia didn't join the children's service but sat between Harry and Miranda.

Rabbi Golden's sermon focused on how to counter anti-Semitism in the guise of anti-Zionism, but Miranda, usually keen on anything to do with her perennially-embattled ancestral homeland, sat there with Julia's hand in hers. The child slumped against her, sound asleep, oblivious to both college students' calling for sanctions and divestment and Middle Easterners calling for the total annihilation of the only country Miranda knew for sure would take her in if she ever had to go there.

When it was time to mourn the dead, Harry gently extricated his hand from Julia's and stood with the rest of the congregation to say the Mourners' Prayer for his mom. For the first time since her own mom died, Miranda remained seated so as not to disturb the little one nestled against her. After the service, Harry gently scooped up the sleeping child. "We won't stay for the potluck. She hasn't gone to sleep quietly like this in weeks. She's exhausted. And she's staying at my place tonight. So would you join us there for supper?"

Miranda nodded, grabbed all three jackets, draped hers over Julia, strode to the front door, opened it, and held it for father and daughter. Julia merely stirred and grunted softly when Harry fastened her into the car seat. "Her mother's got papers due Monday, so I've got Julia for the entire weekend. We'll go to Seattle tomorrow to see my dad and relieve my sister." He got into the car.

"Tell me about your sister."

"Holly's two years older than I am. She's a Seattle city planner. She's been working on a critical project for years now and it's almost happening. This is her first time trying to get a project of her own approved. So Mom's death rocked Holly's world logistically as well as emotionally."

"You're proud of Holly. Your mom would be proud of her."

"You got that." He used the red light to look her way. "Do you have any brothers or sisters?"

"No. But this is beginning to sound like a first date, not me paying a condolence call."

"Actually, it's our fourth date, but who's counting? Our first was a lawyer-client conference at the Canyon. Our second was a kind of surprise party at my house. Our third was a client-attorney dinner, with the attorney getting client privileges, so this shiva visit is our fourth."

After Harry put his sleeping child to bed, he came downstairs and poured them each a glass of red wine. "Shabbat shalom." They clicked their glasses and the host opened his freezer. "We sat shiva for a few days in Seattle at Holly's, but she's a vegan who's into grains I can't even pronounce. So she gave me all this stuff. What'll it be? Frozen lasagna? Beecher's Mac & Cheese? Noodle kugel? Beef stew? Kung bo chicken, chicken enchiladas, or Costco's chicken pot pie?"

"Beef stew or chicken pot pie."

"The pot pie will get done faster. I'm starving."

"Me too." Harry turned on the oven and unwrapped the enormous pie. "Holly gave me a lot of cheese and crackers too, so we can graze while we wait."

Miranda arranged a Dutch goat cheese and a wedge of Brie on a plate with some crackers. "If this is a *shiva* call, I wish I'd contributed something."

"You did." Harry sat down next to her.

Miranda flushed and smiled. "So now, tell me how's Julia doing?" She had relished the grieving child's hug and the way she had snuggled herself to sleep beside her during the sermon.

Harry put his arm around her. "She's a little livelier. She's been up so much at night. But at Temple she just corked off. And she actually talked about her nana to you. Maybe she's at some kind of tipping point. I have an appointment to talk with the grief counselor next Tuesday."

"I hope he gives you good news." Miranda squeezed Harry's hand. "And how are you doing? You look a lot better. The haircut helped." She ran her hand over his fuzzy head.

"You helped. I didn't realize how much I missed you or cared about seeing you. I'm sleeping a lot better too." But then he spoke louder, as if to force himself to hear the truth of what he was saying. "But the thing now is that my dad's situation isn't going to go away. Finding him an affordable and acceptable place to live is a worry and a huge time-suck. Moving him there will be a nightmare too."

"I know. Before my mom got it through her head that her magna-cum-laude college grad daughter couldn't get work, she tried to find a place for my grandma. It's very difficult. If I can help in any way, let me know."

"Do you still babysit? Sometimes I have to go to Seattle to look over a place or to interview a home health aide if Holly can't do it… and Julia's mom's got a lot of papers to write… and an internship…"

Miranda was stunned. There was nothing Harry could have offered her that would have pleased her more. He knew about her arrest and the charge of baby killing and he still considered leaving his precious child in her care. Who knew? Maybe he had other innocent clients falsely accused. She was stammering with excitement when she answered. "I'd be happy to. Julia could stay with me." Then Miranda remembered the armed sexual predator stalking her and the kosherer's killer still at large. She felt the blood leave her face.

"What's wrong?"

"Remember I told you I decided to have sex with you partly because I felt safe with you?"

"Uh-huh. Probably because I know how to deal with rattlers."

Miranda shivered. "Could be. But, I used to feel safe in this valley, too. I came here because I thought I'd be safe from my past out here. Then Isaac Markowitz was murdered right across the street from me and now I don't feel safe here anymore. Not to mention there's an armed sexual predator stalking me and threatening to expose me as an accused baby killer."

"You're helping to bring down Isaac's killer. And you have it in your power to expose that detective and get him locked up where he belongs. But if you're not willing to press charges…"

"Speaking of bringing down Isaac's killer, I mailed off the stuff you sent me from Seattle as I promised. But that inscription in the Bible about the weary traveler is so odd. What do you make of it?" Miranda was glad to deflect the conversation from her unwillingness to have her sad history brought to the attention of her new friends, neighbors, and guests. "I thought it was odd, but when I reread it, it seemed familiar, so I checked the index of that book I told you about, *American Swastika*."

"And?"

"Well, the first part, *For the next weary traveler to lay his head here,* is just an excuse Galen made up for the second part. *Rest At Home O Wanderer Alone.*" The first letters of each word are upper case and they spell RA HO WA which is short for *Racial Holy War*, which is their motto."

"Did you mention that on your Crime Stoppers form?"

"Yup."

"Good work. That info will go a long way towards convincing Carson to pay attention to your claim. How about we talk more over the chicken pot pie?"

Miranda stood and pulled Harry to his feet. "I want to know more about your mom."

"She would have loved you." He ran his hands up and down her torso. Their kiss, sweetened by pity and spiced with promise, lasted a long time.

Miranda finally pulled away. "Let's turn the oven off. The pot pie will stay warm."

Crime Stoppers #44016

Question: Do you know why the suspect boarded in Sunnyvale, not Toppenish where he was working?

#44016: Maybe because from that B & B it looks like he could easily and inconspi-cuously observe and access the processing plant across the street.

Someone in the sheriff's office, possibly even Detective Alex Ladin, began e-mailing her questions about her tips, and Miranda answered them as best she could without revealing her own identity. According to Crime Stoppers protocol, she deleted both questions and answers.

She followed local news, eager to see if the press had gotten wind of the turn the investigation into the murder of Isaac Markowitz had taken. There was no mention of it at all, but Rosemarie stopped by one morning. "Listen Miranda, I know that like me you want this murderer caught. It's scary to think he's still out there." She threw up her hands. "It's sad for that boy's people in New York and it's bad for business here. I'm hurting and that means you're hurting too, right?"

Miranda nodded. "Bookings are down and there have been cancellations. But your referral, Tom Buler, is so faithful. I really appreciate his business."

"He sure likes this place. But listen. I've been bugging my brother, the one who works with the sheriff, not the orchardist, to share anything he knows about the investigation, because all of a sudden, he's pulling overtime. He lives with me, and I know when he starts missing meals that something's up. I was right. You didn't hear it from me, but that fish club doesn't match what the autopsy report said about the wound. It said that club couldn't have delivered the blow the kosherer died from."

"Wow, Rosemarie. That's important, because it means they might have to widen the investigation now that they can't blame the Indians anymore." Miranda pulled some warm cheese biscuits out of the oven. "Help yourself. There's fresh coffee in the pot."

"Thanks. I'll take it with me. I'm showing a house in the area, and I don't want to be late. But after everything you invested in this place, I know you're worried, so I wanted to stop by…"

Miranda provided a recyclable coffee cup with a lid and a few napkins and sent Rosemarie on her way. "Thanks. Keep me posted. And don't worry. I'll keep this news to myself." The realtor was barely out the door when Miranda had Harry on the phone.

"This should force Sheriff Carson to at least consider your pricey shofar as the murder weapon. The timing is good. I wonder if the sheriff heard yet from my lab guy."

"Beats me. But I mentioned that shofar on an earlier Crime Stoppers' form I sent in. I forgot to mention it to you."

"I'll forgive you. Maybe they've got more people working this case now." She heard a doorbell. "Gotta go. Talk to you later."

Miranda appreciated Harry's frequent calls, his interest in her daily life, her baking and laundering, her occasionally idiosyncratic guests, even her bookkeeping. She in turn relished his updates on his grieving family and his work. Their calls connected them in ways that were novel to a woman who had never had an ongoing romantic relationship before. If this gradual meshing of their worlds was what having a boyfriend was like, Miranda loved it. She was very pleased when Harry suggested getting together at her place during Thanksgiving weekend. "This time I insist on the tour."

"Sure. Will you bring Julia?" If Julia was coming, Miranda would buy another air mattress, make chocolate chip cookies.

"No. Her mother's flying her to Spokane and then to her sister's ranch near there after we three have Thanksgiving dinner with my demented dad and completely-crazed sister. Doesn't that sound like fun?" He went on before she could respond. "The trip'll be good for Julia. I told you Julia's done with the diapers, right? And she's sleeping a lot better."

"You did. I'm so glad. That has to be a relief."

"You got that. Yesterday after school she talked to me about how she misses her nana and she cried, but, hell, so did I. The grief guru says she's probably through the worst of it and he's going to cut her loose before the New Year."

Harry called frequently from the car as he drove to and from Seattle where he and Holly still searched for an affordable and suitable place with a reasonable waiting list for their dad to live. As Miranda gradually got to know Harry and learned a little about Holly and their dad and even his ex whom he was putting though college, it struck her as ironic that at this sad time in his life, her boyfriend had even more responsibility than ever before. But thanks to Crime Stoppers, Miranda had a little less.

She no longer felt responsible for solving Isaac's murder herself or with the help of Detective Ladin, and this was a great relief. More confident that Isaac's killer would soon be apprehended, she used a few hours of her new free time to treat herself to some retail therapy with Pauline. As she reported to Harry, "Ever since I eyeballed Rabbi Golden's cowboy boots, I've wanted a pair. Tomorrow Pauline's going to help me look. But she says we have to have lunch at Los Hernandez in Union Gap. I've been sending guests there without having gone myself."

"You'll love it. Have the pork tamales. And then in the spring, I'll take you for some of their asparagus tamales. Unbelievable." And sure enough when they spoke the next evening, he asked, "So, how were the tamales?"

"Amazing. I bought some to freeze. And there were a lot of Western wear shops nearby. Is that a message from God or what? I got my boots in the second place we looked! They're not white like the rabbi's, though. White's just not practical. "

Having indulged her whim, Miranda caught up on her promotional work. She planned a long-overdue open house with the goal of collecting sample menus, flyers, and maps for her guests and of disseminating her own promotional paper. She set a date and e-mailed invitations to the owners and/or managers of mostly Lower Valley tourism-related businesses and city officials.

You're invited to an open house at Breitner's B&B in Sunnyvale

November 16, at 5:30 pm

(See enclosed map for directions).

Network with other Lower Valley entrepreneurs over wine, beer, or cider and goodies!

Bring your menus, your brochures, your business cards to share!

If you want to bring an edible or potable sample of your product, feel free.

Looking forward to meeting you,

Miranda Breitner, Innkeeper.

CHAPTER 22

Guest book: "This is the first guest book I've ever written in. My mom says this place is awesome. The rooms and the food and the cost are all awesome but if you ask me the awsomest thing is Rusty. He's so gentel. I petted him a lot." Gary Howes

She was delighted when almost a dozen folks showed up, not counting Darlene, Pauline, Nelson, and Rosemarie who offered to come "in case nobody else does." The people who did stop by were a lively crew, eager to compare notes and share strategies for attracting clients while they nibbled muffins and scones with tea or washed them down with the cider Darlene and Nelson brought from a nearby mill. Some sampled wine that a new vintner provided, which complemented a longtime local cheese maker's contribution. Oskar Hindgrout walked in with a few jars of jam and a frown, muttering about murderers until Miranda handed him a sugarless cupcake and suggested he lighten up.

Annette showed up with tira misu and Dylan, her small son. Unfortunately, at the sight of Rusty bounding to greet them, the boy stopped short at the door, eyes wide and lips quivering. He refused to cross the threshold until Miranda banished poor Rusty to her second floor apartment. Reassured, Dylan came in, sampled a ginger scone, and fell asleep on the bed in front of the TV in the one empty guest room that Miranda pronounced open for inspection. The mayor of Sunnyvale sent his regrets along with the promise of an extra supply of town maps.

After they all left, Miranda surveyed the used glasses, coffee cups, plates, and crumpled napkins and declared the event a success. Heading up the stairs to liberate Rusty and take him out, she heard the doorbell. She assumed it was Annette returning to collect the mittens little Dylan dropped on his way out, so she ran down to let her in.

But it wasn't Annette. It was Detective Alex Ladin stinking of beer. Brushing up against her, he strode in as if his arrival needed no explanation and he needed no invitation. "Looks like you had quite a party here. Sorry I'm late." He shed his jacket, and when she didn't move to take it, dropped it on a stool.

"It was an open house and now I've got to clean up. My B & B guests are due back soon and I don't want them to return to this mess." She wanted him gone, but she sensed that telling him so would work against her.

"Yeah, I saw your overnight guests leave. All four of them. Said they were going to dinner at Heritage U and to hear some lecture. I gave them directions. They'll be gone awhile." His voice was low, menacing. How long had he been lurking outside, waiting for her open house guests and her B & B guests to clear out? Her gut clenched.

"Any new leads on Isaac Markowitz's killer?" She asked only because he might think it odd if she didn't. She hoped to keep up the pretense that he was calling on police business.

"Yeah." He looked around, eyeing her as she bustled about collecting dishes and glassware and stacking them above the dishwasher. Apparently in no hurry and unconcerned about whether or not his presence was appreciated, the detective ambled over to the counter. He surveyed the room again, toying with a glass empty of all but ice, sliding it from hand to hand along the countertop.

The rattle of the ice in that glass made the hairs on Miranda's arms bristle as they had when she'd seen the rattler that day in Cowiche Canyon. She tried to keep her voice from trembling. "I'm glad there are new leads. I know you can't talk about them, but I'm glad there's some progress."

"Yeah." His second one syllable answer made it very clear that Detective Ladin wasn't there on police business. "So what kinda party was it?" He waved the glass at the stacks of plates.

"Like I said, it was an open house. I'm still trying to get the word about this place out to local business people. I wanted them to see the renovation. Most folks remember this B & B as a ramshackle old farmhouse. I wanted them to see this room and the breakfast setup and a typical guest room." She knew she was babbling, but she couldn't stop. "And I asked them to bring some of their own promotional material for me to share with guests." She pointed to the basket of pamphlets and business cards and began to name the people who brought them. The detective came around the counter and flipped carelessly through the flyers. She was only partway down her list when he jerked his head up and cut into her recitation. "Hey, where's your hound? Wasn't he invited to the party either?"

"Thanks for reminding me." Still jabbering, she turned to climb the stairs. "One of the guests brought her son and he's scared of dogs, so I had to lock poor Rusty in my apartment." Even as these words tumbled out of her mouth, she knew they were wrong. She tried to negate them. "His mom just phoned. She'll be here any minute. The kid left his gloves." She turned and pointed, this time to the small green mittens at the end of the counter.

Undeterred, the detective grabbed Miranda's extended arm and yanked her down the step she'd climbed. He pulled her so close to him she had to breathe his acrid breath. "Don't worry. She won't get in. Looks like we finally got a few minutes to ourselves." He pinned her arm behind her so that her back arched, thrusting her breasts against him. She felt his hard-on pressing her stomach, his breath hot in her ear. She tried pushing him away with her free hand, but he swatted it aside and pawed at her chest. She swallowed a scream. There was no one to hear her but Rusty who was barking.

Continuing to hold one arm behind her back, the detective pushed her to the open guest room and shoved her inside. Rusty's barks were muted. Miranda stood there, numb, dumb, and still as a statue, her spirit breaking along familiar fault lines. He tore open her long denim skirt and pulled it down and off with his free hand. He ripped off her panties with a force that propelled her backward, closer to the bed. "There's your red hair." His voice turned husky. "I remember that head of hair you had. I bet you had on knee socks back then too. You wore glasses." During Detective Ladin's nostalgic monologue, Miranda stood naked below the waist except for socks and boots, passive as a paper doll, waiting for him to pull a gun and rape her.

Finally he released her arm. Her relief was tempered by the realization that he too had both hands free. "Hey, Red, stop acting like you don't want it. You want it alright and you want it rough. I know you do, just like I know you'll keep your mouth shut." With one hand he pulled her sweater over her head and dropped it while with the other hand he opened his fly. He stepped out of his jeans and jockey shorts. She heard a thud as they hit the floor. She knew denim and jersey don't thud, hoped that thud was the sound of his gun hitting the wooden floor. Before she could look, he scooped her up and hurled her onto the bed where she landed hard, limbs akimbo. She heard his next words as a low, scornful hiss. "You'll keep your mouth shut, won't you, Meryl?" Reminding his captive of his hold on her further aroused the detective.

But hearing her birth name on the lips of this pig also aroused Miranda, infused her with adrenaline, and reminded her that she wasn't a naive and helpless thirteen-year-old girl anymore. She was a grown woman, furious, fierce. She didn't have to lie there and let another cop literally fuck her over. No. That wasn't going to happen. She had a promise to keep.

As the leering detective followed his penis to the bed, Miranda sat up, reached behind her, unhooked her bra, flicked it aside, and leaned back on her elbows. She heard his breath catch, saw his eyes widen at her unexpected and seductively deliberate display of her big and beautiful breasts. Focused on them, he didn't notice her bend one of her strong runner's legs until he lowered himself and she kicked him in the balls as hard as she could.

Even as he fell to the floor spitting out the words "Goddamn Jew cunt" over and over, Miranda was on her feet grabbing her skirt, praying her keys and cell phone were still in its pocket. She snatched up his jeans too, but she didn't stop to look for the gun. From the doorway, she pulled her cell phone out of her skirt pocket and snapped a photo of the half-naked lawman writhing and cursing on the floor. Then she locked the room door and sprinted across the lobby. With not a second to spare, she took the stairs to her apartment two at a time and liberated Rusty.

On their way out of the B & B, Miranda pulled on her skirt and held it up with one hand while seizing her parka and Rusty's leash from the hook at the door. She and Rusty took off in her truck. Looking over her shoulder and shaking, she made straight for the Sunnyvale police station a couple of miles away. En route she called 911. She was afraid her voice would break and garble her words, but it didn't. Instead, her successful escape made her voice strong and her message clear. "This is Miranda Breitner of Breitner's B & B in Sunny-vale. Yakima County Sheriff's Deputy Detective Alex Ladin just tried to rape me at my B & B. I kicked him in the groin, locked him in one of my guest rooms, and left. I think he's armed. I'm not safe while he's free and neither are my four guests who're due back soon. I'm driving myself to the police station in Sunnyvale as I speak. My B & B guests need police protection. Now. Tell the cops to break the window nearest the front door if that door is locked."

She parked in front of the police station and ran into the squat stone bunk-er-like building with Rusty at her side. Approaching the desk sergeant, she reached into her parka pocket, pulled out her cell phone and clicked on the photo of half-naked Yakima County Sheriff's Deputy Alex Ladin in the fetal position on the floor of a guest room at Breitner's B & B. She slapped the phone down on the counter without letting go of it. "This sheriff's deputy just tried to rape me." Sergeant Cruz took only one look before Miranda snatched her phone back. "I'm Miranda Breitner."

"Yes, Ma'am. I just sent two officers to your B & B."

CHAPTER 23

Guest book: "This place is homey and the grub's good. And it's a magnet for good lookin gals. The manager's cute enough and nice, but I saw a gal at breakfast who really rocked my world. With scenery like that, who cares if somebody got killed across the street? I'll be back next year." Joecowboy Philadephia, PA

As they talked, the new chief, a serious looking fifty-something man with the loose jowls of someone who'd lost a lot of weight updated her. "According to my officers, he's gone from your B & B, Ms Breitner. But I'm ordering those two men to collect evidence and stand watch there. May I see your photo?"

While keeping her cell phone in one hand, along with the waistband of her skirt and Rusty's leash, she flicked the image to enlarge it with the other and she held it out for the chief to look at.

He rubbed his forehead and sighed. "That's Sheriff's Deputy Detective Alex Ladin all right. How did he get into your place?

"I let him in. I met him when he began investigating the murder of Isaac Markowitz at the plant across the street. He's made moves on me before tonight and threatened to blackmail me when I didn't comply. I tried to discourage him, but I guess I didn't succeed. Also tonight he smelled of beer when he showed up. And he had no police business to bring him to my place."

Chief Walters gave his forehead another rub.

"Chief Walters, what if…"

He looked her in the eye. "Don't worry, Ma'am. He won't bother you again. We've got this. We're going to hunt him down and bring him in. Take a seat, please." He pointed to a lone chair in the nearly empty lobby of the station. "This is the best seat in the house. It's not very private, but it's more comfortable than a bench in the back."

She sat.

"I've already got another two officers tracking him, and we put out an APB. Meanwhile, Ms Breitner, when we get him, we're keeping him right here in Sunnyvale's guest facilities until I have a chat with Sheriff Carson." He hesitated. "Attempted rape is above my pay grade. It's the sheriff's territory. But given that the accused is one of his deputies… Anyway, right now, the sheriff's way up in Naches dealing with some bodies that turned up in a car in a ditch near the river." He shook his head, causing his jowls to sway. "We work with Sheriff Carson, count on his deputies for backup, so we gotta do this by the book, right? We gotta do the paperwork. You say you're pressing charges? "

"Yes." Miranda made her voice loud and clear.

"Good." The chief scratched his head and lowered it just a little. "I don't have a lady here to ask you, but do you have any bruises or cuts or other evidence of physical injury?"

"No. I have my ripped skirt, his jeans and shorts, and a sore shoulder. I didn't fight back until I thought I had a chance of winning." Miranda realized that what she said was true but that it made her sound a lot more experienced with fighting off rapists than she was. She wondered where the words came from.

"I'll get Sergeant Cruz to bring the paperwork out here. What do you take in your coffee? It could be a long night."

"Black is good. Thanks." Miranda couldn't explain it, but she actually felt almost safe in the company of this courteous and seemingly conscientious police officer. He wasn't Olivia Benson, and this small town police station wasn't exactly *Law and Order's SVU*, but at least he knew and wanted to follow proper police procedures.

The Chief turned around and spoke again. "It's bad that cops all over the country are disgracing the uniform. When the public loses confidence in us, it's even harder for the good cops to do their job. And that's not good for the public."

Miranda nodded and let him have his *Blue Bloods* moment. He left her to tremble at her narrow escape, to wish she had on underwear, and to mutter to her dog. Rusty hadn't taken his usual position prone at her feet but stood close enough to her chair to rest his head in her lap. "Jesus, Rusty, that was close. And it's my fault. I never should have locked you up. I'm so sorry." As she violated her vow not to ever become one of those people who talks to her dog, she caressed Rusty's ears and leaned over to kiss the bony spot between them.

Still holding onto the waistband of her skirt, she sipped her coffee. "Remember when that pig first came to the B & B and you shat on his shoes? You never liked him, did you? Somehow you knew. I should've read a little more into that shit 'cause you're a good judge of character, right?" She kissed him between the ears again. "Damn, Rusty, I need a safety pin. Hey, who'm I kidding? I need a whole new life. Again. That's what I need, don't I?" Rusty licked her hand. "But I fended off a rapist! So I shouldn't be sitting here feeling sorry for myself, should I?" Sergeant Cruz interrupted her one-way conversation when he presented her with a clipboard loaded with papers for her to fill out.

As she wrote, police officers brought in a couple of heavily-tattooed young men in handcuffs. Later on, other officers escorted in a cursing stoop-shouldered older woman with a black eye. And finally two cops herded in four young men who couldn't walk a straight line and whose wild eyes screamed drugs. She stopped writing to eavesdrop on the arresting officers talking to Sergeant Cruz. One of the four had driven their vehicle into a truck which burst into flames. The driver was badly burned and apples covered the road, "like a red carpet, I swear." The arresting officers led their prisoners into the back of the station, presumably to be interrogated or to await legal counsel. To her surprise, Miranda was not unduly upset by the presence of these typical police doing their typical police work.

After she and Rusty had been there for well over an hour, Chief Walters approached and handed her a fresh cup of hot coffee. "Good news, Ms Breitner! A guy in a supermarket parking lot near Ellensburg called 911. Said while he was putting his groceries in his trunk. a half-naked man got out of a Sheriff's vehicle and hit him over the head. Maybe with the butt of a gun. When he came to, his pants, groceries, car keys, and his car, an old blue RAV 4, were gone and the sheriff's deputy's vehicle was there with the door open and the motor running."

Miranda nodded and sat there still stroking Rusty in silence and wondering if she should call Harry or Pauline. She was grateful that she had friends she could rely on, but she could handle this herself. Harry had enough on his plate. This was not the time to bombard him with news of this evening's horror. And it was too late to call Pauline who'd wake Nelson and insist on them both coming to the station with clothes and food. Tempting as that prospect was, Miranda recognized it as selfish, too. So she just sat there shivering, muttering, caressing her dog's ear, and waiting.

Chief Walters finally returned. "Now we're really getting somewhere. A state trooper just reported seeing a blue RAV 4 turn onto a maintenance road leading to the Cascades. Those roads are closed for the winter. Maybe your alleged assailant's got a cabin up there or something."

Miranda felt her stomach cramp at the word *alleged.* Didn't Chief Walters believe her? What if Alex Ladin succeeded in discrediting her and no one believed her? She forced herself to listen.

"Anyway, this trooper got ahold of my officers and they all pursued the Toyota and caught up with it, because, wait for it, Ms Breitner, it ran out of gas! The guy he stole it from said he'd planned to gas up on his way home. What a lucky break that was! For us, not for Ladin. He gave himself up. My officers arrested him on charges of sexual harassment, sexual assault, and attempted rape. And I'm no lawyer, but from what you told me and wrote, there may be a blackmail charge in there too. Oh, and the guy he assaulted and whose car he stole is also pressing several charges."

Miranda felt tears of relief welling and she kept listening.

"They're bringing him in, and he's our guest here tonight. So you two can go home now and talk to my officers there and take care of your visitors and get some sleep. You've had a hellish night." He hesitated. "And thanks for pressing charges, Ms Breitner. The gang's victims and their families are almost always reluctant to press charges. It's understandable but very discouraging. You're setting a great example."

"I'm just doing what it takes to put him behind bars, not behind a badge."

Chief Walters' jowls danced again as he shook his head. "Like I said before, these days it seems cops like him are the only ones making the news, and they give the rest of us a real bad smell."

Miranda and Rusty returned to her B & B. Her heart sank at the sight of the telltale yellow tape at the door even as she slipped under it. She immediately fed her hungry dog and put on some more clothes. She gave the Sunnyvale officers her torn skirt and the water glass Ladin had handled. These officers had already photographed her bra, sweater, and ripped panties in the vacant room where they lay, silently corroborating her account. They bagged and tagged these items. Next they showed her the shot-up lock on the door of that room and pointed to a bullet lodged in the hall floor and the broken frame of the window that the fugitive had forced open to use as an escape hatch. Because that window was already shattered, one of the officers had climbed through it to enter the building and then opened the front door for the other. These thorough investigators photographed the lock and the bullet and then dislodged and bagged the slug to take away with them. They agreed with Miranda that Ladin had come into the lobby to look for his pants and get his jacket but when his pants weren't there, he had decided that leaving via the front door would expose his bare butt to too many folks driving by. They photographed the broken window frame. They took more photos, nosed about a little longer, and finally left, taking the yellow tape with them.

Only then could Miranda attend to her befuddled and worried guests who'd returned, been herded into their rooms, and emerged to mill about the lobby. She chatted with them while she finished bringing dirty dishes to the counter and began to arrange them in the dishwasher.

"Was there another murder?" The water management expert who'd spoken at Heritage U wanted to know. "Did that kosherer's killer come back?"

"No. There was no murder here tonight and, as far as I know, Isaac Markowitz's killer has not shown up in this area again."

"So why were the police here? Something sure as hell went on here tonight." The plumber planning to retire and move to the Valley "to grow a few grapes" was curious too.

"Earlier this evening a Yakima County sheriff's deputy attempted to rape me. I, uh, seriously discouraged him, locked him in the empty guest room, and fled with my dog."

"How did you "discourage him?" Are you okay?" The water expert's wife's voice quavered.

Miranda looked up from loading the dishwasher and caught the woman's eye. "I channeled Jane Rizzoli and kicked him in the balls. That incapacitated him long enough for Rusty and me to leave." The water expert and his wife, apparently *Rizzoli and Isles* fans, chuckled audibly and they all clapped.

"What the hell's the matter with your dog?" The other guest, a blogger concerned with Western water issues shot a disapproving glance at Rusty and addressed his next question to him. "Why didn't you take down this creep? You're big enough."

Miranda sighed. "Don't blame him. I held an open house here earlier and a guest's child is afraid of dogs, so I locked Rusty in upstairs. That was my mistake." She shook her head, sprayed the counter with vinegar and water, and started wiping it down.

"Don't blame yourself, either. Are you sure you're okay?" The woman sounded genuinely worried.

Miranda looked around her at the once-again orderly and inviting space and the kindly inquiring faces. "I'm okay, but I'm done for tonight. I'm going to walk Rusty, take a shower, and go to bed. Again, thanks for your concern. I'm sorry you were alarmed and inconvenienced."

As much to prove to herself that she was okay as to give Rusty a little air and exercise, Miranda swapped her boots for her running shoes, kissed her mezuzah, and left. Once outside with her companion so close to her leg she feared he'd pee on her foot, she called Harry. When he didn't pick up, she left word. "This message is for my lawyer. Tonight County Sheriff's Deputy Alex Ladin came to the B & B and tried to rape me. I got away and called 911. I told the Sunnyvale cops I'm pressing charges against Ladin for at least assault and attempted rape. I'm fine and he's in jail here. He'll try to deny the charges by discrediting me. So I'll need your legal services again. It's after midnight now and I'm going to bed. Hope the place you and Holly visited today turns out to be a really good fit for your dad. Good night."

She ran with Rusty through Sunnyvale's quiet streets, some fringed with willows, others bordered by canals. When she saw how the occasional street-lights and headlights transformed trees and buildings into dark shadows on the white snow, she wondered yet again if this valley she'd thought so Edenesque wasn't really "the valley of the shadow of death." But when she and Rusty jogged past the convenience store and the owner, alone for once, returned her wave, she felt better. After all, she'd fought off a brute and said brute was in jail. And with Ladin out of the picture and her Crime Stoppers' tips to work from, it wouldn't be long before the sheriff put Isaac Markowitz's killer behind bars too.

Home again, she organized her breakfast foods, showered for a long, long time, and went to bed. She was afraid sleep, if it came at all, would be troubled by redos of Ladin's attack or dire imaginings of what would happen when he used her past felony arrest and history of suicidal depression to cast doubt on her credibility. She thought about how this latest blow to her reputation and the B & B's, not to mention Isaac's still unsolved murder, would make it impossible for her to make good on her promise to her mother. But instead of keeping her awake, her mechanical listing of these familiar fears, a litany worn to dullness by repetition and no longer even entirely plausible, actually lulled her into a deep, restorative sleep.

CHAPTER 24

Guest book: "Miranda Breitner, Innkeeper, is a smart and gutsy modern woman and she runs an excellent B&B! Helen and I will be back to enjoy the comfortable accommodations and stimulating atmosphere here." John Drew, Water Guy

Local Innkeeper Says Sheriff's Deputy Attempted Rape...

Sunnyvale PD Arrests Armed Sheriff's Deputy ...No Shots Fired

Man Charges Sheriff's Deputy and Accused Rapist with Assault, Theft...

Three Lower Valley Teens Claim Sheriff's Deputy Raped Them...

Miranda couldn't quite believe it, but the fancy footwork that had felled her would-be rapist synced with the general public's growing awareness of the overly aggressive behavior of some police towards Indians, immigrants, and other Valley underdogs to make her a local celebrity-heroine almost overnight. At Pauline and Nelson's groaning Thanksgiving table, she upstaged even the impressive turkey. Before they dug into the holiday meal, the Thurston family and their guests took turns expressing gratitude for their blessings. Pauline, a patina of sweat making her face radiant, was last to emerge from the kitchen and take her place at the table. She was the first to speak. "Thank you, Jesus, for your bounty this year, for our good health, for the mountain snowpack that watered our fields this summer, and for allowing us all to be here together today. And thank you for seeing to it that this year everyone at this table who wants to work has a job. And, last but not least, thank you, Jesus, for bringing Miranda Breitner into our lives and for protecting her from those who would do her harm."

Nelson, as usual, did not waste words. "Thank you, Jesus, for our health, our sun, our water, and for making sure this season's cherry pickers didn't get held up by immigration." He contracted his brow, as if he'd forgotten something, and then, apparently remembering, added, "And thanks for those Hawks." A chorus of amens followed.

The young woman across from Miranda, Pauline's sister-in-law, thanked Jesus for extinguishing a record-breaking wildfire in the adjacent county just hours before it would have destroyed her home. She also thanked him for, so far, preserving the life of her brother on his second deployment in Iraq. It occurred to Miranda that she was not the only one who'd had a stressful year.

But it was the young, fresh-faced guy sitting on her left whose words stirred her most. When he took a seat next to her, he'd introduced himself as Matthew Curtis, a friend of Pauline's nephew. He'd said he was a recent graduate of the Valley's first college for health care professionals and a new nurse at Sunnyvale Hospital. "Jesus, thank you for giving me the chance to earn a living helping sick and injured people. And also thank you for making that disrupting and pointless investigation at my workplace finally go away." Remembering his manners, he added, "Also thank you for this delicious-looking meal and the good company."

Miranda had no chance to ask him about the investigation he'd mentioned before it was her turn. She spoke softly, diffidently, addressing her remarks to her tablemates. "I'm really thankful to be invited here today, to have Pauline and Nelson as friends, and to meet all of you. Another new friend is my dog Rusty. I'm very thankful for him. And also for my good health and strength. And for the guests who come to stay at my B & B." Out of deference to the children at the table she didn't mention how grateful she was to have fended off a brutal rapist.

When everyone had said thank-you and they were all eagerly heaping food on their plates, Miranda held a bowl of string beans while Matthew served them both. "That investigation you mentioned, Matthew, I don't recall seeing anything about it in the *Yakima Herald-Republic.*"

"I've been complaining about it to my friends for weeks, but, understandably, the hospital downplayed it with the press. Out of nowhere, a detective came to investigate our hospital pharmacy for not reporting the theft of a toxin. Clearly this dude thought one of us had ripped off a med, and he challenged our record keeping. He grilled the pharmacy staff and all medical and custodial people for days." Matthew kept talking as he plopped mashed sweet potatoes on each of their plates. "Everybody was suspicious of everybody else. I was sure I was going to lose my job." When she frowned, he shrugged and explained. "You know, last hired, first fired. But this guy wasn't too interested in me. He interrogated this one nurse four times for hours, but she didn't do it. I guess they really got to her though because just yesterday the poor woman quit."

Miranda nodded. "Wow! So what did they find?"

"Nada. What happened is finally the president of the Hospital Board called Lisa, our pharmacy tech honcho and that woman took one for the team. She actually came in from maternity leave with her six-week-old infant! In a few hours, not counting when she was breastfeeding, Lisa untangled the mess the temp made. And she printed out inventory data going forward from the time period in question up until that day, to the hour. Of course the data stream matched up with the stuff in the supply closet every time and showed that every pill and mil of medication was where it was supposed to be and always had been. At Sunnyvale Hospital we're actually very proud of how carefully we control our drugs. The sheriff apologized. Said they'd been following a bad lead."

"Well, I know how disturbing it is to have the cops messing around in your workplace and how much trouble they can cause when they get it wrong." She hesitated and tried to squeeze one more detail out of Matthew. "I know a nurse who works there. She treated me for a bad cut once. Tammy something…"

"Well, for Pete's sake! She's the one. Isn't that something that you should know her?"

"Sunnyvale is a really small town."

"Yeah. You're right. I'm from Boise." He made a grab for the gravy bowl and Miranda spooned some onto his plate. She obliged when he said, "Don't hold back. Pauline is famous for this gravy. And her dressing too. "

Miranda enjoyed meeting Pauline and Nelson's children and grandkids and the other lucky relatives and friends who were regulars at this gathering. After stuffing themselves with turkey and fixings, the kids cleared the table and retired to a bedroom to watch TV. The men took over the kitchen where they divided the leftovers and did the dishes, occasionally glancing at the football game on somebody's laptop. The women settled in the living room to sip wine or cider and chat. This was clearly a time for digesting. Dessert would come later.

After they had critiqued each dish that had been on the table, apparently a ritual, Pauline's sister Pearl hit Miranda with a question. "Miranda, Pauline filled us in on how you fought off that big detective." She shuddered. "I'm glad you did, because you won. But I read that if someone tries to rape you and you even think he's armed, you're supposed to submit to save your life. So why didn't you submit?"

Miranda, usually so secretive, was astounded to hear herself say, "Pearl, I'm really glad you asked me that." And she was. Although she'd never given birth, that Thanksgiving Day Miranda felt there was something in her heart ready to burst out, a dybbuk perhaps. She looked around at the women, all Evangelical Christians and most of whom she'd just met. These kind and friendly people did not know from *dybbuks* and so were unlikely midwives, but they would serve. They had to. A wall around her heart was breaking, and she could feel warm tears leaking down her cheeks.

"Pearl, you're making her cry."

Miranda snatched the Kleenex Pauline handed her and pushed herself to insist. "No, I'm okay. Really." She blew her nose, as if that ability proved her fitness. "So, Pearl, do you want the long answer or the short one?"

"The long one." The others nodded. Pat, Pauline's other sister, put down her knitting.

"Well, when I was thirteen…" They were still sitting there an hour later when Miranda finished describing her concern for Timmy, her arrest and interrogation, how she was arrested and charged with shaking the little boy to death. She explained that the detectives had not followed procedure when informing her of her rights and also how the judge decreed there was no evidence to justify bringing her to trial. She laid out her years as a pariah, her cutting, her suicide attempt, and then she talked about her grandma, her mother and father, their divorce, and her schooling. The women sat riveted, taking in every word, sometimes nodding, other times shaking their heads, dabbing their own eyes. When Miranda recounted suing Seattle PD and winning, everyone clapped. Finally, when she detailed her makeover and her move to the Valley, they cheered.

"So all this is why I had to fight back. I wasn't going to let another bad cop literally screw me over as if I were still a helpless kid. Been there. Done that."

"Did you pray on it? While you were lying on that bed deciding what to do?" Pauline really wanted to know.

"I didn't have to. I'd heard that gun drop. If I just lay there and let that bastard rape me, I'd die inside. I was fighting for my life. And I'm Jewish and we believe every human life is sacred." The "J" word had slid out like afterbirth. That's when Miranda realized she no longer felt pregnant. Instead she felt reborn, new. Pauline, Pat, Pearl and the others began to chat about experiences of their own her story had evoked. When Nelson interrupted to announce dessert, they kept talking as they made their way back to the table.

On Saturday of the holiday weekend, after the last B & B guest left for the morning, Miranda and Harry savored a cup of coffee.

"I'm glad you "came out" to all those folks. You've been so caught up in your own secrets, you haven't even asked me about mine."

"I didn't know you had any."

He took her hand. "Everybody does. You know, you're the first woman I've ever dated who didn't quiz me about my ex."

"You're right. Should I start?"

"Yes, but not today. Today you should know that I hate the thought of how much and how long you suffered because of those bullheaded cops. And I really hate that bastard who attacked you the other night. I hate that you had to go through that. You must have been so scared to get so brave."

"I was scared until I got mad. It makes me mad all over again to learn that that man was repeatedly raping underage girls by threatening to report their parents to immigration." She slapped the newspaper on the counter where, earlier that morning, she'd seen that headline. "I bet that creep had some terrible childhood trauma of his own to make him so screwed up. But I can't start feeling sorry for him." She refilled each of their coffee cups. "Anyway, enough about me. I did all the talking last night, and I'm still at it. Tell me, how's Julia? Your dad? How was your Thanksgiving? It had to be hard for all of you without your Mom. "

She saw Harry blink, and when he spoke, he didn't mention his mother or the holiday meal. "Julia told Holly and my dad that you're a Hanukah person and she wants to have you with us when we light the menorah. And I want you to meet the rest of my family, at least my dad and Holly."

"I'd love to. When you give me a date, I'll sign up Darlene. How's your search for a place for your dad to live going? I guess it's on hold for the weekend. That's frustrating."

"What's really frustrating is making my sister understand how frail and far gone my father is now, what kind of care he needs. He doesn't need a place with trips to the theater, flower arranging classes, and trendy food. He's eighty-eight and his heart is weak. His mind is, too, and his arthritis is bad, and his hearing's shot. Christ, he can't always make it to the toilet. And he's stubborn." Harry lowered his head and mumbled, "He needs a place where some kind, strong, patient person can be with him most of the time and help him get through the day like my mom did. He keeps asking where she is."

Miranda kept quiet, sensing there was more.

"This afternoon Holly and I are interviewing a new caregiver to stay with him while she's at work. The last one quit on Wednesday. And we have to talk about selling the condo." He sighed. "So I really gotta go." He kissed her. "Please take care of yourself. And don't worry about that hospital snafu. I'm betting the FBI will be involved soon. And one bad lead won't stop those guys. It'll motivate them. You'll see. If there was supposed to be a poisoning, they'll find out." He gave Rusty a final head scratch. "Now go answer your fan mail."

To Miranda's astonishment, she actually had fan mail. Although heavily populated by underdogs, the Valley wasn't exactly a leader in the struggle for civil rights. But when one of those underdogs stood up for herself, her action struck a chord with the others. She figured that was why as soon as news about Ladin's attempt to rape her got out, PE teachers at both Sunnyvale and Topp-penish High Schools invited her to speak on self-defense for women and girls and Pauline's church wanted her to participate in a panel on that topic for their Ladies Auxiliary. A Heritage University prof asked her to address her women's study students. Even Rabbi Golden pressed her to write an article for Temple Shalom's newsletter on how her Jewish background helped her escape rape. "You could title it 'Nice Jewish Girl Kicks Ass.'" Miranda's favorite invitation came from the new owner of the old Western wear shop in Union Gap where she'd bought her cowboy boots. He wanted her to model them and be the spokesperson in the store's ad on local TV. "We're announcing our new slogan, 'Boots on the Ground.'"

She decided to put off accepting these invitations and setting dates until after the holiday weekend. Just then she wanted to know more about why Nurse Tammy was quitting her job. So as soon as Harry left she tore through her chores and ran with Rusty. As they passed Darlene's house she waved to Josefina and her grandma who were building a snowman. Miranda hollered,

"Back soon. Tea?" Seeing Josefina playing outside on Darlene's front lawn prepared Miranda for the closed blinds and *To Rent* sign on the lawn of the pumpkin house. A couple of the property's signature orange globes lay smashed in the snow below the front steps while a lone jack-o'-lantern sagged sadly next to the door.

This was the first thing Miranda commented on later when she and Rusty were warm and snug in Darlene's kitchen and the women were sipping tea with Josefina and her doll. "Yes, they're gone, those tenants! It's some kind of miracle. I left for Spokane to bring Josefina here for the weekend and when we got back the house looked like now. The sign was up, the place was empty. Nobody around here knows why they left."

Miranda figured that the FBI's hospital investigators' intense scrutiny of Tammy had warned the nurse and her husband. Even though Tammy hadn't stolen poison, once Steve Galen was arrested both she and her husband could be charged with harboring a killer and planning a hate crime. They were on the run. "I'm glad they're gone. Tell me about your Thanksgiving. How was it without Javier?"

"Our holidays are always a little, you know, a little sad. Geraldo's chair is empty. Now Javier's is too…. But my whole family thanked God that you're safe." She shuddered and began to button her sweater. "That detective was a bully. He really wanted to get his hands on Javier. He said if Javi would just come back and confess to killing that kosherer he'd get a reduced sentence. But if they had to wait, he'd get life or the death penalty. That man sat right in that chair where you are now for an hour every day for weeks and watched me cry."

Josefina patted Darlene's shoulder. "Don't cry, abuela. Javi's okay."

Miranda registered the girl's remark and the quick headshake it evoked from Darlene. It was tempting to tell her friend that wherever she had stashed him, her grandson was no longer suspected of killing Isaac Markowitz. But that would be premature. Instead she said, "We don't have to worry about Alex Ladin anymore. He's the one going to jail. He won't even get bail." Then she spoke to the girl and her doll. "Josefina, tell me, did you ever dunk your churro in your cocoa? It's really delicious that way." And she demonstrated.

She left Darlene's place frustrated again by the snail-going-backward pace of the investigation into Isaac's murder. She hoped that perhaps the FBI detectives were making more progress than they were revealing to the press and tried to put it out of her mind. She answered her e-mail, paid bills, and went grocery shopping. It was while in line at the supermarket that Miranda con-sulted her phone and read a post by a local blogger. "According to an anony-mous source close to the investigation of the murder of Isaac Markowitz, a witness has come forward with new information about the identity of the young man's killer and is willing to testify! She says she was inspired by the "*cojones* of that Breitner woman."" Miranda was elated. While the clerk rang up and bagged her order, she checked obits to see if a certain old woman living in Sunnyvale had died of cancer recently. There had been several such deaths, but only one that took place at the home of the deceased's daughter with that daughter in attendance. That night Miranda told Harry, "Now that her mother's no longer in danger of being deported, Carmen's doing what's right."

"The FBI could have shown Carmen photos already and they could be arresting Isaac's killer right now. Then you can really kick back and put this whole thing behind you."

"Oh no I can't. I still think Galen went to the processing plant to poison wine, to kill or sicken lots of Jews, not just to kill one. But let's not argue about that again." She hesitated. Harry found her insistence on this point unreasonable. Should she be worried? No. Couples weren't always in accord on everything. "How did the interview go? And the meeting with the realtor?" Before he could answer, Miranda heard the doorbell ring. "Somebody's at the door. Gotta go. Talk later."

Even without the gold star on his chest and the requisite white cowboy hat, Miranda would have found Sheriff Ethan Carson a formidable figure because of his size and stance. Although only about five-ten, the lawman stood tall in the B & B doorway, his boots planted below substantial hips, his hands bracketing those hips, and his gray eyes busy sizing up a place he clearly felt he had every right to be. His all-business crew cut was a faded brown with just a few flecks of gray. Girded with a gun and assorted gadgets, his midsection threatened her door-jamb as he made his way in.

"Yakima County Sheriff Ethan Carson here. Ms Breitner?" He extended a hand, not to her, but to Rusty who sniffed it and registered acceptance if not approval by retreating to his cushion. Miranda, who once recoiled at the sight of a badge, was pleased to see Sheriff Carson. Maybe she could pry out of him a shred of information about the slower-than-frozen-molasses investigation into Isaac Markowitz's murder.

"Forgive me for bargin' in without callin'. I won't be long, but I wanted to tell you myself how bad I feel about the, uh, alleged behavior of my soon-to-be former deputy." His tone was apologetic, humble. He lowered his head for a moment while gripping his hat in both hands and revolving it.

"I appreciate your apology, Sheriff." This was an understatement. Miranda, who had thought she'd never see the day a cop acknowledged, let alone apologized for his own or his underlings' screw ups, took special pleasure in the sheriff's hat-in-hand *mea culpa*. Even so, she thought Sheriff Carson ought to be out trying to find Isaac's murderer instead of there at her B & B apologizing.

Having said what he said he'd come to say, the sheriff looked around. "Nice job you did here. I hope that killin' across the street didn't cause you too much grief. Terrible thing."

"Actually, it did. It still does. I grieve for the victim and his family. Isaac Markowitz was very young and newly married." She considered stopping there, but she didn't. "Another thing is, Sheriff, I'm Jewish, so it scares me knowing there's still a killer on the loose, especially one who targets Jews. Not to mention that having someone murdered right across the street and his killer still at large has been very hard on my business."

"Then you'll be glad to learn that with Detective Ladin shall we say, "otherwise occupied," I've taken over the investigation myself. It won't be long before that young man's killer is in custody. And, Ms Breitner, for once the press got it right about that witness you inspired to come forward. She sure is a big help." He glanced at her, his eyes newly narrowed, probing.

Sheriff Carson's scrutiny made Miranda wonder if he'd come not to apologize for having hired a sicko rapist but rather to size her up, get something from her. Had Carmen Esposito mentioned her visit? Did the sheriff suspect that she was the one supplying Crime Stoppers with leads? She felt a chill run through her. If he suspected her, Steve Galen could too. After all, who else had a bird's-eye view of the processing plant parking lot, would have spotted the telltale smoke signals sent by the unwitting Carmen during each of her forays to the niche to smoke?

Before Miranda could work herself into total panic mode, the doorbell rang again and this time when she opened it Michael Wright walked in. "Michael! I was going to call you. Sheriff Carson, meet my friend Michael Wright. Michael, Sheriff Carson." The two men nodded at one another warily, each no doubt recalling the sheriff's deputy's attempts to pin Isaac's murder on Michael or his grandfather when the family fish club turned up covered in blood at the crime scene. Sheriff Carson did not apologize to Michael for the careless detective work that led to that fiasco.

"Hey, Ms Breitner. Glad you're okay. Me and my sister think you're a warrior! And we heard you have a busted lock, a bullet hole in your nice new floor, and a busted window pane and frame." He grimaced at the extent of the damage. "So I'm going to fix them at no cost to you." He hesitated and smiled sheepishly. "Colestah also said I should drill a hole in your front door and put in a peephole so you can check out who's there before you let them in."

Sheriff Carson's nod indicated his unsolicited approval of the peephole.

But it was the clairvoyant Colestah's approval and the siblings' generosity that pleased Miranda. "Thanks, Michael. I didn't want to interfere with your long weekend, so I was waiting until Monday to call you."

"No problem. I need a break from the books. I'm just glad you're okay. What do you want me to start with?"

"That room is booked for tomorrow night, so a new lock and window would be good. I boarded up the window as best I could this morning. I guess you'll have to order a whole new window, right?"

"Most likely."

"Okay. I'll cut the room's per-night charge until it's replaced."

"But meanwhile I can seal it to keep the heat in."

"Great. I'm hoping my insurance company will pony up the cost of repairs. They sent an inspector."

"You can discuss that with my sister. I'll check out the lock and the window and hit Home Depot and be back to seal that window and put in a new lock. I'll repair the floor later in the week." He headed down the corridor to the guest rooms.

"You're a busy woman, and I've taken up enough of your time." The sheriff shifted his considerable weight from one foot to the other as he spoke, so Miranda suspected he had more to say. She was right. "But before I go, would you give me a list of the guests who were here three days before and after the day Isaac Markowitz was killed? I need their contact info too."

Miranda was stunned. She'd sent Steve Galen's contact info to Crime Stoppers. Surely Sheriff Carson didn't think one of her other guests killed Isaac Markowitz. "Yes, I guess so. But why?"

"Routine. After a homicide we knock on the doors of all the neighbors to see if any of them saw anything or heard anything. Detective Ladin should've interviewed each of your guests individually." The sheriff scowled. "Turns out you're the only one he talked to here." He rolled his eyes. "So I'm just tryin' to dot all the i's and cross all the t's and move things along. That's all." He shrugged.

"Why don't you help yourself to a cup of coffee and a gingerbread scone while I print out that list? I have only four rooms here, so it won't take long."

After the sheriff left with the list, scary possibilities whirled around in Miranda's head. It wouldn't take Steve Galen long to figure out that it was she in her crow's-nest who spotted Carmen Esposito and recruited her as a witness. He'd really hate her for this, possibly come after her. Or he might come after Carmen. Then she reassured herself that that snake must be holed up some place where he felt safe, confident that sooner or later the authorities would arrest a gang banger for the murder of Isaac Markowitz. But she couldn't leave it at that for long. Steve would've heard that Tammy was grilled about stealing poison. So he'd know she and her husband had been outed as haters, possibly as collaborators. Thus warned, maybe Steve had already shed his art restorer persona and established a new identity for himself. But by the time Miranda had run with Rusty, baked several batches of cranberry muffins, and caught Harry up on the sheriff's visit, she'd reassured herself that it would be dumb for Steve to return to the scene of his crime in any guise, and he wasn't dumb.

Almost a week later, as Miranda swirled environmentally friendly cleanser around a guest's toilet bowl, she shooed Rusty away. She'd still not managed to cure him of quenching his thirst with *eau de toilette*. She addressed the unrepentant animal sulking in the bathroom doorway. "You just like to push my buttons, don't you? This stuff may not hurt the ecosystem, but it would really mess up yours, trust me." She sponged off the base of the toilet and the rim and was swabbing the seat itself when she flashed on one of the names on the list of guests she'd given the sheriff. Kneeling there on the bathroom floor hyper-aware of Rusty's bad habit, she read new meaning into that name: *Angela Lacey*. The pleasant pregnant pharmaceutical rep came to the Valley wheeling a suitcase full of sample meds to leave with doctors. Angela could have supplied Steve Galen with poison. How hard would it be for a charming pharm rep to get her hands on a chemical suitable for poisoning large quantities of grape juice? Easy peasy.

Sheriff Carson wasn't just dotting his i's and crossing his t's. No, he was trying to figure out if the art restorer had a co-conspirator besides Nurse Tammy and her hubby. Finally, thanks to her Crime Stoppers submission, he was investigating a hate crime as well as a homicide. She hoped the sheriff would do a background check on Angela Lacey, learn how she earned a living, and investigate whether or not she'd provided the poison.

Miranda should have felt elated, but instead she felt a little queasy. The bedroom she'd just aired out had been Steve's. Maybe Angela had given Steve the poison and he'd prepared the toxic concoction right there in the sink she'd just scrubbed. Then maybe he'd flushed away the excess in the very toilet bowl she'd just disinfected. Or not. Maybe he forgot to flush. It amazed her that so many of her guests were averse to flushing. If Rusty'd had a chance, he'd have helped himself to the contents of that toilet. She glanced over at her still pouting pooch and remembered that she'd caught him in the act of drinking from Steve's toilet on the morning Isaac met his death. And she also remembered that Rusty had seemed out of sorts later that day and squirted out liquid shit that evening when Alex Ladin showed up bringing word of the tragedy across the street. Maybe Rusty pooped funny not because of his instant dislike for Alex Ladin, but because he drank poisoned water.

Miranda fled the bathroom, slamming the door behind her, and flew to her laptop. She checked her guest records, looking for the exact date Steve Galen left the B & B. Then she opened the lab report Dr. Cynthia had sent on Rusty's only stool sample, produced shortly after he'd thrown up on the same day Steve Galen checked out. If Isaac Markowitz interrupted Galen before he actually put the poison he and Angela had prepared into the juice enzymes, then surely he'd have gotten rid of the stuff before leaving the B & B. Poor Rusty. She dropped to her knees and threw her arms around her dog.

In the note accompanying the lab report Dr. Cynthia had typed, "Don't worry! He's fine. But try to keep him from eating plants." Miranda felt reassured. The cooler weather and coming snowfalls would make plants scarce anyway. She hadn't even bothered to read the lab report. But reading it after Sheriff Carson's visit, she saw that "Rusty's stool sample contained trace amounts of only one chemical that might have caused him to vomit, oleandrin." Riddled with guilt, she Googled *oleandrin* and learned that it's found in oleander, a flowering shrub originally grown only in Asia. Now this deadly plant is also grown in the US in warm places like California where it's often used to decorate highway dividers. Because dogs have been adversely affected by eating its leaves, oleander is considered part of the dogbane family. Its leaves are also particularly toxic to children.

Recalling how warm and friendly Angela Lacey had seemed, Miranda shuddered and hugged Rusty again. She would know about oleander and be able to get it. How could that woman, a mother-to-be yet, conspire to poison children? Miranda knew she couldn't very well use Crime Stoppers to direct the sheriff to Angela Lacey without risk of revealing her own identity. But if Carson didn't unmask her himself and fast-forward the investigation soon, she might have to.

She finished her chores mechanically, without taking her usual pleasure in the fresh scent of just-dried linen and the reassuringly antiseptic aroma of her vinegar-based cleanser. When Michael arrived with a floorboard and drilled a peephole, she made cheese quesadillas for the two of them. As they ate, she didn't say anything to him about her new insights, but pumped him for news of his classes and of Colestah. When he began to work, the drone of his power tools and the banging of his hammer bugged her, even when she took refuge upstairs. She had to get out of the B & B for a few hours. "Michael, I need a change of scenery. I'm going to take a ride to one of those tourist attractions that I've sent guests to but never visited myself."

"Cool. Which one?"

"The Stonehenge replica in Mary Hill. It's not far, so I'll be back by six. The only new guest coming tonight is due after that." Wearing snow boots and her parka, she leashed Rusty and set out in the truck.

The snow-sprinkled fields and hills glittered in the sunlight so that they looked like what Mona had called "Christmas card scenery." The wind turbines whirling atop the white hills warmed Miranda's eco-friendly heart. But she was sorry not to see any of the wild mustang ponies. There weren't many cars, either. She speculated that a few of the passenger vehicles sharing the road were headed for the Mary Hill Art Museum just a few miles beyond the Stonehenge replica. The acclaimed gallery was on her list too, but that afternoon she wanted to take Rusty with her, and she doubted that her energetic hound would be welcome in an art museum.

She couldn't miss the large circle of tall uniform columns overlooking the Columbia River. From the monument's parking lot, Washington's own Stonehenge seemed more Roman coliseum than Druid calendar and shrine. She wasn't surprised that on that day in late November her truck was the lonely only vehicle in the lot. Because they had the place to themselves, she unleashed Rusty who raced off to explore. She, too, explored the standing stones and a flat man-sized altar, all encircled by those identical gray columns.

Miranda read the plaque explaining that a Quaker named Sam Hill who made his fortune paving area roads built the monument out of poured concrete. She also read that he believed, perhaps mistakenly, that Druids created the original Stonehenge to offer human sacrifices to their deities. Hill's version of Stonehenge opened in 1918 and was designed to memorialize Klickitat County soldiers killed in WWI and also to show that Americans still sacrifice people to the gods of war. The dead soldiers' names were etched on the stelas inside the circle of columns. The center of the monument supposedly aligned with the sunrise during the summer solstice. Miranda found the place too grim to offer the pleasant change of scene she'd hoped for. But the view of the river below redeemed it, so while Rusty gamboled about, she stepped between the columns behind the monument and took pictures of the mighty Columbia down below and the tiny town of Mary Hill nestled on its bank.

Then dutifully she reentered the monument and began to circle the interior standing stones. The sun was lowering and the stelas cast long shadows. It occurred to her that the least she could do to pay proper respect to the named war dead was to say Kaddish for them even without the requisite ten other mourners and even though most if not all of the dead soldiers weren't Jewish. So first she walked from stone to stone reading aloud the names on each. That done, she chanted the "Mourners' Prayer." Finished and feeling a little better, she walked over to the altar, brushed off the snow from a spot on one end of it, hoisted herself up, and perched there. She didn't feel like a human sacrifice. She felt like a protein bar. She unwrapped the one in her pocket and contemplated the neat circle of boot prints she'd made in the virgin snow.

She looked up when she noticed some footprints she hadn't made intersecting with hers at the circle's edge. She assumed they signaled the arrival of another off-season tourist, but when she glanced around, she saw no one.

She was peering between stones and columns in an effort to see the parking lot when a woman's shrill voice distracted her. "Miranda Breitner. Small world, isn't it?" The speaker stood in the shadow of one of the perimeter pillars, so it took Miranda a moment to recognize Spa Lady, the B & B guest who owned a spa in Napa Valley and had come to the Yakima Valley looking for property where she could build a second one. Her real name was Gloria Derrinsman, but Miranda thought of her as Spa Lady because that was part of her e-mail address. She was on the list Miranda had given Sheriff Carson. The woman had left a glowing review in the B & B guest book. So if she was visiting the Valley again, why the hell wasn't she staying at Breitner's?

"Hey, Gloria. What a surprise!"

It wasn't until Miranda jumped down from the altar and walked towards the newcomer that she saw the gun in Gloria's suede-gloved hand. She froze midstride, her heart racing and her brain struggling to make sense of this armed apparition.

"It's your last surprise."

"I don't understand." Gloria had been a model guest. She must be having a psychotic episode. Maybe she was drugged. "Are you okay?" Miranda heard her own voice, thin and high pitched.

"No. I'm not okay. But I'll feel better after I shoot you and leave your body here for the wolves and cougars."

"What are you talking about?"

"I'm talking about how, in a minute or two, I'm going to kill you."

Miranda wanted to keep her talking. "What'd I ever do to you, Gloria?" That's when Miranda realized that it wasn't Angela Lacey who supplied Steve with poison. It was Spa Lady. She'd mentioned several times that her spa's masseuses used only organic herbs to make their "emollients." Spa Lady knew from poison.

"Steve says you're the only one who could've seen that Mexican whore and realized she could ID him. And it was you who got her to testify. She said so. All you muds work together." Miranda was close enough to see Gloria's eyes gleam. "So Steve'll go to prison. And for what? Ridding the world of one more Jew? That's a public service. You Jews are taking over this country, running it down. Steve and I were just trying to get rid of a few more Jews before they got old enough to be really dangerous. Our plan was foolproof. No one would connect us to puking and dead Jew brats all over the country." Gloria sighed and stopped talking.

"How did you know I'd be here?"

"Your redskin houseboy told me." Miranda saw Gloria shudder. "He took a message. But you won't get it."

After fighting off Alex Ladin, Miranda thought she was pretty tough. But lust had literally disarmed him. The hate that animated this crazy-eyed aspiring child-killer spewing venomous clichés was different. Spa Lady clung to her gun, and that gun was a game changer. There would be no chance for heroics.

Gloria shook her head and spoke again. "But Steve's not stupid. They'll take a few years off his sentence if he gives them a name. That name would be mine. That bastard will give me up in a heartbeat." Miranda heard her captor choke back a sob. "He couldn't have set up this operation without me. When Tammy said she wouldn't be able to rip off poison from the hospital, I stepped up. I grew those plants in my herb garden and drove them all the way up here. And I chopped all those fresh leaves. But when that damn Jew came in asking questions like he owned the place Steve lost it, couldn't resist killing the mud. I even helped him with that later on. I took that goddamn bloody antler off his hands and cleaned it up and got rid of it for him." Gloria's voice was no longer shrill. It was flat and low, the voice of a robot. "I've loved him for years, but he'll give me up. So I have nothing left to lose. I'll let the cops finish me off. But I figure before I go down I might as well get rid of one more Jew. And that would be you." She actually spat on the snow before she stepped forward, raised her arms, and, holding the gun in both hands, aimed it at Miranda's head.

Only about six feet away, Miranda couldn't stop staring at the little hole in the revolver that the bullet would come through. She closed her eyes and prayed aloud. "The Lord is my shepherd...." She hadn't even gotten to the part about green pastures when, Spa Lady screamed.

Miranda opened her eyes to see Rusty gripping one of Gloria's forearms between his sharp-toothed steel-trap jaws. Her other arm flailed about in the air. She didn't have the gun anymore. Miranda spotted it and rushed over to pick it up where it lay just outside a circle of snow yellowed by the pee trickling over the would-be shooter's running shoes. Miranda watched as Gloria cursed and struggled to free her arm from Rusty's grip. Then she stiffened where she stood until she was still and silent as the stela behind her. The red stain blossoming on Spa Lady's khaki sleeve told Miranda that any motion Rusty's captive made only cued the onetime army-trained animal to tighten his grip.

"Good, Rusty." Miranda held the surprisingly heavy handgun gingerly as if it were a tongue-flicking serpent or a lit firecracker. But then, picturing NCIS's Ziva David, she pointed the business end of the firearm at the chest of the woman who had intended to kill her, held the weapon steady in one hand, and repeated, "Good Rusty. Good job."

With her other hand, she reached in her pocket for her cell phone, prayed for a connection, and, when it came, dialed 911.

CHAPTER 26

Guest book: "Nice place you got here. I been away for a while, it surprised me to see how solid you made this old place. They were going to tear it down. It was nice staying here even if I was back here for a funeral."

"By now you probably have 911 on speed dial, Ms Breitner." Sheriff Carson's quip was wasted on Miranda. She'd driven with Rusty from Mary Hill to the sheriff's bustling office in Yakima where, with Harry and Rusty at her side, she'd been answering questions and filling out paperwork for hours. She wasn't in the mood for witticisms.

"My arm was tired. I was real glad when those two FBI agents showed up."

Sheriff Carson nodded. Harry paled. She'd called him from her truck on the way there. She didn't want her lover to learn about her latest brush with death via the local TV news, and she wanted her lawyer with her when she pressed charges. Again.

"Sheriff, what made you call in the FBI?" She admired Harry's ability to compartmentalize. Her lover looked sick, but her lawyer was on task.

Sheriff Carson leaned back in his padded swivel chair and guzzled water from a bottle. "When I took over the investigation of Isaac Markowitz's murder from Detective Ladin, I reviewed all the paperwork. In his autopsy report the doctor said the tox screen showed no poison in Isaac's system." The sheriff shrugged. "So because Isaac wasn't poisoned, Detective Ladin wasn't inclined to look for a toxin. And for the same reason, our own overworked state lab techs never tested Isaac's clothes specifically for traces of toxins."

The sheriff whirled back and forth in his chair, as if to signal a change of subject. "Another thing is Detective Ladin doesn't set much store by Crime Stoppers. But when I read the leads coming in from that site, I realized that we might be looking at more than a homicide. We might be looking at a hate crime. So I shipped everything I had to the FBI lab and put a rush on it. They tested Isaac's clothes and, would you believe, they found tiny oleander leaf particles on his shirt and pants and even stuck to his bootlaces."

Miranda just couldn't let this sloppy police work go unremarked. "I understand their reasoning and I know you're understaffed, but your deputy and your lab techs cut corners, right?" Harry gave her a look.

"Now you're starting to sound like a reporter."

Harry was quick to defuse any developing friction with a less hostile question. "Okay, so, Sheriff Carson, tell me how did the FBI get a handle on this Gloria Derrinsman who tried to kill Miranda today?"

"The FBI did detailed background checks on the names on the list Ms Breitner gave me. There weren't many names, and the feds have a data base you wouldn't believe." Sheriff Carson shook his head to stress the bottomless depths of the FBI's file. "They really liked a young mom for a co-conspirator, because she's a pharmaceutical rep, so she might have been able to access poison. But her mother is Nez Percé, so she's not likely to belong to a white supremacy group. The feds kept digging and found that this Gloria Derrinsman's been charged with discriminatory hiring practices at her members-only spa. She settled out of court. Membership at that spa is limited to white Christians. She's on a Southern Poverty Law Center watch list. Talk about red flags!" Carson waved his hands in what Miranda assumed was his "impersonation" of a flag.

"So the feds put eyes on her and early this morning she flew to Seattle. Two Seattle FBI field agents began tailing her as soon as she got off the plane." He paused and drank from his water bottle again. "We needed her, because thanks to Crime Stoppers we were onto Galen, but we couldn't find him. The feds figured Gloria might lead us to Galen."

"Instead, thank God, she led them to Miranda." Harry took a deep breath and exhaled. Miranda noticed that his color was returning.

"Thank God and Rusty." Miranda's hand met Harry's as they both stroked the big dog. "But they didn't find Galen. Remember, Sheriff, I told you Gloria said she got rid of the murder weapon for him. I guess that means you'll never find it or him now." Miranda wanted to hear if the shofar she'd gone to such trouble and expense to provide offered any evidence of Galen's guilt.

Sheriff Carson's phone rang. Later Harry swore that the lawman's ring tone was a few notes of the theme from *Longmire*, a western series featuring a squeaky clean Wyoming sheriff that Miranda hadn't watched. Carson took the call. His contributions were short and mostly questions. "Where?"

"Which Vancouver? BC or Washington?"

"You've gotta be kiddin'."

"In this weather?"

"No problem. We don't need DNA."

And finally, "Nice work."

He jammed his phone back into the holder on his belt and his smile broadened into a satisfied grin. He leaned back in his chair, inhaled, and announced, "We got 'im."

"Where?" Harry and Miranda spoke in chorus.

The sheriff stood and pointed to the window through which they could see a couple of TV cameras and several people standing around with mics and phones and tablets poised. "I gotta talk to those reporters in a minute. They've been pickin' at me for weeks like wolves on a sheep's carcass. Finally I got a fresh kill for 'em." Miranda thought the successful manhunt had revived Carson's sense of how a western sheriff ought to sound, because he began dropping his selected initial consonants and final gs.

"You're not leaving this room before you tell us where they found Steve Galen." Harry made his voice playful, but the sheriff sat down again.

"The bastard's been hidin' in plain sight, workin'. He's been restorin' stone monuments honoring Civil War Veterans who served in the Confederate Army at Jefferson Davis Park near Vancouver, Washington. Just off Route 5."

"Here in this Washington? Not DC? We have a Jefferson Davis Park? Are you serious?" Disbelief sharpened Miranda's voice.

"Yep, Ms Breitner, I'm serious. It's a private park and they got a Confederate flag flyin' alongside a Betsy Ross one with the thirteen colonies on it. A smart state trooper made inquiries there and recognized him from that photo we have. He tried to get himself shot, but the trooper took cover behind one of them monuments and let him run out of ammo and then arrested him." The sheriff shook his head and stood again as if he were about to dismiss them.

Miranda and Harry remained seated and Miranda spoke. "But, Sheriff, you were going to tell us about the murder weapon? It wasn't the fish club, so what was it?"

This time when he answered the sheriff sounded tired. "It was some kind of Jewish musical instrument made out of the horn of some animal. It belonged to the deceased who had it on 'im at the time. The instrument had no DNA, but its size, shape, and striations match the wound as described in the autopsy report. And some of the prints on it are Gloria Derrinsman's." Sheriff Carson sat down of his own accord. "The press can wait a few more minutes. What else do you two want to know?"

Miranda forced herself to keep quiet about the provenance of the shofar and its monetary value. After Steve Galen was convicted, she'd try to get it back to the Markowitz family if, considering what it had been used for, they wanted it. If they didn't, they could sell it. It belonged to them. All she said was, "That instrument is called a *shofar.*" Sheriff Carson grabbed a yellow pencil from a Seahawks mug and scribbled the word on a small notepad pad on his desk. To Miranda the note pad and pencil looked like artifacts extracted from a time capsule.

"In view of what she endured today, how her business has suffered, and how she was sexually assaulted by the previous investigating officer, Miranda deserves to know whatever else the FBI found out about this case." Harry spoke in what Miranda thought of as his "Julia voice." It usually masked impatience.

"They gave some samples of this Galen's handwritin' to their handwritin' analyst to compare with the taggin' on the Toppenish Murals, and her report indicates that Galen tagged those murals himself! Can you believe that? It's as if I rode into town, robbed a bank, and then applied for the job of sheriff in that same town!"

"Right." Again Miranda and Harry spoke in unison. Miranda remembered the pride Steve Galen took in his ability to restore the murals. How he must have been laughing at her gullibility. At everybody's gullibility. He was smart. Who was he, really?

"What did the FBI's background check of Steve Galen reveal about his past? Has he committed other hate crimes?"

"He grew up poor in West Virginia and had an abusive and usually unemployed father who did time for domestic violence and theft." Carson stroked the strings of an imaginary violin with an imaginary bow as he spoke. "In prison his dad joined the Aryan Brotherhood. His son liked to draw and made posters and designed tee shirts and tats for them and before long he joined too. They encouraged him to go to college so he could find a good job and contribute to their cause. He got a scholarship to the University of Delaware and majored in art. But he got arrested for forgin' copies of paintin's and sellin' them as originals. That was the end of his formal education. He had a reunion with the Brotherhood when he went to prison. Once he got out, he learned about art restoration on a job he had workin' for an older restorer, one Max Feldenstein. One day Feldenstein 'happened'"— the sheriff formed air quotes with the fingers of both hands— "to fall from a ladder and die. Galen took over his regular clients and set up for himself. Galen still kept up with the Brotherhood, though. He'd go to a town on a job, usually a small rural place, and, would you believe, everywhere he worked, while he was in town, bad things happened to minorities and immigrants? The feds are still compilin' data on that. And they're givin' Feldenstein's death another look too."

"So as far as we know for sure, Galen is being charged with homicide, conspiring to commit mass murder, defacing public property, and fraud." Harry was ticking off the crimes on his fingers as he spoke.

"And he stole my handyman's fish club too." Miranda remembered well the anxiety Steve Galen's greedy grab had caused the Wright family.

Sheriff Carson threw up his hands. "Yeah. I guess now that you mention it, he did."

Miranda wasn't done. "Since that fish club wasn't the murder weapon, and since it is stolen property, would you return it to my handyman, Michael Wright? It's a family heirloom."

"I'll see. It was stolen and then used by Galen to mask his involvement, so it's still part of the homicide investigation." Miranda gave him a look. "But, I'll see what I can do. It'll be awhile before all this dies down, but maybe then."

As soon as Miranda got home, she read a text from Harry. "Work 4 me part time as an investigator? Seriously. Think about it." She was too tired to think about it. There was also a text from Michael, who'd agreed to stay until the guest came when she'd called from the sheriff's office. "Sarah Marcus checked in about seven thirty." Miranda took Rusty out for a final pee, fed him, and gave him a huge treat. When she crawled into her sleeping bag and he stretched out on his cushion beside her, she hugged him. In case her hug didn't say it all, she whispered into his ear, "You saved my life today, Rusty. Thank you."

She was up early the next morning, eager to catch the local news online. It was gratifying to see videos of both Steve Galen and Spa Lady in handcuffs. She herself was alive and pretty sure that now she could keep her promise to Mona. She'd come to this valley for a new start in life, for a second chance, and those hate-fueled criminals' murderous doings had threatened her efforts. But then both she and her B & B had been given a rare gift, a second second chance. A wider-than-usual smile animated her face as she served breakfast while kibitzing about the big news with her guests.

When Sarah Marcus emerged from her room, Miranda thought perhaps they'd met before. The young dark-haired woman with her straight features and piercing hazel eyes looked so familiar. Miranda was annoyed with herself for not being able to place her. "Good morning. I'm Miranda Breitner. Welcome!" Hoping for a hint as to where they'd met, she asked, "What brings you to the Valley, Sarah?"

When the girl answered, her voice was low, her smile puckish. Miranda figured she couldn't be more than nineteen or twenty. "I'm here for a family reunion."

That was no help at all. While Sarah ate a hardboiled egg and buttered a scone, Miranda wondered where she'd seen that impish smile before. After the other guests left, she tried a more direct approach. "Sarah, you look familiar. Have we met?"

Sarah giggled. "Just once. Briefly." Then, more serious if not more helpful, she added, "It was a long time ago and we both looked different then."

Miranda tried to keep her voice from betraying her pique. "I give up."

"My real name is Casey Weintraub. I'm your half-sister."

"What?" Miranda sank onto the nearest stool, bent over, and put her head between her knees to prevent herself from losing consciousness.

"I read in *The Seattle Times* about how you escaped from that rapist and I saw your picture. I showed it to Dad, and he recognized you. I Googled you and your B & B and found out more. You're my sister."

When Miranda looked up, Casey moved towards her, arms outstretched, clearly expecting a sisterly embrace, a hug. "I have no sister. My mother had only one child."

She could tell from the way Casey's chin stiffened that this hybrid twig on the twisted Weintraub family tree wasn't going to just break off and disappear.

"But your father had two. You and me. And now he's got emphysema and is under Hospice care. He wants to see you before he dies, wants to ask your forgiveness."

"I don't know if I can ever forgive him. His damn cigarettes killed my mom and he actually thinks I killed a child. He wouldn't leave me alone with you or even let me hold you."

Casey blanched at this version of family history. But she recovered and her words came fast. "Maybe you haven't forgiven him, but I've never done anything to you, and I'd like to know you, to have you in my life." When Miranda didn't reply, Casey slowed down and embellished her pitch. "Things have changed. My mother left us both back in 2008 when Boeing cut dad loose. I was 13." She hesitated again, still hoping for a response. When none came, she shrugged and reached into her jeans pocket. "Okay. Here's my contact info. Think about getting in touch with me when you've had a chance to recover from all that you've gone through recently. By then it may be too late for you and dad, but you and I still have time to get to know one another. We're both a little short on family." She turned and then turned back. "Please. I want my sister in my life."

Desperate for someone to share the latest episode in the soap opera that was her own life, Miranda headed on foot for Pauline's. On the way, a familiar white Subaru stopped alongside her and Rabbi Alinsky rolled down the window on the passenger side. She stuck her head in to greet him. "Thank Hashem you are alive and well. He was listening to my prayers and those of my crew. We and the Markowitz family too are grateful to you for how you got rid of that incompetent and immoral detective. How you made them see that hate was at the bottom of Isaac's death. Isaac's life has new meaning because, thanks to you, we know he prevented another terrible crime." The rabbi paused. "That sheriff says he got his leads from Crime Stoppers." He paused. "Stoppers, Schmoppers..." Miranda thought she saw a smile behind his beard. "What do they know from *shofars*?"

Miranda ignored his attempt to out her as a contributor to Crime Stoppers. "I remember you telling me about white supremacists. Who knew from haters? Anyway, I'm relieved for all of our sakes that these criminals will be brought to justice and that we can go about our business normally again." She wrapped her arms around herself against the cold. "I take it that RCK, Inc., will continue to kosher juice grapes here and that you'll continue to supervise their kosherers."

"Yes. In fact, I'm in the Valley today to make agreements with the processing plants we'll serve next fall." Her self-embrace and hopping from foot to foot did not escape his attention. "You go along. I see that you're cold."

"Good to see you, Rabbi. Check in with me when you get back in the fall."

When Miranda and Rusty arrived at Pauline's, Darlene was just leaving with a basket of eggs. "What's the rush? Where're you off to?"

"Thanks to you, I'm on my way to Spokane to get Javi and bring him home." The woman looked ten years younger.

"That's great news! I suspected you'd hidden him away somewhere safe. Where the hell was he?"

"Where he belonged. In a suicide watch group's safe house." Miranda figured her puzzlement showed because Darlene rushed to explain. "It's a group of people who try to prevent others who speak of suicide or who appear to be thinking about it from ending their lives" Darlene couldn't have sounded prouder than if her grandson had been at Harvard. "My priest told me about them. They saved Javi's life." She winced. "Javi was filled with despair, afraid that no matter what he did, a gangbanger would kill him. And he was also filled with grief over what they did to his brother. So Father Lonagan and me, we took him to members of this group that Father knows in Spokane. A man and his wife took him into their home. The woman, she runs the after-school program at their church and Javi helped out. She also home-schooled him a little in math and psychology. And he had to keep a diary. And now he loves to write!" Darlene's grin only expanded when she added, "And he is over that bitch who used to boss him around and who gave him up."

Miranda hugged her friend. "Good job, Grandma! Who knew there were such groups?"

"Who knew how to almost get herself raped and shot without even trying? I'm so glad you're okay. And this big lover boy saved you!" She gave Rusty a head scratch. "I always knew he was special. I'll be home tonight. Come by for tea."

Pauline welcomed Miranda with a hug. The chickens were in the barn, so Rusty settled down at Miranda's feet. "Hot cocoa? Or coffee?"

"Cocoa, please. And I brought some gingerbread. Just nuke it a minute."

"Well, you sure don't look like the heroic woman I've been reading about. What happened? What's wrong? What can we do?"

Miranda peeled off her parka, sat down, and burst into tears. On cue, Rusty thrust his head into her lap. "My half-sister whom I don't know at all showed up and told me that my father's dying and wants me to forgive him, which I don't. And I'm getting really serious with a guy I hardly know. He wants me to work part-time for him and meet his family! I don't even know my own family!" Miranda hadn't expected to mention her growing concern that she and Harry were moving too quickly, that she still had so much to learn about him. She felt guilty for telling Pauline this before saying anything to Harry.

Pauline talked while she served them cocoa and nuked the gingerbread muffins. "Pearl is my half-sister...

It was Pauline's revelations about the ancestry of her beloved older sister and about the daughter born to Nelson's first girlfriend and whom Pauline raised as her own that Miranda was recalling when she entered Temple Shalom that evening. By the time she left Pauline's, she'd decided that the next day when she visited Seattle with Harry and Julia she would stop by the hospital to see her own father and sister before meeting Harry's dad and sister. Pauline was all about faith and family. But, unlike the Thurston's faith which seemed simple and straightforward, the Thurston family was complex and tangled, just like Miranda's, and, come to think of it, just like those families in the Torah.

The sight of the children clustering around Rabbi Golden distracted her. The rabbi stood poised to light the candles and bless the wine and the grape juice. But when she spotted Miranda, she asked her to light the Sabbath candles. Touched by this honor, Miranda approached the table and smiled at the healthy, happy youngsters circling her and at the adults, including Harry, a bit farther back. Little Julia grinned up at her. She struck the match and put it to the wick which obligingly flamed. While the rabbi said the blessing, those assembled joined in and then they all sang the lovely prayer. Miranda remembered her grandmother saying that Jews all over the world would be welcoming the Sabbath similarly and, for the first time in many years, Miranda felt at home in that world.

Selected Resources

Books: *American Swastika: Inside the White Power Movement's Hidden Spaces of Hate* by Pete Simi and Robert Futrell; *Back to the Blanket: A Native Narrative of Discovery* by James A. Starkey, Jr.; *Everything You Wanted to Know about Indians But Were Afraid to Ask* by Anton Treuer; *Images of America: Yakima Washington* by Elizabeth Gibson; *Kosher Nation* by Sue Fishkoff; *Ruby Ridge: The Truth and Tragedy of the Randy Weaver Family* by Jess Walter; *Skinheads: A Guide to an American Subculture* by Tiffini A. Travis and Perry Hardy; *Strangers on the Land (A Historiette - of a Longer Story of the Yakima Indian Nation's Efforts to Survive Against Great Odds); The Land of Yakimas* by Robert E. Pace; *The Toppenish Murals* by The Toppenish Mural Society.

Periodicals: *Intelligence Report* from The Southern Poverty Law Center; *The Jewish Transcript; The New Yorker; River Journal: Yakima River; The Seattle Times; Yakima-Herald Republic.*

About the Author

Jane Isenberg wrote the prize-winning memoir *Going by the Book* (Bergin & Garvey), *The Bel Barrett Mystery Series* (Avon/HarperCollins), and the WILLA Award winning historical mystery *The Bones and the Book* (Oconee Spirit Press). She earned degrees from Vassar College, Southern Connecticut State College, and New York University and taught English for nearly forty years, first in high school and later in community college. Now retired from teaching, she writes in Issaquah, Washington where she lives with her husband Phil Tompkins.

Visit her website www.janeisenberg.com and her blog www.notestomymuses.wordpress.com.

CPSIA information can be obtained
at www.ICGtesting.com
Printed in the USA
LVHW090526271118
598379LV00002B/496/P